THE DANCE OF THE DAGGERS

BOOK THREE OF

THE TALES OF THE TERRITORIES

PETER WACHT

Kestrel
Media Group, LLC

The Dance of the Daggers
By Peter Wacht

Book 3 of The Tales of the Territories

Cover design by Ebooklaunch.com

Published in the United States by Kestrel Media Group LLC.

ISBN: 978-1-950236-36-7

eBook ISBN: 978-1-950236-37-4

Library of Congress Control Number: 2023904674

❀ Created with Vellum

THE SYLVAN CHRONICLES

(Complete 9-Book Series)

The Legend of the Kestrel

The Call of the Sylvana

The Raptor of the Highlands

The Makings of a Warrior

The Lord of the Highlands

The Lost Kestrel Found

The Claiming of the Highlands

The Fight Against the Dark

The Defender of the Light

THE RISE OF THE SYLVAN WARRIORS

*Through the Knife's Edge (short story)**

* Free short stories can be downloaded from my author website at
PeterWachtBooks.com. My books are also available on Amazon.

YOUR FREE SHORT STORY IS WAITING

THE DIAMOND THIEF

This short story is a prelude to the events in my series *The Tales of Caledonia* and is free to readers who receive my newsletter.

Join Peter's newsletter and get your FREE short story.
PeterWachtBooks.com

SETTING THE STAGE

The Tales of the Territories continue the adventures of Bryen Keldragan and Aislinn Winborne as they travel across the Burnt Ocean to the Territories, what will eventually become the Kingdoms of *The Sylvan Chronicles*.

The events occur more than one thousand years before the happenings in *The Sylvan Chronicles* and take place in the lands far to the west of Caledonia that have been opened for colonization thanks to territorial grants from the deceased King Corinthus Beleron. There they will take on new challenges, make new friends and enemies, and continue to battle those who have turned to the Curse.

In the Territories, sometimes called New Caledonia, as in the other Realms, the ability to use the Talent sets apart the person gifted with this unique skill. But being able to use the Talent is only part of the dynamic. For if a Magus chooses to follow a darker path, the Talent becomes the Curse.

The Sylvan Chronicles, The Tales of Caledonia, and *The Tales of the Territories* are a part of the larger world of *The Realms of the Talent and the Curse.*

1

COMBAT IN THE MURK

Jakob spent a long, restless night in the heart tree.

He dozed on occasion, not by choice, his exhaustion getting the better of him, although never for more than a few minutes at a time.

The rough bark dug into his back. The cold prickled across his skin, the damp fog caressing him, the plummeting temperature making the moisture feel like ice.

He was tired.

He was sore.

He was heartbroken, memories of his father popping unbidden into his mind.

The most frequent scene the last one. His father draped across the slaver he had just killed so that Jakob could escape. Dougal's last words haunting him.

"Go. Now. Into the mist. Please. For me."

He didn't bother trying to sleep. He didn't want to sleep.

Not tonight.

Not after what happened to his father.

Not with the Wraiths still hunting for him.

He searched with the Talent constantly. Fearful that the

monsters in the mist would find him before he found his way off the plateau and out of the Murk.

Time and again he pinpointed the exact location of the fist of Wraiths he had barely evaded. Thankfully, they remained more than a mile away in among the heart trees to the north.

He had fooled the monsters, sending them to one side of the plateau while he went to the other. He doubted, however, that his deception would continue to meet with its current success for much longer.

He assumed that the Wraiths knew that he was still on the plain.

They just didn't know where he was.

He wanted to keep it that way until he found a path that led away from his predicament. Either to a place where he could hole up until the Murk drifted back to the north or out of the fog entirely.

Because he had no doubt that if he stayed on this hidden steppe, the Wraiths would find him.

With the pitch black of the fog shifting to a dark grey, Jakob judged it to be the right time to continue on his way.

He was still several leagues away from safety.

He needed to be careful. Smart. Patient.

Those characteristics are what had allowed him to escape the Wraiths yesterday. He hoped that they would be enough for him to do the same today.

As Jakob made his way slowly down the trunk of the tree, the challenges facing him dominated his thoughts. Yet even with the urge to increase his pace growing more and more insistent within him, he couldn't rush. If he fell and twisted an ankle or broke a leg, he was done for.

Of course, he might be done for even if he didn't.

When he reached the forest floor, he stood there for several minutes.

He saw nothing but the wispy dull grey of the haze.

He couldn't hear anything. The squirrels, birds, and other animals of the Highlands had gone to ground with the coming of the Wraiths.

He wanted to get a feel for what was around him. He needed to know when his hunters would come for him.

A bolt of fear wiped away the remnants of his exhaustion upon searching through the grey for the hundredth or more time in just the last few hours.

The Wraiths were leaving the forest to the north and making their way back across the small plateau. They were taking their time, moving methodically, seemingly confident that he couldn't leave the plain before they found him.

The monsters just might be right.

He needed to move. Now.

Jakob used the Talent as his guide so that he could navigate the thick fog. He headed toward the south, moving in the opposite direction from the hunting Wraiths.

He knew that's where the edge of the fog was.

Yet knowing that didn't give him any additional confidence that he would succeed.

The entire time, two critical questions plagued him.

How far must he go before he escaped the fog?

And would the Wraiths catch him first?

The monsters in the mist continued to make their way toward him at a steady pace. Apparently, they had decided that since they failed to find him among the heart trees to the north that this was the only direction that he could have gone.

It was sound logic.

Logic that very likely would lead to Jakob's death if he didn't get out of the Murk in time.

Still, that knowledge didn't faze him. Jakob had grown accustomed to playing this game of cat and mouse with the Wraiths.

He just needed to stay calm. Focused. And, most important, quiet.

As he did the day before when the fog first drifted in from the north to cover the Highlands, he worked his way across the plateau in an erratic manner, never taking a straight path, always shifting this way and that, more concerned with stealth than speed.

Never rushing.

Never doing anything that would give himself away too easily.

Without making a sound, he glided through the Murk as if he was a part of it. Being able to see everything that was around him with the Talent gave him a boost of much-needed energy, the grey haze no longer a hindrance.

But he didn't allow his early success to go to his head, understanding the consequences if he did.

His objective remained the same.

He walked toward the south in a pattern that couldn't be discerned. To have any chance of finding him, the Wraiths needed to detect some sign of his passage across the plateau, which based on how he was moving could lead them in multiple directions if they weren't paying close enough attention.

Consequently, the monsters gained nothing by trying to get ahead of him. They would be taking a shot in the dark.

That meant that they would have to move more slowly than they would prefer. They would need to take their time and check every one of his false trails. They would question their decisions.

He hoped that all that increased his chances of getting out of the fog before the Wraiths slit his throat.

Even so, despite his best efforts, he felt as if the Wraiths were slipping a noose around his neck. That they were giving him just enough rope so that he could hang himself.

The monsters were working their way across the plateau in a pattern that slowly but effectively narrowed the space in which he could be hiding.

A frustrating reality, and one that he could do little about.

Jakob had to admit that because of his much-too-frequent experiences in the Murk and his use of the Talent, he was learning quite a bit about Wraith tactics. Whether he'd ever be able to make use of that information and the other knowledge that he was acquiring during his attempted escape ...

He feared that he knew the answer already.

He just didn't want to admit it to himself.

He forced that draining thought out of his mind.

There was nothing to do but keep trying.

His father had fought for him. Died for him.

Jakob wasn't about to let Dougal's sacrifice go to waste.

THE WRAITH SCOUT worked his way slowly, diligently, across the plateau. His comrades were spread out around him in a broad arc that resembled a crescent moon.

He had just missed his prey the afternoon before. He had been so close, in fact, that at one point he believed the boy had been no more than a few yards away from him. Maybe only just a few feet.

But the boy had kept silent. Kept himself under control. Demonstrated a skill that made him think the boy was more Wraith than human.

That thought irritated the Wraith Scout. He should have completed this hunt by now.

But the fact that his prey was still alive also impressed the Wraith Scout. It took a spine of steel to maintain your composure when faced with certain death.

In all the time that he had hunted south of the Wyld, he

had yet to find in any of the other humans he had killed the iron will and calm self-possession this boy had when faced with the inevitable fate of a bloody end.

Nevertheless, that held little meaning to the Wraith Scout. He would still kill the boy. It was only a question of when.

Because unfortunately for the boy, his luck was going to run out this morning.

The Wraith Scout would not miss him again. He would bring this chase to a close, running the steel of his dagger across the boy's throat.

The Wraith had been right to wait in the forest during the night. There was no easy way off this plateau, so he was certain that his prey remained close.

Closer than he had thought, in fact.

As soon as the fog began to brighten to a dull grey, the Wraith Scout assumed that the boy would slip out from wherever he was hiding.

It was the only choice for the boy to make.

And if he was to evade his hunters and break free of the Murk, there was only one direction for him to go.

With that thought guiding him, the Wraith Scout had ordered his hunters back toward the south, working their way in a very precise manner through the Murk. They broke their search into quadrants, hunting across every foot of ground in each one before moving on to the next, ensuring that their prey had no opportunity to double back on them.

Every so often he and his hunters stopped.

Waiting.

Watching.

Listening.

Searching for any sign of movement up ahead.

Hoping for any sound that might betray their quarry.

Whenever they did, however, there was nothing but silence and the slowly drifting grey mist.

Challenging.

Frustrating.

Fun as well.

Each time they waited, the Wraith Scout smiled menacingly when they had no choice but to continue toward the south as they sought to flush the boy from his hiding place.

Their prey truly was a worthy target. Finally, beyond the borders of their homeland, he and his hunters faced a real challenge, a true test of their skills.

He and his comrades had a good idea as to where the boy might be now. They had made swift though thorough progress across the steppe.

Now the only question that bothered the Wraith Scout was whether they would catch him before he escaped the fog.

He pushed that concern to the side. They still had time.

Based on where they were on the plain, they couldn't be more than a few hundred yards behind him, and the outer edge of the Murk was still several leagues distant.

Plenty of time and space to conclude the hunt.

Besides, the boy was about to reach a harsh conclusion. There was no way to get off this plateau without coming back toward him and his hunters.

Therefore, there was no need to rush their search. Better to be precise in their work.

The Wraiths continued to adhere to a strict pattern with their hunt. They searched for any hint of their prey's passage through the long grass, understanding that if they could find the right trail, it would lead them directly to him.

The Wraith Scout stopped again, his hunters doing so as well. They waited for several minutes, seeking any sign as to where the boy could be.

No sounds.

No movement.

Nothing to reveal their quarry.

Frustrating and fun indeed.

The Wraith Scout's eyes widened in delight. The boy truly was a worthy opponent. But as he had learned time and time again, everyone made mistakes.

Rather than beginning the search of the next grid, the Wraith Scout knelt, his clawed fingers reaching down to brush the crushed grass.

Picking up his gaze, he grinned, running his tongue across his sharp teeth.

The boy had been here. Lying on the ground. Based on how flat the grass was and how little dew had collected on the stalks compared to the grass around this crushed space, it hadn't been very long ago.

Less than an hour.

The Scout stood carefully, then walked to his left for a dozen yards.

He saw exactly what he was looking for in the dirt. The faint trace of a boot.

He followed the tracks, needing to go slowly because the impressions were barely there. The trail led him thirty yards to the south.

The Wraith Scout stopped again, kneeling, wanting to make sure.

The boy stopped here as well. He was certain of it. His razor-sharp fingers traced the faint marks in the dirt and grass.

The Wraith moved to the left again, this time for ten yards, then he strode toward the south again for another thirty yards.

He stopped abruptly, fearing that he had lost the trail.

No, he hadn't lost the trail. His prey was simply trying to make it more difficult for him.

Looking behind him, the Wraith Scout saw how the boy had backtracked, returning toward the north for a dozen yards before walking to the right for twenty yards and then continuing again to the south.

The boy was smart. He knew what he was doing. He didn't seem to mind being in the Murk.

Maybe the Wraith Scout's first assumption had been correct when he lost the boy last night.

No human ever had escaped him in the Murk.

Until now.

Maybe this human truly was the same one who had shamed the Wraith Hunter.

The Wraith Hunter had said that the boy had moved within the Murk as if he belonged in it.

As if he was a part of it.

As if he was a Wraith himself.

This boy certainly met those criteria. He moved almost as well as his hunters, flowing in and out of the grey as if he were born to the Murk.

Still, his unique abilities when it came to the grey would not save the boy.

The Wraith Scout had yet to fail on a hunt, and he wasn't about to start now.

He called to one of his hunters with a sharp, shrill whistle. The Wraith appeared right next to him, coalescing out of the fog as if he were a part of it.

After the Scout issued a few brief instructions, the Wraith sped off, moving toward the southwest.

The Wraith Hunter now knew where their prey was. If the hunter just sent ahead didn't kill him, he would keep the boy in place so that the Wraith Scout could do the honors himself when he arrived.

The hunt had almost come to an end. Soon the Wraith Scout would slide the bone-white steel of his blade across the boy's throat.

Soon he would taste his prey's blood.

2

DON'T PICK THE WRONG FIGHT

"Three days until we reach Ballinasloe," said Captain Gregson.

Despite the heavy chop, the bandy-legged sailor with a neatly trimmed beard that framed his face, his upper lip free of whiskers, leaned casually against the back rail that ran along the length of the helm. Clearly, he was more comfortable on water than he was on land, his body moving easily with the rhythm of the ship and the sea.

When in port, he tended to be grouchy at the best of times, slightly on edge. When at sea, he was always in a good mood, even while navigating the worst of storms or guiding his ship through a dense fog that turned the world to twilight as he sought to escape what had been more tale than truth until he had seen the mythical monsters with his own eyes.

His smile broadened while he watched his wife spin the wheel one rotation, the *Freedom* responding with a pleasing grace and slicing toward the northwest. Emelina was working to get as much speed out of the strong gusts blowing at their backs as she could.

"Maybe four at the most," he continued. "Though I doubt it

with Emelina at the tiller. The wind seems to find her, just as it's doing now."

"It'll be nice to finally set foot on dry land again assuming that when we do, we won't have to worry about being slaughtered by the Kraken," mused Declan.

They were more than a week past the Jagged Islands. Even so, the harrowing experience of their brief time within that archipelago would never be forgotten by any of the Blood Company.

Declan still woke up in a cold sweat on most mornings. Not fearing that he lost a combat with those creatures from the deep, but rather that he lost Bryen during the young man's duel with the King of the Kraken. That was a loss that he didn't think he could bear.

"I wouldn't be too sure about that," joked Bryen. "From what Aislinn told me after she spoke with her father, Ballinasloe can be a little rough."

"That it can," agreed Captain Gregson, "as can all of the Territories. Keep in mind that much of New Caledonia, most of it I should say, is still wild. As a result, some of the people living there have adjusted their standards accordingly, and not always for the better. Those are the ones you have to watch out for."

The Captain of the *Freedom* pushed himself off the rail and with the pipe that spent more time between his fingers than between his teeth gestured toward where Majdi and Jenus engaged in a vigorous practice session near the mainmast. The two men were so large in both height and breadth that both were unwelcome riders on the backs of the Griffons, the animals tolerating them only if there was a desperate need.

That was fine with both of the men. They preferred to keep their feet on the ground. Or the deck as it were.

The gladiators lining the training circle shouted encouragement as Majdi and Jenus honed their skills with a blade, not only seeking to get the better of the other, which was reason enough to strive for victory – bragging rights of course, but also to win the pot of coins hanging from the mast.

After fighting their way through the Kraken, Declan thought that some distraction would be a good idea for the gladiators to take their minds off their latest travails. A tournament -- with the restriction that no blood be spilled, or at least not a lot -- had done wonders for the spirits of the men and women who had once fought in the Pit.

"Although I doubt you and your Company of Blood will have much to worry about," concluded Captain Gregson. "A few thugs, thieves, or wannabe heroes don't compare to the Kraken."

"I won't disagree with you there," said Declan. "Most people, at least the sane ones, tend to stay clear of us."

The former Master of the Gladiators turned away from the combat. He already knew how it was going to end.

Majdi and Jenus were the best of friends and were a match in skill and strength. They would beat on each other until they both decided that it was a draw.

That way they both could enjoy the spoils and the acclaim. Until they decided that they were done, though, they would put on a good show for their fellow soldiers of the Blood Company.

Declan's thoughts inevitably drifted back to the fight against those monsters in the mist. It had been a hard one. More difficult than he had anticipated.

He had feared that they wouldn't get away, the creatures swarming the ship, even Rafia with her strength in the Talent struggling to hold back the creatures from the deep.

If not for Bryen and Aislinn's timely arrival on the backs of Banshee and Astuta, the other Griffons right behind them, and the savagery of their attack, ripping into the Kraken with talon and Talent, they would all likely still be in Solace Sound. Either slaughtered by the monsters that came out of the fog or in the bellies of the great white sharks that patrolled the waters around those islands.

"That was not an enjoyable encounter," grumbled Captain Gregson. His smile remained in place, although it seemed more forced as his thoughts returned to that harrowing experience. "The Kraken King? Who would have thought? A myth come to life. You know, thinking about it now, I would have much preferred the Kraken to remain just a frightening story. But I guess that would have been asking too much."

For a time, the three men stood there quietly, enjoying the blustery wind that kept them cool despite the hot sun, that chilling encounter with the creatures that had slaughtered the previous inhabitants of the Jagged Islands replaying through their memories.

With the Bakunawa pursuing them, and killing those sea dragons a beast of a job as Davin had joked one too many times, they had few options for escape. They chose what they judged to be the least terrifying course of action at the time.

Sailing into a massive storm rather than risking the wrath of a massive sea snake hundreds of feet long that was intent on taking them beneath the waves.

Thankfully, they had escaped the Bakunawa by the skin of their teeth.

They had not avoided the fury of the storm, which threatened to sink them dozens of times if not for the bravery and skill of the *Freedom's* crew and the strength of the three Magii working with them.

Because of the incredible power of the storm, their only choice was to ride the waves and allow the horrific weather to take them where it would. They finally broke free far to the south near the Jagged Islands, hundreds of leagues off-course.

Not unexpectedly, they had to make several repairs before they could resume their journey across the Burnt Ocean. To do that, they risked taking refuge in Solace Sound, hoping that they could complete their work and be on their way in only a few days.

Bryen grunted at the memory of gliding into the calm waters of the protected bay, one of Sirius' favorite sayings passing through his mind.

"Hoping doesn't make it real."

His grandfather's words rang true then just as they always did. As the Blood Company foraged for the supplies they needed, they discovered that the stories about the Jagged Islands and what stalked the remote atoll were all too true.

Since evading the Kraken, they had enjoyed an uneventful journey. The only excitement had been the many pods of whales and dolphins that appeared without warning, the sea dragons that had pestered them farther to the east and forced them into the tempest nowhere in sight.

The crew had succeeded in repairing most of the damage caused by the storm and the Kraken, and the Blood Company used that quiet time to recover from what seemed like their never-ending struggles between life and death. He was grateful that no one from the Pit was killed during the clash with the Kraken, though several gladiators were seriously wounded. Bryen and Aislinn used the Talent to heal those who required their assistance, speeding their recovery.

"That seems to be the way of the world, Captain Gregson. Myths are no more than stories that have stood the test of time. There's a reason for that. There's always a nugget of truth hidden within each one. Unfortunately for us, in addition to making a myth real, we got to create a story of our own."

"Right you are, lad," agreed Declan.

After much prompting, Bryen had told Declan of his and Aislinn's exploits in the mountains as they sought to escape the Kraken King and his Horde. If it hadn't been Bryen relating their experience, Declan would have scoffed at what he revealed, not believing any more than every other word.

However, because it was Bryen, Declan assumed that the young man was offering him a very brief, succinct version of events, leaving out more than he was sharing. He had to talk to Aislinn to get the full story, and what a story it was.

"You certainly do seem to lead a charmed existence, Lord Keldragan," Captain Gregson offered. Bryen had told the master of the *Freedom* multiple times that he wasn't a lord, that he should call him by his first name, yet that instruction never stuck with the ship captain. "Killing the Ghoule Overlord. Fighting Bakunawa from the backs of Griffons. Escaping the Kraken King. Two of those monsters often used to frighten children into their beds, the other to gain the attention of drunken sailors."

"I wouldn't describe my life as charmed having to combat monsters such as those," murmured Bryen with a small smile that seemed more resigned than anything else. "Cursed likely is the better term."

"I can understand your perspective," chuckled Captain Gregson. "Even so, many say that in life we rise to our appropriate level, whether shop owner, ship captain, or monster slayer. It's not something that can be avoided. We are who we are, no matter how much we try not to be."

"Perhaps so," Bryen said, not in the mood to engage in a philosophical dialogue, in part because in that moment Captain Gregson very much sounded like Declan, and in his opinion one Declan was more than enough. "And if that truly is the way of the world for me, still, I wouldn't mind a break from such creatures as the Kraken King. At least for a time."

"You say that, Lord Keldragan, but do you believe your own words?"

Bryen stared at Gregson for quite a long time before responding, his usual hard gaze, not intended to demonstrate anger or irritation, at least not in this instance, making the captain slightly nervous.

"Sometimes," he admitted, his smile returning along with a wink. "When I need to."

"So will they believe you, Captain?" asked Declan, recognizing that Bryen wasn't interested in continuing down the current path of the conversation.

"What do you mean?" asked the ship captain, distracted, turning his gaze away from Bryen and toward the cargo ship that was passing them about a quarter mile to their north, the large vessel heading toward the east and Caledonia.

Several ships had hailed them during the last few days as they drew closer to the New Caledonian coast, the ocean becoming more crowded. They were swiftly approaching where the Burnt Ocean met the Sea of Mist, the fogbanks so common to those waters beginning to take shape at the edge of the horizon.

All the ships they were coming across appeared to be what they were. Merchant vessels, nothing more.

Even so, Captain Gregson didn't demonstrate much in the way of trust for his fellow mariners. He never allowed the *Freedom* to get too close to any of those ships, and they never slowed.

A few times Gregson even asked Declan to position the Company of Blood along the rails when a ship that he wasn't sure was a cargo carrier exhibited too much interest in them.

Declan appreciated the Captain's caution. There was no cause to make the lives of the pirates plaguing the New Caledonian coast any easier than they already were.

"The Kraken."

Captain Gregson smiled at that. "Me? No, probably not. Not at first anyway. But when the crew starts telling tales, those stories will spread through the harbor taverns faster than a wildfire. Then every captain in the port will want to talk with me."

"You can probably get a few free drinks once that happens as well as some useful information."

"I expect that I can, and I plan to do just that, in fact. Captains and sailors are always hoping for a good tale. The hard part will be getting them to believe that it's more than a tale. Any other ship caught in the Jagged Islands like we were would have ended up at the bottom of Solace Sound."

"Which is why you didn't repair all the damaged railings and left many of the scars on the hull, isn't it?"

"You found me out," admitted Captain Gregson. "Many will doubt what I have to say. Some evidence of the battle will help to convince them along with the items we recovered."

"Smart man," said Declan.

Once the *Freedom* was clear of Solace Sound and the fog controlled by the Kraken King that sought to descend upon them, Captain Gregson had tasked some of his sailors with throwing the bodies of the dead Kraken littering the deck into the sea.

He also had them collect their very unique weapons. No one would be able to dispute what Captain Gregson had to say once he showed them all the spoils that his sailors had gathered.

"Cautious man," Gregson corrected, "and it could prove profitable when I bet those who don't believe and show them the proof of what came for us."

"What do you make of those ships?" asked Bryen, nodding to the northeast, having paid little attention to the conversation, instead watching the dark smudges gain greater clarity during the last few minutes. The three vessels were arcing across the water, the swirling wind pushing them directly toward the *Freedom*.

"Wary of everyone and everything," murmured Captain Gregson, shifting his gaze in the direction Bryen indicated. "I

can see why you're still standing and your adversaries are not."
He frowned, then pulled his spyglass from his belt.

"I had cause to be so," confirmed Bryen.

"That you did," agreed Captain Gregson, keeping his spyglass trained on the approaching cutters.

If he had been forced into the Pit and survived for ten years, Captain Gregson believed that he would be much the same way as Lord Keldragan. In fact, his wife had already told him that he was much like the Volkun to begin with, at least with respect to his wariness. His martial ability was another matter entirely. He doubted that he would last more than a few seconds if he faced off against the Lord Keldragan.

Captain Gregson lowered the spyglass for just a moment, staring at the three black dots that were growing steadily larger, before putting the spyglass back to use.

He didn't like the look of those ships heading toward them. Not at all. They were the size of frigates, smaller than the *Freedom*. Also faster. On their own they presented a mild threat. Together, they could give him and his crew a real challenge.

That was his concern. As was the fact that whoever was leading them certainly knew the sea, the vessels' bulging sails catching every last burst of speed the wind offered them.

Of course, that, in itself, wasn't necessarily worrisome. There were many excellent captains in these waters, although none who could handle a ship as he could, he thought modestly.

No, what bothered him, what finally forced the smile from his face, were two key details that he had identified during his initial survey of the frigates. First, the three vessels didn't fly any colors. Second, and more concerning, their sails were black.

Admittedly, that didn't confirm what he feared. It did, however, suggest that what he had hoped to avoid as they made for Ballinasloe couldn't be avoided.

He wouldn't be able to confirm their intentions until the ships came a little closer. Still, he preferred to assume the worst.

"You're right not to be trusting," said Captain Gregson.

"You're worried about those three vessels?" asked Declan, who now was staring in that direction as well.

"I am and with good reason. As I mentioned before, piracy has become a major problem here on the New Caledonian coast and it only seems to be getting worse. Every time I make port another of my friends has been lost at sea. It could be the weather," said Captain Gregson, motioning to the fog that was billowing several leagues off their port side, "it could be Baku-nawa or just bad luck or poor seamanship. More likely, though, it's the pirates who infest these waters like the swarms of mosquitos you find in a marsh."

"Nothing is being done to stop these pirates?" asked Bryen, although he guessed at the answer before he even asked his question.

"Governor Winborne and the other lords responsible for their Territories have done nothing about the hazard these blackhearts present. The powers that be offer words, not action. Without their assistance, we must face this peril on our own."

"What aren't you saying, Captain Gregson?" asked Bryen.

During his time with Aislinn in the Southern Marches, he had learned a great many things. One of the most essential, Bryen believed, was that often what was left unsaid was just as, if not more, important than what was said. And clearly, Captain Gregson wasn't telling them everything.

"Emelina, take a look, would you?" the Captain asked his wife, handing her the spyglass, not responding immediately to Bryen's question. He wanted to confirm his suspicions first.

The helmswoman kept a hand on the wheel as she shifted her gaze toward the northeast. Her husband might command the ship, but no one touched the helm unless she permitted it.

"I normally don't talk about rumors," began Captain Gregson, although his expression said that his words didn't match his actions. Because just as Declan had said with respect to stories and myths, there was always a kernel of truth to be found in a rumor.

"But ..." prodded Declan.

"But I've heard stories that perhaps the pirates are working with or for those ruling in New Caledonia. That's why the Governors and their cronies aren't doing anything to stop them. They're the ones who are actually profiting from those blackhearts' efforts."

"That's quite a charge," nodded Declan, although he wasn't really surprised. "You have proof of this?"

"No, not yet, although I've heard that some of the merchants based in Ballinasloe, one in particular actually, are trying to gain the evidence necessary to prove that theory. That's why I was reluctant to mention it since it's more supposition than fact." Captain Gregson shrugged, then grimaced, almost as if he were apologizing in advance for what he was about to tell them since the argument admittedly was fairly weak. "But the last time I made this voyage some sailors were talking in one of the taverns in the port."

"Sailors are always talking in taverns, Captain," said Declan.

"Indeed, they are, my friend," agreed Captain Gregson, his eyes never leaving those three ships as they drew steadily closer. "I won't dispute that. However, these sailors were different from the others who I've come across. They certainly weren't the type of mariners who I would allow on my ship."

"What was the topic of their conversation?"

"They were discussing an offer they had just received from one of the less reputable agents who makes a living by filling berths on ships crossing the Burnt Ocean. Apparently positions paid not only with a daily wage but also in prizes taken. Or so I heard."

"And you believe these men were mulling the possibility of ..."

"Joining a marauder? Yes. It only made sense."

"That information could be accurate, but why would you and some of the other captains think that the lords governing the Territories would have anything to do with it? It puts them in a potentially very dangerous situation. It puts at risk all that they have attained."

"True, but taking such a risk offers a great deal of profit as well. The ship these sailors were supposed to join was docked at the Governor of Fal Carrach's dock. Circumstantial evidence at best, I know, but it makes you wonder, doesn't it?"

"That it does," agreed Declan, who turned a pointed look toward Bryen. Based on Bryen's cynical expression, he was thinking the same thing that Declan was.

After having to deal with Marden Beleron, why would they not give some credence to the rumors that some of these lords were attempting to supplement their income in nefarious ways? In their experience, the greater someone's power and wealth, the greater their greed as well, and the greater their willingness to do whatever was required to achieve their objectives.

"And what of these three ships coming up on us from the northeast?" asked Bryen, his deep grey eyes fixed on the vessels that cut more sharply through the waves toward the west on a path that would see them come alongside the *Freedom* in a quarter hour at most. Obviously, these black-sailed ships had every intention of catching up to them.

"We should be able to stay ahead of them for a little while longer on this course," concluded Emelina, handing the spyglass back to her husband and returning her attention to the *Freedom's* passage through the rolling waves. "They'll have to come at us from the stern as they've misjudged the angle of approach just enough to give us a chance. When they're in a better position to make a run at us, we'll have some decisions to make."

"They're faster than us," grumbled Declan.

"Yes, that can't be denied," said Captain Gregson. "My sailors and I will do all that we can to stay ahead of them. We can do that for only so long, however. Even with our extra sailcloth, we're too large, too heavy. So long as this wind holds in their favor, they'll catch us."

"Uplifting prediction, Piotr," offered Emelina.

"I aim to please," Captain Gregson replied, his telltale smile back as he offered it to his wife. "In the meantime, I'd suggest that you and your Blood Company get ready for a fight. Just in case."

"Wary of everyone and everything, Captain?" asked Declan with a sly grin.

"Just so. It's why I'm not yet shark bait."

~

"Is it as we thought?" asked Bryen.

The three ships were almost upon them. They still didn't fly any colors to show who they were, although their black sails confirmed for the crew that they had become the next prize for the pirates haunting these waters. Assuming the brigands caught them, of course.

The captains of the vessels were quite skilled. Throughout the chase, the three ships remained in a tight, triangular formation, tacking easily in response to whatever direction Emelina turned the wheel as she searched for any additional speed that she could find as the gusty wind pushed them closer to New Caledonia. Even so, despite her obvious competence, slowly but steadily, the distance between the ships shrank.

Just as Captain Gregson suggested they would, at the outset of the hunt, their hunters attempted to curl in toward them.

They tried to time their approach so that they could pull up along both sides of the *Freedom*, thereby boxing them in.

Emelina refused to allow that to happen, demonstrating a rare skill as she milked even more speed from the wind, seeming to have a preternatural ability to keep their vessel on course while finding an even stronger blast that kept them just ahead of their pursuers.

The vessels behind them had no other option but to adjust their approach because of Emelina's unique ability to frustrate their efforts. Missing by just a few minutes the spot where their paths would have brought them right up against the *Freedom*, the hunters shifted their focus to tracking the *Freedom* from the rear, knowing that with time, the speed of their lighter, smaller ships would play to their advantage.

Therefore, even with Emelina's masterful efforts to stay clear of the sea dogs barking at their stern, eventually the race would come to an end, and not in their favor.

Bryen watched all this from the Griffons' deck, smiling every now and then, appreciating Emelina's skill and experience. The helmswoman usually took them no more than a degree or two to port or starboard as she allowed the wind to guide her, each time she did so thwarting another attempt by their pursuers to draw alongside.

His smile slipped, his usually grim visage returning, when he saw the two ships flanking the lead vessel break away, curling farther to the east and west respectively. He didn't understand why they would do that, seemingly giving up the chase, until he glimpsed two more dark specks emerge from a fog bank to the southwest that Emelina had been heading toward.

He was about to call out, but there was no need. Emelina saw these two new arrivals to the hunt the same time Bryen did, Davin's cry from his place in the crow's nest offering an additional warning for all aboard.

With the two new ships, both with black sails, only a few hundred yards off their bow, Emelina turned the wheel sharply, making more for the northwest.

A smart move, Bryen thought. The pair of frigates that sailed out of the fog cut across their wake, missing them by only a few hundred feet.

Their prize having eluded them, the pirates scrambled across the rigging of their ships, adjusting the sails so that these two frigates could join the chase.

And because they were so close, Bryen heard the curses from the captains standing at their helms fly across the space separating them. The raiders had not expected such a bold move from such a large ship.

The only move really, Bryen knew, but it came with a cost. Because now the *Freedom* was hemmed in on both the port and starboard sides by the ships that had been pursuing them from the start.

Emelina's only choice now was to run with the wind for as long as she could, all the while knowing that the frigates on both sides of her would slowly but surely cut in toward her until the boarding ropes were flung across.

"Does it look as bad from up there as it does from here?" asked Bryen, turning his gaze toward the low-lying clouds above them, a consequence of the fog bank that they had been skirting. He couldn't see who he was looking for, but he didn't have to. He knew where she was.

"It doesn't look good," Lycia replied in Bryen's mind, the Protector connecting to the gladiator with the Talent.

Lycia often spent much of the day flying above the *Freedom* riding on the back of Arabella, she and the Griffon having become fast friends. Hidden in the clouds, she offered Bryen a bird's-eye view and perhaps a few useful options as well.

"How long before they're on us?"

"A quarter hour at most," Lycia replied. *"Those two ships that*

sailed out of the fog are coming back around. They're less of a concern for now. But those two ships blocking you in, there's little that Emelina can do about them with that third vessel closing in on the stern."

"Positive as always," murmured Bryen.

"Just telling you how it is."

"I would expect nothing less. What are we facing?"

"Give me a moment to get a better count."

"What do you see, Lord Keldragan?" asked Captain Gregson. He stood next to his wife at the wheel, though he was careful not to get too close so that he didn't interfere with her as she searched for some way to break free from the frigates pinching at both sides.

"You were right to be wary," said Bryen, not bothering to remind the shipmaster that he didn't care for titles. "It almost seems like they knew we would be here."

"It does, doesn't it. I had never imagined that pirates could coordinate their efforts so effectively."

Captain Gregson wanted to think more about what Bryen had just said, but he didn't have the time to consider how these raiders might have known of their passage, especially after the delay caused by the storm. "Any information our eyes in the sky would be willing to provide would prove helpful."

Just then, Lycia spoke again in Bryen's mind. *"On the two ships to the port and starboard, more than fifty men are preparing to board. So more than a hundred in all."*

"And on the ship at our stern?"

"More than the other two combined. A hundred and twenty. Maybe a dozen more than that, but I can't get a good count. There are too many of them running around the deck like their breeches are on fire."

Bryen gave Captain Gregson a quick update on what they were facing. He believed that the Blood Company could handle those numbers. What were several hundred pirates compared to the Kraken or Ghoules?

Even so, he preferred not to take the risk if he could avoid it. As Declan liked to say, the best battle was the one you didn't have to fight.

"You can deal with that many?" asked Captain Gregson.

"If necessary," Bryen replied, "but you know from experience that you never know what could happen in a fight. Once the blades are out, all bets are off."

"Right you are," agreed the Captain. He took a few seconds to think, an idea coming to mind. His only idea, in fact. "Maybe there's something we can do to improve our odds. If we can't dissuade these pirates from following us, perhaps we can reduce their numbers so that when they do try to board us, it will be a more certain clash." He turned toward his wife. "Emelina, please take us into the Floe."

Captain Gregson said it as if he were making a simple request, but Emelina clearly didn't take it that way. Her look of concern mixed with excitement when she glanced back at her husband made Bryen think of Davin's constant need for a new adventure, usually the riskiest and most dangerous one possible.

"Are you certain?" she asked, her eyes sparkling with anticipation. "You're not teasing me?"

"Well, if you don't think you can manage it, I can always take the wheel."

"Not even when I'm dead," growled Emelina, a broad smile breaking out on her face.

Her eyes sparking dangerously because of her new assignment, with a harsh turn of the wheel, the *Freedom* heeled hard to port, cutting right in front of the pirate ship on that side. Emelina avoided a collision by no more than fifty feet.

In fact, they were so close that the pirates actually shot flaming arrows in their direction. None struck home, however, all of them falling into the sea. Emelina's surprising maneuver had caught them off guard.

Bryen turned his gaze to where they were headed, less concerned by the pirates shifting course to pursue them than the challenge they now faced. The hazy line of white that was still a league distant gained greater clarity as the *Freedom* sliced through the waves.

Captain Gregson had told him about the Floe. A field of icebergs that drifted from the south to the north, melting as they floated into warmer water, pushed there by the current created by the Sea of Mist meeting the Burnt Ocean.

Bryen had been curious about what Captain Gregson had described. However, that didn't mean that he had any desire to sail in among the mammoth icecaps at speed.

"Can we go any faster, Captain Gregson?" asked Davin, a wild grin matching the spark in his eyes. He had climbed down from the crow's nest, wanting to jump right into the fight that he expected would be upon them soon. "Our pace is a bit staid at present."

"You want to go faster through a field of icebergs?" muttered Captain Gregson, shaking his head in disbelief. He cringed on the inside every time Emelina steered the *Freedom* around a floating deathtrap, which was quite often, knowing what would happen if she misjudged by just a whisker. His wife was relishing the challenge while at the same time giving him an ulcer.

Sometimes, she avoided the sharp edges of the floating hulks by no more than a few feet. And that was with the wind still filling their sails as they made their way through the churning water that marked the end of the Burnt Ocean and the beginning of the Sea of Mist.

Did Davin not understand the danger that these icebergs presented? One good strike, even just a thin scrape in the wrong place along the hull, and they'd all be swimming for their lives. Until they drowned, froze to death in the frigid water, or were plucked from the ocean by the pirates chasing them to serve as entertainment before they were put to death.

"Are you all right in the head, lad? After you took up diving off the crow's nest, I worried about you. I wondered even more when you surfed right next to the Bakunawa and treated that monster as if you were spearfishing. This request seems to confirm my suspicions."

"My sister thinks I might have been hit one too many times in the head when I was in the Pit. I never really kept track, though, so I couldn't say for sure."

Davin stood at the helm, a broad smile plastered across his face. He savored every second of the *Freedom* slaloming through the treacherous obstacle course. Even so, he thought that it could be made a touch more exciting.

He had asked Emelina if she could bring the ship even closer to the icecaps. She told him to bug off.

He had been disappointed, although not surprised. So, all he had left as an option was more speed.

Next to him stood Captain Gregson, nervous, fidgeting behind his wife, issuing orders to the sailors scrambling around the deck and in the rigging as he watched Emelina navigate their large ship through the dangerous Floe.

Maybe Davin's sister was correct, Gregson thought. Maybe there was something off with the red-haired gladiator.

Then again, the salty mariner had to admit that his wife was doing a masterful job, cutting in between the icebergs with a delicate, experienced touch.

It would have been fun to watch if not for their dire circumstances and his increasing fear as to how this chase was going to end.

He was growing tired of this particular adventure. And he worried that eventually their luck would run out.

The current that carried the icecaps varied in width, although never by less than two leagues. Based on what Davin had told him in terms of the breadth of the obstacle course when he came down from the crow's nest, Gregson assumed that they were about a third of the way through the field with a league, maybe a little more, to go.

He didn't doubt his wife's abilities to guide them through the moving maze. He feared that the pirates pursuing them could cause them to falter at the worst possible time.

The three ships closest to them were gaining, just as he assumed that they would. The hounds appeared to be unconcerned about where they were headed and the dangers they faced, more concerned about losing such a large prize.

And he knew that their attempted escape would only become more difficult. Captain Gregson assumed that the two pirate ships that had failed to take them when they came out of the fog and that were farther behind than these three vessels would be entering the Floe right about now.

Thankfully, the frigate that had been tracking them on their starboard side had dropped off the pace. The captain, eager to bring his vessel alongside them, had cut too close to what looked like a small icecap but was actually quite a large one, the ice spreading out a good distance in all directions beneath the water. An unseen jagged spike ripped open the hull below the waterline.

Gregson didn't feel any sympathy for them.

Although the wounded vessel tried to continue to maneuver through the Floe, Captain Gregson knew that they wouldn't make it. The ship was listing badly to the port side.

It wouldn't be long before they were dead in the water. Soon after, they'd be beneath the waves, the current of the Floe forcing the floundering ship into an iceberg.

The ship on the port side had sailed almost a quarter mile away from them, not wanting to meet the same fate, prepared to cut back toward them when the time was right.

The third ship remained locked onto their stern, no more than a thousand yards behind them, attempting as much as possible to mimic their movements as they slowly closed the distance between them.

Despite the white-knuckle danger, he could tell that Davin loved every second of the chase.

Captain Gregson almost envied him. Almost.

He could only imagine what the lad might do if he ever faced a situation where the excitement that he craved was unavailable.

Actually, he already knew the answer. He'd find trouble for himself like diving out of a crow's nest.

"She might be right, lad," Captain Gregson muttered under his breath.

"You have nothing to fear, Captain Gregson," said Bryen. "Davin is just addicted to the adrenaline of a good adventure, even when he claims that he's not. It's a common result for those who spend too much time in the Pit. In fact, it's often a requirement if you wish to survive that experience for more than just a few weeks."

"Then how come it doesn't seem to affect you, Lord Keldragan? I haven't seen you jump out of the crow's nest a single time."

"Because I wasn't hit on the head as many times as Davin was," Bryen replied with a straight face.

Captain Gregson chuckled at that, even as his eyes crinkled with worry. "Watch the port side, love."

"Have no fear, I see it," replied Emelina, turning the wheel less than a degree. It proved to be just enough to avoid the hidden ice. The part of the iceberg that stuck out of the sea resembled a dozen masts bonded together, so not a very large obstacle. But the helmswoman knew from experience what waited for them beneath the surface. "Now stop telling me what to do. Right now, this is my ship, not yours. Got it?"

"Sorry, love," murmured Captain Gregson, not wanting to risk distracting her at the worst possible time. "I'll leave you be."

"Funny, very funny," said Davin, missing the conversation between husband and wife.

"I do what I can when I can," Bryen replied with a smile.

"Don't I know it," grumbled Davin, "and it's not always as you say it is. I wasn't making any such claims when we were fighting our way through the Lost Land to the Temple of the Ghoules. I was not enjoying that adventure one bit."

"You both entered the Lost Land?" asked Captain Gregson, needing something with which he could distract himself.

He was fighting hard not to offer more advice to Emelina, even as his hands moved in front of him, mimicking the movements of his wife at the wheel. He hated not being in control at a time like this, but he was willing to acknowledge that Emelina was much more skilled at the helm than he was.

"No one has ever entered the Lost Land and survived other than that Magus during the First Ghoule War," the Captain continued.

The two gladiators both gave the Captain of the *Freedom* knowing looks.

"Have we got some stories for you." Before Davin could begin a tale, Bryen challenged him once again.

"Say what you want, but I find that hard to believe. Not even when we were swinging on those vines across that acidic river, and you made that throw with your spear and killed the Echidna waiting to rip out my heart?"

"An Echidna?" wondered Captain Gregson, having a difficult time keeping track of the conversation between the two gladiators while also keeping an eye on his wife as she spun the wheel hard to port, seeking to curl away from an icecap that was drifting right toward them and was at least as large as a small castle. "What's an Echidna?"

"Think of a Ghoule crossed with a snake," replied Bryen.

"I don't think I want to," admitted the Captain.

Davin's expression shifted slightly because of Bryen's question, his eyes sparking brightly. "Well, you have me there. That was kind of fun."

"Even though we almost died multiple times?"

"That added some spice to it all," Davin admitted grudgingly.

"I thought you were enjoying yourself," nodded Bryen.

"That was quite a throw, wasn't it?" said Davin, not yet ready to let the topic go. "While swinging on a vine across an acidic river, no less. I'm sure that no one else has done that before, and certainly not with my accuracy."

"Nor will anyone else ever do it again," offered Bryen, seeing instantly how his words brightened Davin's mood.

"You're probably right about that. Did you tell Dorlan about that throw like I asked you to?"

"I did."

"How did he react? Was he angry that I made a better throw than he did when he was fighting that dragon in the Pit?"

"He didn't say anything at all."

"He didn't say anything at all?" Davin was shocked. "What do you mean he didn't say anything?"

How could he not? They had been trying to one up the other with the spear for years. And, in Davin's opinion, after that experience with the Echidna, he had won the contest.

"He didn't say anything at all. Dorlan just looked at me, harrumphed as if it wasn't as impressive as I was making it out to be, then shrugged his shoulders and walked away."

"He did what?" Davin exclaimed. "How could he do that? My throw had to have been better than his!"

"He didn't seem to think so. You'll have to talk to him if you want an explanation. I can't tell you what he was thinking."

"Can we get back to what's going on in the here and now?" asked Captain Gregson in a sharp tone, not understanding how the two gladiators could become so easily engrossed in something that had nothing to do with the two ships swiftly bearing down on them. The one on the port side was arcing toward them now on a broad curl, seeking to exploit an opening in the icebergs flowing up from the south.

"Right ... sorry." Bryen shifted his focus back to the ships weaving through the icecaps and preparing to attack.

Although heading into the Floe had taken one ship out of the race, unfortunately the two that continued their pursuit were gaining on them, avoiding the lethal obstacles with a practiced ease. The pirate ships, smaller and faster, were demonstrating a maneuverability that the *Freedom* couldn't match, even under Emelina's skilled hands.

"On its current course, the ship on our port side could be on us in minutes," said Captain Gregson.

The pirates manning that vessel seemed to agree, standing at their starboard rail, grapple hooks in hand, waiting for the right opportunity.

"Perhaps Lycia," suggested Davin.

"I was thinking the same thing," said Bryen.

"Any thoughts on how you could slow down the ship that's almost upon us?"

"We'll figure something out," she replied, Bryen detecting a distinct note of pleasure in her voice.

"The ship on our port side shouldn't be a problem for much longer, Captain Gregson."

"What's she going to do?" asked Davin.

"She didn't say," replied Bryen. "I have no doubt that it will be quite final, however. You know your sister."

"That I do. This is going to be fun to watch."

"What's who going to do?" asked Captain Gregson.

"Lycia," replied Bryen, as if that were answer enough.

"Do you think whatever she does will work?" asked Davin.

Bryen looked at Lycia's twin. "We are talking about your sister you know. I've yet to see her fail at anything she puts her mind to."

Davin nodded. "Right, sorry. Whatever it is she does, as I said, it should be quite a sight."

"Here she comes."

Bryen, Davin, and Captain Gregson looked to the port side. The pirate ship curling in toward them had been forced to make a last-second adjustment, slicing right past an iceberg that wasn't moving as fast as the others.

To do that the captain of that vessel needed to turn more sharply than he wanted to, his ship's prow now lining up directly with the port side of the *Freedom* rather than angling toward it so that he could come alongside.

Needing to bring his ship around so that his pirates could board, the captain turned the wheel hard, the ship heeling over sharply to avoid the collision.

Emelina seemed unconcerned by the proximity of the pirate vessel. She kept the *Freedom* on its current course.

They all saw why just a second later. An iceberg was coming up fast on their port side, the pirate ship now on a course to crash into it.

The captain of the frigate turned the wheel hard to starboard then, almost recognizing the danger too late. The ship avoided the bulk of the hazard by only a few yards, although a long sliver of ice that extended up and out of the water did slice across the ship's hull, leaving a long gash just above the waterline.

Though slowed by the scrape, the damaged frigate continued on its course, curling back toward the *Freedom*.

Emelina had gained the distance that she wanted thanks to

the captain's miscue, and now their attacker was aimed toward the stern rather than the bow.

Based on what he saw happening on the deck of the marauder, Bryen assumed that the pirates were congratulating themselves for avoiding an almost lethal collision, and they were likely praising their captain for his seamanship. Instead of a watery grave, they would be back in a position to board the *Freedom* in just a few minutes, an open path appearing in the Floe for the next few miles.

Bryen hoped that the men shouting curses at them were enjoying their temporary reprieve, because the pirates had made a lethal mistake. They had failed to consider what might be above them.

In a streak of auburn fur and feathers, Lycia dove down out of the clouds on Arabella's back, coming so fast that even the pirate manning the crow's nest didn't have the time to call out a warning.

Their attack took less than five seconds. The damage, however, was irreversible and fatal to the ship and pirates.

Arabella smashed down onto the wheel, using her powerful paws to crush the captain into the wreckage. She then kicked with her back paws, destroying what was left of the tiller just to make sure.

In a flash, the Griffon was gone, lifting herself back into the sky with her powerful wings.

Lycia offered a few choice curses as the pirates on the main deck watched, stunned, never having seen the like, some barely believing what had just happened. The men with crossbows in their hands failed to even raise their weapons.

The effect of Arabella's attack was immediate. With the wheel destroyed, the pirates had no way to maneuver their vessel. Worse, the cutter was at full sail.

Already curling toward the *Freedom*, the ship continued on its arc, past the stern of the large merchant ship, missing it by no more than fifty feet, sailing through its wake, then continuing on an unavoidable and disastrous track.

Just seconds later, the pirate ship was sinking. The frigate slammed into an iceberg prow first and then scraped along the side of the cap, the stern disappearing beneath the waves after the hull cracked and then split apart near the mainmast.

Another ship down, three more left by Bryen's count.

"That woman is well named," muttered Captain Gregson, having heard tales of the Crimson Devil fighting in the Pit.

"That she is," agreed Bryen. "It's a good thing that she's on our side."

Lycia jumped off Arabella's back when the Griffon landed on the deck, nodding to herself in satisfaction.

She had killed men. She had killed women. She had killed beasts and monsters. Not because it had brought her any joy or pleasure. It was always for one reason and one reason only. To stay alive.

And now she had killed a ship for that same reason.

That was something that no other gladiator could claim. Not even her brother.

She felt slightly sickened knowing that so many pirates were drowning that very second, but she had little sympathy for them. They had sealed their own fates as soon as they decided to make her ship a target, and she had no doubt what would have happened if they had taken the *Freedom* as a prize.

Rubbing her forehead against Arabella's fur just below her neck, Lycia scratched beneath the feathers near her eye and then along her beak. The Griffon purred contentedly.

Once done, she strode across the deck to the helm, musing on what she could do to improve their odds of reaching Ballinasloe. If she and Arabella could take out one ship, why not another?

"You outdid yourself," said Davin.

His voice suggested that he was a little jealous that he hadn't been up in the sky with her. Her brother seemed to have forgotten that his stomach rarely agreed with him when he flew on the back of a Griffon.

"I did, yes," Lycia replied matter-of-factly. She then turned her attention to Bryen, who was speaking to Declan, Aislinn, and Captain Gregson. "Do you want me to go back up and try for the other ships? I don't think the one at the stern saw me. They were still behind an iceberg when I attacked and the clouds are quite low, so they probably won't see me coming either."

Lycia's expression was hopeful. She was more than ready to have another go at their pursuers.

"We could take a different approach," Aislinn said. "We could use the Talent to set our hunters on fire."

For just a moment, Bryen thought that she was about to do it, sensing her reaching for the power that she could employ.

"I appreciate your desire to remove the threat the pirates present," Bryen said quickly, "but let's hold off for now."

"You're taking all the fun out of this," muttered Lycia.

"You've got that right," agreed Aislinn. "We could end this now. Doing so would help us and any other merchant ships plying these waters."

Bryen ignored them both, having learned that it was never a good sign when Aislinn and Lycia agreed on something. He turned his attention to the helmswoman. "Emelina, how much longer until we're past these icebergs?"

"A league, no more, Lord Keldragan," Emelina having the same habit as her husband of giving Bryen a title that he didn't want. "Probably less. Then open seas once we're past them."

Bryen nodded, thinking.

"What do you have in mind, lad?" asked Declan. He was quite familiar with Bryen's expression.

"I'm thinking that we should have a talk with our pirate friends. What Captain Gregson said about our attackers having potential benefactors piqued my interest."

"Now you're really taking all the fun out of this," said Davin, offering his support to Lycia and Aislinn.

"Only for a time," replied Bryen. "The pirates will get what's due to them. Can you keep us clear of the vessel at our stern until we're free of the Floe."

"Of course, Lord Keldragan," replied Emelina.

Bryen nodded, expecting no less. "Once we're through the Floe, we'll let the pirates catch up to us. I want to find out who they are, who they're working for, and hopefully determine if what Captain Gregson suspects is accurate. There's only one way to do that."

"And if they don't want to talk?" asked Declan. He understood the value of Bryen's idea, but he also knew that no strategy, no matter how well thought out, ever worked as you expected or wanted.

"Then we sink them," Bryen said, his eyes hard, his voice cold. "But we'll let the pirates decide."

3

SENSE OF LOSS

"Kerala! Kerala!"

The young man kept shouting out the name impatiently as he lumbered across the battlements of the Stone, the fact that those battlements were still under construction an obvious annoyance that stoked his always ready anger. Growling under his breath, he worked a few of his stubby fingers in between his black leather armor and his crisp white shirt, which flashed when it caught the sunlight as he advanced down the parapet.

Although immaculately clean and of obvious quality, his armor had been constricting him more than usual the last few weeks. And at that very moment he felt like he could barely breathe.

It was as if the leather was shrinking, fraying even. Like he had worn it out in the rain for the last few months. Every day. All day.

But he hadn't. He'd been careful about that.

He would need to speak with his armorer about how this could even happen, disappointed in the shoddy craftsmanship. And it wasn't a conversation that his armorer was going to enjoy. Not with the punishment he had in mind. Before that though he needed to complete another task.

The stonemasons scrambled out of the way as he trudged by, forgetting their work for a few seconds. Mortar dripped from their trowels as they pressed themselves against the outer curtain and dipped their heads the barest amount required in order to avoid any claim of disrespect by their employer.

They felt no love toward the lord who demanded their service at the expense of their other work.

Work that actually paid.

But they weren't in a position to deny him.

They had felt the wrath of Torstan Sharperson one too many times and had no desire to experience it again. It was better to stay clear and beneath the notice of the Governor of the Highlands when he was in such a mood.

"Yes, Governor Sharperson," replied a small man who stepped out of the shadowy entrance to the tower that soared a hundred feet into the sky.

Once the spire was finished, it would allow the Governor to gaze upon his domain all the way to the northern border of the Territory. Assuming it was ever completed.

He was having some difficulty acquiring the necessary stone that would take the tower three hundred more feet into the sky.

Governor Sharperson designed the tower so that at the very top a massive pyre would burn day and night, serving as a beacon for those coming to the Stone. A guide to the travelers on the road and a reminder of the might of the man who ruled in the Highlands.

The chamberlain's job was to make certain that this second spire was better built than the first one. Kerala was doing all that he could to ensure that happened.

He didn't want to relive the horror when the original tower

collapsed. He didn't want to consider what would happen to him if this second tower followed the first.

"What is the matter, Governor Sharperson?" asked Kerala obsequiously.

"Come with me," he ordered, every few seconds his fat fingers working their way between his shirt and armor, trying and failing to give himself more room to breathe.

Clearly furious, the Governor of the Highlands stalked down the circular steps of the turret, ignoring the pounding coming from above. A constant cloud of grime filtered through the air as the stonemasons worked at all hours to raise the tower to the height demanded by the youngest son of the Lord of Sharston.

Huffing and puffing his way down the steps, his face turning red because of his infrequent exertion, finally he appeared in the bustling courtyard where his workers gathered the supplies they required while at the same time even more materials were brought in on wagons.

A never-ending process. Or so it was supposed to be. It had slowed almost to a crawl during the last few weeks, Sharperson finding it more difficult to obtain the resources he needed to complete the construction of his citadel.

The Governor paid no attention to what was going on around him, striding down the wide road that led away from the keep. The workers dodged out of his way as if he were the shark and they the minnows.

Sharperson did not seem to notice, nor did he even acknowledge the men and women responsible for creating the reality and the perception that he sought for himself. Seemingly in a world all his own, he viewed himself as well above all these commoners.

These people were nothing more than tools to him. To be used as needed, not deserving of his notice. Unless they failed to do as he required.

Then he paid attention to them. In the worst possible way.

When he reached the guardhouse, the portcullis being put in place at that very instant, Sharperson turned around. He took a moment to examine all the work being done, although he had an ulterior motive. He was winded from his brief exercise.

Of course, he would never admit to himself or anyone else that he had stopped to catch his breath. That was a sign of weakness.

And he was not weak.

As he had learned while growing up at his father's knee and having to deal with six older brothers, Talus being the worst, displaying any sign of weakness simply led to a rash of continued abuse and humiliation.

He had experienced it much too often when he was a child.

And he would never experience it again.

Ever.

He nodded with pleasure as he gazed upon the cranes, scaffolding, and many stonemasons, carpenters, and other skilled craftspeople scurrying about, seeking to complete construction of the Stone before winter came. Now just a season away.

Not much time to complete the work. But they would. Of that Sharperson was quite confident.

His workers didn't have a choice. More than their livelihoods depended on it. He had made that perfectly clear.

"Impressive, isn't it, Kerala?" nodded Sharperson, his initial anger cooling to just a simmer, replaced by the contentment that he likened to a father gazing for the first time upon his just born child.

He had waited almost a decade to make this happen. But he wouldn't have to wait much longer.

His time was coming. He could feel it.

For him to be who he truly was, who he truly was meant to

be, he needed a fortress that reflected his power in this Territory. In all of New Caledonia, in fact.

Now, finally, his dream, the symbol of his power, was well on its way to completion.

Once he was done, all would know the name Torstan Sharperson. On both sides of the Burnt Ocean.

A name that all would remember. A name that all would respect. A name that many would fear.

A name that would overshadow every other lord in Caledonia, New and Old, and particularly the names of his brothers.

The work on the Stone had been slow to begin, in fits and starts as he struggled to pull together the necessary resources and materials. More times than he cared to count the construction ground to a halt.

Growing tired of the excuses he instituted a program to motivate the workers. That it was based on fear didn't bother him in the least.

Time in the dungeon for poor craftsmanship or mistakes that caused unnecessary delays, maybe even a hanging if the error was particularly egregious. As a result, the skilled craftspeople of the Highlands, who were required to devote a good portion of their week to working on his keep, had been more than happy to intensify their efforts.

What was it to him if a man died when the scaffolding on the west wall collapsed? Or if the retaining wall crumbled because the tower that he wanted to build as a shining example of his beneficence and fortitude, and of course his power, proved to be too tall and too heavy for the foundation?

The stonemasons losing their lives were of little concern. Speed was rewarded above all else.

"Quite impressive, yes, Lord Sharperson. I've never seen its like."

Wiping a clean cloth across the sweat bubbling up on his bald head, Sharperson smiled at the perceived compliment. He scanned his creation one more time, thrilled by how the walls of the Stone zigged and zagged as they worked their way up the incline of the monstrous rock that served as the base of the fortress. And at the very top, his private keep, the tower that would be the beacon of his rule rising in the very center.

Anyone entering the Stone from this direction, as would be the case at the north gate as well, would be given the impression that as they advanced deeper into the fortress they were walking into the maw of a sharp-toothed monster.

Like the dragons of old, he believed. Just as he demanded. Just as he wanted.

He had learned from his older brother Talus that appearance and perception were just as important as the force of arms when exercising power. Allowing that critical knowledge to guide him had led him to this specific design.

His brother would be jealous if he could see all this. Knowing that, in and of itself, made all the nagging frustrations and delays worthwhile.

Once complete, conquering the Stone would be all but impossible.

For the many travelers who would have no choice but to stop here, Sharperson's citadel straddling the primary route that led toward Shadow's Reach to the north and Ballinasloe to the south, it would leave an indelible impression. As well as a good number of golds in his pockets.

He had no doubt that word of his greatness would spread throughout the Caledonian Territories. Likely to Old Caledonia as well, finally reaching his cursed brother. Let Talus simmer in his own jealousy for once.

"I'm glad you agree, Kerala, otherwise I'd have to throw you in the dungeon."

With a bark of laughter, his heart no longer beating so fast that it felt like it was going to burst through his chest, Sharperson strode out from beneath the gate and down the road for fifty yards. At a small stone marker by the side of the road he turned to the right, then followed a narrow trail that was barely visible in the brush.

Kerala, feeling uneasy, just as he always did in the presence of the Governor, had no choice but to follow.

The taxes that the Governor imposed on the people of the Highlands went a long way to supporting the construction of the Stone and the opulence to which Sharperson wanted to grow accustomed. However, in addition to learning the meaning of real power, he had absorbed from his profligate brother another critical lesson.

To solidify his hold on all that he had acquired and to ensure that he was in a position to build on that power, he needed more than one source of revenue.

Taxing the Highlanders was a good start, a foundation of sorts, but it wasn't enough. It would never be enough for what he had in mind.

Thus, the placement of the Stone.

The merchants and settlers winding their way through the Highlands were required to pay a toll for the use of the road. That was proving to be an excellent income stream as well. They had no way to avoid the fee because this was the only trail through the spires that could manage anything with wheels.

The Highlands was too imposing. The many tracks winding their way in among the peaks were too small for wagons. And they were too dangerous for those seeking to make the journey on foot. Too much risk and not enough reward for what you could carry on your back.

Of course, as Governor, he could take action against the threat haunting the peaks, but he had other issues at the top of his mind.

Besides, why would he do anything that would benefit others that would only harm his interests over the long term?

Sharperson had two good sources of revenue that helped to

fill his coffers. Profitable, yes, though not as profitable as they needed to be.

Because his treasury was being depleted just as fast as it was being replenished.

The taxes still weren't enough for him to achieve the place that he so deserved in New Caledonia. Therefore, a third source of revenue was required, and this stream had proven to be the most lucrative of all.

Once Sharperson reached the bottom of the trail that ended a hundred feet below the winding road, Kerala right at his heels, he cut down off the dirt track, walking along the precipice upon which the western wall of the Stone rose. He followed the well-trodden path around the edge of the cliff and then stalked through the forest below the keep.

He emerged near the base of the massive peak that rose to the northwest of the Stone. He walked out from between the trees and into a large clearing that was invisible to any who might look in this direction from the road above.

The Stone would be Sharperson's masterpiece. A testament to himself and who he was.

But this small settlement right next to the mountain, the first that he had built when he assumed control over the Highlands upon receiving his charter from Corinthus Beleron, was the primary driver of all that he sought to accomplish in this Territory.

One of the first settlers to arrive at this ramshackle village had named it Miser's Way. Sharperson hated that appellation.

He offered a different name instead. A better name.

It did little good. It never stuck.

Sharp's Glade had such a nice ring to it. Yet even under threat of a whipping the people living in this small town ignored his order and called the settlement what they wanted to call it.

A small sign of defiance. At first, it worried him. He had

learned over time, however, that some flexibility was required regarding matters of little importance so long as that flexibility did not extend to matters of great importance.

In the end, despite several attempts to change the name to what he believed it should be, he simply accepted Miser's Way.

What did it matter anyway? It wasn't like any of these people would ever be leaving this village.

And, strangely, as the years passed, he began to feel a sick sense of pride at what he had accomplished. After all, he put very little into supporting the people living in this hamlet, even as they put everything they had into making him rich.

"Any problems today, boys?" asked the Governor in a tone that suggested there better not have been any as he walked right through the small gate. The squad of soldiers standing guard nodded in respect, even offering a few "Governors" and "Lord Sharpersons" as he passed.

"Of course not, Lord Sharperson," said the Sergeant in charge of the detail.

"Then we'll need to agree to disagree," murmured the Governor, although only loud enough for Kerala to hear.

Ignoring the soldiers' salutes, Sharperson glanced at the semicircular wooden wall of the stockade that ran around the village and butted up against the mountain on both sides. He was pleased to see that as he required a soldier stood every fifty feet along the parapet that rose twenty feet off the ground.

Unlike on the battlements of the Stone, however, these soldiers were focused on what was going on within the village rather than on what might be occurring beyond the wall.

Sharperson would be the first to admit that the compound wasn't much to look at. Nevertheless, Miser's Way served its purpose. And, even more important, it was cost effective.

Ever since Sharperson had arrived in the Highlands, he had used indentured servants to form the bulk of his work force. For the cost of passage, these men and women were required to provide him with seven years of labor, during which time they would be given the opportunity to pay off the debt they owed him.

A fair deal at first glance. At least that's what those who put their names or marks to paper thought.

Yet no matter how hard they worked, they never could pay off the debt.

Because of the high cost of food, housing, and medical care, and the plethora of other fees and expenses that was often lost in the fine print of the contract signed by the people leaving Caledonia in search of a better life, the likelihood of gaining their freedom and working for themselves was virtually nonexistent.

In fact, most of the original workers who came across with Sharperson ten years before were still here. Those few who weren't were more likely to have died in the mine than to have fulfilled the terms of their agreement with him.

As a result of the financial success of Miser's Way, Sharperson had applied the same model elsewhere, creating a dozen more villages throughout the Highlands. Just like Miser's Way. All designed to support the incredibly productive mines that he owned as part of his contract with the Crown.

Each village was constructed and managed in the same way. The latrines were dug in the same location in every camp. The food hall was built in the same spot. The administrative office was always set against the mountain to the right side of the entrance.

Everything, from the housing for the single miners and those with families to the supply sheds to the tracks for the carts used to bring the ore out of the mines, was placed in a very precise, time-tested way. Everything that happened in the village occurred according to a specific process.

Sharperson liked that. He preferred employing strategies

and methods that had proven their efficacy over time. Efficiency was important to him, as it meant lower costs.

Because in his mind that's what a successful business was. A combination of procedures and processes designed to gain the highest possible profit from the resources applied to make that business function.

The model, though not necessarily one that favored his workers, certainly favored him and his treasury.

"Has our special cargo arrived, Kerala?"

"Yes, Lord Sharperson. Just last night as you said it would."

"No difficulties, I hope." Sharperson said it as if there better not have been.

Kerala hedged a bit before replying, shrugging his shoulders as if to say it was really not a matter worthy of the Governor's attention. Not wanting to be the bearer of what could be perceived as bad news.

"Out with it, Kerala." Sharperson's volcanic temper, never far from the surface, already was in danger of erupting. "I heard a concerning rumor this morning during breakfast. Is it true?"

"We had a minor incident," Kerala finally admitted, sweat breaking out on his forehead despite the cool fall afternoon. "Nothing that we couldn't handle, my Lord. We didn't want to bother you with it."

"What kind of minor incident?" hissed Sharperson, his face scrunching up into an angry scowl. He wanted to hear what happened from Kerala in his own words.

"It's really not worth your time and attention, my Lord."

"Spit it out, Kerala. I'll decide what's worthy of my time and attention."

Kerala nodded and then gulped at the same time, trying to gain control over his jittery nerves. "It seems that the delivery coincided with an escape attempt."

The Governor halted, a red rage coloring his expression. After all that he provided to the people of Miser's Way, still they felt the need to ignore his largesse and challenge him? To attempt to escape the debt they owed him? How incredibly ungrateful.

"Explain."

His voice was soft. Dangerously so. Kerala knew the risk of not responding immediately and succinctly.

"It seems that a handful of the villagers decided to attempt their escape at the same exact time that the cargo we received was being put in place." Kerala always made sure that he used the term "villager" whenever speaking with the Governor about the people of Miser's Way, knowing how much Sharperson disliked the many other terms used by the Highland Guard that put such a negative light to what was being done in this town and the others built around the various mines located within the Highlands. "Captain Hippolates and the soldiers weren't aware that these villagers were hiding right where the cargo was to be stored."

The Governor's anger began to dissipate, a small smile breaking out on what slowly had become a murderous visage. "That must have been quite a surprise for the villagers foolish enough to try to break their contracts."

He could almost see what happened in his mind, enjoying every aspect of the gruesome images. He almost wished that he had been here to watch. A small part of him, the more rational part, was glad that he wasn't.

"It was, indeed, Lord Sharperson." Kerala sounded as if he was going to be sick to his stomach as he recalled what he had seen.

Captain Hippolates had called him to the mine after what had occurred. He'd likely never be able to get those scenes of the aftermath out of his mind. Biting back the bile rising in his throat, he continued.

"The cargo sensed the hiding villagers and forced its way past the soldiers. Before they could get the beast bound once again, the cargo killed two of the would-be escapees. Captain Hippolates allowed the cargo a good portion of its meal, the stupor of the beast gorging on the villagers aiding his efforts to regain control."

"A smart man," admitted Governor Sharperson. If he was in Captain Hippolates' position, he likely would have done the same. "None of the soldiers were hurt?"

"No, none were hurt. Not even touched by the beast. The restriction remained in place. The cargo didn't care about the soldiers. It cared only about the hiding villagers. They were not protected like the soldiers were."

"That's good to hear," replied Sharperson. Not so much the news that none of his soldiers were harmed -- if any of them had died, well ... they were soldiers after all -- but rather that the constraint that was supposed to protect him and his soldiers had worked. "And the villagers who survived?"

"The cargo was satisfied, at least for a time, with the two people it killed."

Sharperson nodded. "Where is the cargo now?"

"We have the cargo in an unused shaft. A guard has been set. Not for the cargo so much as to ensure that none of the workers wander down that way."

"There's no chance of the cargo getting loose before time?"

"Captain Hippolates assures me that there is nothing to worry about, Lord Sharperson. He was quite insistent. The cargo can't break the chains. And with no prey so close to them, apparently they've settled down. They've satiated their bloodlust."

"Good. We'll let the cargo loose the day after tomorrow. Continue to make certain that no one goes down that shaft. I don't want any more incidents. Do you understand, Kerala?"

"Yes, Lord Sharperson," the chamberlain nodded swiftly. "Captain Hippolates said it would be so. He said that you have nothing to fear."

"If Captain Hippolates said it, then it will be as he said," confirmed Governor Sharperson. The Captain of his Guard never failed to keep his word, even with the most disturbing, ghastly assignments.

That issue addressed, his original reason for bringing Kerala down to the village popped back into his mind. He turned on a heel and stalked through the camp toward the main shaft that led down into the mountain. These particular veins, so close to the Stone, had proven their worth since he began mining here shortly after he arrived in the Territories.

He had discovered a variety of jewels, although predominantly diamonds the last few years as his miners dug deeper, as well as several good veins of gold. Sharperson had put most of what they had found into the construction of the Stone and expanding the size of the Highland Guard.

It was the right thing to do in his opinion. In his mind, a Guard was much like a fortress. The bigger the better.

Both in terms of reality and for appearance's sake.

Finding soldiers to serve in the Highland Guard had been easy. He need only focus on those who were willing to cross a certain line if it meant better pay.

However, he had made clear that crossing that line could only happen at his command. And he had not ordered what he saw rising before him.

His anger began to simmer once again, steadily increasing to a boil.

Two men and a woman swung from the gallows.

"Explain this to me, Kerala," said Sharperson in a very soft, menacing tone. "Explain why this was done without my knowledge."

"These are the three surviving villagers who tried to escape, Lord Sharperson," Kerala said, "or I should say they were the surviving villagers. Captain Hippolates said that an example needed to be made."

"I decide who lives and dies here, Kerala." The Governor, who was at least twice the size of his chamberlain, stepped in close to Kerala, his presence making the smaller man even more nervous than he was already. "No one else, Kerala. Only me. I thought you and Captain Hippolates understood that?"

"I do, Lord Sharperson. We do. I promise you. Have no fear of that. But we didn't really have a choice."

Sharperson bent down so that he was looking Kerala square in the eyes. His own blazed with a white-hot rage that almost made Kerala release his bowels.

He had seen that look before from his Lord. Usually it appeared right before Sharperson sent someone to the gallows or some other grisly death.

"Then how did this happen, Kerala?"

The little man explained as quickly as he could. "When the physick was binding their wounds, two factors led to the decision that I made in consultation with Captain Hippolates. We didn't want to wake you since the sun was only beginning to peek above the horizon, and I knew that you hadn't gotten much sleep because of your endeavors from the night before."

Kerala hoped that by looping Captain Hippolates into the explanation -- Governor Sharperson's current favorite -- that he could not only spread the blame, but also potentially avoid a punishment. Still, just to be safe, he brought in his Lord's escapades between the sheets hoping that it would help improve the hulking Governor's mood.

And it did, seeming to have an immediate effect. The taller man's grimace that appeared to be almost painful flickered to a softer expression of amusement and gratification.

"The physick said that the wounds the three villagers had taken were severe, that they had little time to live," continued Kerala. "An hour, no more. We didn't want to lose the opportunity to make an example of them, so we told the physick to bind the wounds so that their injuries could not be seen. We then placed the hangman's noose around their necks when the night shift was leaving the mine and the morning shift was coming from the village. That way we ensured that all the miners got a chance to watch the spectacle."

Kerala gulped and then nodded when Lord Sharperson motioned with his hand to continue. The rage hiding in the Governor's eyes appeared to have faded, memories of the pleasures he had enjoyed the night before dancing behind his eyes.

"Captain Hippolates told the villagers that these three had attempted to steal some of what they had found during their shift, and that the other two had died in a tunnel collapse. He also informed the villagers that the five had not met their quota for the month, which the villagers immediately understood affected them as well, since everyone is required to contribute toward that larger objective."

"Was their production going down, Kerala?" Sharperson's anger had turned to curiosity, knowing how his chamberlain's devious mind worked. That's why he kept the little man alive even when Kerala displeased him on occasion.

"It had, Lord Sharperson." He motioned to the three villagers hanging from the scaffold. "As was the production of the two killed by the cargo. When the physick was binding their wounds, he told me that he had identified signs of the black lung disease. Their performance was suffering because they were. That might explain why all five were seeking to escape. Knowing that the black lung disease cannot be cured, perhaps they thought to enjoy their last days beyond the gates of Miser's Way."

"Perhaps, Kerala," Sharperson muttered. "Perhaps." His chamberlain had offered a good, convincing argument.

"In the larger scheme of things, Lord Sharperson, removing these five from the workforce will aid us in the long term. We will not have to feed, clothe, house, or care for villagers who cannot work and could linger for months as they waste away from their illness. And, with the next batch of indentured servants expected to make port in Ballinasloe in just the next few days, we lose very little in terms of production. No more than a few weeks will be affected. Probably even less than that."

"You and Captain Hippolates have done quite well with this situation, Kerala. Still, there is that matter of possible lost production until the new villagers arrive. That could be several weeks from now as you said. We can't afford any drop off in our take. Not now. The stream of revenue must continue to flow unimpeded."

"There's nothing to fear in that regard, Lord Sharperson. Captain Hippolates made it clear that the other miners would still be required to meet the quota despite the loss of those villagers who sought to escape. They were angry at that, though more at their peers who had put them in this situation than you. They know the rules. They know the consequences when those rules are broken."

"That they do, Kerala. You're right. I spent a lot of time and effort making sure that they did."

"Yes, you did, Lord Sharperson. That's in large part why everything is running so smoothly now. From what Captain Hippolates' soldiers have reported this morning, there is already an added sense of urgency among the day shift. I expect the same will happen tonight. They seem quite intent on avoiding the punishment to be levied out if the monthly quota is not met."

"Are you trying to flatter me, Kerala?" asked the Governor.

Kerala didn't see the anger in the back of Lord Sharperson's eyes any longer. Although his voice had hardened, whatever thoughts of pleasure that had taken up residence there had been replaced by the cool calculation of a man intent on making more out of his current position than most would think possible.

"Of course not, Lord Sharperson. I am simply speaking the truth."

For several long seconds Lord Sharperson stared at Kerala, his eyes narrowing, his posture becoming more threatening. Then he leaned back and chuckled.

"That you are, Kerala. I just wanted to have a little fun with you. I would have kept going but I feared that if I did you might soil your pants."

"Right you are," chuckled Kerala, his laughter forced, sweat dripping from his brow.

Kerala's hands clenched into fists to control the shaking that threatened to erupt. He quickly forced his fingers open once he regained some measure of composure, not wanting Lord Sharperson to see what he was doing. Not wanting him to think that he was anything but what he appeared to be.

"I have to hand it to you, Kerala. You're a crafty devil."

"Thank you, Lord Sharperson. I thank you for the compliment. I have learned quite a lot in your service."

"One thing, though, Kerala. Next time, if anyone needs to hang, you come to me first. No matter what time it is. No matter what I'm doing. As I said, I decide who lives and dies in the Highlands."

"Yes, Lord Sharperson," Kerala replied with a slight stutter.

"And if you don't heed my warning, you'll be the one swinging from the gallows. Understand?"

Kerala nodded and gulped again, hating himself every time that he did, the sudden rush of fear that surged through his body drying up his words.

"I'm glad we understand each other, Kerala," said the Governor as he turned back toward the main gate, wanting to return to the Stone so that he could keep an eye on the work, knowing that Captain Hippolates would have everything well in hand here in Miser's Way.

Kerala had made a good business decision. Sharperson valued that. He wasn't displeased by what had happened.

He had an analytical mind, so he agreed with the solution applied by his two subordinates. It all made perfect sense.

His workers were simply tools to be employed. When those tools could no longer be used then they should be tossed away, just as Kerala and Hippolates had done.

No, what bothered Sharperson was that a unique pleasure had been denied him. He relished exercising his power over life and death. Of seeing the look in another person's eyes when they realized the control he exerted over them.

He thrived on it.

He lived for it.

And in that moment, he felt the need to fill that sense of loss.

He knew exactly how to do it.

4

FIGHTING IN THE FOG

Jakob had enjoyed more success than he had anticipated that morning. Evading the Wraiths. Continuing to make his way to the south.

His approach had proven to be a good one. Nevertheless, staying ahead of the monsters in the mist was becoming more difficult just as he thought it would.

Because they, too, had implemented an effective strategy. One that was swiftly reducing his odds of escape.

Despite all that he had done to avoid a confrontation, he was certain that it wouldn't be long before they located him.

He would have to fight.

Using the Talent, he identified the first of the Wraiths in the mist. He still had a good lead, and he had reached the far southern edge of the plateau.

Nevertheless, he didn't believe that his current progress would be enough. The fog was still as thick as it was back near the heart trees. And he still had several leagues to go before he was free of the Murk.

More concerning, his hunters were no more than a few

hundred yards behind him now, having closed the distance between them with an infuriating speed.

Worse, he was running out of space. He had no good way to exit the plateau on this side.

The hidden steppe ended in a drop of several hundred feet just a half mile further on. There were no paths or crevices like the one that he had used to reach this plateau from the larger one above.

He only had two options now. Go back the way he had come and try to climb back to the plain above or continue toward the southwest to a small ridge that extended out from the steppe and over another forest of heart trees that waited a few thousand feet below.

The first option didn't appeal to him. He doubted that he could make it back past the Wraiths without being discovered.

The other option didn't really appeal to him either, because all he was doing was giving the Wraiths what they wanted. He was allowing them to trap him against the edge of the cliff.

Of course, he didn't really have much choice, did he? At least at the top of the ridge, Jakob would have a better chance of defending himself if the Wraiths found him.

When the Wraiths found him, he corrected, as he reached the beginnings of the slope that led to the top of the spine.

Better to be realistic regarding his chances.

He had gotten this far, so there was no point in stopping now. He dug his boots into the soft earth and began to make his way up.

He could see thanks to the Talent that the Wraiths were moving much faster now, coming right at him. They had a good sense of where he was.

He increased his pace. He couldn't afford to be caught on the slope.

That realization gave him an extra burst of energy as Jakob pulled himself to the top, using the rocks and long grass to help him. Instead of taking a moment to get a better idea of where he was and where the Wraiths were, he stayed low to the ground, ducking and rolling across the wet grass.

One of the Wraiths, likely the advance scout, almost ran right into him. The monster was just as surprised to see him there as he was to see the Wraith.

Yet, even with that momentary shock, the monster still had the wherewithal to swipe wildly for his throat with his three-foot-long, double-bladed daggers.

Back on his feet in a flash, Jakob sprinted to the south for several dozen yards as if he were trying to flee. He then skidded to a stop and spun around abruptly, pulling the daggers out of the sheaths on his hips and turning to face his adversary.

There was no point in trying to escape now. The Wraith was too fast. So Jakob used the only advantage that he had against this monster of the mist.

Surprise.

The Wraith was sprinting right at Jakob, never believing that his prey might have some bite. Not really thinking about his environment.

The Wraith slipped in the wet grass when he tried to stop himself from running right onto Jakob's daggers. Forced to reach down with one arm so that he didn't fall to the ground and potentially all the way back down the slope, the Wraith lost track of his target for just a heartbeat.

A costly error.

The Wraith felt a burn across his shoulder, a sharp blade slicing deeply into his flesh. And then again in his side, a painful stab into his lower back that just missed his spine.

Regaining his balance, though because of his wounds not without more of a struggle than he would have liked, the enraged Wraith hissed menacingly as he faced off against his prey. That anger was joined by an unexpected and unwanted trace of concern.

The boy should have been frightened, even terrified to stand against him. Unable to see him in the mist. Unable to defend himself.

But that didn't seem to be the case at all.

Jakob stood calmly atop the ridge, well balanced, well positioned, his eyes never leaving the Wraith as he moved through the fog. Every time the Wraith tried the maneuver around him, Jakob shifted his positioning just a few feet to the left or right, unperturbed by the threat the monster presented.

Jakob watched the Wraith closely. He could tell by the monster's hesitant movements that his hunter was beginning to understand that the stealth that he usually enjoyed when hunting in the Murk would be of little value to him in this combat, the injuries that Jakob had exacted upon him only making an already difficult situation more challenging.

Because of that, in the place of stealth, the Wraith selected speed, rushing toward Jakob in a grey blur.

Jakob sidestepped the attack, running the dagger in his left hand across the Wraith's ribs, then pivoting to avoid the back-handed stab the monster aimed for his eye.

The furious Wraith didn't stop there. Ignoring the pain of his new wounds, he lunged with the dagger in his right claw, aiming for the throat.

Jakob was ready for the attack, barely needing to move, simply adjusting where he stood so that when the Wraith's bone-white steel slid by his face, his own dagger, held out in front of him, cut across the Wraith's claw, slicing off two of the monster's needle-sharp fingers.

The Wraith reared back in shock and pain, dropping the blade.

Despite his success -- the Wraith down to a single dagger while nursing several severe wounds, including a claw that he could no longer use -- Jakob knew that he needed to be careful. A single mistake against his adversary would cost him his life.

He also realized that he had made the right decision to take on the Wraith with his daggers. Attempting to use his sword against the wickedly fast creature would have been a useless effort.

Even with the Wraith only able to attack with one weapon, the monster pushed Jakob to the very limit of his abilities. Several times Jakob had to employ the manacles on his wrists to defend against one of the Wraith's unceasing stabs and slashes. And if not for the Talent, none of his efforts to protect himself would have mattered. He wouldn't have been able to see the Wraith in the mist until it was too late.

Jakob was pleased with himself despite the challenge of the combat. Even as he became more and more certain that he only had a few minutes at most to live.

He could sense the other Wraiths climbing up the ridge. The one he was fighting now had shifted his focus more to holding him in place rather than killing him, waiting for his comrades to join the fight.

The change in tactics only made sense. The Wraith's wounds were beginning to slow him down and prevent him from taking the fight to Jakob as the creature would have preferred.

That didn't mean, however, that the Wraith still wasn't ready to try to kill him if the opportunity presented itself.

Sensing Jakob's brief moment of distraction, the Wraith lunged, aiming a stab for Jakob's groin.

He dodged out of the way. But the Wraith stayed with him, refusing to allow him to disengage.

For the next several seconds, the constant chatter of steel striking steel drifted through the fog. Jakob defended against every thrust and stab, some so close that he felt the monster's blade slice a whisker off his cheek several times.

An intensifying growl made Jakob smile. His adversary was hurt and angry. Frustrated as well. Likely getting anxious.

More important, the Wraith still wanted to kill him before his brethren arrived. That meant that Jakob might have a chance to get in a strike before the odds turned against him for good.

He discovered that his assumptions were correct just a few seconds later. In a lunge that was no more than a faint shift in the fog, the Wraith stabbed for Jakob's eye.

It was just a ruse, however. The Wraith shifted the positioning of his arm so that he could scrape his steel across Jakob's throat instead.

The speed of the assault didn't bother Jakob. He saw it all. Thanks to Aloysius' training, time slowed for him, giving him the chance to respond accordingly.

Parrying the cut aimed for his neck, at the same time Jakob spun away from his adversary and kicked out with his right leg.

The blow slammed into the back of the Wraith's legs, sending the creature toppling to the ground, the monster knocked off balance so easily because he had overextended himself in his lust to kill his prey.

Jakob continued with his motion, forcing the Wraith down to the wet grass, putting his knees on the Wraith's chest, crushing the breath from the creature at the same time that he stabbed the dagger in his left hand straight through the monster's neck.

The Wraith emitted a soft gurgling sound, all the creature's energy leaving him along with the gush of blood that spurted from the wound when Jakob pulled his weapon free.

Jakob sighed with relief. At least he had killed one of the Wraiths pursuing him.

A small victory, and likely his only one.

Sensing that he had a few seconds to study his enemy, he finally got a good look, the Wraith no longer just a moving shadow.

His dead opponent was tall. Taller than him by a head or

more. He was also thin, almost emaciated. The monster's greyish white skin, matched with his grey leather armor, allowed him to blend into the fog almost perfectly.

The Wraith's hands were more like claws. What was most striking, however, was the gaunt, almost skeletal face. That feature made it seem as if the Wraith's skin was pulled too tightly over his bones.

Realizing that his time was up, Jakob pushed himself off the Wraith and sprinted along the ridge toward the very end of the ledge.

The other Wraiths hunting him were there.

They had heard the fight. They were closing in on him.

Jakob knew that he couldn't escape. But he could try to find a place where he could better defend himself.

Thanks to the Talent, he knew just the spot.

Reaching the small summit of the cliff, Jakob stopped and turned, daggers held at the ready. The rocks that marked the border of the ridge rose up behind him and would prevent the Wraiths from coming at him from behind.

That was the best that he could do. There was no more space and no more time to run.

He didn't have long to wait.

The Wraiths coalesced out of the mist, four all told. They were about ten yards away from him, no more than dim images in the swirling fog.

If not for the Talent, he wouldn't have even known that they were there. With the natural magic of the world within his grasp, he could see the monsters as clear as day.

It had been a good run, Jakob thought. His father would have been proud of him for surviving so long.

Yet it seemed that his luck, what little that he had, had just run out.

For the next several minutes there was nothing but silence.

Apparently, his adversaries wanted to get a good look at him before they killed him.

Jakob forced himself to not take a step back when the Wraith in the center stepped forward, the creature not stopping until he was only a few yards away. Even with the lack of distance between them, Jakob still would have had a difficult time making out the monster in the mist if not for the help of the Talent.

He assumed that this was the leader. The other Wraiths had remained in place, deferring to him.

Jakob could sense the tension within them. The desire to kill him. The monsters were working very hard to restrain that urge, that privilege apparently falling to the Wraith standing before him.

"You've run as far as you can, rabbit," hissed the Wraith. "You have nowhere else to go now. Nowhere else to hide."

"I can always fight my way through you and your friends," Jakob replied, trying to infuse his voice with a bravado that he wasn't feeling.

His comments earned a soft chuckle from the Wraith Scout. "I appreciate your courage and your confidence, but that matters little in your current circumstances. All that matters now, in this moment, is your skill. Do you have that skill, boy? I'm not sure that you do. I am sure that I will be taking your head back to the Wraith Hunter. He will want to gaze upon the face of the quarry who has proven so difficult to kill. The quarry who has culled one from the Horde."

As he listened to the words drift out of the fog, Jakob realized that this was the Wraith who had spoken to him just yesterday during the beginning of the hunt, trying to spook him, to get him to reveal where he was.

Strangely, instead of the Wraith's promise filling him with terror, Jakob was curious. He wanted to know who the Wraith Hunter was.

Of course, that really didn't matter now. All that mattered in that moment was doing all that he could to extend his life for as long as he possibly could.

"You seem awfully confident that you can kill me," Jakob said. "I just killed one of your fighters."

"I will give you the credit you deserve for killing my hunter. However, you need to understand that I am not my hunter. I am more than my hunter." The Wraith Scout took another step toward him. "I am just speaking the truth."

"Then don't hold it against me when I prove you a liar."

"Strong words, boy." The Wraith Scout's laugh sounded like a saw cutting through wood. "But I expect no less." The Wraith snorted. "So, tell me, boy, are you ready for the Dance of the Daggers?"

"Always," Jakob replied in a strong, soft voice.

Jakob didn't wait for the Wraith to attack, wanting to catch his adversary by surprise with a stab aimed for his left thigh.

The Wraith slipped to the side, avoiding the jab.

But the monster in the mist didn't evade the primary attack, which actually was the dagger in Jakob's other hand that he had kept down along his thigh. He plunged the steel hilt deep into the Wraith's right knee.

The Wraith shrieked in both anger and pain, Jakob stepping back before the monster could catch him across the chest with a slice of his double-bladed dagger.

"That is the last of the blood you will draw this day, rabbit," hissed the Wraith, gliding forward with a remarkable speed, though slower than usual thanks to the wound that Jakob had just given the creature.

Jakob had hoped that getting in that blow would disable the Wraith. No such luck. Although it did make it somewhat easier for Jakob to defend himself.

Still, that's all that he was able to do for the next few minutes.

The Wraith ignored the severity of his wound and applied constant pressure. His twin blades sliced through the fog with a speed that proved mesmerizing if Jakob watched the pattern too closely.

Yet through it all, Jakob unable to break away from the Wraith, the creature seeking a way past his defenses, the monster failed to deliver the final strike, which clearly annoyed the Wraith.

"You fight well, rabbit, but I have never failed on a hunt. I will not fail now."

"Say what you want. There's a first time for everything."

Jakob's retort lacked the confidence that he wanted it to have. Despite the Wraith's wound, the monster was proving to be a challenging opponent, his speed almost getting the better of Jakob several times.

And now, after more than a week on the run, after watching his father die, after not getting any sleep for several days, Jakob was tiring. He was finding it more and more difficult to stay in the fight.

His movements were becoming slower. More sluggish.

A few times he slid across the wet grass, thrown off balance, luckily always keeping his feet and avoiding the slash that the Wraith inevitably sent his way in an attempt to make him pay for his clumsiness.

Of course, those slashes didn't miss by much. They were coming closer to cutting into his body each time.

The Wraith noticed how Jakob was beginning to falter, sensing that his opportunity to end this combat had arrived. The monster in the mist became a whirlwind of motion. It was as if Jakob's stab into the creature's knee had no impact on him whatsoever.

Jakob defended himself as best as he could. But finally, after several long minutes of escaping the Wraith's dagger, he felt the slice of the bone-white steel across his cheek and brow, a fiery pain spreading through his body.

He ignored the heat and the warm blood trickling down his face. He couldn't afford to allow himself to be distracted. Not now.

Right after he received his wound, Jakob stumbled in the slick grass, one foot slipping too far to the side.

Recognizing his chance, the Wraith lunged with the dagger in his left claw, slashing for his prey's throat, believing that the boy finally was his.

The Wraith didn't realize until it was much too late that Jakob's clumsiness was just a feint. The ploy earned Jakob the opportunity that he had been seeking that he wasn't sure he would ever get.

Jakob glided to the side, avoiding the Wraith's cut. Before the monster could recover, he drove the dagger in his left hand up through the creature's jaw and then into his brain.

With a hard shove of his shoulder, Jakob pushed the Wraith off his steel, the monster collapsing to the ground, a look of permanent surprise serving as the Wraith's death mask.

"As I said, there's a first time for everything," Jakob offered to his former adversary, his blood up. He turned quickly toward the lip of the ridge, preparing himself for the remaining Wraiths who still stood no more than ten yards away.

They appeared uncertain. Not sure what to do. Not expecting their leader to die.

He was thrilled that he had survived the combat, but as he watched the Wraiths, he understood that his success had only bought him some additional time. The three Wraiths would come for him, and they would finish him quickly, because he didn't have the energy to fight so many of the creatures at one time.

And even if he did, they still would have killed him. Taking on one of the monsters on his own was challenge enough.

Jakob would put up the hardest fight that he could, but the result had already been determined. The best that he could hope for was that he take one more of the creatures with him to the other side.

"Grab the rope, lad," said a deep voice from far above him. "It's your only chance."

Jakob risked a glance behind him, seeing a rope swaying in and out of the fog.

He shook his head in disbelief. He had been mistaken when he reached the top of the ridge.

He hadn't been forced to stop because of the stone of the cliff, but rather because of the stone of a tall tower built at the very edge of the ridge. He had been so focused on the Wraiths pursuing him that he had completely missed the structure rising behind him, believing that it was a natural landmark.

Not wanting to miss his opportunity, Jakob held his dagger in one hand and reached for the rope. In an instant he was twenty feet off the ground and rising through the haze.

And just in time.

The Wraiths lunged for him, missing him by no more than a hair as they rushed out of the fog, seeking to sink either their daggers or their claws into his flesh.

They weren't particular. They just wanted to kill the boy and claim the credit for his death as their own.

When he was about one hundred feet in the air, Jakob came to a stop. Then he felt himself being swung to the right. It wasn't long before he dropped down onto the top of the tower, several men already wrapping the rope around their arms as they made their way toward a small opening in the stone roof.

"There's definitely going to be a scar there," said the man who stood before him. His rescuer motioned with a large hammer to the thin scar that cut across much of his own shaved head and then toward the bloody slice that Jakob had received. "Your days as a handsome young man have come to an end."

"I'd rather just be alive," Jakob replied, feeling incredibly tired, even jittery, as the adrenaline that had helped him take on a fist of Wraiths began to fade within him.

"That's the spirit, lad." The fellow smiled and gave him a nod of respect upon seeing the manacles on his wrists. Those told him all that he needed to know about the young man.

About where he had come from. What he had been through.

Few escaped the slavers. No one escaped the Wraiths. Except for him.

"You're brave lad, but foolish," his rescuer continued. "Standing against a Wraith like that is a death wish."

"I didn't have much of a choice."

"I guess you really didn't, now did you? How long have you been in the fog?"

"Since yesterday," Jakob replied. "Several times before that as well."

"You've been out in the open ever since you escaped the slavers?"

"Yes." Jakob didn't have the energy to provide his interrogator with any more information than that.

"How long have these particular Wraiths been hunting you?"

"Like I said, since yesterday."

That caught the man's attention -- he didn't know anyone who could say the same -- as did the young man's performance against the Wraiths, although he had listened to the combat more than watched because of the denseness of the fog.

Few survived in the fog without locating a strong, defensible fortification. None could say that they had killed a Wraith and lived to tell the tale, much less two of the monsters.

"How did you evade the Wraiths for so long?"

"I applied a lot of what my father taught me," murmured Jakob, wanting nothing more than to lie down and rest for several days, knowing at the same time that he couldn't do that. Not yet. "And a lot of luck."

Jakob wasn't comfortable saying much more than that, not wanting to reveal to a complete stranger that he could use the Talent. Not everyone viewed his unique ability to make use of natural magic in a positive light, and he had no desire to be left outside the tower with the Wraiths. He could tell by the sounds coming from below that the monsters were beginning to climb the stone of the tower.

"Your father still out in the fog?" The man who had saved Jakob already knew the answer, or at least he suspected that he did. Nevertheless, he felt the need to ask.

Jakob looked at the fellow who had saved him. He saw the hope in his eyes. He appreciated that. But he also saw the hint of reality that was there as well, the acceptance of what must have occurred.

"No. He's not." Jakob said no more than that, not yet ready to share the story of what had happened to his father, what his father had done for him, with anyone else, especially someone he didn't know.

The man stared at him for several seconds, apparently unconcerned as the sounds of the Wraiths digging their claws into the side of the tower became more pronounced. Jakob thought he saw a hint of sympathy behind the man's hard eyes.

"The name is Dargenton Westgard, but everyone calls me Duff."

"I'm glad they do. That's a mouthful." He said it was a small grin. "Jakob."

Duff stared at Jakob for several seconds more, then laughed heartily. "A sense of humor after what you've had to deal with? What's not to like? Come on."

Duff motioned to the trap door in the roof, leading him

down into the tower, the men who had stowed the rope waiting for them so that they could pull the steel door shut and lock it in place.

"We'll wait out the Wraiths," Duff explained. "We can move on when the fog clears. You seem to have no problem killing those bastards, but I don't feel like trying my hand against three today."

"Thank you. I appreciate the help." Jakob kept his hand along the inside wall, fearing that he would miss a step, the last of his energy draining away. "I owe you a debt. If not for you and your men, I'd be dead."

"Don't worry about that, Jakob. Just doing what needed doing." Duff motioned to the manacles circling his wrists. "We can get those off you. We can't do it here, but we can where we're going. We've got a blacksmith's forge in the village just a few leagues to the south."

Jakob considered the offer for a moment, staring at the steel around his wrists. "Thank you, but no. I'm not taking these off until every person enslaved in the Highlands is free."

Duff's smile broadened as he headed down the steps again, not moving deeper within the tower until he heard the telltale pinging and pounding that confirmed for him that the steel trap door above them had been locked and secured.

Just in time too, because he heard, as well, the soft thump of the first Wraith to step onto the top of the tower right before the steel fit into place.

"I like how you think, Jakob. I get the feeling that we're going to get along just fine."

5

ALWAYS A PRICE

"You're certain, Captain? No doubt?"

"No doubt whatsoever, Governor Winborne," replied Argenta Rensom, Captain of the Northern Guard. She stood at attention with her shoulder blades almost touching, stretching her leather armor and exposing multiple scratches and tears. Her eyes focused on some point on the wall just above her commander's head. Few had the courage to challenge her with steel to begin with, her height and hard expression only making her more intimidating. "At least three dozen Wraiths fought their way onto the northern parapet. It was the largest attack that we've repelled to date."

"How many men died to keep those monsters out of the city?"

"Twenty-two dead, fifteen wounded. Of the wounded, a third will probably die in the next day because of the severity of their injuries."

"How many Wraiths did we kill?"

Captain Rensom hesitated before responding, chewing her lip, obviously not liking the answer she needed to give him. "I don't know, Governor Winborne. There were signs of Wraith blood on the battlements but no bodies."

"Just like every other engagement we've had with them."

"Yes, Governor Winborne. Unfortunately so. I assume they carry off their dead. Although with the fog, I have yet to find any evidence that we have done anything more than wound a few of the creatures."

"That's a heavy price to pay, Captain Rensom."

He raised his hands to calm her, seeing that she was becoming agitated. An uncommon reaction for her. She usually kept her emotions in check.

But that was hard to do when she bore the weight of every soldier lost on her broad shoulders, as if she all on her own could have somehow kept them all alive against the unstoppable creatures they fought.

"That is no criticism of the Northern Guard," he explained quickly. "And it is certainly no criticism of you. Our soldiers fight as well as can be expected when they are fighting with one hand tied behind their backs because of this infernal Murk."

"Yes, Governor Winborne. Thank you."

Captain Rensom let out the breath that she had been holding. She chafed at the restrictions of their current situation. She could do nothing but defend, and it didn't seem as if they could even do that to the best of their ability with this cursed fog. Especially not after what she had discovered earlier that morning.

"As you know, it is extremely difficult to battle these monsters in the mist," she continued. "Nothing we have tried has helped us. Even placing massive fire pits along the wall to break the gloom offer little assistance. The Murk is so dense that the light those braziers provide offers no value. It simply reflects off the haze, making it even more difficult to see at times."

"We will find a way, Captain. Have no fear. Now what was it that you needed to tell me? The message I received said that it was quite urgent that I speak with you."

Kendric sat behind his desk, the huge tabletop carved from the trunk of a heart tree. The towering, majestic spires, which rose three or four hundred feet into the sky and were a common sight in the Highlands and along the ridges of the Northern Peaks, were said to be a marker of the health of the world.

Ancient and powerful, the stories suggested that the heart trees first appeared when the magic of the world was split into two streams both flowing from the same source, the Talent and the Curse coming to be. It was also said that when a heart tree fell, it was a sign that the Curse was winning its age-old battle against the Talent.

In Kendric's opinion, that tale was no more than that. A fable.

As a result, that story had not stopped Kendric from making use of the wood of several heart trees in the ongoing construction of the Shadow Keep. The strength and beauty of the carved timber was second to none and a needed resource if he was to build the citadel he had in mind. That he deserved.

Right now, the polished wood of his desk gleamed brightly thanks to the sunlight streaming through the windows to his front, pinpricks and splashes of burnt oranges and reds dazzling his eyes. To his right there was a flash of silvery grey, the light bouncing off the desk and striking the weapon set on the wall that was unique in both its design and use.

Supposedly crafted by the Giants of the Rime, it was actually three daggers forged into one, the grip in the center. Each of the blades a foot and a half in length. Each one spaced evenly from the next.

It took some effort for him to pull his gaze away from that

very arresting weapon. But he did, needing to focus on what Captain Rensom had to tell him.

"Governor Winborne, when the Wraiths came at us on the wall this morning, the fog snuck down from the north during the night at a faster rate than was usual."

"You can skip that part, Captain Rensom. As you know, I was there." He leaned forward, his eyes blazing with anger. Not at his Captain. Rather, his rage and hatred was reserved for the creatures lurking in the fog that were demonstrating quite clearly that they were a major threat to his rule. "I am always there on the wall when the Wraiths come. I want to kill one of those monsters just as much as you do."

"I know, Governor Winborne, my apologies. I didn't mean to suggest otherwise. Your leadership and courage on the battlements is appreciated and valued by every soldier of the Northern Guard." She took a deep breath to calm her frazzled nerves, beginning again. "As you know, after the fight on the wall, the fog cleared quickly. Rather than taking a day or two as is its usual wont, it only took a few hours for the Murk to return to the north."

"You find that strange, Captain?" mused Kendric. "I found it to be a gift."

"I do find it strange, Governor Winborne. It's never happened before. The Murk has always been consistent in its movement and pacing. Until today."

"We should go to a gambling den tonight," prodded Kendric, the hint of a smile on his lips, hoping to change his Captain's sour mood. "We've simply been blessed with good luck. We should take advantage of it while it stays with us. Why are you so concerned about that?"

"Because the Wraiths only come in the fog, and they like to stay because the fog stays as well. There is never just one fight along the wall. It is always a series of clashes that last for several hours. The Wraiths climbing, fighting, disappearing, then doing the same thing somewhere else on the parapet. But not today. One attack and they were gone. Didn't you find that a bit odd?"

"I did, Captain Rensom. I also found it to be a good thing." Kendric leaned forward then, arms crossed, wanting to get to the point. "What are you trying to say, Captain? Just spit it out."

"I believe that this morning's fight was less a clash and more a test."

"Every clash on the wall is a test, Captain," countered Kendric, not understanding why his usually calm captain was becoming so agitated.

"Yes, it is. That can never be denied. But this morning's fight felt different. The fog came quickly, the Wraiths came just as fast. They left even faster. They did that for a reason."

"What reason would that be other than the fact that we sent them fleeing back to the north? They couldn't hold against us, so they left before we slaughtered them."

Captain Rensom needed to take another deep breath in order to calm herself. Governor Winborne's uncalled-for confidence, which bordered on arrogance and she assumed he used to hide his own fears, threatened to send her off on a tirade that she reserved normally for new recruits to the Northern Guard.

"They breached the wall," she said slowly, quietly, biting off the words individually. "The Wraiths. Breached. The wall."

"What do you mean they breached the wall!" shouted Kendric, pushing himself up from his seat, sending papers flying in every direction. "That isn't possible. I was there. I don't care how well they do in the Murk. None of those monsters could have gotten past us. Not a single one!"

"They did, Governor Winborne. I'm sorry, but they did."

"You better be able to back up that claim," he said harshly.

"During our normal sweeps through town after the fog

cleared, two of our patrols came upon houses that had been attacked. One a few blocks from the northern wall. The other only a few blocks from the Shadow Keep. Both were broken into by the Wraiths. The monsters slaughtered the people living there. There were no survivors."

"That cannot be possible," Kendric hissed. "We would have known if the Wraiths got past us. I would have known. I'm certain of that."

"It is more than possible, Governor Winborne. It is a fact. It cannot be any clearer. The wounds on the victims are consistent with the preferred killing style of the Wraiths. A slice across the throat. Every one of the them. Men, women, and children. And to ensure that there was no mistake as to who did the bloody work, one of those cursed double-bladed daggers that the monsters prefer was punched into the wood on each of the doors." Captain Rensom closed her eyes in frustration. "There is no mistake, Governor Winborne. It was the Wraiths. They got by us on the wall and then murdered two families who had sought shelter."

"They must have been living in the older houses, not the ones that are being built now." Kendric's voice sounded almost like he was pleading for his statement to be true.

The houses now being constructed in Shadow's Reach were all following the same model, the residence just as much a fortress as a home. The beams of the roof were set so tightly together that there was less than a foot between them. A hard tile that shattered only with the most powerful of blows was then nailed to the wood to further deter any attempt to get into the dwelling from above.

Rather than a wooden frame, the walls were built with stone that was always at least a foot thick, often more than that, and the windows were too small for anyone but a small child to climb through. The doors themselves were said to be impregnable.

A solid piece of oak several inches thick that was wrapped in steel bands, imitating the entrances to the brochs said to be used by the Highlanders to stay safe when the Murk descends. There was no way to open those doors other than from the inside when they were closed and locked, a bar of steel running across the internal frame as a final defense.

Captain Rensom shook her head sadly. "The people living there were well off. Traders. Their homes were of the new style. I believe that the Wraiths selected those homes on purpose. They wanted to make a point. They wanted us to know that they could get to anyone."

Kendric considered her theory for a moment, becoming deflated as his anger faded, replaced by a sense of defeat. He had a hard time disagreeing with the conclusion Captain Rensom offered.

If those monsters could break into the dwellings that were designed specifically to keep them out, what did that suggest to the many residents of Shadow's Reach who were clamoring for these apparently useless homes?

Anyone living in Shadow's Reach now was no more than a sitting duck.

He had worked on the design personally, helping to perfect it. Or so he had thought.

If the design failed to protect these people, what did that say of him?

"If these were the more defensible homes, then how did the Wraiths get in? That isn't supposed to happen unless the residents invited in those monsters."

"The doors. They went right through the doors."

"How could that even be possible? I watched when the door was placed in the first of the new homes that was built. They struck that door with a battering ram more than a dozen times and there wasn't even a dent. It's a version of what the Highlanders use to protect themselves, blast it! How could the Wraiths do that?"

"I don't know, Governor Winborne. We're looking into it now. We've called in every blacksmith and stonemason in the city in search of an answer. Somehow, the Wraiths ripped the doors free from the stone."

Kendric slumped back down in his chair, the sense of defeat almost crushing. His face ashen, his eyes were wide open though he saw very little, even as his mind worked frantically.

These new truths upset the very boundaries of his world. They put at risk everything that he had been trying to achieve.

The Wraiths had gotten over the wall without them knowing.

The Wraiths had run rampant through his city.

The Wraiths had slaughtered two families.

They had done it in less than an hour.

And then they had left.

Without being discovered.

With impunity.

Not a single Wraith killed.

There was only one conclusion that could be made upon staring at those facts for any length of time.

No one was safe in Shadow's Reach.

And he had failed.

He was responsible for those families dying.

"They weren't testing us, those bastards were showing us what they could do," Kendric murmured, his hate leaking out in his voice, needing some other emotion to prevent him from being overcome by his rising fear. "They want us to know what they have in store for us. What they plan to do when they attack Shadow's Reach in force."

"My feelings exactly, Governor Winborne." Captain Rensom wished that she could offer her lord a different response, but to do so would impinge upon her need to speak honestly even when doing so put her in a poor light.

Kendric barely heard her, sitting in his overlarge chair for several minutes more before he finally spoke again.

"How many soldiers in the Northern Guard are fit for service?"

"Only two thousand, Governor Winborne. We have lost several hundred during the past few months, the Wraiths increasing the frequency of their incursions to almost one a week. Sometimes more. As a result, our recruitment efforts have slowed to the point of being nonexistent."

Two thousand soldiers was a fairly large number. Especially for the Territories. Only Sharperson had more in the Highlands, and he had his own problems to deal with.

Kendric understood why Captain Rensom had said it that way. Two thousand soldiers had no chance of defending the entire city wall when the fog drifted in. Not if the Wraiths came at them in greater numbers. Not if they assaulted more than one wall. Not if they could slip by the defenders on the parapet without being noticed. Without consequence.

And he was certain that the Wraiths would employ that strategy now. It was just a question of when.

The monsters had learned what they had needed to learn. Next, they would do what they needed to do.

"Thank you for your update, Captain Rensom. Please see to the dead and the wounded. I will visit the wounded later today."

"Thank you, Governor Winborne. The soldiers will look forward to your visit."

"Tomorrow we will talk again first thing. We will discuss what strategies we can employ to better protect ourselves against the Wraiths now that the situation has changed. We will have no choice but to change our tactics as well."

"Of course, Governor Winborne," replied Captain Rensom.

She tried to keep her customary energy in her voice but failed. She was at a complete loss as to what to do next.

They had put in place a host of new schemes to defend against the Wraiths, including the new construction design for the homes, new methods for defending the wall, even fixing steel spikes and wire to the battlements to prevent the monsters from even reaching the top.

Yet all to no avail. It seemed that nothing could stop these predators.

What else could they come up with in the next day that would protect against these monsters of the mist who had yet to demonstrate any weaknesses? Little else came to mind.

After Captain Rensom left with her head bowed, Kendric remained in his chair for more than an hour. Too tired to move. Too dejected.

He watched the sun set. The shadows lengthening across the surface of his desk. The darkness beginning to settle around him.

The Murk and the creatures lurking within it that threatened the very existence of Shadow's Reach were looking more and more like insurmountable perils.

What was he to do?

This was his Territory. So, it was his problem to solve.

But he had no idea how to address this challenge. Everything that he had tried so far had failed.

Kendric had come to his office earlier that afternoon to go through his ledgers, thoughts of his success at keeping the Wraiths from coming over the wall that morning still dancing through his head.

He shook his head in frustration. How quickly the sweet taste of perceived success had turned bitter. Building the Shadow Keep was getting more expensive than he had budgeted originally. The need to strengthen the fortress' defenses in light of the brazenness of the Wraiths, as well as some of the other extravagances that he and Ursina could not do without, only added to the already steep cost.

The revenue that he had expected from the taxes he imposed and some of his other endeavors to raise money weren't providing him with the resources to do all that was required.

Worse, he couldn't pay for the work as quickly as he had before. He was several months in arrears to many of the artisans and craftspeople and, as a result, and not unexpectedly, the work was dragging.

He might need to put in place the approach that Torstan Sharperson employed to build the Stone in the Highlands.

Kendric hadn't wanted to take that path. He didn't fancy taking advantage of the people who owed him their allegiance. Now, however, he might not have any choice.

He shook his head in frustration again, this time with more vigor, stifling several curses that sought to slip between his lips. He couldn't believe that this was happening to him.

But then again, he should have assumed that it would. This seemed to be a common pattern in his life that had started when he was growing up in the Southern Marches.

The Shadow Keep was supposed to be a testament to his power as an independent ruler. A beacon for all that he had achieved in the Territories. A taste of what he would do in the future.

He was tired of being the younger brother, of being second best to Kevan, of always being in his shadow. And coming here, building his own fortress, pushing the town toward becoming a city, governing his own Territory that could one day become something more than just a far-flung province of Caledonia, was supposed to allow him to do that.

Serving as the Governor gave him the chance to make his own name. To chart his own course. To show his brother that purchasing the grant to the Northern Territory was the right thing to do. Not the necessary thing. And deservedly so.

Kevan hadn't said it, but Kendric had known what his brother was thinking. That time away from the Duchy was the only way to ensure that Kendric could become more than he already was.

Kevan had been right. Kendric would grant him at least that.

But he would never admit that to Kevan. He was his own man, casting his own shadow. He no longer walked in the shadow of his older brother.

The Shadow Keep was to be the most obvious example of that change for Kendric. A visible reminder of what he had become, of what he was responsible for, of what he had earned. And how so much farther he could go. Therefore, the redoubt needed to be completed as swiftly as possible.

But not just for that reason now.

The citadel could serve an even more urgent need. The Shadow Keep was so large that even with the growth of the town surrounding the bastion, it could house every resident of Shadow's Reach if there was cause to bring the inhabitants behind the walls.

It would be much easier to defend against the Wraiths along the parapet of the Shadow Keep. The walls were higher and the battlements not as long as those of the city.

Whether he liked it or not, at least in one respect his path was clear. He would do as Torstan had done. Beginning tomorrow, the stonemasons and every other artisan would be required to work on the Shadow Keep for several days a week until it was complete, regardless of what other work they might have. Regardless of what he owed them.

Payment would be deferred against the costs of defending the town and its residents from the Wraiths.

A fair trade. And if anyone failed to meet this new requirement, he would take whatever action was necessary to educate them on the folly of doing so.

He was certain that Ursina would be happy to help him with that. She had a knack for bringing recalcitrant people around to their way of thinking.

One problem solved, and yet so many more remained. And so many questions continued to bother him.

Did he really want to cede the walls of the city to the Wraiths?

Would that not demonstrate his weakness?

Would that not diminish him in the eyes of the people who relied on him for their protection?

He shifted his positioning on the chair that he had sunk into for the first time since Captain Rensom left more than an hour before. He looked at the wall to his right.

Mounted on the stone hung the Blood Dagger. It was a strange weapon. The steel caught the faintest glimmer of light, making the weapon shine brightly even as the shadows gained dominance in his office.

It was said that those who mastered the weapon could throw the dagger for a hundred yards or more and it would return to his or her hand. Every time.

Because of the magic used to forge the weapon, the person to whom the weapon bonded would always be able to catch the dagger without having to fear the sharp blades that never dulled with the passage of time.

Kendric believed that was a myth. He had tried it once and the blades had almost taken off one of his fingers. Even now, that finger ached when the weather turned cold or it began to rain.

Ursina gave the Blood Dagger to Kendric as a wedding present, explaining that it was crafted by the Giants of the Rime. Therefore, it contained several special qualities. He took her at her word, although a worm of doubt made him question her claim after his attempt to use the weapon.

Of course, he never voiced his suspicion out loud. His wife was not one who liked to have what she said challenged, even by the man she loved.

Kendric shook his head again, this time in disappointment. Maybe if the Blood Ruby that was supposed to be in the center of the blades was actually there, he'd have had better luck.

Ursina believed that the jewel had been lost at some point in the past, the weapon passing through many hands before she acquired it through a strange quirk of fate.

In the end, it was really just the stuff of nonsense to him. A reminder as well that in the real world nothing could ever live up to expectations. That you could never quite make the world what you wanted it to be.

For him, the Blood Dagger served as nothing more than a reminder of his wife's love for him. She knew of his interest in daggers as evidenced by the dozens of weapons resting on the table and affixed to the walls around him, so she had added to his collection. She had gifted him a dagger and attached a good story to it.

"You are sitting in the dark, husband," said Ursina, the Lady of the Northern Territory gliding into his office from a hidden door built into the wall at his back, several lamps fixed along the wall flickering to life as she passed.

She understood the value of shadows. She was more than willing to make use of them if that served her purposes. She just didn't have need of them now.

"It is a dark day, Ursina." He took a few minutes to update her on what Captain Rensom told him. "I have been wracking my brains for some solution to this threat. Nothing that we have tried has worked. So long as those Wraiths come in the fog, they will beat us every time. Of that, I have no doubt. We are powerless in the Murk."

"Not powerless, husband. Simply at an extreme disadvantage."

"Is there a difference?" Kendric asked, continuing on before Ursina could reply, his anguish clear in his voice. "And these Wraiths proved earlier this morning that they could get into the city. We know that now and so do they. There is nothing that we can do to stop them when they do it again, and they will do it again. The fate of every person living in Shadow's Reach is in my hands, and I have no good way to protect them. We are at the mercy of those monsters."

"You do yourself a disservice, Kendric," said Ursina, her voice, once comforting, now as sharp as the blades on the Blood Dagger. She disliked it a great deal when he fell into one of his moods. "You do me a disservice as well. True, what we have tried against these Wraiths has not worked. But I must remind you once again that we have not tried everything."

"Ursina, we have spoken about this before. Many times, in fact, and ..." Kendric began, clearly not wanting to engage further on this topic.

"And we will continue to speak about this until you finally see reason," cut in Ursina.

She took a few seconds before continuing, needing the time to gain better control over her rising anger. The solution to this challenge was so simple, yet her husband still balked at it. She could not understand why he didn't have the courage to do what must be done.

If he was to rule all of New Caledonia, decisions such as these needed to be made in an instant. Without remorse. Without concern. Without second thoughts.

She tried again in a much gentler voice, seeking to nudge him in the direction she wanted him to go.

"Kendric, my love. I understand why you hesitate. I have listened to your reservations. We have discussed each one. And we have agreed that this is the only way to protect our claim in the Northern Territory."

"Ursina, please. Hear me out. Just one more time. If we go down this path, do we not run the risk of unleashing a potentially even more terrifying plague upon us?"

Kendric raised his hands to head off the protest that he knew was coming from her. He had heard it many times before, just as he had forced her to listen to his.

"I know what you're going to say. So far, the experiment has worked for the most part. We have had very few problems, and those that have occurred we both agreed were a small price to pay for what we learned. They were necessary, because it allowed you to fine-tune what we were doing. But on the scale that you propose ..."

Kendric sagged back into his chair. Ursina knelt next to him, her warm hand gripping his forearm gently. She began to run her hand up and down his skin, recognizing and wanting to alleviate her husband's distress.

He was a good man. That was one of the reasons that she loved him.

But she also believed that his wanting to always do good, to always do the right thing, was a weakness. If they were to have any chance at removing the Wraiths as a threat, at solidifying and strengthening their position in New Caledonia, then no weakness could be permitted.

"You know what we must do to stop these Wraiths, Kendric. Now is the time to decide. If the Wraiths can scale the wall and enter the city without us knowing, then we must do this. It is the only way. You know that just as well as I do."

"But what if something goes wrong?"

"Kendric, you must listen to me now," said Ursina, her eyes shining brightly in the candlelight, latching on to her husband's and not letting go. "If something goes wrong then something goes wrong. It happened when we tested this approach, and it will happen again. This is an art, not a science. We cannot plan for every eventuality. We do not know what will happen in the future. We can only do what we believe is necessary to ensure that we have a future."

"Yes, my love, I know," replied Kendric. His wife's sharp eyes and her gentle touch were making him feel better, his worries dissipating. The sense that sparks of energy were reaching all the way down to his bones sent a comfortable warmth spreading through him.

"And we do know what will happen with the Wraiths if we do not do this," continued Ursina. "We've known it since these attacks began."

She leaned in closer to the man she loved, who had given her so much and who could still give her so much more. She trailed her lips on his cheek, her warm voice now only inches away from his ear.

"It is the only way, Kendric. You are right. Everything else we have tried has failed. That cannot be denied. But we have not tried this as we said we would. This is the only path that gives us any chance at success."

"It comes at a terrible cost, Ursina."

"Yes, it does, Kendric, and a comment such as that is one of the reasons I love you so. You always think of others before you think of yourself. But is our freedom not worth that cost? Are not our lives and the lives of those who depend on us worth that cost? Better to pay the price with some rather than all."

"I was hoping that we wouldn't have to continue. I can't deny our success, but the whole thing makes my skin crawl. Whenever we're done, I feel as if I've bathed in a pool of filth. And I hate to see you sullied so. I know it bothers you as well."

"It is just another price that we must pay, my love. Besides, as my former instructor and mentor used to say, hoping doesn't make it real."

"You're right, my love. You're right. We keep having this conversation, and the fault for that is mine. But you are right. We must do what must be done if we are to protect the Northern Territory."

6

A NEW START

"It looks like you made quite an impression," said Duff, trusty hammer in hand, though he had no plans to use it. At least not then.

"I guess I did," replied Jakob. "It seems that they're not done with me yet."

He and Jakob stood at the entrance in the base of the tower, the steel-bound oak door open for the first time since the fog drifted in several days before. They had spent the rest of yesterday and then the night within the broch, safe from the Wraiths, Jakob catching up on some much-needed sleep.

Only now was the fog finally receding. And with it, the Wraiths.

The Murk slowly. The Wraiths reluctantly.

From where Duff and Jakob were standing, they could make out the dim shapes of the monsters in the mist at the very edge of the fog. Every so often, the Wraiths stepped back, always staying within the mist, as it slowly drifted back to the north.

Thanks to a gust of wind, Jakob made out the large lumps draped over the shoulders of two of the Wraiths. Something else that Jakob deemed worth knowing. The Wraiths took their dead with them.

Even from where he stood, Jakob could sense the monsters' hatred. They wanted him. Badly.

They believed that they had a debt to pay. Why he believed this, he didn't know. But he was sure that he was right.

Rather than retreating with the fog at the first opportunity, the three Wraiths who had hunted him kept their places at the border of the grey. Watching him. Measuring him.

The Wraiths stepped back when the grey haze thinned. That's when he could see their eyes. Pitch black in the grey. Burning with the promise of what would happen the next time they caught Jakob in the Murk.

Jakob's first reaction was fear, but that quickly subsided.

These monsters were standing there just for show. If they tried to exit the fog, they would die.

He was safe. For the moment.

They were only trying to intimidate him.

And after all that he had been through, after all the time he had spent in the Murk, that wasn't going to happen.

The Wraiths were there because he had proven something to them that they never thought possible. These monsters in the mist couldn't kill all the prey they hunted. They were not invincible.

Jakob had proven something to himself as well. He could survive in the Murk. He could hunt in the Murk, just like the Wraiths did.

Strangely, he welcomed the Wraiths' attention. Because he wasn't as afraid as he used to be when he heard that whisper in the grey blanket that told him the Wraiths were nearby.

Instead, he felt on edge, balancing on the tip of a blade.

His father would call him a fool, because he was actually thinking about going after the monsters now. Of joining them in the Murk.

Some part of him wanted this fight. He needed the release.

And he welcomed the challenge. Because he knew that he could kill them.

If he was being completely honest with himself, however, he also wanted to enter the Murk because he didn't want to deal with the emotions welling up within him. During his time in the broch, he had thought of little else but his father's death.

As Dougal had liked to say, better to be doing than thinking.

Better to be fighting than remembering.

His expression hard, Jakob moved from Duff's side, striding toward the very edge of the fog.

"Lad," Duff called to him, the Highlander making no move to follow him.

Jakob ignored his new friend. His hands went for the daggers on his belt, and he began to reach for the Talent.

Better to do than think. Better to fight than remember.

He stopped himself at the very last second. He stood no more than a few feet away from the Wraiths. The thin wisps of grey never came close to touching him, which meant the Wraiths couldn't either.

His caution proved unnecessary.

The Wraiths stood there, not moving. They simply stared at him, their gleaming black eyes burning brightly in the fading Murk.

"This isn't over," said Jakob, not understanding why he felt the need to do this. Why he was saying this, antagonizing creatures whose only desire was to gut him. Yet he couldn't help himself. "The next time you come with the Murk, I'll be coming for you."

"Brave words," hissed one of the Wraiths, "when you stand outside the Murk. Why not come for us now?"

"Do you not have the courage to join us in the mist, boy?" taunted another of the Wraiths. That one's shoulders were free of the bodies of the dead Wraiths. He stood poised for a combat, a bone-white dagger in each clawed hand. "Are you afraid of the Dance of the Daggers?"

The third Wraith remained silent, though he took a half step forward even though he bore the weight of one the Wraiths Jakob had killed across a shoulder. He pulled his foot back just as quickly, hissing in pain as the dim sunlight touched the grey leather of his boot, a tiny whisper of steam drifting into the air and dissolving just as quickly as it had appeared.

"I killed two of your brethren in the Murk," replied Jakob, watching with a great deal of interest what had happened with the overeager Wraith. Another useful piece of information. "In the very world that you supposedly dominate. Why do you think I can't kill you as well?"

That silenced the Wraiths in an instant.

He could sense their frustration.

Their anger.

Their desire for revenge.

Their desire to kill.

It was almost palpable.

For just a second, Jakob thought the one who appeared to have become the leader was going to lunge for him despite what had just occurred with his comrade. He almost wished that the monster would.

The desire to fight, to do anything but think, still surged through him. He was still on edge, and he would have welcomed the chance for another combat.

It would help to clear his jumbled mind.

He was also curious to see what would happen if the Wraith stepped out of the fog entirely, assuming that the creature even could. But it wasn't to be.

The Wraith kept himself under control, all three taking another step back as the fog receded once more.

"We will return, boy," said the Wraith. "We will be looking for you as well. Beware. You won't see us coming."

Jakob smiled at that, choosing not to reveal that, in actuality, he would see them well before they came close to him. But they could learn that on their own and to their regret.

"Don't keep me waiting. The next time you come with the fog, I'll come hunting for you."

The Wraith snorted at that. Perhaps the monster enjoyed Jakob's brief attempt at bravado. Perhaps he was insulted.

Jakob didn't care. The comment did as he intended. A tiny barb that would stick in the monster's craw.

Because he knew that he would be facing these Wraiths again. He still owed them a dance.

Jakob stood there for several minutes more, simply staring at the dim shadows, the creatures stepping back in time to the fog drifting slowly toward the north, ensuring that they remained protected within the Murk. When the Wraiths were ten yards away, the fog pulling back at a faster pace, Jakob turned.

The Wraiths were gone, heading back to wherever they came from. So he returned to Duff's side.

"What was that all about?"

"We needed to finish the conversation that was interrupted yesterday."

"A conversation?" Duff stared at Jakob for several seconds as if he might be daft. "You're done then? You're not going to go after them? Because it looked like you were."

"I thought about it, then thought better of it."

"I'm glad," said Duff, shaking his head as if to say that he wasn't quite sure what to make of the young man he had just met. "You're done? We can get moving?"

"For now. I just wish I had finished all those bastards. I wish I killed the entire fist instead of just the two."

"Me too, but that would have been a tall task, lad, and not easily accomplished. Not without you coming out with a wound or two worse than the one you suffered. If you came out at all."

Jakob nodded, not in a position to disagree with that statement. "Still, a worthy task."

"True," Duff agreed. "You should feel good about what you've accomplished. I don't know of many others who have survived the Wraiths, and no one has killed any of the creatures. You took down two of the monsters. That story will spread far and wide in the Highlands."

"How do you know that's going to happen?" Jakob really didn't care for the attention.

"Because I'm going to be the one who starts the spreading," smiled Duff. "With the Murk coming in so frequently now, we need stories like yours. They give the Highlanders hope, which has been in short supply since the Wraiths first appeared."

"It offers little solace when you consider what these monsters have done to the people of the Highlands."

"I can't disagree with you about that," admitted Duff. "Nevertheless, we need to start somewhere if we're to rid the Territory of this menace."

"I can't disagree with you about that."

"I'm glad we've come to a meeting of the minds, lad." Duff turned toward the west, striding through the long grass, jumping or climbing over the rocks that stuck up from the ground, seeking the curling path that was a mile farther along the ridge that would allow them to get down to the forest far below them. "I do have to say that those three gave me the shivers."

"Me as well."

"Certainly didn't look like it, lad. Seemed to me that you weren't concerned in the least. That you were raring to have another go at them."

"That thought had crossed my mind. In the beginning at least. Then I came to my senses."

"I'm glad you did, lad," said Duff. "I would have hated to have gone to so much effort to save you yesterday and then have to bury you this morning."

"I'm glad that I didn't prove to be such a burden for you."

"Me too, lad," snorted Duff, enjoying Jakob's dry humor. "If nothing else, it seems that we share a similar perspective on the world."

"How so?"

"We both appear to subscribe to the philosophy that the only good Wraith is a dead Wraith."

"I won't disagree with you about that either."

Duff turned toward Jakob with a curious look. "I need to ask. I know you killed two of those bastards, so I don't doubt your skill. But do you really think that you can kill three Wraiths at one time?"

Jakob thought about the Highlander's question for almost a minute before responding, following Duff onto the trail that switch-backed along the steep ridge for more than a mile before reaching the heart trees far below. "Yes, I do."

Duff snorted again at that, but he didn't laugh. He had learned during his brief conversation with Jakob in the broch that he was a serious young man. He wasn't joking.

Duff didn't take him to be a braggart either. Rather, he had learned that Jakob told you what he believed. No more, no less.

Another reason he already had come to like the lad.

"I'd like to think that you're jesting or offering a bit of bluster, but I don't think that you are. I get the feeling that you're being completely serious. That you believe what you say."

"Does that worry you?" asked Jakob, having fallen into step next to Duff, watching as the Murk continued to recede to the north. By the end of the day, the Highlands should be free of the fog. Until the blasted Murk returned, of course. And when that would happen was anyone's guess. Only the Wraiths knew.

"For some strange reason, it doesn't. Confidence can be a good thing so long as it doesn't become arrogance."

"I'm glad to hear it, and I'll keep that in mind." He chose not to tell Duff that what the Highlander had just said was exactly the same maxim that his father used to tell him, and much more frequently than he cared to recall.

"What did you say to them?"

"That the next time the fog came I'd go hunting for them."

Duff shook his head in wonder. "You do recall what I just said about the difference between arrogance and confidence?"

"Don't worry, Duff, I know what I'm doing."

"If you say so," muttered the Highlander. "I don't know if you're just being incredibly brave or you're just being a fool."

"Probably a little of both."

Duff laughed at Jakob's response. He believed that you needed to find the humor in life whenever you could, especially here in the Highlands. "Come on, lad. We've got a ways to go, so we need to pick up the pace."

For much of the day, Duff led Jakob to the south. If the former soldier wasn't offering bits and pieces about his time in the Highlands, then he was digging those bits and pieces out of Jakob.

It was hard for Jakob to keep the focus on the Highlander, Duff having a knack for conversation. Whenever Jakob succeeded, rare though it was, he pushed for as long as he could.

Just as much as he wanted to get a real sense about what was happening in the Highlands, he also wanted to get a better feel for the man who had saved his life.

In the end, he concluded that Duff was someone who he could trust. Up to a point.

When the Highlander asked him about how he had escaped the slavers, kept himself and his father alive for so long with his father being hurt so badly, and then killed two

Wraiths, Jakob had offered all the information that Duff could possibly want, except for the most critical part.

The Talent.

That was a variable that Jakob wasn't quite ready to share.

He had remembered Aloysius' warning. "Trust when you must," the old Magus had told him almost every day that Jakob worked with him. "Not because you want to."

By late afternoon, they were making their way down the crest of a mountain and into a small valley. When he saw what waited before him, Jakob stopped, needing to take it all in before following Duff down the winding trail that led into the hollow.

In the center of the vale stood a tower that was the mirror image of the one he had hidden in to escape the Wraiths. This broch was built in the center of the village, which clearly was growing. There were several dozen cottages arrayed in neat, orderly rows, a dozen more under construction, along with a large meeting hall and paddocks running toward the fields that were deeper within the dale.

Behind the tower was a green that extended for several hundred yards to the west. What really caught his eye was the large open space that circled the tower, none of the homes any closer than one hundred yards.

"Impressive," said Jakob, stopping when they reached the blacksmith, who was located at the very perimeter of the village, a good distance away from the other homes. There appeared to be no shortage of work as Jakob watched a rather large man train a half dozen apprentices.

"I like to think so," replied Duff.

"Was the killing ground your idea?"

Duff beamed at the question, pleased that Jakob had noticed. The more time he spent with this young man, the more Duff liked him, and not just because he came across as a fighter at heart.

"I did learn a few things when I was in the Royal Guard. I had a very good Captain. He was a stickler for details."

"And those details can mean the difference between life and death."

"Exactly so," replied Duff, giving Jakob a strange expression. "Where did you learn that?"

"My father." With his emotions so raw, he wasn't willing to say more than that.

"Your father served in the Royal Guard?"

"For a time."

"What's your family's name?" asked Duff, curious if he had ever served with him.

"Nothing worth mentioning," Jakob replied, brushing off the question. "How long has this village been here?"

"Almost a year now," explained Duff, choosing to let go of Jakob's unwillingness to respond. This young man wasn't the only one who came to the Territories looking to work from a clean slate. "This village is just one of many."

"Each one with a tower."

"Yes, always with a tower."

"So back where we came from? A village will be built there too?"

Duff nodded. "The tower always comes first. Once the tower is done, the village follows."

"Smart. How many villages are there now?"

"Twenty right now, three more about to be built, one of those around the broch we stayed in last night."

"No lack of demand, then."

"No lack of demand. More than we can handle, in fact. Unfortunately, we can only build the towers so fast. But the people understand that, so they won't move until the tower is complete. Without the brochs we have no way to protect against the Wraiths and slavers both since Sharperson offers no help whatsoever. He seems to only care about the Stone and the mines he has deeds to."

"There's a reason the Governor doesn't offer any assistance."

Duff's expression shifted, becoming shrewd. "It's true then? The Governor rules the slavers?"

Jakob nodded. "From a slaver's mouth to my ear."

"I assumed as much. Many of us did, although we had little to back up our beliefs. Where is this slaver now?"

"Dead."

Duff smiled upon hearing that. "You know a slaver is much like a Wraith. The only good Wraith is a dead Wraith."

"And the only good slaver is a dead slaver," Jakob finished for him. "I couldn't agree with you more."

"Another meeting of the minds," murmured Duff. "I like it. You did the deed?"

"I killed several of the other slavers who were trying to capture me and my father, but not that one. A Stalker took care of him for me."

"A Stalker? I've never heard of those monsters ever bothering any of the people being sent into forced labor or the slavers themselves. How did that come about?"

Jakob provided a brief recounting of what happened in the valley and how he worked to get his father to safety, only to lose him to the slavers right before the fog blanketed the Highlands.

During Jakob's clipped retelling, Duff just listened, holding back the many questions that came to mind. He observed Jakob, his eyes never leaving him.

Trying to see the young man behind the persona he put forward. He didn't think there was much difference between the two.

Not judging him. Not measuring him. The lad already had proven his mettle.

He had caught glimpses of the lad's combat against the Wraiths below the tower, although not much. The fog was too thick to see much more than a few dim figures moving in the mist.

Still, he had seen and heard enough to know that this young man was a good fighter, one to be respected, perhaps even feared with a bit more seasoning. That was important if you wanted to make your way in the Highlands, particularly these days.

He was getting another feeling about this young man as well. A sense of quiet purpose. Commitment.

Someone who could be trusted.

Someone who would watch your back in a fight.

Someone who when he made a promise would do all that he could to keep it.

Here within these peaks that was just as if not more important than his skill with a blade.

"Will you be staying with us or seeking to make your own way?" Duff asked once Jakob recited the events of the last few days. "We're always looking for anyone able and willing to contribute."

Instead of responding immediately, Jakob took his time to consider the question. He hadn't really thought about what he was going to do next. After his first night in the Highlands, his primary objective was to escape the slavers and get his father to a safe place. He had achieved that goal, but for all too brief a time.

When he lost his father to the slaver's steel, his priority shifted to escaping the Wraiths. Now that he had done that, he hadn't thought much about what was next, still trying to process all that had occurred.

He could go off on his own and try to start a new life for himself. Yet that idea held little appeal for him. That was a path that he was going to take with his father. Now ...

Now he was alone.

First Senna.

Now his father.

Then his thoughts turned to all the other people who had been enslaved. To the many others who every day were being made to work in the mines. To all the ones who had not escaped the slavers.

How not only the slavers but also the Wraiths were terrifying the Highlands. Making what was supposed to be a new beginning a bloody end.

Jakob shook his head, although the movement was barely noticeable.

He couldn't do it.

His father had always said that he had an overdeveloped sense of right and wrong, that the world was grey and that he'd only get himself in trouble if he looked at it as black and white.

But here, in the Highlands, he could see little grey, other than that of the Murk. Here, after his experiences with the slavers and the Wraiths, it was only black and white.

No, he couldn't focus on himself right now. Not when there were people in need.

For just an instant, he recalled the faces of the men and women who had been prisoners with him and his father. The old and the young. All different, yet all the same.

All wanting to make a new life for themselves.

All seeking something better for themselves and their families.

All gone.

Their hopes and dreams had been stolen from them. First by the slavers, then by the Wraiths who slaughtered them, only he and his father escaping the monsters in the mist.

He couldn't walk away. Not now. Not when he might have something valuable to contribute. Not when he could fight for what he believed to be right.

He would be the first to admit that revenge was a part of his thinking. He felt that he had unfinished business with the slavers, one slaver in particular.

The Wraiths as well.

But it wasn't the only part. It wasn't even the largest.

These people here in this village and the others dotting the Highlands were trying to make a life for themselves under extremely difficult circumstances. That was something that appealed to him. Something that he thought that he might want to be a part of.

"If I stay, will I get the chance to kill more Wraiths and the occasional slaver?"

"I can almost guarantee it," replied Duff with his characteristically broad grin.

"Then I'd like to stay and help."

"Good lad," said Duff, giving him a companionable slap on the back. "I was hoping you'd say that. You'll start as a hunter. Not only will you be responsible for bringing in game for the entire village, but you'll also defend against any threats that might come our way."

"That works for me," nodded Jakob.

"I thought it might. Hunters are the last ones into the tower. They're responsible for getting everyone to safety before they seek safety themselves. Whether Wraiths or slavers, it doesn't matter. Are you ready to make that commitment?"

Once again Jakob didn't respond immediately. The last man in. He mulled that requirement for a few seconds. For some reason that he didn't quite understand the risk appealed to him.

"Yes, that works for me."

"Good. You start now."

"He can start in an hour," called a sharp voice, Jakob turning as a young woman maybe just a few years older than he was strode down the path leading from the broch.

She stepped up right next to Jakob. She was about his

height, her long brown hair braided down her back. For just a second, he saw a little bit of Senna in the shape of her face, even more so in the mischievous spark that flashed behind her eyes.

What he noticed first about her, however, was the long dagger on one thigh, the hilt of another dagger visible at the small of her back. He got the sense that she was exceedingly competent with those blades and likely could gut him in just a few seconds if she felt the need to do so.

Although that wasn't her intent at that moment. The woman placed a hand gently beneath the slash that ran from his brow down to his cheek, taking a close look at the angry wound. Jakob had washed it as best as he could, but he didn't have the supplies that he needed to do the stitching.

"It's stopped bleeding, but it looks like a horrible mess," said the woman. "First, I want the physick to look at this. Then we can get who started?"

"Jakob," offered Duff. He then nodded toward the woman. "And this is Saraa."

"A pleasure to meet you," said Jakob.

"Tell me that after I put you through your paces. You might have a different opinion of me then."

"I should have been paying closer attention," said Duff, motioning toward Jakob's wound and the blood covering his face. "I forgot all about that."

Saraa snorted in response. "How could anyone forget about that?" she said, pulling her hand away. "Even when Fenrick is done with him, Jakob will have a nice scar that neither he nor anyone who sees him will be able to forget. He'll probably scare the children just as he's doing now. I haven't seen a wee one since he walked into the village."

"Maybe so, but you know what they say."

"I don't, Duff, and I don't want to know."

Duff told her anyway. "In my experience, most women like

scars. It makes a man seem dangerous, and some women like a little danger, don't they?"

"I doubt you have much experience with women," Saraa countered. "Besides, that is no more than speculation."

"It got you here, didn't it?"

Jakob grinned at that, although he was careful not to laugh. He didn't think that Saraa would appreciate it and he didn't want to give Duff more credit than he deserved.

"If I didn't have better things to do, I'd give you a slice just like Jakob's." She shook her head with disappointment, although that spark of amusement remained in the back of her eyes. "You're insufferable, you know that?"

"I've been told that many times, and I'm sure many more to come," Duff admitted with a grin that suggested he viewed such a criticism as anything but. He then turned his attention toward Jakob.

"Saraa has been with us for more than a year. She's a hunter as well. She'll show you the ropes. After you see the physick. We don't want you scaring the children, after all."

Jakob nodded, offering Saraa a smile, then taking a longer look at her. She was a beautiful young woman. Made even more so by the bow and quiver of arrows on her back, as well as the long daggers that could function as short swords if there was a need. Clearly, she could handle herself.

Saraa returned his look with just as much interest. After several uncomfortable seconds passed, she nodded and then smiled.

"Come on, Jakob. I'll show you around. But first to Fenrick." Saraa turned and started walking back toward the broch, though she had only taken a few steps before she looked back over her shoulder, that spark in her eye still there. "Make sure you stay close."

7

FRIEND AND FOE

"There's something that you need to know," said Aislinn, having joined Bryen on the helm.

"You're rethinking your decision to come with me?" asked Bryen with a straight face, although his eyes flashed with a hint of amusement.

"Funny, Protector. Very funny indeed." She punched him lightly on his arm. "You said you wanted me to come. So you're stuck with me, whether you like it or not."

"Much like an albatross around my neck," Bryen mused.

This time Aislinn hit him a little bit harder, making him wince. "Are you sure you want to continue with your humor, Protector? If so, you might need some protection from me."

"No, I'm done," Bryen said, raising his hands in surrender.

"Good. Now can we talk about a more serious matter?"

Emelina had guided the *Freedom* through the Floe, dodging the last of the icebergs with a consummate skill. They were now on the eastern boundary of the Sea of Mist. Because the two bodies of water met here, it would be rough seas for the next few hours.

That was a small price to pay, however, as they were now

only three or four days from the coast of New Caledonia. Depending on the winds and the weather, of course.

After several months' journey, it felt good to know that their ultimate destination, Ballinasloe in Fal Carrach, was less than a week away.

Because of that Bryen felt more relaxed than he probably should. Well, that and the fact that they had removed two cutters from the chase and the two others that were still afloat likely were caught among the icebergs.

Therefore, he wasn't too concerned about the single pirate frigate that was just now emerging with some difficulty from the Floe. The cutter barely made it past the last iceberg that drifted in front of it, the captain attempting to turn sharply, the ship responding sluggishly, the portside hull scraping across a keen edge of ice that extended out from beneath the water.

The soldiers of the Blood Company who were tracking the vessel from the stern cheered when a long gash appeared in the side when the ship finally broke free, a few groaning when they realized that, luckily for the pirates and less so for them, the damage was above the waterline.

Bryen actually grinned upon seeing that. The time for running had come to an end, although they didn't want to be too obvious about it. Captain Gregson already was ordering his sailors to prepare for a fight, Emelina turning the vessel in wide curls that were designed to slow their progress and allow their hunter to overtake them.

He didn't believe that seizing the damaged ship would prove to be much of a challenge. Not with the other frigates yet to come through the Floe.

If they captured the ship quickly, they would have some time to speak with these pirates and make them see the error of their ways before they needed to deal with the rest of their pursuers. Assuming, of course, the two ships stuck further back in the Floe made it through the icy obstacle course.

"What would that be?"

"Have you been searching around us with the Talent?"

"No, I thought you were doing that."

"I am," confirmed Aislinn. "Look to the south. You should be able to see them now."

Bryen quietly berated himself for not paying more attention to the larger picture, as he had focused primarily on the ships chasing them from the east. When he located what Aislinn had been tracking, he was even angrier with himself. It was foolish to think that he could let go of the stresses plaguing him even for a time.

Because now they had more threats to overcome than just the one damaged ship coming upon them from the rear.

The pirate frigates that had emerged from the squall and that Bryen thought would be close on the sterns of the other cutters that chased them through the Floe instead had raced through the icebergs on a different track farther to the south.

It seemed that they had little difficulty finding a way through the flowing field of ice, because those two frigates were now coming toward their port side. Worse, there were two more frigates with them, likely the stragglers who came out of the fog after the *Freedom* had entered the Floe.

Five pirate ships in all. Seven if you counted the two that were now out of service if they had not yet slipped beneath the surface.

Even as Bryen thought about what to do regarding this new, more challenging dilemma, a part of his mind was considering the larger implications of what was occurring.

This wasn't happenstance. These pirates knew that the *Freedom* was going to be here around this time, even with the delays they faced thanks to the Bakunawa, the storm, and the day they spent introducing themselves to the Kraken on the Jagged Islands.

How that could be, he didn't know. But he meant to find out because he was sure of his worrisome conclusion.

To do that, Bryen definitely needed to have a conversation. That desire guided the strategy that he was constructing for the engagement. And as part of that strategy, first he needed to remove several of the threats they faced so that when he had that conversation with the captain of one of the pirate frigates they weren't rudely interrupted.

"Even after all the delays we faced in crossing the Burnt Ocean, I really get the feeling that these pirates were waiting for us," murmured Bryen, shaking his head as the final pieces of his plan fell into place.

"What makes you say that?" asked Aislinn with a sardonic twist to her lips, realizing that Bryen was more talking to himself than talking to her. "The fact that there would be seven ships here if not for us removing two from the fight already? Seven pirate ships to take just one vessel? That's excessive don't you think?"

"That I do," Bryen said, turning his wry smile toward her. "You really are spending too much time with Lycia."

"Why do you say that?"

"Because her sarcasm is washing off on you."

"That's not necessarily a bad thing," Aislinn replied.

"It's not necessarily a good thing either," countered Bryen. "One Lycia is enough." He turned his attention to what was going on below the helm, sailors and soldiers moving to their assigned positions as Captain Gregson and Declan both issued a series of clipped orders. He nodded to himself, certain now of what they needed to do to ensure that they maintained the upper hand. "We're going to adopt a new approach."

"You don't think they'll make this easy for us? They won't want to just come on board for a nice chat if we offer them tea and sandwiches?"

"No, I don't." Bryen gave Aislinn a sideways look. "Again with the sarcasm. It's getting tedious already."

"Sorry, I just couldn't resist." It was her turn to raise her hands in surrender. "What do you have in mind?"

"Forcing the pirates overtaking us from the east to capitulate by demonstrating why the Company of Blood is so named."

"Simple and effective. I like it."

"Prepare to repel boarders!" shouted Declan as he strode past the helm toward the starboard railing, the pirate ship at their stern coming up on them on that side. "Just remember that I want some of them taken alive!"

"But that's only a part of the strategy," prodded Aislinn.

"Correct," confirmed Bryen. "Let's find Lycia and Davin. It's time to demonstrate to these marauders that they came for the wrong prey."

"I have to give them credit," said Davin.

"What do you mean?" asked Lycia. "Give who credit?"

"The pirates. They certainly are offering an energetic defense."

"They haven't hit any of us. They haven't even come close."

Lycia, Davin, Aislinn, and Bryen soared in and out of the low-hanging clouds, Banshee and the other Griffons circling around the fight developing aboard the *Freedom* and then curling around the attacking vessels that now were sailing around the prize they sought to take. They had to be careful not so much of the archers who had climbed the rigging, hoping to gain a lucky strike, but rather of the large crossbows set into the fore and aft decks of the ships.

Each bolt that streaked through the air from those devices was six feet long and would do a great deal of harm to the Griffons if the pirates' aim was good. Even though trying to hit a flying target was exceedingly difficult and required a good bit of luck, particularly because of the rough swells that lifted and dropped the ships in a stomach-churning rhythm, they didn't want to put the Griffons at an even greater risk.

"True. But they don't seem to be as scared of the Griffons as I thought they would be." Davin had been surprised by that finding. Most people never saw such animals unless they traveled into the wilds, such as the northernmost mountains of the Shattered Peaks, and if they did, they tended to give them a very wide berth.

"I think it's because they're so scared that they're offering, as you said, such an energetic defense. The Griffons terrify them, which is likely part of the reason why their aim is so poor. Their nerves are getting the better of them."

Davin mulled that prospect for a moment as he rode on Fuerza's back, running his hands through the auburn feathers and fur that ran down the back of the Griffon's head all the way to his front paws. "You could be right about that."

"Of course I'm right," confirmed Lycia, her Griffon, Arabella, gliding comfortably next to Fuerza.

The two gladiators watched with interest as the damaged pirate ship that had been chasing them finally came up alongside the *Freedom*. The buccaneers flung more than a dozen grappling hooks across the space, the steel biting into the wood railing, allowing them to bring the two ships closer. As soon as the hulls slammed together, several pirates attempted to swing across from the rigging.

That proved to be a poor idea. The Blood Company archers who had positioned themselves on the *Freedom's* yardarms and at various spots along the length of the ship made quick work of them, most of the pirates attempting to board falling dead before they even had left their own vessel.

Dissuaded from continuing to employ a losing and fatal tactic, the pirates instead concentrated their efforts along the starboard side railings, seeking to force their way past the defenders' shield wall. That only served to frustrate them as well.

After several minutes of fierce attacks, none of the pirates had yet to set foot on their prize. The large, curved scuta the Blood Company employed proved to be too much of an obstacle for them, the challenge of getting past the shield wall made all the more difficult because every so often a spear appeared randomly over the steel rim of a shield.

That, in itself, wasn't unexpected. What was surprising to the attackers was that those spears never missed.

The soldiers standing behind the shield bearers struck with an uncanny precision. Throat or chest, every time, until ten pirates littered the deck of their own ship, bleeding out and bogging down the flagging efforts of their brethren.

Davin shook his head in disappointment because of the obvious lack of imagination. It wouldn't be long before the pirates rued their decision to even give chase.

He could just imagine what had been going through their minds when they first saw the *Freedom* compared to what was going through their minds now.

Because of the size of the vessel, he assumed that the marauders believed that the ship would be an easy target. That this prize would offer them a big payday.

Now, the pirates likely were beginning to wonder whether with these veteran fighters on board if they were the target rather than the other way around.

At least the smart ones would be thinking that, Davin assumed. Because the pirates who were so foolish to lash their vessel to the *Freedom* were indeed the prey now.

As Davin and Lycia focused on the activity around the *Freedom*, Bryen spent more time keeping an eye on the other frigates, which were doing their best to maintain their positioning around the battle. The choppy water and the unpredictable currents caused by the Floe on the far eastern edge of the Sea of Mist were hindering their efforts to come up on the *Freedom's* port side and contribute more fighters to the clash.

Bryen wasn't worried if one of the pirate captains actually succeeded in gaining the port rail. He was certain that the Blood Company could manage another attack while still keeping their current aggressors in check.

Even so, Bryen didn't want the gladiators to have to deal with that additional pressure if it could be avoided.

Catching the attention of Aislinn, Davin, and Lycia, he signaled to his friends what he had in mind. Receiving nods in return and a broad grin from Davin, who for the moment seemed to have forgotten that he usually didn't enjoy riding on the back of a Griffon, Bryen whispered a few words in Banshee's ear.

In a flash, the Griffon dove down toward the cutter that was curling toward the *Freedom* from the northeast.

Banshee twisted and turned during her rapid descent, demonstrating a remarkable agility as she avoided the two large crossbow bolts shot toward her by what Bryen saw were some very desperate pirates.

At the very last second of her approach, the Griffon tipped her wing, soaring sideways through the air, parallel to the frigate. No more than fifty feet above the waves, she gave Bryen the perfect angle for what he wanted to do.

Reaching for the Talent, Bryen shot a rapid-fire burst of white-hot spheres from his left palm, his right hand grasping Banshee's feathers to keep himself in place. He was past the ship in just a few heartbeats, but that was all the time that he required.

He didn't need to see what happened to judge the success of his efforts. He could tell by the screams of terror that echoed in his ears as Banshee pumped her powerful wings to get them back up to the cloud cover.

When he finally looked down upon regaining his perch, every single one of the ship's sails was on fire.

Aislinn, riding on Astuta's back, attacked right after he did. The Griffon dove down toward the ship that was following the one Bryen had set aflame. Tucking in her wings, staying just above the frothing waves, Astuta sped below the steel bolts that passed harmlessly above her.

As she streaked past the vessel, Aislinn fired a stream of power that struck the sails rigged to the foremast. Not bothering to be precise, she maintained her attack, the energy blasting across the deck and into the mainmast and then the mizzenmast.

As Astuta peeled away, Aislinn looked back over her shoulder. The fires were spreading swiftly, all three masts burning, the flames already licking down into the hatches.

Two vessels removed from the fight in less than a minute. A good piece of work in Bryen's opinion.

Now the pirates on those ships had a much more intense and personal concern.

Thoughts of gold and other riches melted away in a flash, replaced by the impossible aspiration to save their ships and themselves. Any desire to continue after the *Freedom* fled as soon as the first spark struck their sails.

Bryen and Aislinn watched from above as Davin and Lycia concentrated their efforts on the ship behind the two cutters that were swiftly becoming flaming hulks. Arabella hurtled down toward the vessel, the pirates having lost track of the Griffons flying above them, for the moment focused solely on turning their ship to avoid colliding with the two floundering and burning frigates that were now blocking their way.

The pirate captain started to shout an order to the helmsman to turn hard to starboard. He never got out more than a few words.

The Griffon slammed down into the helm with a sickening

crunch, catching the captain with one sharp paw and the helmsman with the other.

Right behind Arabella and Lycia came Davin and Fuerza, their focus the now spinning wheel that because of the lack of control already was taking the ship off course, the rough water forcing the vessel back toward the Floe.

With a few fast and furious kicks, Fuerza destroyed the wheel, removing the only tool the pirates had to navigate through the choppy seas.

Leaping back into the air, the two Griffons with their claws extended sliced through the sails rigged to the foremast and the mainmast, shredding the cloth. Fuerza also knocked down the mainmast with a jarring kick.

In seconds, a third pirate vessel was out of commission, its main deck shattered by the falling mainmast, the timber smashing through several more decks and sending thousands of pieces of splintered and cracked wood in all directions. The now useless sailcloth drifted slowly down and draped itself over the several dozen injured and dying pirates trapped beneath the wreckage.

In Lycia's opinion, the imagery was only appropriate, the black sail offering a visual testament as it settled onto the deck. There was only one price that the pirates would be required to pay for their greed.

Death.

"ARE you sure you don't want me to play a larger role? I'm more than happy to do so."

"Not yet," replied Declan, noting and ignoring the excitement he heard in the Magus' voice. "We don't want to scare them away just yet."

"Fine," Rafia grumped.

She had restricted her use of the Talent during the fight. Bryen wanted to eliminate all the marauders in a single play. To do that, she understood that she needed to allow the pirates to think that they had a real chance to take the *Freedom* so that their compatriots circling around them didn't get spooked and make a run for it.

Therefore, she limited herself to the raiders who had climbed the rigging. She made sure that when they fired crossbow bolts down at the Blood Company that they always missed, the shafts knocked off target with the Talent or clunking uselessly against the shields that she crafted as needed.

"But I don't know how much longer I can manage the boredom."

Declan chuckled at Rafia's remark. He understood the Magus' perspective. Her patience tended to wear thin quite quickly.

Declan and Rafia stood on the helm as the Blood Company, lining the starboard rail, prevented the pirates from boarding with a coordinated, unwavering defense. Just as Declan expected of them.

Not a single pirate had managed to fight his way past the shield wall, and he knew without a doubt that none of them would.

In fact, Declan recognized the exact moment that the pirates, after more than a dozen unsuccessful attacks on the wall of steel, seeking some kind of weakness yet finding none, realized that they had bitten off more than they could chew. He could see it in their eyes, a hint of fear mixing with a frantic desire to break away from these hardened soldiers who couldn't be killed, at least not by them.

Unfortunately for the pirates, they were committed now. With their ship lashed to the *Freedom*, they had no way to break away without risking being slaughtered themselves.

"Why don't you clear the rigging then," suggested Declan. "I'd like to avoid any lucky strikes when we move to the next step in our plan."

"With pleasure," murmured Rafia, her eyes sharpening, becoming predatory.

Reaching for the Talent, she sent bolts of energy no larger than the size of sewing needles toward the dozen pirates positioned in the shrouds and lines who were taking potshots at the gladiators.

The pirates never saw what killed them, the streaks seeming to be nothing more than flashes of light.

However, the effect of those splinters of energy was immediate and devastating. The miniature bolts shot right through the pirates, some of the crossbowmen slumping dead on the ropes, others getting tangled in the rigging or falling to the deck far below, only adding to the horror their friends faced against the scuta of the Blood Company.

"That was quite fast and quite effective."

"I aim to please," Rafia replied.

Declan nodded, not saying anything immediately, instead looking at the wild-haired Magus who clearly was where she was meant to be. In the heat of a battle.

"I don't know if I agree with that statement," Declan finally murmured, but saying it softly so that Rafia couldn't hear him. There was no reason to start an argument while in the midst of capturing the pirate ship.

Tehana and Asaia barely noticed the pirates who fell out of the rigging and crashed down onto the far deck. The two gladiators were too busy, Asaia with her much-preferred whip and Tehana with her shortened trident reaching over the shoulders and shields of Majdi and Jenus. Combined the two huge gladiators in that part of the shield wall took up as much space across the railing as six men standing shoulder to shoulder.

The two friends never failed to make their presence known.

Each pirate foolish enough to test their skill against them fell away with a scream of pain and a shower of blood.

Not unexpectedly, the soldiers of the Blood Company were getting a little bored. It wasn't an easy task to extend a fight that they could have ended within the first few minutes of its beginning.

Still, that was their assigned lot, so they demonstrated a great deal of restraint, not eliminating the pirates with a cool efficiency right at the start of the clash despite having multiple opportunities to do so.

Finally, their patience was rewarded. They heard the command that they had been waiting for just a few seconds later.

"Over the rail!" roared Declan in his stentorian voice. "Take the ship!"

"It's about time," grumbled Tehana.

"I couldn't agree with you more," replied Asaia.

The tenor of the battle changed in just seconds. Majdi, Jenus, and the others holding the rails stepped back and kneeled, placing their shields above their heads. Asaia, Tehana, and the other gladiators behind them took a few steps back, then sprinted forward, each one planting a foot on a scutum and leaping through the air.

A flight of arrows preceded them, knocking back a dozen shocked and terrified pirates as the gladiators landed on their vessel hungry for blood. Whip, trident, sword, and dagger flashed with a blinding speed, never failing to find flesh.

Majdi and the other shield bearers scrambled across the lashed together railings right behind the first wave, the archers keeping up a steady fire to keep the way clear and increase the pressure on the pirates.

It was just a matter of time before the marauders, who struggled to mount an effective defense, broke. The gladiators just needed to give them one final push.

That none so gentle shove came when several squads of the Blood Company, who had been hiding in the hatchways, swarmed across the railings. At the same time, Dorlan, Kollea, Chesin, and a few others who had climbed the rigging when Majdi and the other shield bearers leapt the railing swung across to increase the pressure on their adversaries.

The pirates, already beginning to waver under the lightning-fast onslaught, crumbled completely just a few seconds later. Those not overrun by the gladiators sprinted for the hatches, hoping to get below decks before they were cut down.

Less interested in defending themselves. More interested in running for their lives.

The marauders didn't realize that regardless of their efforts, whether standing and fighting or running and hoping to escape into the tight passageways below, they didn't stand a chance. They had sealed their fates as soon as they had come alongside the *Freedom*, because the Blood Company was not in a merciful mood.

Declan knew what the outcome of the fight would be before it even started. If the Ghoules and the Kraken couldn't kill the gladiators of the Blood Company, then a band of pirates, no matter how many, certainly stood little chance.

He almost felt bad for the bastards.

Almost.

With his gladiators sweeping the deck of the pirate ship clear, the Sergeant of the Blood Company climbed down from the helm, Rafia right behind him.

"Shall we?" he asked, offering the Magus his hand.

Rafia gave him a smirk, ignoring the assistance he offered her and vaulting over the rails, daggers in both hands.

Declan could only shake his head in wonder. Always looking for a fight, even when this one was almost over. Placing a hand on the chipped and blood-splattered handrail, he vaulted after her.

"I want prisoners!" he shouted, reminding the gladiators what he had required of them.

The main deck was covered by dead and dying pirates, rapidly expanding pools of blood staining the wood. Hopefully he would find one or two marauders still alive below.

BANSHEE GLIDED in a broad circle a few hundred feet above the waves. She was preparing to dive a second time toward one of the ships yet to be attacked. She held back, however, Bryen whispering into her ear, asking her to wait.

She did, grudgingly. The delay chafed, at odds with her aggressive nature.

Bryen took a few seconds to take stock of what was occurring across the surface of the Sea of Mist. They had disabled three of the pirate ships. Two of those ships were on fire, the blazes out of control, pirates jumping into the sea, willing to take their chances in the frigid water rather than risk being burned alive.

The third ship, her helm ruined, sails torn, and the black cloth covering the deck that had been shattered by the collapsed mainmast, was drifting at the whim of the volatile currents right toward the Floe. It was only a matter of time before a collision with an iceberg sent the vessel to the bottom.

He could see as well that the Blood Company had everything well in hand. They had taken the pirate ship lashed to the side of the *Freedom*, turning the tables on the pirates with a little trickery and a shocking demonstration of skill, force, and will.

Declan stood on the deck of the prize, Majdi and the others bringing up through the hatchways those pirates who didn't want to brave the water, instead foolishly trying to hide somewhere on the ship. And if he wasn't mistaken, it appeared that

Asaia and Tehana had captured the captain, the man bloodied and battered, dazed, though still on his feet.

Good. He was exactly the person Bryen wanted to talk to.

He doubted that any of the other captains on the surviving ships would have much more to offer than the one he now had in hand. So he could turn his attention toward eliminating the last two pirate ships, which were now sailing at all possible speed toward the west.

Fleeing.

A smart move on the part of their captains. They saw what happened to their comrades, and clearly they believed that discretion was better than a certain bloody end.

Nevertheless, their moment of clarity wouldn't save them. Bryen wasn't in a merciful mood today.

Rather, he believed that a statement needed to be made. Removing seven pirate ships from the waters along the New Caledonian coast was a much louder declaration than eliminating five.

"Ready?" called Aislinn.

"Let's hold off for a moment," said Bryen, earning a shriek of disappointment from Banshee when he asked her to wait a little longer. "I want to see what's going to happen."

Aislinn shifted her gaze to the west when Bryen nodded in that direction. Three sleek frigates were coming in fast, slicing across the top of the waves.

"Who could they be?" asked Aislinn.

"I don't know, but if they're going after the pirates, they might be worth getting to know better."

The three ships were flying the same colors, fields of green with what they took to be bunches of dark purple grapes in the very center. They had no idea who the flags belonged to, but they doubted that they were in league with the pirates.

Bryen was impressed as the frigates drew closer. The hulls were modified, wings along the side lifting the vessels completely out of the water as the wind stretched their sails to capacity. While running fast, these ships resembled catamarans.

He had watched those vessels on occasion during his time in Battersea, taken with the design since it lessened the drag of the hull across the water, providing several more knots to an already fast craft.

You needed to be a skilled mariner to manage a ship such as that correctly, as the greater speed also increased the risk of capsizing. And clearly, the commanders of these three vessels knew what they were doing.

Bryen and Aislinn didn't have much longer to wait to see how the drama was going to play out. The three ships steered directly toward the two pirate frigates that were sailing side by side, clearly intent on escaping a promising battle that quickly had become a disaster.

"They don't stand a chance," said Bryen, meaning the pirate ships. The three corsairs had adjusted their spacing, ensuring that the lead ship cut right between the two ships coming from the east, the other two along the outside of each vessel.

"No, they don't," agreed Aislinn, observing with a wicked smile as long steel spikes that extended out for more than ten feet curled down the sides of these new arrivals and then locked into place.

That was a clever innovation, Aislinn thought. She had never seen anything like it while growing up in the Southern Marches.

Certain now as to the fates of the fleeing pirates, neither Bryen nor Aislinn felt an ounce of sympathy. As the three corsairs glided more than sailed across the waves, the steel spikes scraped along the sides of the pirate ships, leaving several long gashes and holes above the waterline, and just as many below.

The impact of the devastating damage was immediate. Both

pirate ships slowed drastically, taking on water, struggling in the rough seas, pirates running around frantically, trying to keep their vessels afloat even though they knew that the odds were against them to begin with and were only worsening with every passing second.

"Now that is quite effective," said Davin, coming up next to Bryen on the back of Fuerza. "Clever. Tricky. Impressive."

"I thought you might enjoy that," replied Bryen as he watched the three vessels circle back around to finish off the two pirate vessels, although from where he flew above the battlefield, he could tell that another attack wouldn't be necessary. One of the ships was already listing badly, its sails dipping closer to the waves. The other was sinking rapidly, its bow already submerged. "They don't even have to risk their lives boarding the ships. If the pirates want to live, they'll have to beg to be taken aboard."

"So clever, tricky, impressive, and efficient," offered Davin.

"I can't disagree with you about that."

"I'd like to meet the captain of this flotilla," said Davin. "A man after my own heart. Brutal, but in a nice way."

"You know what you just said is somewhat contradictory, right?"

Davin nodded. "I can't disagree with you about that. But it seems like the best way to describe whoever's making the decisions down below us."

"Let's see if we can give you the chance to introduce yourself to the captain," Bryen said, ignoring Davin's attempted humor. "Come on. Let's get back to our ship and let our new allies finish what they're doing. I have a feeling that whoever helped us will want to have a chat."

8

SECRET REVEALED

"You never told me you were a Magus," whispered Saraa. She tried to add a touch of pique to her voice. She failed miserably because of her excitement.

"I'm not a Magus. I never passed the Test. Never even took it. I just know how to use the Talent."

"Passing the Test isn't relevant. Being able to use the Talent is relevant." She rolled her eyes and shook her head in wonder. "Do you try to be difficult, or does it just come naturally to you?"

"It comes naturally," Jakob replied, glancing over at Saraa and giving her a wide grin. "You could still go with the others. Duff can come down and take your place. Are you sure you want to do this?"

They crouched next to a heart tree. The Murk had drifted over the mountaintop, hiding almost everything around them, including the broch that was only a few hundred yards to the north.

"Are you trying to get rid of me?" Saraa demanded, her voice taking on the hard edge with which Jakob was all too familiar.

"No, of course not," he replied. "I just want to make sure that you want to do this. There are no guarantees that it will work."

"I'll take that chance," Saraa confirmed. "I'm not leaving all the fun to you. Besides, I'm just as good a fighter as you are."

"I didn't say that you weren't. I just have a few advantages because of the Talent that you and the others don't have."

"You have got to stop throwing that in my face. It's getting tedious."

"I'm not throwing it in your face," Jakob replied with a touch of heat. How could this woman make him smile so easily and then aggravate him with barely any effort just a heartbeat later. "I'm just stating a fact."

Not known for having a great deal of patience, Saraa grumbled softly to herself, a fairly common occurrence for her when she was in the midst of an argument that she didn't believe was necessary. They had already decided this between them. There was no reason to revisit it.

"That's all well and good, but we're here now. I'm not going anywhere. So stop complaining so that we can focus on the work that needs to be done. You need a Highlander to see if this will work, and that Highlander is me. Deal with it."

"I'm not complaining ..." Jakob stopped himself, then shook his head with his eyes closed for just a few seconds, knowing that Saraa could barely see the motion because of the dense fog.

There was no point in arguing with her. It wasn't worth the time or the effort. Because even when Saraa was wrong, you weren't right. She always made sure of that.

Besides, the reason for them being out in the Murk rather than safely behind the stone walls of the tower needed to take precedence. He could sense the Wraiths approaching.

"It sounded like you were," Saraa countered.

"All right, enough," replied Jakob, his irritation plain.

Jakob's response brought a smile to Saraa's lips. She had achieved the effect that she desired with very little effort. If she couldn't win an argument, she was more than happy to make the other person not want to continue the argument. She viewed the latter as a victory as well, because it meant that she still got what she wanted.

"The Wraiths are close," Jakob continued after taking several deep breaths. "Let's see if I can do this now as I did it before."

"And if you can't?"

"Then run for the broch and hope that Duff is willing to let you in with the Wraiths on your heels."

"I'm not running away, so make sure you do it right," Saraa replied, reaching out blindly in the billowing mist and squeezing Jakob's forearm warmly when she found him.

"Why are you always so difficult?" mumbled Jakob, not thinking that Saraa would hear him. But she did.

"I'm difficult because being difficult helps to keep me alive. You should know that by now." Saraa gave him one more stronger squeeze before releasing his arm. "Besides, you like it when I'm difficult. I keep you on your toes. You'd be bored otherwise."

"That's one way to put it," he replied, this time making sure that what he said was under his breath.

Reaching for the Talent, Jakob extended his senses out into the Murk. It didn't take him long to pinpoint what he was looking for.

More than a dozen Wraiths hunted within the fog, all of them within a league of where he and Saraa were hiding.

Three had broken away from the other Wraiths and were coming in their direction. These three were only a few hundred yards away and closing quickly.

He would have preferred just one Wraith for this experiment, yet there was nothing that he could do about it now. He could only hope that he and Saraa could maintain the element of surprise, because if they didn't, they were dead.

"Ready?"

Saraa nodded, her expression both anxious and excited.

Jakob nodded as well, taking a deep breath to calm his nerves, hoping that what he was about to do worked, because if it didn't, they were well and truly dead.

Reaching out a hand, he touched Saraa's forehead, a thin stream of the Talent connecting them.

He was done in a heartbeat. Saraa's look of amazement confirmed for him that he had succeeded.

Back in Caledonia, Aloysius had taught him some interesting ways to employ the Talent that Jakob believed would be of use to him and the Highlanders in their fight against the Wraiths. During the last few days, he had trained hard to perfect those skills.

By sending a stream of the Talent directly into Saraa's mind, he was able to connect with her so that she could see what he saw when he used natural magic to navigate the Murk.

If she could see what he could see when he extended his senses around them, then she could follow the movement and positioning of the Wraiths all on her own. She would know how to move and where to move.

Most important, she could fight unimpaired.

Jakob had just succeeded in eliminating the key advantage that the Wraiths enjoyed.

Their stealth.

These monsters were lethal fighters, although few of them had yet to engage in a real fight in the Highlands. Instead, they always relied on the benefits given to them by the thick grey mist.

They had not been challenged in any way until they had come across Jakob.

But that was about to change.

"Three Wraiths coming this way. Two from the west, one from the north," Saraa said. She was ecstatic that what Jakob did worked for her. It had just leveled what had been an uneven playing field. In fact, it might have tilted that field in her favor. "The one on his own is about one hundred yards away from the others."

Jakob nodded, both pleased and relieved that he had succeeded. He had worried that he had sentenced Saraa to her death by taking her out into the Murk to challenge the monsters in the mist. "Let's start with the Wraith coming from the north. He's the closest."

"Got it," Saraa replied, her eagerness palpable.

Since she had first come to the Highlands a few years before, every other time the fog drifted down from the north she had no choice but to make for a broch or some other highly defensible fortification. Now she didn't have to. She could finally take the fight to these monsters.

Living or dying wasn't her primary concern, although she certainly preferred to live. What really stuck in her craw had been the running.

"Remember how we're going to move," Jakob said as he began to walk slowly through the fog. Saraa followed him, mimicking his actions.

He never took a straight path toward where he wanted to go, striding forward ten feet then back five. Cutting to the left, then back to the right. Forward again, then back. Back again on an angle after stopping for several seconds, then to the right.

Stopping again, listening, fading into the fog, becoming a part of it. Forward again, the thick grey threads reluctantly giving way before them. Back ten steps, then toward the right once more.

Saraa couldn't identify a pattern to Jakob's movements. He seemed to move as the whim took him, ensuring that there was no rhythm to his motion, that there was no pattern that the Wraiths could discern.

Leaving Jakob to the task of getting them where they needed to go without being discovered, Saraa shifted her focus to the vision that had appeared in the back of her mind. All the critical missing pieces that the fog had cut out had been put back in place with an even greater clarity.

Even better, not only could she see everything that was close to her. She could sense everything else that was in the mist with her for ten leagues around.

"Don't get too excited," Jakob whispered in her ear when he stopped for a few seconds, Saraa almost walking right into him because she had allowed herself to become distracted by her new ability.

He could sense her exhilaration. He didn't want her excitement to get the better of her.

She nodded, then thought that Jakob wouldn't see the movement in the fog. She stopped herself from saying anything at the very last second, realizing that thanks to the Talent he could see her motion, even as she could see his smile despite the grey mist.

"Do you remember the plan?" he whispered, his breath warm in her ear, bringing a touch of heat to her cheeks to match the enthusiasm surging through her.

She nodded.

With that, he was gone, leaving her in the Murk right next to a heart tree. She tracked him through the swirling haze as he moved in a disjointed pattern to a position about twenty feet to the north, right next to another massive tree trunk.

They settled down to wait. Neither moving. Both barely breathing. Blending into the fog as if they were a part of it.

And they were, Jakob applying a separate stream of the Talent to complete that task. Even if the Wraiths stood no more than a foot away and stared right at him or at Saraa, the monsters wouldn't see anything but the Murk.

Unless either of them betrayed themselves by moving or making a sound. Any motion or disturbance would break the illusion.

Despite the distance between them, Jakob could sense Saraa's agitation as they waited for the Wraith that they had targeted to approach. The monster didn't appear to be in a rush, taking his time as he glided through the grey mist. Stopping for five minutes, even ten minutes at a time, just to see if he could flush out any prey who might be hiding close by.

Through it all, as the tension increased, Jakob was pleased that Saraa was able to control her anxiety. Here, in the Murk, success, and by that he meant staying alive, depended on patience. Something that she often had in limited supply.

Jakob pulled his attention away from Saraa, focusing again on the Wraith. The monster was just a dozen yards to his side now, gliding closer. In a few more steps he would be right in front of Jakob.

The seconds passed agonizingly slowly.

One step. Then two. A third. Almost there.

Then the Wraith stopped.

For just a moment, Jakob worried that the monster had sniffed out where he was.

But no, just a false alarm. All was still well.

The monster was just doing as was his practice. What Jakob had done. Halting every so often to see what might happen while he waited.

The instant that the Wraith took another step forward, Jakob stabbed with his dagger.

The Wraith caught the movement out of the corner of his eye, the motion breaking the illusion.

It didn't matter. Jakob was too quick.

The Wraith twisted away incredibly fast, although not before he hissed in pain, the sharp steel sliding into his kidney on his right side. One clawed hand dropped a dagger and pressed on his wound, trying to stanch the flow of blood gushing down his side.

The other claw sliced up toward where he thought his attacker's throat would be, his double-bladed dagger tight in his grip leading the way.

The monster never got his weapon above his waist. Before he could, a sword slid through the Wraith's back, the sharp tip appearing through his chest.

The Wraith's strength faded as soon as the blade was ripped free. Dropping to the damp ground, the Wraith realized his error as his blood pooled around him, his strength fading quickly.

He had come to the Highlands multiple times. He had never been attacked. Not once. Not until now.

The Wraith had never thought that it could happen.

He had never considered the possibility that there might be humans waiting for him in the Murk, and that they would find him before he would find them.

He had never believed that these humans -- weak, slow -- had any bite.

"Congratulations," Jakob whispered.

Saraa nodded, thrilled as she gave Jakob a feral grin. She wanted to hug him in thanks, but she restrained herself. Now wasn't the time.

She had hoped that Jakob's idea would work, she was desperate for it to work. Although just like Jakob, she worried that it wouldn't.

Now that they had tested this application of the Talent, all of her doubts vanished thanks to the body crumpled at her feet.

With this new tactic, the Highlanders no longer had to fight from a defensive position unless they chose to do so.

They wouldn't have to run and hide every time the fog appeared.

They could stand and fight. They could make these Wraiths pay for the terror and murder they had inflicted upon the people living in these mountains.

So long as Jakob was here, they could take the fight to these monsters.

That would change the dynamic of the current conflict rapidly.

To the good for the Highlanders.

To the bad for the Wraiths.

"There are two more Wraiths just to the west. Two hundred yards or so. Should we make a play for them?"

"You can talk in my mind as well?" Saraa failed to keep the shock from her voice. She was speaking directly to Jakob without saying a word! Another incredibly useful tool for them to implement.

"Yes, I just didn't want to throw too much at you at one time."

"This will make our efforts in the Murk so much easier."

"It should, yes."

"You know, you could have shown me this before we got started. You didn't have to hold back."

"I know that now," replied Jakob, ignoring the gentle chiding, not wanting to get into a muted argument at this very moment. *"Now about those other two Wraiths?"*

"Lead the way."

Saraa would raise the issue with him once they were done hunting. If for no other reason than to make sure he didn't get too comfortable.

She liked him best when he was a little on edge. When he settled into the quiet that he preferred, she didn't know how to interact with him.

She also wanted to know what else Jakob might be able to do with the Talent that could prove useful to their endeavors against the Wraiths. But she would dig that out of him later. Now, she had the chance for another kill.

Jakob and Saraa headed toward the west, taking their time. Moving as they did before. Not giving the Wraiths hunting for prey in the Murk any patterns that would make it easier for the monsters to find them.

"Are you certain?" asked Jakob. *"They're close together, so we'll each need to take on one."*

"I welcome the challenge," Saraa replied. Not arrogantly. Just with a spirit that she hadn't felt in quite a long time.

"Are you never not confident?"

"Never."

Both took the same approach as they did when dispatching the first Wraith. Using the clear vision that the Talent gave them, they selected positions along the path the pair of monsters were taking as they glided through the wood. Jakob and Saraa ended up about twenty yards away from one another.

With Jakob using the Talent to blend them into the Murk, they just had to wait. Their prey would come to them.

Their task was made easier because unlike them, the Wraiths moved on a more direct path. They didn't have anything to fear in the fog.

Or so they believed.

Both Jakob and Saraa hoped to disabuse these two hunters of that notion.

For Saraa, it was just as agonizing as the last time. The Wraith approaching her never came straight on, stopping and starting with an annoying regularity.

She understood now why Jakob moved as he did in the fog. He was mimicking the actions of the Wraiths to a very large extent.

Tricky and effective.

Saraa tensed, then forced herself to relax. The Wraith was just fifteen feet away from her now.

Then ten feet.

Five.

Three.

Saraa punched forward with her sword, driving the steel through the Wraith's gut. Knowing the danger of the monster's double-bladed daggers, she pulled her sword free and ducked. Rolling to the right, she swung backward with her blade. The sharp steel sliced across the back of both of the monster's legs.

The Wraith collapsed to the ground, groaning in agony.

She never allowed the monster to scream. She pushed down hard with a boot on the back of the monster's head, crushing his face into the leaves and dirt, holding him in place as she drove the tip of her sword through the back of his neck.

Her target eliminated, she was about to go to Jakob's aid when she realized that it wasn't necessary. He was walking toward her, bloody daggers in hand. He wiped the weapons with a cloth that he had cut from the Wraith's shirt before sheathing the steel.

"*Come on,*" he said in her mind, continuing through the Murk, using that disjointed walk of his to move through the mist. "*There are more Wraiths coming our way. Too many for us to fight. Once the Wraiths find the ones we killed, we'll lose the advantage of surprise. So it's time to take our leave.*"

Even though her blood was up, even though she knew that she was close to being invisible, even though she believed that she could do anything in the mist, finally having buried a blade in the creatures who had been terrorizing the Highlanders for so long, Saraa agreed with his decision.

Three kills. That was an excellent morning. And now it *was* time for them to take their leave.

When they reached the broch, a length of rope dropped down the side as they approached. Saraa took one more look around her with the natural magic that Jakob was sharing with her.

Nine more Wraiths were moving toward the broch now. Fast. No more than a mile away.

It was definitely a good idea to quit while they were ahead.

They must have found the bodies.

Saraa grabbed the rope and started to pull herself up, speeding her climb by walking up the rough stone. Jakob was right behind her.

"Don't do what you're doing."

"What am I doing?"

"You're looking at my rear."

"What are you talking about?"

"You're looking at my rear end as I climb. I know you are. I don't even need to look down at you to confirm it. Stop it."

"I'm looking at where I need to place my hands so I don't slip and become easy meat for the Wraiths," Jakob replied, a touch of exasperation in his voice as he pulled himself up the tower, making sure that he never lost track of the Wraiths who were now less than a quarter mile away and swiftly closing the distance to the broch. Making sure as well that he wasn't looking at Saraa's rear, even though he found it incredibly hard not to do so since she was talking about it.

"Likely excuse," murmured Saraa, although Jakob could tell that her mild outrage was feigned.

He was certain that she was enjoying this conversation, particularly because it was taking place at his expense. Knowing that, he sought to turn the tables on her.

"You're just saying that because you want me to look at your bottom."

"Quite full of yourself, aren't you?"

"I'm just telling you how I see it."

"And what do you see right now Jakob Kestrel?" Saraa didn't let him reply. "My rear."

Jakob bit back his next response, knowing that it would only take this conversation down a path he didn't want to take. "Next time I'll go first and you can look at my bum. How's that?"

"You promise?"

Jakob shook his head as he continued to climb, trying to keep the smile that threatened to break out on his face from doing so. Describing Saraa as difficult was an understatement in his opinion.

Although she was right. She did keep him on his toes.

"Do you know what this means?" asked Saraa as she pulled herself over the parapet, Duff and a few other Highlanders waiting for them by the trap door, anxious to get inside, knowing that the Wraiths were almost to the base of the tower.

Jakob grinned as he climbed over the parapet, pulling the rope up behind him so that the monsters wouldn't have an easy time of it when they climbed the tower themselves. "The hunters have just become the hunted."

"That they have."

9

LEGENDS MADE REAL

"They appear to be little different than the pirates we just dealt with," said Rafia.

The three cutters circled the sinking vessels several times, the sailors on those ships selectively rescuing the men who had ended up in the rough sea. The waterlogged marauders pulled from the waves were either thrown into chains and herded away or thrown back into the ocean after their throats were cut.

"Actually, they're quite different."

"What do you mean?" The Magus was surprised by Declan's acceptance of the savagery being applied to the pirates.

"It means that though our new friends are employing a very harsh measure, it's justified. Keep in mind that the penalty for piracy is death by hanging. There is no cause for trial or delay. The sentence may be carried out immediately if they're caught in the act."

"Even so, it seems a bit harsh."

"This from a woman who takes particular pleasure in killing Elder Ghoules through the application of lightning?"

Rafia ducked her eyes, trying to appear chastened. It didn't really work, the effort only making Declan smirk.

"Fine, fine, I'll give you that," conceded Rafia. "It is a hard world we live in, you're right."

"Thank you for that," nodded Declan, not expecting Rafia to shift her perspective so swiftly. "Besides, they certainly don't deserve our mercy. Not from what some of Captain Gregson's crew have been telling the Company about the atrocities being committed by men such as these all along the New Caledonian coast. If they had taken our ship, our roles would be reversed, and they'd be feeding us to the sharks right now after they'd had their fun with you and the other women."

"Point taken. Then what are they doing?"

"They're taking the ones who are not too badly injured in the hope of gleaning some information from them," interjected Captain Gregson, who came to stand next to them on the helm. "They're leaving the dead to float. They don't deserve any more than they're getting now. And they're giving mercy to those pirates with wounds from which they have no chance of recovering."

"So a kindness," murmured Rafia.

"Yes. They're ensuring that their suffering isn't prolonged. They're not acting like pirates ..."

"They're acting like soldiers," finished Declan.

"Correct."

"Do you know from the flag who these ships belong to?" asked Declan.

Captain Gregson turned his head, glimpsing the field of green with the purple grapes in the center. He nodded. "I do, although I've never met her."

"A her?" asked Rafia, intrigued.

"Yes, she owns a shipping company sailing out of Ballinasloe."

"If she owns a shipping company, then why is she attacking pirates?" asked Rafia.

Captain Gregson lifted his eyebrows at the question, as if to say the answer was fairly obvious. "Wouldn't you do the same if these pirates were threatening your interests? On the high seas, I've always thought it better to act than react."

"So how would you like to handle this?" asked Aislinn, who had stepped up next to Declan, Rafia, and Captain Gregson, Bryen right behind her, having heard Captain Gregson's answers to Rafia's questions.

"We have little to fear," said Bryen. "Five Griffons, three Magii, and a Company of itchy gladiators? This pirate hunter will visit with us once she's done. When they hail us, let a few of them come aboard. We need to have a talk."

THE SHIP that led the attack on the pirates, the name *Swift* emblazoned on its hull, which was now settled back in the water, the wings that had given the vessel such tremendous speed once again submerged, slowed right next to the *Freedom*.

The frigate didn't stop, however, continuing to glide past, only a few feet separating the two vessels. The close distance allowed the captain to jump across, landing deftly on the deck.

It was a maneuver designed to demonstrate the skill of the *Swift's* crew, a fact that no one aboard the *Freedom* would deny after watching the risky maneuver with bated breath. Expecting a collision any second, they breathed again once the frigate sailed past and took up its position in the pattern with the other two vessels that had cut through the pirates so easily and quite literally.

As the ships circled around the *Freedom*, sailors and soldiers watching from the railings, they resembled sharks preparing to attack. If there was a need to do so.

After the ship passed, all eyes turned to the woman who had jumped aboard. She had come across on her own, which testified to her bravery. Although the hard look in her eyes suggested that she wasn't too concerned by her new surroundings, not with three of her crews ready to come to her aid.

She wasn't very tall, and she had a pixie-like face, making her appear more petite than she really was. Her hair, so blond that sometimes it flashed pink in the fading daylight, was cut short along the sides, curly locks hiding her forehead and drifting into her eyes at the whim of the wind that gusted across the deck.

The woman stood there calmly, more curious than worried, taking in all the people who stared right back at her. The sailors moving around the deck performing their various duties and Captain Gregson on the helm ordering a small crew to cut the ropes so that they could scuttle the pirate ship tied along the starboard side didn't bother her in the least.

Clearly, she was used to what was going on around her. It was an environment in which she was quite comfortable.

Talia took her time observing the happenings aboard the ship. When she shifted her gaze away from the familiar activity on deck, she used every ounce of self-control to ensure that she didn't reveal her anxiety regarding the more than fifty soldiers standing and sitting casually about the deck.

They looked as if they knew what they were about. Their success against the pirates so foolish to attack them certainly confirmed that for her.

That and the fact that she sensed that these men and women, although they were calm and composed at present, were just a heartbeat away from the violence with which they were so conversant. They appeared to be relaxed, but she could tell that they were not.

These soldiers were on edge. She assumed that was the only way they knew how to be.

That thought unsettled her, yes. Although that conclusion didn't frighten her.

She could deal with soldiers. Things tended to be straightforward with them. You could interact with them in a direct manner and expect the same in return.

She didn't get the same feeling when she shifted her gaze to the small group of people standing right in front of her. They sent a shiver of fear down her spine that she needed all of her self-control to keep hidden.

An uncommon reaction for her, since it so rarely occurred. Fascinating as well, because she wanted to know why these people had such an effect upon her.

The man and woman off to the side and leaning against the railing, both with red hair, obviously were twins, the similarities between the two too much to be ignored. The woman scowled at her while the man smiled, even giving her a nod and a wink.

She had to look at him twice just to make sure that she hadn't been mistaken. Clearly, the similarities between the brother and sister did not run to temperament.

Another man and woman stood beneath the helm, the man leaning back against it casually, a double-bladed spear gripped in his hand. The woman stood right next to him, arms crossed, a sword sheathed on her back. The woman stared at her with interest, long auburn hair braided and resting over her left shoulder.

She felt as if the woman was taking her measure, searching for secrets that Talia didn't even know about herself. She probably was. An ingrained authority radiated from the woman. Once she was done with her examination, the woman offered her a brief smile.

The man standing next to the woman not only frightened her but was also an enigma to her. She couldn't get a read on him at all, other than a sense of coiled aggression that she believed could spring free faster than a scorpion's tail.

His hair was white, prematurely she guessed, because he didn't appear to be any older than the young woman standing beside him. His deep grey eyes, which carried both a hint of sadness and ice, suggested that he had seen more of the world than anyone several decades older than he was ever should.

Those eyes sent another shiver of fear down her spine. They showed absolutely no emotion whatsoever.

For just a second, her own eyes were drawn to the scars on his cheek and neck. What had caused such a grievous injury, she had no idea. She was simply amazed that he was still alive.

But what really caught her attention was the silver collar around his neck. He didn't seem the type for such adornments. Could it be more than just an affectation?

When she realized what she thought it could be, she tried to keep the surprise from her face.

Could he really be wearing a Protector's collar?

She had to put some effort into pulling her gaze from him, even as her mind worked furiously at what her discovery could mean. She turned to the last couple, who stood right in front of her, no more than ten feet away.

A grizzled veteran of some Caledonian Guard was her first guess. She assumed that the older man with the short grey hair was the leader of this troop of soldiers.

When she saw the scars that ran up and down his arms, she adjusted her perspective ever so slightly. Looking at the man made her think immediately of the one with the double-bladed spear.

Same posture, same stance, same hard look, as if you were nothing more than another opponent to be dealt with in a combat. She was certain that the two warriors were connected in some way. Perhaps they had survived many of the same challenges.

When she finally looked upon the woman in the multicolored robes, her breath caught for several seconds. She needed to remind herself to breathe.

She should have expected as much after glimpsing the streaks of energy that lit up the sky as she and her ships approached the sea battle from the west.

A Magus.

She could sense the power held in check by this woman with the mane of wild hair. Surprisingly, she had a warm smile and her eyes appeared to welcome Talia, although there was a hardness to them as well. A warning, perhaps, that she was not what she seemed.

Whether it was a ruse, she didn't know. She didn't have much experience with Magii, other than to understand that it was better to stay away from them whenever possible.

"Thank you for allowing me to come aboard, Magus," she said, her inspection of those greeting her complete, nodding toward the woman in respect, assuming that she was the one in command.

Rafia smiled and nodded as well, seeking to make their visitor more comfortable.

Although the woman didn't show it, Rafia could tell that she was nervous, and justifiably so, in her opinion. Jumping aboard by herself and then coming face to face with such grim characters was a daunting demand.

"You're quite welcome. And you are?"

"Talia Carlomin."

"Talia Carlomin," repeated Rafia, seemingly mulling her name. "You are the leader of this small fleet?"

"I am."

Talia said it calmly, as if it was of little matter. Rafia liked that about the young woman, as she did several other qualities she sensed just beneath the surface.

"I am told that you are a sailor. That you own a shipping company in Ballinasloe."

"I do." Talia said it with pride, pleased that her name had preceded her. But there wasn't a hint of conceit in her tone.

"And you hunt pirates as well."

Talia shrugged at that. "I do what I must, Magus."

"As do we all," she agreed. "I am Rafia Riverstone, Master of the Magii."

"An honor, Magus Rafia. I never expected to find someone of your power or your position on a vessel such as this one."

"When duty calls, we all must answer," Rafia replied cryptically, "or as one in our small troop likes to say, you must do what you must do."

"I couldn't agree with you more, Magus Rafia."

"So, Talia Carlomin, are you a pirate like these others?" She nodded toward the men who had been chained and were being led away toward the brig, Captain Gregson's crew being none too gentle with the tamed marauders. "Seeking to profit through the acquisition of ill-gotten gains? Or perhaps even achieve a larger objective?"

Rather than getting angry, Talia smiled at the questions. They were a test, she knew.

Rafia Riverstone was curious as to how she would respond to the challenge she had laid out before her. Although Talia wasn't certain exactly what the Magus could be referring to with her last inquiry about a larger objective.

She felt the eyes of everyone on deck on her, particularly that of the tall soldier with the red hair standing next to his sister. Although his expression differed from that of the others.

Despite the seriousness of the situation, he gave her another nod and wink.

That more than anything else set her nerves on edge. His attention was proving more concerning than the lack of attention by the other soldier standing in the shade of the helm.

"No, I'm not a pirate," she replied simply, understanding that demonstrating any anger or other emotion in that moment would lower her in the eyes of the Magus.

"So a pirate hunter indeed," offered Rafia, nodding sagely. "A woman giving herself the responsibility of clearing the Sea of Mist of this pestilence."

"I guess that's a good way to put it," Talia replied, realizing that she had passed the test. Until the next one. "I believe my actions confirmed my intentions."

"For now," Rafia replied. "You seem to be quite skilled in your chosen profession."

Talia smiled at the statement. She had never thought of what she was doing as that, but it wasn't too far from the truth. Until she had eliminated every single pirate from the New Caledonian coast, all her other goals were secondary.

"I wouldn't call it a profession, Magus."

"Then what would you call it?"

"A duty, Magus."

Rafia smiled, her eyes crinkling. She was impressed by how the young woman threw her own words right back at her. She was beginning to like this one.

Talia Carlomin was as sharp as a blade, seeming to have a personality similar to that of Bryen's. She had liked the Protector the moment she had met him, Rafia getting the same feeling now with Talia Carlomin as she did then.

"Why did you help us, Talia Carlomin? And how is it that you knew where we were?"

"To your first question, you know the answer," said Talia. "As you said, hunting pirates has become my profession for now. My primary duty. As to your second question, I received word from several of my eyes and ears that a small fleet of buccaneers was coming this way. Because it's unusual to have so many of them together at one time, I wanted to know why. Now I do."

"You came here with only three ships? To take on as many as seven?" Rafia's tone suggested that she was both fascinated and concerned by the decision that she made in the face of such odds.

Talia shrugged. "As you have seen, my crews and I know what we're doing. I don't view seven pirate ships as much of a challenge. Rather, I see it as an opportunity. It allows me to complete my mission all the faster."

Rafia smiled at that, turning her head just enough to give Davin a sideways glance to remind him to stay quiet since their visitor's answer had drawn a short, sharp bark of agreement from him. When she turned back, Rafia watched as the woman pulled her gaze from Davin as well, clearly not pleased by the interruption.

When she set her eyes back on Rafia, Talia's seeming calm had returned in an instant. This Talia Carlomin certainly didn't lack confidence or composure.

"And now that you've helped us, Talia Carlomin, what is it that you seek?"

Talia thought about the question for a few seconds. She could dissemble. She chose not to. Not with this Magus who she sensed could sniff out a lie with ease.

"I seek information, Magus Rafia."

"What kind of information?"

"I seek to know why so many pirates came for you, Magus Rafia."

"We're a large ship with a large cargo. It only makes sense, doesn't it?"

"No, it doesn't," Talia Carlomin replied finally, having hesitated for a moment, distracted by the strange expression the red-haired soldier was giving her now. He seemed amused by her exchange with the Magus, as if she and the Magus were acting out a scene and they had reached the climax. Thinking about it, perhaps he was right. "No, they would only need two or three ships to take you as a prize. Or they would have if not for you and your company of soldiers."

"And what does that tell you, Talia Carlomin?"

Talia looked at the Magus for quite some time, not so much pondering the question as pondering the woman. For some strange reason she felt as if she were back in school, called on by the docent to answer a question, the eyes of every other child in the room locked onto her, waiting for her to make a mistake.

"They weren't here for the cargo, Magus. They were here for you. They wanted to make sure that you never reached the Territories."

Rafia stared at Talia for several heartbeats, her eyes narrowing dangerously. Then she let out a melodic laugh that startled both Talia and the soldiers standing on the deck.

Talia watched, slightly confused, somewhat bemused, as the Magus grabbed the arm of the man at her side and gave it a warm squeeze that clearly didn't bother him. His eyes never left Talia, however, his gaze remaining fixed on her, unyielding though not menacing.

Not yet. Not unless he deemed her a threat.

"You're a sharp one, Talia Carlomin. I'm going to enjoy getting to know you better."

"What do you mean by that, Magus?"

Rafia ignored Talia's question, not feeling the need to remove the mystery just yet. "I agree, these pirates are likely here for us, not the cargo. But you are mistaken in one respect."

"And that would be?"

"The pirates are not here for me."

"But you're the Master of the Magii," challenged Talia, not quite understanding. Her instincts in situations such as this one rarely were wrong.

"The pirates, or rather those funding the pirates, who

indeed do not want us to reach New Caledonia, are more likely to be here for those two."

Rafia nodded toward the scarred man with the double-bladed spear and the woman with the sword on her back. She saw it then. Beneath the chilling coldness of the soldier's eyes.

A flash of power much like that of the Magus'. Still, why would these two be of such interest to the pirates and their benefactors?

"Not you, Magus? I find that hard to believe."

"No, not me," confirmed Rafia. "I'm just along for the ride."

Talia turned her attention to the couple beneath the helm, both of whom were staring right at her, the woman with a smile, the man with ... she didn't know what to make of how he was looking at her. That expression of his made her feel colder than when she stood on the helm of one of her frigates during an ice storm.

"And they are?"

"They're the ones you need to talk to."

It was then that the man and woman standing below the helm stepped forward, the woman gripping the Magus' arm in thanks as she walked past her. The man followed a step behind. She caught a flash of fading sunlight off the silver collar. She was certain now.

Her father had schooled her in the history of Caledonia as a child, and she had always gravitated toward the stories involving magic, impossible quests, and unrequited love.

The man with the double-bladed spear had to be a Protector. It was a rare practice, she recalled, halted decades before, although apparently that was incorrect.

Rumors she had heard in the taverns on the docks of Roo's Nest before making her way across the Burnt Ocean flitted through her mind. At the time she had been in such a rush that she had paid them little heed, her mind on what she perceived as more important matters. Something about a Protector who had also been a …

The larger picture was finally coming into focus for her. If he truly was a Protector, then the woman was …

"You're Lady Aislinn Winborne, heir to the Southern Marches, daughter of Duke Kevan Winborne."

"That I am," replied Aislinn, impressed that Talia knew who she was. "It is a pleasure to meet you, and many thanks to you and your crews for your help."

"We did very little, Lady Winborne. Based on what I saw, I doubt that you and your company would have had any difficulty with those last two pirate ships."

"Probably so," admitted Aislinn. "Still, we do appreciate your assistance. You are based out of Ballinasloe, Ms. Carlomin, are you not?"

"Talia, and yes, I am." Talia's eyes narrowed, the puzzle that she had figured out right before meeting the Lady of the Southern Marches just became a bit more complicated as the full implications of who she was speaking to now hit her. "You are also the niece to Governor Kendric Winborne."

Aislinn nodded. "Yes, do you know my uncle?"

"Only by reputation, Lady Winborne."

"Aislinn," she corrected. "And if you don't mind my asking, what is my uncle's reputation in the Territories?"

Talia hesitated before responding, although it didn't take her long to decide how she would handle this potential snare. Honesty had proven to be the correct approach ever since she had stepped onto the deck of the massive ship.

"That would depend on who you spoke to, Aislinn."

Aislinn nodded at that.

"I'm speaking to you, Talia."

Talia smiled at that, recognizing the trap that she had just walked into. "Complicated."

Now it was Aislinn's turn to smile. This pirate hunter was

cautious. An important trait based on her current circum-stances. She appreciated Talia's diplomatic response.

She definitely wanted to talk more with the pirate hunter about her uncle. Her perspective would prove useful to Aislinn's larger endeavor. But now was not the time to pursue that line of questioning.

"This is Bryen Keldragan," Aislinn said, placing her hand on the arm of the man who stood just to her side.

Talia found it difficult to look directly into those unfor-giving eyes. She had been right. This man was a Protector. Lady Winborne's Protector.

Or at least had been. The stories in the taverns hadn't touched on that all that much, instead focusing on the role this gladiator had played in taking down a three-hundred-year-old dynasty in a matter of days.

"You're the Volkun," said Talia, doing all that she could to ensure that she maintained control over the slight tremor of fear that threatened to set her body shaking.

"Guilty."

Talia's eyes widened. If he was the Volkun, then the soldiers standing and sitting behind him were ...

"And this is the Blood Company."

"Unfortunately so," Bryen replied, pleased by the woman's knowledge. He was also struck by her lack of fear -- or maybe she refused to let it show, as well as the directness of her next question.

"Why are you here?"

"To start new lives just like everyone else in the Territories," Bryen replied, "although it seems that we have yet to escape our old lives."

"So tell me, do you have a nickname? If you're a pirate hunter, you really should have a good nickname."

Talia Carlomin stared at Davin, having been introduced to him just minutes before. He hadn't told her that he fought in the Pit, something that she gave him credit for. But it was quite obvious that he had.

If Bryen Keldragan was the Volkun, then the twins obviously were the Crimson Devil and the Crimson Giant. An apt nickname for the fighter who had taken an interest in her as soon as she sat down on one of the barrels the crew had set below the helm so that they could engage in the conversation that was required.

A conversation that for Talia, upon learning who these people were, could prove quite helpful to her efforts to rid the coast of the constricting menace offered by the pirates.

"Some have taken to calling me Captain Scar," she replied finally, hesitating.

She hadn't been certain that she should reveal what to her sounded so foolish. She gave in, though, because she realized that he would learn soon enough so there was no cause to withhold it.

"Captain Scar," Davin repeated, clearly intrigued. He stared at her for several seconds, not seeing any imperfections on what in his opinion was quite a lovely face. But he smartly kept that to himself, having been told too many times by his sister that it was better not to share everything that crossed his mind without at first thinking about how others might react to what he wanted to say. Maybe the scar wasn't visible. He frowned at that possibility. "Were you flogged? Is that it?"

"No, why would you think that ..."

"Were you stabbed with a hot poker?" Davin already having moved on to the next option that came to mind.

"No, I was not stabbed with a hot poker. What are you ..."

"Sliced across the chest with daggers?"

"Daggers across my chest?" Talia's gaze narrowed. "Why are you thinking about my chest?"

That stopped Davin from offering the next possibility that had come to mind, his face flaring when he realized how what he had just asked could be interpreted. "I wasn't thinking about your chest. I was just wondering ..." Davin spluttered, finally stopping himself when Talia broke out into a broad smile, the first that he had seen from her since she had stepped on board the *Freedom*.

"You're playing with me," Davin said, although his face still burned.

"I am," replied Talia. "I can see why they named you the Crimson Giant."

Davin stared at Talia for just a few heartbeats. Talia worried that she may have overstepped, not knowing how volatile these gladiators who made up the Blood Company could be. Her concern dissolved when Davin broke out into a belly-shaking laugh.

"That was a good one," Davin said, his eyes still twinkling with delight when he could catch his breath again.

"Thank you. My sailors and soldiers would have been impressed."

"Why do you say that?"

"Because I'm not really known for my humor."

"What are you known for?"

Talia opened her mouth to reply, then closed it just as quickly. He had taken her by surprise. What was she known for? That was an excellent question.

"You'd have to speak with my sailors and my soldiers."

"Now you're just being evasive," challenged Davin. "What do your sailors and soldiers say about you?"

Becoming increasingly uncomfortable, not liking being the center of attention, Talia attempted to turn the tables on the gladiator who always seemed to have a smile on his face.

"How would your friends describe you?"

Davin leaned back from Talia, arcing his eyebrows as he did so, his expression thoughtful. He knew exactly what she was doing, although he didn't mind.

He was having fun engaging with her. Having spent so much time aboard the *Freedom* with the same people while crossing the Burnt Ocean, it was good to have the chance to speak with someone new, someone who challenged him, though not in the way his sister did.

Lycia carried the baggage of them growing up together, viewing him as her younger brother who needed to be watched over, even though he had proven to be one of the deadliest fighters ever to set foot in the Colosseum.

Talia Carlomin didn't know his full story.

How much she did know, he wasn't sure yet, although it really didn't matter to him. What mattered was that she was speaking to him as if he were someone worth speaking to, and he both valued and appreciated that.

"Impulsive. Passionate almost to a fault. Fun-loving when I likely shouldn't be. Quick to anger, just as quick to apologize."

"That's not necessarily all to the good."

"No, but it's honest. It's accurate." Davin shrugged. "They would also say that I do whatever must be done. No matter the consequences."

"That's not necessarily all to the good either."

"No, sometimes it's not. But it's honest."

"Are you always this honest?"

Davin didn't even wait before replying. "Yes. I see little point in not being honest. I am who I am. There's no reason to try to be anyone else."

"That sounds incredibly insightful ..." began Talia.

"For a gladiator," Davin completed. "I know. Me and my friends," he motioned to the men and women talking in small groups across the deck, many of them sharpening their weapons, "just because we fought on the white sand doesn't mean we aren't more than that. Most important, I think my compatriots would say that I could be trusted. That if I say that I'm going to do something, I do it. And if I can't do it, then I'm dead."

Talia stared at him for a very long time, never having engaged in a conversation like this one before. Never having heard someone speak of his own death as if it was of little consequence. Not knowing what else to say, her reply was quite simple.

"I believe you."

"So, what do your soldiers and sailors say of you? I've told you quite a bit about me. Now it's your turn."

Talia gave Davin a smile that more resembled a grimace. "I was hoping that you had forgotten the original question."

"I don't forget anything," said Davin. "It's another of my faults."

Talia leaned back this time. "They would say that I'm fair, that I do what I say that I'm going to do, and that I can be trusted, no matter the situation."

Davin nodded. He didn't doubt it. He could sense all that within her. "So, there are some similarities between us. And how did you earn the nickname Captain Scar?"

"I thought you might have forgotten that as well."

"As I said, I don't forget anything."

"So I'm learning." Talia pushed her blonde, curly hair that covered her forehead to the side, revealing the mark on her brow that she tended to hide now by growing her hair longer. "Though I have to be honest with you. That's really not my nickname. Or at least the one I prefer."

Davin smiled. She had been playing with him, and he didn't mind in the least. "What's the name that you prefer?"

"The Huntress."

"That's much better," he replied after mulling it over.

"Although that really is an impressive scar. Let me show you this scar of mine that might compare. I earned it when I was fighting a pack of starved lions in the Pit."

He started to pull up his shirt, Talia's eyes widening, not anticipating such a display. Bryen's hand on Davin's shoulder stopped him.

"Another time perhaps?" Bryen suggested, sitting down next to Davin, Aislinn and Rafia joining them, Lycia and Declan standing behind them.

Davin smiled then, nodding.

"Right." Then he turned his focus to Talia, giving her another wink so that she knew he hadn't meant to make her uncomfortable. "Sorry. As I said before, impulsive and all that."

"Yes, I'm beginning to understand," she replied, more amused than insulted, appreciating how he had returned the favor.

"As are we," said Aislinn, who leaned in toward Talia.

The Lady of the Southern Marches was still smiling, although Talia could see the flint in the back of her eyes.

"What is it that you're understanding, Aislinn," said Talia, a challenge in her voice.

"That a woman willing to take on seven pirate ships with only three at her disposal is both driven and ambitious."

"Ambition is not a bad trait."

"No, it's not," Aislinn agreed. "Not when it's directed toward the greater good. As appears to be the case with you."

Talia nodded, comprehending now the point of this conversation. This was another test. "You want to know if you can trust me."

Aislinn nodded. "We do. Your actions speak loudly, but we've seen those actions without a larger context."

"So, a broader perspective is needed."

"It is," confirmed Aislinn. "How was it that you became a pirate hunter?"

Talia closed her eyes, taking a deep breath. Many possible responses came to mind. She settled once again for the truth.

"The pirates have been a problem ever since I arrived in the Territories. For me, for all the other merchants. The Governors of the Territories made noise about addressing the issue, but noise only. They've done nothing, and it appears that they have profited from the marauding along the coast."

"You believe that the Governors may be responsible," said Aislinn, nodding. "Receiving a cut of the spoils?"

Talia's eyes narrowed. It seemed that the Lady of the Southern Marches was just as sharp as the sword on her back.

"I do, as do most of the merchants who are working with me."

"You have proof of this?"

Talia smiled at that, her grin savage. "I do."

"And what have you done about this finding?" cut in Rafia.

"Nothing directly, not yet," replied Talia. She shrugged. "There is little that we can do at the moment. The Governors are stronger. They have more soldiers. They have more resources. If we take them on directly, then the Governors will take action against us. They are already making our lives and our businesses more difficult. We are not yet ready to challenge them as they deserve to be challenged."

"You seek to cut at the edges for now. Eliminate the pirates and you weaken the Governors," prodded Aislinn.

"Yes, and if we weaken the Governors enough, we may have the chance to take them on directly."

"Is my uncle involved in this?"

"I don't know," Talia replied honestly. "The Governor of Fal Carrach, yes. The Governor of the Highlands, most likely. The Governor of the Northern Territory ..." Talia shrugged. "I have no evidence linking Kendric Winborne to the pirates. I do believe, however, that he and his wife may be responsible for some of the other threats we face in the Territories."

"You don't believe that he is blameless," suggested Aislinn, who wanted to dig deeper into the topic, although she understood as well that they could pursue the details of Talia's last comment later.

They needed the big picture now. The smaller glimpses could be gleaned when there was more time.

"I don't. Just because I can't see the connection doesn't mean it's not there."

Aislinn nodded. She couldn't fault Talia's reasoning.

"What evidence do you have to support your claims?"

"As you have seen, we've been quite effective in our battles against the pirates. Several of the captains have been taken. They have been quite forthcoming in terms of the arrangements they have with the Governor of Fal Carrach."

"And you believe them? They're raiders and cutthroats. They would say anything if it meant saving their own skin."

"As far as I can throw them," Talia replied.

Her comment drew a sharp laugh from Davin. Instead of the interruption irritating her, it made Talia smile.

"But with respect to what they're saying about Hakea Roosarian, yes, I do believe them. Everything that I've learned from the pirate captains has been confirmed through other sources."

"There's more to this than just that," said Bryen.

He had been studying Talia Carlomin while Aislinn questioned her. His initial impression of her told him that she was not only exceedingly competent, as she had demonstrated when sinking two pirate ships in a matter of minutes, but also driven, perhaps even to a fault.

Yes, she was combating the pirates because they threatened her business interests and those of the other merchants. That only made sense. He could tell, however, that there was something more personal about her decision to take on at least two Governors of New Caledonia.

And now, Talia Carlomin was studying him. The fear that had been there the first time she had looked at him had faded, replaced by an appraisal without any judgment. She could sense his loss, just as he could sense hers.

"You're familiar with vengeance," said Talia, her eyes never leaving his.

"I am," he admitted. "We are very good friends."

Talia nodded at that. They understood each other then.

"The pirates and Hakea Roosarian were responsible for my father's death," she said softly, although everyone caught her words.

Davin leaned in upon hearing that, his eyes sparking with rage. "You haven't gained your revenge yet?"

"No, not yet."

Davin nodded, as if he were contemplating something quite serious. Although Talia barely knew him, she believed that was a rare endeavor for him.

"Why should we believe all that you've told us?"

"You shouldn't," Talia replied calmly, fighting to keep the emotion welling up within her upon thinking about her father from leaking into her voice. Now wasn't the time for memories. Now was the time to conduct business. "Let me show you."

"Show us what?"

"You need to see it to believe it," said Talia.

"That's not an answer."

"It is, just not the answer you were expecting. Let me show you what's going on, what's happening to those not enjoying the protection of the Governors."

"You want us to trust you?" asked Aislinn. "Good impressions aside, you're asking quite a lot."

"What do you have to lose but a little time?" countered Talia. "You want to know what's really going on in the Territories before you make your way to Ballinasloe. I can give you that."

"We could lose more than time."

"Perhaps, but then again you have on board not just the Master of the Magii, but also two others skilled in the Talent, do you not?" Aislinn smiled and then nodded to Talia, demonstrating her respect for her figuring that out. "You also have Griffons. How that could be, I do not know, although I surely would like to learn. I don't have Magii with me, I don't have Griffons, and although my soldiers are quite competent against pirates, they are no match for the Company of Blood. You could have sunk us anytime you wanted, but you didn't. You still can, of course."

Talia leaned forward then, allowing her eyes to settle on each of the individuals seated around her before she continued. "All I ask is for a few days. You are sailing to the west anyway, so what do you truly have to lose?"

Rafia studied Talia with a great deal of interest as the woman made her request. She had found the pirate hunter interesting upon meeting her, even more so now. Her instincts were excellent to have sniffed out more than one Magus aboard.

She was brave. She was sharp. And she was driven. Definitely someone worthy of their time. She nodded toward Aislinn and Bryen. It wasn't her decision to make, but she wanted to relay her support for the concept.

"We'll go with you," said Aislinn. "Your ships can follow."

"But you'll stay with us," added Bryen.

"I expected no less."

"Do you agree to the terms?"

Talia gave Aislinn a smile, pleased that her decision to listen to the intelligence that she had received had allowed her to make the acquaintance of such powerful potential allies.

"I do."

"CAN WE TRUST HER?"

Aislinn asked Bryen the question as they walked through a hatch that led to one of the smaller holds in the stern.

"Until we can't."

"Fair enough. One of Sirius' sayings? Or perhaps Declan's?"

"One of mine, actually."

"Wonderful," muttered Aislinn, seeing that Bryen appeared to be quite pleased with himself. "As if Sirius and Declan offering maxims all the time wasn't enough."

Bryen ignored Aislinn's comment that was heavily tinged with sarcasm. "Besides, we have the chance now to get a better feel for what's going on before we make landfall. We won't have to rely entirely on the efforts of the Blademaster. And we should be able to get corroboration on most of what she told us."

"True," agreed Aislinn. She nodded toward the end of the hallway, where Majdi and Jenus lounged against the wall. "Did you want me to begin with him?"

Bryen smiled at the offer. "Let me try first," he replied, his eyes turning even colder than they usually were. "I'll soften him up, then you can start asking the questions."

"Soften him up how?" asked Aislinn.

"Don't worry," Bryen replied. "I know that we're no longer in the Pit."

"Sometimes I wonder about that," murmured Aislinn.

"Funny," Bryen replied. "Any problems?"

He and Aislinn stopped at the entrance to the main hold, their arrival halting the constant bickering between the two friends. From what Bryen could gather, they were arguing about who got the most kills while capturing the pirate vessel. It wasn't a conversation that he had any desire to engage in. He already had enough bad memories to last him a lifetime.

"None," Majdi replied. "He hasn't moved. He hasn't said a word. He should be ready for you."

Aislinn was about to walk in. Bryen put a hand on her arm. "Give me a moment. Let me put him in the right mood first."

Aislinn nodded. "Remember, we need him alive. For now."

"No worries there," Bryen replied.

Bryen stopped at the entrance to the hold so that his eyes could adjust to the dim light provided by the torches lining the walls. Those pirates who survived their skirmish with the Blood Company were being held in the brig.

Bryen had Majdi and Jenus bring the captain here so that he could contemplate the unique challenge of his current circumstances. How alone he was. And what fate would befall him if he failed to cooperate.

"You are?" asked Bryen quietly, stepping forward out of the shadows.

The man looked up. He was sitting in a chair just a few feet away.

Bryen could see it in his eyes. The captain was terrified, although at present he was succeeding in controlling his fear. Just barely, however.

The two gladiators standing guard hadn't bothered to tie him up. Why would they? What would be the point of the captain trying to get past them? An early death? And once the captain had reached that conclusion, it had terrified him even more.

He had become a pirate because it was an easy way to make a lot of golds and silvers. Now, he was beginning to regret that decision. He'd gladly give back all the money he had earned to escape the dead grey eyes of the man who approached.

"Anders," the captain replied.

He could have been difficult. He could have stayed quiet. But, again, what was the point?

He had lost his ship. He had lost most of his crew. He had lost his freedom. His life likely was next, unless perhaps he could prove his utility.

His benefactors only cared about him if he was giving them the percentage they demanded. Now, they would care less about him. He was just a liability, and he knew that.

Bryen could only imagine what might be going through Anders' mind, but he had an idea. He had a feeling that this interrogation was going to be much easier than he had anticipated.

"Anders, you know of Talia Carlomin."

"I do," he whispered.

"What can you tell me about her?"

"She's the bane of every pirate on the New Caledonian coast," he said softly. "The Huntress has built quite a reputation for herself. Deservedly so, in fact."

"The Huntress," Bryen thought. That must have been what Davin was talking with her about when he interrupted their conversation. "Is that so?"

"It is. I wouldn't lie to you. There's no reason to."

Bryen nodded. "Then we agree on something." He stepped closer to the pirate, who cringed as he approached, trying to sink into his chair. Bryen loomed over the man for almost a minute before finally leaning down so that he could look Anders in the eyes. "You know, I've built quite a reputation for myself as well."

"Really," said Anders, his voice beginning to shake, just as his body was, the self-control he had been exhibiting quickly disappearing. "And who are you?"

"The Volkun."

Anders didn't say anything, his mind needing a few seconds to process what he had just heard. When he did, his face turned white.

In a rush of movement, Anders pushed back with his feet, scraping the chair against the floor, trying to get as far away as he could from the man who had earned a reputation for spilling gallons of blood on the white sand. A reputation that had followed him to the Territories.

With a loud jolt, Anders slammed into the crate behind him. His eyes widened in terror, the fear that had threatened to consume him as soon as he had been placed in this hold freezing him, both mind and body.

He had nowhere to go. Nowhere to hide.

He could only stare in terror as the Volkun glided through the shadows, reaching for him.

10

THE MARCHERS

"Do you think this is actually going to work?" asked Duff.

"Do you want me to tell you what you want to hear, or do you want me to tell you what I actually think?" replied Jakob.

Duff stared at Jakob with an expression of annoyance mixed with amusement. In that moment, he seemed to regret saving Jakob's life.

Although the former Sergeant of the Royal Guard was less than pleased, Duff's sour expression only made Jakob's grin expand, not fazed in the least that his friend didn't really care for his response.

Jakob could understand Duff's discomfiture. Standing out here in the open, the Murk having settled over the Highlands once again, certainly could be unsettling for those unused to navigating the dense covering. To say nothing of the threat presented by the Wraiths who were coming toward them.

Finally, seeing that Jakob wasn't going to offer anything more, Duff gave in, even though he didn't want to. Jakob always seemed to be able to wait him out, never bothered by the impatience that tended to build within Duff whenever he believed that the young man – or really anyone for that matter -- was being unnecessarily difficult. With respect to Jakob, in Duff's opinion, that recalcitrance seemed to raise its head much too frequently.

"An honest answer would be appreciated," he grumbled.

Duff almost wished that he couldn't see in the fog as Jakob's grin widened into a smile. But he could, and that only served to increase his irritation even though the Highlander would be the first to admit that it was a welcome change.

In the past, when caught in the Murk, standing right next to Jakob, Duff would have seen no more than a dim shape in the swirling grey. If that.

Sometimes the fog was so thick he couldn't even see his hand if he put it right in front of his face.

That's the way it had always been since the Wraiths had begun to terrorize the mountains several years before, the fog creeping across the Northern Steppes and blanketing the Highlands after smothering the Northern Peaks.

But no longer.

Now, Duff could see Jakob's irritatingly confident visage. Just as he could look upon the other Highlanders spread out around them as if the fog that had drifted in from the north wasn't even there.

It truly was remarkable, what Jakob was doing. He could sense the mist, even feel it, but it no longer impeded him in any way.

Duff had been skeptical at first when Jakob had proposed the experiment, never really putting much faith in something that he didn't know to be real. Of course, it didn't help that when Jakob had revealed his skill in the Talent, his first reaction was one of distrust and concern.

He had allowed his ingrained suspicion of anyone making use of natural magic to color his perspective despite Jakob demonstrating time and again since he had found his way to the broch that he always had the best interests of the High-landers at heart.

To get past the worries of Duff and many of the other High-landers, none wanting to risk an encounter with the Wraiths from a position of weakness, Jakob had proposed a test.

Many of the Highlanders had balked. Saraa had not, trusting Jakob implicitly and refusing to allow anyone else to take her place.

Their success against the Wraiths in the Murk had convinced the Highlanders of what could be done. So much so that Duff had needed to deny many of the requests from High-landers who wanted to join them on their current expedition.

He could understand why.

The Highlanders hated to run.

They wanted to fight.

They wanted revenge.

Once Jakob used his natural magic to link him and the Highlanders with them so that they could see what he could see in the Murk, Duff realized instantly that he had been a fool. He had allowed his superstitions to get in the way of the gift Jakob had given them.

The gift that could mean the difference between living in fear or living the lives the men and women of the Highlands most desired and deserved.

Jakob nodded, contemplating Duff's comment for a few seconds before responding. "I think the strategy has a good chance of working so long as everything goes according to plan."

Duff stared at him again, this time with an expression saying that Jakob was the fool, not him. "That's not very help-ful. How often do things go according to plan?"

Jakob turned his smile toward Duff again, even clapping him on the shoulder. He had been expecting the question. "Rarely. Or as my father liked to say, never."

"Your father was a smart man," muttered Duff, his eyes widening as Jakob used the Talent to search around them once again.

As he studied the picture that Jakob shared with him, Duff realized that their tactical situation hadn't changed much. Duff was glad for that. The opportunity they had been hoping for was still there for the taking.

As Jakob had said, they just needed to follow the plan. Until that plan changed, Duff's natural cynicism would prevent his confidence from becoming arrogance.

If he ever allowed that to happen, as he had seen many times before, he knew what the result would be. He would be a dead man. It was only a matter of time.

"He was," Jakob replied so softly that Duff almost didn't hear him. Jakob's thoughts drifted in Dougal's direction for a few seconds. He pulled them back swiftly to the task at hand, not wanting to get caught in those memories. Not with the threat that was coming toward them. "He taught me a great deal."

Jakob had been tracking what hid within the Murk since the fog first drifted over the peaks yesterday. Going against their almost ingrained inclination to take shelter, the Highlanders from his broch and two others that were only a few leagues away followed Jakob to where the fog reached down into a small valley where an unfinished tower stood, the work having halted with the arrival of the thick grey tendrils.

Jakob and the Highlanders had come here for a very specific reason.

They knew that the Wraiths liked to visit those parts of the Highlands where the brochs had yet to be completed. Once the towers were constructed, the monsters in the mist found it much more difficult hunting in those valleys, the Highlanders too well trained to be caught out in the haze if it could be avoided.

Better for the Wraiths to try for their kills in those areas where the Highlanders could not yet enjoy the benefits provided by the towers.

Jakob, and through his use of the Talent the Highlanders with him, knew exactly where the Wraiths were now. He had stolen the monsters' most devastating attribute, their invisibility in the grey mist.

They just didn't know it yet.

Two dozen Wraiths were hunting within the fog. Half were moving toward the gulley that led to the incomplete broch. The same crevice in which he, Duff, and a score of Highlanders had hidden.

The rest of the monsters hunted along the rim of the dale and were still a good distance away.

Those Wraiths who were farther away weren't an immediate concern. Jakob and the Highlanders with him just needed to worry about the monsters that were approaching them from the north.

A large number, true, but still manageable.

Jakob could sense the excitement that the several dozen Highlanders waiting in the gap were struggling to contain. He could understand why.

They watched the Wraiths' progress just as Jakob did. For the first time, these men and women didn't have to run when the Wraiths came. They could stand their ground. They could meet steel with steel.

It would be a fair combat, unlike all the other slaughters that had occurred before.

"They're coming."

Duff turned his attention back to the gulley that ran to the north. "How far would you say?" The former Sergeant was enjoying the perspective that the Talent gave him, but it was new to him, so he hadn't yet mastered the ability to judge distance.

"Less than a minute."

"And our rabbits?"

"Just a few dozen yards ahead of them."

"She's cutting it close."

"You know how she is."

"I know how she is," Duff grumbled. "She takes too many chances."

"She wanted to make certain. If the Wraiths didn't take the bait, then we'd need to start again. That could put us in a dangerous position."

"I know, it's just a big risk."

"We're all taking a big risk. That can't be avoided. Besides, do you want to be the one to tell her to be more cautious? Because I certainly don't."

"No, not me." Duff shook his head emphatically. "She'd as soon as gut me as talk to me if I raised that issue with her."

"That's my point," replied Jakob. He pulled the long daggers sheathed on each thigh. "Just a few seconds now."

An instant later, the rabbits were there. Saraa and the squad of Highlanders with her sprinted down the gap, going right through the small opening the Highlanders had left for them before quickly closing the breach in what was a very loose shield wall.

Duff didn't want to fight from a defensive position. He wanted to ensure that the men and women with him had the ability to engage their opponents aggressively.

He also didn't want to risk having any of the monsters getting by them. So, he thought that the modified approach that he had taken would work best for them.

Block the narrow opening in this section of the gulley. Allow his fighters to attack, but only after ensuring that none of the monsters got behind them.

Simple, Duff thought. Although nothing was simple once a fight began.

Jakob bent his knees, standing on his toes, one foot slightly in front of the other. The hilts of his daggers felt good in his hands. He was looking forward to this. He had been ever since he and Saraa had proven that his application of the Talent could work.

Saraa and the other rabbits had started with a lead of a little more than a quarter mile. The pursuing Wraiths had closed the distance to almost nothing in just a matter of minutes.

As Jakob watched the Wraiths race toward them through the Murk, for the first time, he could see in their dark black eyes that the Wraiths were overcome by the bloodlust of the hunt. The predators weren't standing still as was their habit now that they had their prey in sight. They weren't listening, waiting, or searching for a hint of a sound or movement.

The Wraiths were gliding across the ground with a frightening grace and speed. And he could sense the barbarousness radiating from the monsters.

Their blood was up. They were only interested in one thing.

The kill.

And they could taste it.

Good. Jakob was glad for that. Rather than frightening him, his discovery pleased him.

Because the strategy that he and Duff had worked out depended on the Wraiths doing just what they were doing now. They meant to make use of that unfettered ferocity.

The Wraiths were no more than ten yards away when Jakob heard the welcome twang from just above him, the archers perched atop the massive rocks that lined the gap more than happy to employ the sight given to them by the Talent to lethal effect.

Three Wraiths fell dead, pierced by arrows that flew straight and true through the Murk, before they could take another step.

Even more surprising for the nine surviving Wraiths, all of

whom skidded to a stop upon seeing their brethren fall, was the large number of shadows standing right to their front. For just a moment, they weren't sure what they were gazing at, never expecting something like this to ever happen.

But there was no mistaking it now. The leader of this band of Wraiths, who stood a few feet in front of his hunters, smiled viciously upon seeing what waited before him. Their prey, usually hidden away in their stone burrows, had come out to play.

A large group of Highlanders.

More Highlanders, in fact, than the Wraith had ever seen in the Murk since the first few times he had begun to hunt within these mountains.

For just a few heartbeats, the Wraith and his hunters struggled to comprehend this new reality. This wasn't supposed to be how things worked.

Since they had first entered the Highlands with the fog, their efforts always had been just a hunt for them. A simple task made that much easier because of the many advantages granted to them by the Murk.

What had changed?

These Highlanders were not struggling as they normally would in the fog. They were not fleeing, seeking some terrain or hideaway that was more defensible. They were standing their ground, staring right at them, apparently having no difficulty whatsoever picking them out of the Murk. A realization that had struck all the Wraiths at the same time.

For the first time since coming into these mountains, the Wraiths experienced an unexpected and unsettling feeling.

Fear.

The Highlanders could see them clearly. They knew exactly where they were.

That meant that this was no longer a hunt as they all assumed it to be. This was a battle.

Not wanting to suffer the same fate as their comrades who had been cut down from above, the Wraiths raced toward the Highlanders, desperate to get in close so that the archers would have a more difficult time trying to take them out of the clash while engaged with their prey.

A smart decision, but their brief moment of hesitation proved costly. The three Wraiths at the back of the group who were slower than their comrades to charge toward the Highlanders fell almost as one, another wave of steel-tipped barbs whistling through the fog and slamming into the creatures, two of them with three arrows sprouting from their chests and for the third a quarrel through the eye.

The Highlanders maintained their calm as they watched with a great deal of satisfaction the number of attackers drop again. The Wraiths were still dangerous opponents. But the Highlanders outnumbered their adversaries two to one now.

That and the fact that for more than a year they had been forced to hide away from these monsters filled them with a rage that they could barely control.

That they didn't want to control.

They wanted to vent their anger on the source of their fears, and they did.

As one, the Highlanders rushed forward, no longer able to manage their desire to gain vengeance on the monsters who had terrorized them and their families for so long.

In just seconds, the larger fight broke into a smattering of smaller clashes. Although driven forward by their rage, the Highlanders still maintained their discipline, employing the tactics they had practiced until they were second nature, forming into small squads, each one now harrying a single Wraith.

They weren't in a rush to kill the Wraiths they faced off against. They still were wary of the monster's speed.

Instead, the Highlanders sought to tire their adversary and

take advantage of the mistake that they knew would come. Because the Wraiths weren't prepared for this.

This unanticipated patience demonstrated by what just moments before had been their prey, more prone to fleeing than fighting, frustrated the trapped Wraiths, who, instead of attacking as was their habit, shifted their focus to defending themselves. A position with which they were quite unfamiliar.

They were used to killing the Highlanders as if they were no more than animals. The Wraiths were not accustomed to fighting for their lives against those they viewed as nothing more than chattel. Vermin. A species to be exterminated.

Because of the Highlanders' momentary lack of order, two of the Wraiths made it through the charge unscathed, slipping deftly by the Highlanders.

The two hoped to come at their prey from behind. But no such luck.

Duff and Jakob stood there waiting for them. Unafraid. Expecting that this would happen.

Another part of their plan, in fact. Worried that some of the Wraiths would be fast enough to breach the Highlander line, they wanted to be ready for just such an occurrence. And they were.

Duff attacked his adversary with a calm viciousness, swinging the large blacksmith's hammer that he favored in a two-handed grip, one hand by the end, the other about halfway up the haft.

At first, the Wraith thought that he was in for an easy combat. Not so.

Duff destroyed that misconception in an instant, keeping his cuts through the air with the steel head short and compact, never allowing himself to be pulled off balance, always ensuring that he could bring the shaft up to block the many attempts the Wraith made to cut across his throat with his double-bladed daggers.

What had started as a promising chance for the Wraith, the monster believing that the Highlander would be easy meat just like all the others he had come across, instead devolved into a life-or-death struggle to stay clear of the hammer head that with every swing kept getting closer and closer to cracking his skull.

The Wraith was so focused on preventing that very final ending from happening that he soon lost track of exactly where he was in the canyon.

Duff, on the other hand, knew exactly where he was and what he was doing. He had maneuvered the Wraith back toward the side of the gap, just as he wanted to.

In a moment of awkwardness, the Wraith fell onto his back on the rough ground, his ankle caught between two of the many jagged rocks that littered the canyon. The monster shrieked in agony as the bone in his lower leg snapped.

Duff felt no sympathy for the monster's plight. The Wraith only was getting what he deserved.

In a swift motion, Duff brought his hammer down, smashing the Wraith's head much like he would a small stone. A gruesome conclusion for the Wraith, although a very satisfying one for the former Sergeant.

His opponent dead, he turned around quickly to determine if he needed to assist in any of the other clashes. He smiled wickedly.

The Highlanders who had herded the Wraiths away from one another already had finished their bloody work. All of the Wraiths but one were dead, several with arrows sprouting from their backs and chests, the archers assisting in the kills whenever they had the chance.

The only combat that continued pitted the Wraith who was the leader of this decimated troop against Jakob.

Duff was certain of his assessment of the Wraith because the last surviving monster demonstrated a confidence – some

would likely call it a swagger -- and skill that suggested that he
was used to being in command and that he was not used to
being in his current position.

He was fighting for his life, having to move around the floor
of the gulley as Jakob decided. The young man demonstrated a
speed and intensity that was frightening and exhilarating both
at the same time.

Clearly, the Wraith understood the position that he was in,
having caught out of the corner of his eye the bodies covering
the ground. None of them Highlanders.

Knowing that he would receive no assistance, the Wraith
attempted to shift the momentum of the duel, throwing himself
with an almost wild abandon at the Highlander who dared to
challenge him, the white steel of his blades cutting through the
fog in a blur, barely visible in the swirling mist.

Yet despite his best efforts to break free, the Wraith realized
that it was already too late. The other Highlanders had circled
around him and the boy facing off against him, eliminating his
chances for escape.

Nevertheless, if he could kill the boy, the Wraith believed
that he still had a chance. He could try to cut his way between
the Highlanders at his back, then make for the north and his
comrades who were only a few leagues away.

A good plan, in his opinion, though no more than that
when he took in the archers who stood on the rocks above him,
bows drawn, arrows nocked, just waiting for the chance to
finish him.

It was then that the Wraith realized that he wouldn't be
leaving this gulley alive, and when he stared into the eyes of the
boy who had the audacity to believe himself his equal with
steel, the Wraith understood that the boy knew it as well.

In fact, Jakob had known how this combat would end for
quite some time. So he had allowed the Wraith to tire himself
out and reach this inevitable conclusion on his own.

Making peace with what was to come, the Wraith stepped back. The monster stood there calmly, allowing the swirling fog to settle around him. He was curious.

Only seconds into his combat with the boy, he had concluded that the Highlanders could see him clearly in the Murk. He badly wanted to know why that was the case.

But the Wraith saw no point in asking. The Highlanders would never reveal their secret.

The Highlanders were inferior to the Wraiths, true, but they were not fools. He had learned that in just the last few minutes.

Certain of his fate, the Wraith waited for the steel-tipped arrows to pierce his flesh. Much to the Wraith's surprise, he didn't hear the tell-tale whistle of the shafts streaking through the air.

The Highlanders above him certainly were more than willing to do the deed, but a raised hand from the boy who stood against him held them back.

"You are the one," said the Wraith. "I am sure of it."

The Wraith had heard stories of a boy who glided within the Murk as if he were a part of it. This had to be him. His silky movements betrayed him.

It was the only explanation for the ease with which the boy had stood his ground against him, never taking a step back, always advancing, forcing him this way and that as he chose, not feeling the need to hide behind a long length of steel, instead engaging the Wraith in a fair combat, dagger against dagger.

"The one what?" Jakob was more than happy to allow for the break in their combat, certain that this monster couldn't evade the Highlanders arrayed around him. Besides, the conversation might prove useful. What better way to learn more about his enemies?

"The one who lives in the Murk. The one who is of the Murk."

"I'm only here because of you," Jakob replied. "If you weren't here, I wouldn't need to be in the Murk."

"You should give yourself more credit. Even now your reputation is growing among the Horde. Many want to challenge you. Many want to cut your throat and take your head back to the Wraith Hunter. It would be a great honor for them to do that."

"I care little for my reputation. I care even less about the Wraith Hunter."

"You should care. You were lucky the first time you met him. He will not be taken by surprise a second time. You will die by his hand. The Wraith Hunter has said so. When the Wraith Hunter speaks, all must listen."

"You must listen. Not me. The Wraith Hunter is nothing to me."

"You speak out of arrogance or ignorance. I cannot tell which."

"I speak based on what I know, Wraith. I speak the truth. Tell me, if my surviving the Wraith Hunter was based on luck, then how do you explain what happened to you and your brethren just now?"

The Wraith was about to offer an immediate reply, enraged by how the boy had insulted him and his leader, but he kept those words to himself. This boy was much more than he seemed.

Besides, it was a good question. The Wraith could offer some useless response, yet what was the point of doing that? The boy wasn't taunting him. He was simply speaking from what he knew.

Another reason this boy who lived in the Murk was a worthy kill. Unfortunately, the Wraith knew that the kill wouldn't be his.

At first, that realization had galled the Wraith. Now, he accepted it with resignation. There was only so much you could control in life. And right now, he exercised very little control at all.

"I cannot," the Wraith admitted. "Still, I suggest that you be wary. Don't allow this one lucky success of yours to color your perspective. The Wraith Hunter will come for you. He will kill you."

"So you say," scoffed Jakob.

"So I know," hissed the Wraith, for the first time anger resonating in his voice. "The Wraith Hunter knows who you are."

"And who am I?" Jakob was too curious not to ask.

"The Wraith who is not a Wraith."

Jakob didn't have a chance to think about what the Wraith had just called him, the monster flashing forward with a speed that he could only track thanks to his use of the Talent.

Bringing his daggers up just in time, Jakob parried several slashes and stabs with his blades, the sound of steel striking steel echoing off the rock of the gulley. It became almost a sustained tenor because of the incredible pace of the Wraith's assault, resembling what it would be like to hear Duff's hammer hitting an anvil in a constant rhythm.

Through it all, Jakob held his ground.

He could have stepped back. He could have allowed the archers poised above him to kill this Wraith.

He chose not to.

He wanted to make a point, as much to the Wraith as to himself.

The Highlanders no longer fled from the Wraiths. Not now. Not again.

The Highlanders would stand and fight, just as he was doing now.

The end came unexpectedly fast, drawing several gasps, even a few exclamations of shock, from the men and women watching the combat.

The Wraith was so focused on slipping one of his daggers past Jakob's defenses that he never considered the possibility that the Wraith who is not a Wraith had figured out the pattern of his attack, the monster running through a methodical series of cuts and slashes before beginning the sequence over again.

A dangerous habit against any adversary. Deadly against one with Jakob's skill.

As soon as the Wraith pulled back the dagger he held in his left hand, preparing to slash Jakob's throat, Jakob ducked and in the same motion kicked out with his left foot. His boot connected with the Wraith's knee and bent the leg back at an angle that led to several audible pops and a crack, the Wraith falling backward to the ground, ligaments torn and bones broken.

Before the Wraith even hit the ground, the monster was dead. Jakob followed the Wraith toward the rocks and drove the dagger he held in his right hand into the Wraith's chest, giving the monster a final twist of his blade, ignoring the Wraith's painful gasp.

His strength fading, the Wraith's daggers slipped from his claws.

"Remember what I said Wraith who is not a Wraith," the monster's voice thick from the blood pooling in his lungs even as his eyes took on a faraway look. "We come for you. We will not stop coming until you are dead. The Wraith Hunter knows you. He hunts you."

Jakob stared down at the Wraith, watching as the light left the monster's black orbs, the creature's last breath a strangled wheeze as blood trickled out of the corner of his mouth.

Jakob should have been pleased by his success, having killed the Wraith with little risk to himself. But he wasn't.

Instead, he felt cold inside. Not because he killed the monster, but rather because of the Wraith's words, which continued to play through his mind.

"The Wraith Hunter knows you. He hunts you."

He didn't know for certain who the Wraith he had just killed was talking about, but he had an inkling. The first Wraith he met in the Murk. When he was trying to escape with his father from the slavers and then the monsters in the mist.

The Wraith who had stared at him from the edge of the fog when he had gotten his father free of the Murk and they had climbed a tree just in case the grey tendrils reached for them once again.

It had to be. He didn't know why he thought that, but he was certain that he was correct.

That Wraith had been an excellent fighter. He had also proven to be smart, cunning, tenacious, and, worst of all, patient.

A lethal adversary if ever there was one.

Nevertheless, that was a worry for another time. He and the Highlanders were not yet done with their current exercise.

Jakob stared at the Wraith he had just killed a moment longer, taking in the monster's slackening features, before he wiped the Wraith's blood from his dagger on the monster's leather armor and then sheathed both blades. Hesitating for the briefest of moments, he then reached down for the Wraith's double-bladed daggers, testing the weight in each hand.

He nodded in appreciation. The white steel was the lightest metal that he had ever carried, the blades razor sharp. For some unknowable reason, he got the sense that these blades could not be broken, although that was a test for another time.

How the Wraiths made their weapons, he had not a clue, but he did like the feel of them in his hand. The curved daggers were well balanced, and they felt as if they belonged between his fingers.

"You going to keep those?"

"I think I will," Jakob replied as he pushed himself up off

the ground. "Well done, by the way. Although you didn't have to cut it so close."

"Do I sense a note of concern?" asked Saraa, her eyes sparkling with delight, believing that she was correct.

"For you and the others," Jakob clarified.

"If you say so," Saraa replied with a lift of her eyebrows and a broad grin.

She'd take what Jakob was willing to give her. For now. She wanted more from him, but she knew that he wasn't ready yet.

He had revealed bits and pieces of what had happened to him in Caledonia, why he needed to leave for the Territories with his father. She could tell that the shadow of all that remained with him, darkening his thoughts and his emotions. So, she returned to the business at hand, knowing that this wasn't the time to press him.

"We needed to be close," Saraa clarified. "It was the only way to draw the Wraiths in."

Jakob was about to challenge Saraa's statement, not wanting her to put herself in such a dangerous position again. Instead, he held his tongue. He knew that any request or warning he offered to her would fall on deaf ears.

He could never win an argument with Saraa. She had a way of twisting his words around so that her perspective was always the right perspective.

And in those few instances where she couldn't do that, she would simply ignore him. So, there was no point in wasting his breath.

Rather, he turned his focus to a more practical purpose. Using the Talent to search for the other Wraiths who weren't a part of this group of hunters.

"Anything to worry about?" Jakob asked as Duff approached out of the fog. He walked confidently, unworried by the rough ground thanks to Jakob giving him the clarity of vision that made the Murk no more than an inconvenience rather than the deathtrap that it had been until now.

"No one hurt badly. Just a few scratches. The archers and our greater numbers made sure of that. We took the Wraiths completely by surprise." Duff gave Jakob a companionable slap on the back. "I've got to say, lad, I could get used to this."

"That's good to hear, because so could I," Jakob agreed. He caught all the nods from the Highlanders who had joined them on this expedition, the men and women circling around them now that they had dispatched all of their enemies. Their expressions eliminated the need for words. They were expectant. Hopeful. Confident. He was glad to see it. Because he was feeling the same way. "Shall we give it another go?"

"The other dozen?" asked Saraa, her eyes flashing with a bloody hunger.

"Yes. They're about three leagues away. I doubt they have any idea what happened here. They were moving away from these Wraiths."

"How long do you think the fog will last?"

"Who can say?" replied Jakob, answering Martin's question with a shrug. The former soldier who had served with Duff in the Royal Guard was a blacksmith by trade now, although he was more than happy to revert to his old ways if it meant ridding the Highlands of more of these monsters in the mist. "If past experience is any guide, we should get to a point where we can ambush the Wraiths before they escape with the Murk."

None of the Highlanders missed the use of Jakob's word *escape*. That's what they had done whenever the fog came in before. Or they had. Until now.

The irony wasn't lost on them, their drive to pursue the remaining Wraiths only heightened by the fact that in their minds, thanks to Jakob and the Talent, the roles had been reversed.

The Wraiths weren't the hunters anymore. The Highlanders were.

Duff was nodding his head, his small grin expanding to a broad smile in just a few breaths. Although the smile wasn't crafted of humor. Rather, it was formed from a darker emotion. A necessary emotion.

He was met as well by similar smiles and the dead-eye stares of men and women keen for revenge.

"What say you, Marchers? Shall we have another go at these monsters?"

Saraa had proposed the name for their small fighting force based on the fact that they had covered ten leagues during the night to get to this exact location so that they could catch the Wraiths by surprise. Not everyone had agreed at first with the suggested appellation.

Some other options were bandied about. The Racers or the Runners seemed to have support. No one could agree, although the discussion had kept them distracted during the long run.

The argument ended when Duff finally grew tired of the bickering, declaring that they would be named the Marchers or nothing at all.

That had settled it. As soon as Duff had stated his opinion, it was a done deal.

There were no shouts or roars of acclamation in response to Duff's question. Only soft murmurs of agreement and a few nods, the Highlanders' already hard looks becoming flintier.

For the first time the Highlanders had engaged in a fair fight with the Wraiths, and they had won. Without the loss of life themselves.

They all had friends and family who had fallen victim to the monsters in the mist. And now they believed that they could change the dynamic of this struggle.

"Then off we go," said Duff. "The Marchers go to battle."

The former Sergeant nodded to Jakob, who was already

trotting at a rapid pace through the fog toward the northwest, the Highlanders at his back having little trouble staying with him, their desire for vengeance pushing them forward.

Jakob already had a plan in mind for this next group of Wraiths. If they could get ahead of the monsters, they could come at them when they were moving back through the Highlands toward the north. The Wraiths would never expect the Highlanders to be waiting for them there, having already cleared the land through which they had traveled to come this far in among the snowcapped peaks.

As his father liked to say, there was nothing better than an unfair fight.

Jakob agreed with him.

11

DIVERGING PATHS

"Do you see it?" asked Talia. "Just a hundred yards beyond the surf."

"Barely at best. That dark shape that looks to be made of black granite?"

"Yes. That's it."

Davin and Talia hid atop a rocky promontory that stretched out over the waves crashing against the shore. Their roost would have given them an excellent view of the Highlands to the west. At present, though, they couldn't see the snowcapped peaks, the darkness only lit now and then by the inconsistent light of the full moon sneaking through the shroud of clouds that strayed above.

Despite the prevailing gloom, they could pick out the beginnings of the sandbar that connected the island to the mainland. No more than a hundred yards wide, in that narrow space, when the tide was out, the water came no higher than the waist of a tall man. On each side, however, the sea floor dropped precipitously, falling away to an unknown depth.

You could walk the sandbar depending on the pull of the moon. You just needed to stay on the path, just like the creature was doing now as it strode toward the beach. Otherwise, you ran the risk of coming face to face with the great whites and Great Sharks that patrolled these waters much like they did those surrounding the Jagged Islands.

Every so often, when the moon broke through the drifting clouds, Davin caught the flash off a large fin cutting through the waves, the great white swimming parallel to the channel. Davin assumed that the animal's interest came from the creature daring to cross the watery path. The great white could sense the disturbance in the water, yet the animal could do nothing to quell its hunger.

"You're right," agreed Davin. "The monster blends into the darkness quite well. If not for the moonlight the beast would be all but invisible."

"And thus, the difficulty in killing these creatures, among other reasons."

"You've come up against one before?" asked Davin.

"Not on the sea," Talia replied, "not yet. However, I do have some experience in the suffering these monsters can cause when they take their prey. Three attacked one of my crews. Half the sailors were killed before they were driven from the ship."

Talia chose not to share any more than that. She had no wish to relive the gut-wrenching experience of watching her father die on their dock in Ballinasloe, the victim of a Stalker's claws.

Davin glanced toward his companion, noting the tightness of her jaw and the flintiness in her eyes. She wasn't telling him all that she could, but that was her right. She had a grievance against these Stalkers, and he didn't begrudge her that in the least. He also had no desire to push her on a matter that clearly was quite painful.

"This creature reminds me of the Slayers we fought on the Breakwater Plateau."

"Slayers?" asked Talia, unable to keep her curiosity from her voice. "What kind of monsters are those?"

Davin was about to explain in all the detail that he could muster, even wanting to share the story of how Bryen had named him the Slayer of Slayers because of his success against the creatures. Yet even with the first words on the tip of his tongue, he chose to stay quiet instead, which was an uncommon decision for him.

Usually, he was more than happy to regale others with stories of his adventures. He doubted that the woman crouching beside him would be impressed with his retelling.

She was all business, all the time. Besides, the Stalker was almost to the shoreline, and he didn't want to miss what was going to happen next. He decided to keep his response brief.

"Something much like this Stalker you described to us, only a little nastier. The creatures were always hungry."

"What does hungry have to do with this?"

"The Slayers were the assassins of the Ghoule Overlord. Their purpose was to kill his enemies. They were very good at it. And when they were done, they always ate what they killed."

"I'm glad you didn't share that when we were eating dinner this evening," Talia said drily.

"You're welcome," Davin replied, his characteristic grin returning, as if he had done her a favor.

"You're not just pulling my leg?"

"No, I wouldn't dream of doing that," replied Davin, a broader smile playing across his lips, the gleam in his eye suggesting to her that he wasn't being entirely truthful. "Sirius said that Slayers could wipe out a small town, slaughtering everyone and then feeding on them, in less than an hour. After coming up against those monsters, I had no cause to disbelieve him."

"Do we really need to be talking about this now with what's coming toward us?" chided Talia.

"I was just answering your question." Davin shrugged, not understanding why she seemed to be just a tad irritated. After all, she had started the conversation. "That's all."

The *Freedom* and the Carlomin Trading Company frigates had reached the Isle of Mist the evening before, sailing into a small cove on the northwestern side that allowed them to hide from any passing ships.

Although the precaution seemed unnecessary. They hadn't seen another vessel since they had anchored. Even better, since leaving the pirate vessels burning and sinking at the edge of the Floe, they hadn't run into any other problems, whether pirates, Bakunawa, or bad weather.

During that time, if Talia wasn't talking with Bryen, Aislinn, and Rafia about what they needed to be aware of before they made land in the Territories, she spent most of her free moments, which were few and far between, near the helm or the bow staring at the sea, lost in thought. Davin had watched her from the crow's nest, forgoing the dives that had become so routine for him.

He was curious about this young woman, the memories and concerns that tugged at her. Who, not long after coming to the Territories, had made it her mission to rid the Sea of Mist of the pirates haunting its waters.

She had a purpose in life. Several, in fact.

Inexplicably, he felt a connection to the woman also known as the Huntress. Much like him, Davin could tell that she had a restless spirit.

Rather than diving into the ocean with a rope tied around his waist, he had climbed down and started to talk with her. A few times anyway. Trying to figure out why he was drawn to her.

They were never long conversations. A few minutes at most. It was clear that Talia Carlomin preferred the quiet to chatter.

Yet during those few minutes she came alive in a way that

he had never anticipated. Maybe she sensed the same thing in him that he sensed in her.

Always on edge. Always needing to do. Always needing to move. Never really feeling alive unless there was some risk involved.

He shared some of his experiences in the Pit with her, although he was always succinct, not feeling the need to add the many explicit and gory details that he usually included when telling others. He also touched on some of the challenges they faced while overthrowing Marden Beleron and then freeing Caledonia from the dark shadow of the Ghoule Overlord.

Talia seemed to appreciate his restraint. She even offered some hints as to what she had been doing during her voyages through the Sea of Mist, talking about some of her engagements against the pirates and what she and her mother were attempting to do in Ballinasloe.

But just like him, she gave Davin nothing more than the facts, not feeling the need to provide a colorful story.

Talia also told Davin much of what she talked about when she met with Bryen, Aislinn, and Rafia, as well as what they could expect when they reached the Isle of Mist. He had not believed some of it until he had seen it with his own eyes.

A very large village, almost a town, had sprouted on the western side of the island just a league from where they were hiding now. The huts and cottages were ramshackle at best, but they provided some shelter from the elements.

It was a sad affair in many respects. No one had taken charge of the settlement, so basic services, such as sanitation to prevent the spread of disease, were nonexistent.

To Davin's way of thinking, it appeared as if the people who had come to this very small island hadn't given much consideration to what they would need to do once they made it here. They had thought no further than just getting there.

Of course, thinking about the many challenges facing those coming to the Territories that Talia had explained to him, he could understand why so many of them were stuck in what he viewed as a strange limbo. Unwilling to leave, although just as unwilling to set down roots.

Many of the people who had crossed the channel to the island had come to Fal Carrach or the Highlands with the belief that they could start a new life in a world that was not bound by the strictures that governed their existence in Caledonia. A life that could give them a measure of independence and security that they had failed to achieve on the other side of the Burnt Ocean.

Or so they had hoped.

Those hopes had been dashed with the arrival of the fog and the creatures lurking within as well as beasts like the one just about to step onto the beach.

"You're right," murmured Davin. "That looks like a dreadful piece of work."

"Will your friends be able to manage the Stalker?"

Davin grinned at the question. "Just watch."

They didn't have long to wait.

THE DARKNESS WAS COMPLETE, the thick clouds covering the full moon, the thin haze beginning to form off the coast of the Isle of Mist dampening any sounds and hiding the faintest of movements. The only disturbance was the gentle push of the creature walking through the surf.

As soon as the beast set foot on the shore, a sphere of energy burst into the sky right above the Stalker, illuminating the beach for several hundred yards as if the noonday sun was shining down.

The light gave all those standing on the sand a good chance

to study the monster, which was forced to shield its blood-red eyes against the glare.

"Much like a Slayer," murmured Aislinn. She noted the creature's coloring and hardened skin that resembled wax in certain places. She guessed that it served as a type of armor.

She stood with Rafia and Bryen, right in front of Lycia and Declan, who had formed the Blood Company into a semicircle that touched the surf in two places, scuta at the ready to prevent the Stalker from attempting to escape into the heart trees growing just a hundred yards up the sandy shore.

The shield wall wasn't necessary, not with three Magii standing with him. But Declan was who he was.

He preferred to prepare for every eventuality. He didn't like mistakes and he hated bad luck, and he believed both could be countered with proper planning.

"Yes, it does look like a Slayer, doesn't it? At least in some respects. No tail, thankfully," murmured Rafia. "I hated the tails. Very unpredictable weapons."

"What's it waiting for?" asked Aislinn.

The Stalker stood on the beach, staring right at them, its blood-red eyes blazing with hate. Talia had said that the Stalkers were vicious monsters, slaughtering any unlucky enough to cross their paths during the night. But now, Rafia had stolen the comfort and safety of darkness from this creature, and it hadn't yet figured out what to do next.

"Us," Bryen replied. "It's used to being in the shadows. It doesn't like being seen so clearly."

Before Bryen had uttered his last word, in a burst of speed also reminiscent of a Slayer, the Stalker sprinted out of the waves, clawed feet digging into the sand, its shrill shriek preceding the monster as it raced up the beach right toward the three Magii.

The Stalker didn't get far. Rafia shot a streak of energy into the monster's chest, knocking the beast back toward the waves, its scream dying in its throat after it had gone no more than a dozen yards.

The monster landed on its back, its sternum blackened and scorched, the bones beneath the flesh and muscle charred. The stench of burning meat filled the air until the steady breeze that blew down from the mountains that formed the spine of the island swept it across the channel toward the Highlands.

The three Magii walked over to the dead Stalker, Declan and Lycia joining them, as did Davin and Talia after they climbed down the rocks and made their way along the surf having observed the spectacle from afar.

They all took in the monster's greyish black flesh that looked to be as hard, if not harder, than the leather armor the Blood Company wore. And the skin did, indeed, resemble wax, as if whoever had made these monsters had hung them in flames to complete the process. The clawed feet and hands reminded them of the Ghoules, although this creature didn't carry a weapon.

Running through several of their minds was the thought that they had left one continent, tired of fighting against monsters that for centuries had been no more than stories, only to arrive on a distant continent and find themselves in much the same predicament as they were before. Monsters of yore walking the land, endangering all who came upon them.

"Many people seeking to settle in the Highlands and to the south are here because it's not safe with terrors like these running about," explained Talia. "But even here, these creatures remain a threat. Everyone on this island simply wants a chance to make their own way without having to worry about some creature stalking them in the night. Yet there really are no safe havens."

"Is this what also hunts in the fog?" asked Rafia.

The monster lying at her feet didn't bring to mind any of the creatures that she had come across while fighting against the Ghoule Overlord, although there were some similarities. Briefly catching the eyes of Aislinn and Bryen, they both nodded, letting her know that they were thinking much the same thing that she was.

This Stalker wasn't a natural being. She was certain that it had been made. Molded into what it was now. Crafted with the Curse.

The trace of Dark Magic was unmistakable.

The key question now was who in the Territories had the capacity and knowledge to create this monstrosity?

"No, I don't believe so," replied Talia. "From what Jakob and Duff told me the last time we spoke, the monsters in the mist blend almost perfectly with the fog. Clawed feet and hands much like a Stalker, yes, but they have a greyish white coloring. They're not so broad or so muscled as this." She motioned toward the Stalker, restraining the urge to spit on the creature, her seething hate threatening for just a second to get the better of her. "Those monsters in the mist are tall, thin. Rather than employ their claws with any regularity, they prefer to use double-bladed daggers that resemble the haladie of ancient times for their bloody work."

"They sound like a pleasant lot," commented Davin in his characteristic dry humor that fell flat on his current audience.

"Those haladie are nasty weapons," Declan murmured. Rare in his experience and exceedingly effective in the hands of someone with the requisite skill to use them.

"What are those creatures called again?" asked Aislinn.

"Wraiths."

"Seems like a fitting name if they look as you say they do," murmured Rafia distractedly.

Her mind had already begun to work on the challenge that just seconds before had been set before her. Who could have employed the Curse in such a way as to make a monster like this? Some new threat with which she was unfamiliar? Some old peril that was raising its head once again?

She didn't know. And she didn't know how to find out. Not yet. But she would.

Shaking her head in frustration, the Magus turned her attention back to the conversation. She could take up the new puzzle later. Perhaps Bryen could reach out to the Ten Magii through the Seventh Stone. They might be able to give her a place to start her search.

"And who are Jakob and Duff?" asked Declan.

He would make sure that every soldier in the Blood Company took a good look at this Stalker. He had a feeling that this wouldn't be the last time that they would be coming up against these monsters.

"They're Highlanders."

"You're going to have to tell us a bit more than that," prodded Declan.

"They've been leading the defense against the Wraiths in the Highlands."

"They work for the Governor of that Territory?" asked Aislinn.

Talia snorted softly at the thought. "They have no love for the Governor of the Highlands. If they came upon him, they'd likely treat him just as they do the Wraiths."

"What do they do to the Wraiths?" asked Lycia, her curiosity piqued.

"Kill them whenever they can," Talia replied with a cold-bloodedness that instead of surprising Davin actually appealed to him. In his experience, there was only one way to deal with your enemies.

"From what you said, it's smarter to hide or find a fortification that you can defend when the Wraiths come," said Declan.

"It is, and that's what the Highlanders have been doing. However, in speaking with Jakob and Duff, they've been testing some new approaches for challenging the Wraiths. They weren't specific. I just sensed that they had grown tired of always running and hiding. That they wanted to hunt the Wraiths rather than be hunted themselves. And so far, from what I've heard, it appears to be working."

"Why the bad blood with the Governor?" asked Declan. He wanted to determine if the two Highlanders could be viewed as allies or potential obstacles before he made a decision on them. Although hearing that they preferred to fight from the front foot rather than show their backs already had put them in a positive light for him.

"Torstan Sharperson has ignored the pleas of the Highlanders for assistance and protection against the Wraiths, the Stalkers, and the slavers. Jakob and Duff have taken it upon themselves to do something about it."

"Much like you with respect to the pirates," offered Davin.

"I guess so," Talia replied, slightly uncomfortable. "I really never thought of it that way before."

"It sounds like they have their hands full," commented Aislinn.

"They do," agreed Talia with a sharp nod. "Because the Governor has offered no meaningful aid other than platitudes, and, in fact, is potentially complicit at least with respect to the slavers, Duff and Jakob have been doing all that they can to protect the Highlanders from these threats."

"How do they do that with the fog?" asked Lycia. "From what you were saying aboard the *Freedom*, it's so dense that you can't see a thing. That you're blind and at the mercy of the Wraiths who move through the mist as if they're made from it."

"I haven't spoken with them for a few weeks, so I don't know all the details. Nevertheless, they've been proving successful in their efforts, at least based on the stories that I hear in the Ballinasloe taverns. Moreover, they've gained the attention of the Governor. He's declared them and any Highlander working with them to be criminals despite all that they're doing for the people living among the peaks."

"Why would he do that?" asked Davin. "I would think that he would be happy if someone else was doing the work that he should be doing."

"They're a threat to him," answered Aislinn.

"Just because they're doing something that this Torstan Sharperson should be doing?"

"Exactly so," continued Aislinn. "They're usurping his authority. When it comes to power and politics, perception and reality are often indistinguishable. If Torstan Sharperson isn't exercising the authority that he should be, and these two Highlanders are, then they're gaining power at his expense. He can't permit that if he wants to maintain his own power."

"That's a harsh way of looking at the world," Davin said sadly.

"It's really no different than the Pit," grumbled Declan. "Kill or be killed."

No one standing with the Master of the Gladiators had cause to disagree with him, least of all Bryen, Davin, and Lycia who had spent so much time on the white sand.

"The Lady Winborne is absolutely correct with her assessment," said Talia. "There's another factor involved as well."

"What would that be?" wondered Davin.

"Taxes."

Aislinn smiled and nodded upon hearing that, already figuring out what Talia meant.

"What do you mean by taxes?" asked Davin.

"Duff and Jakob and the many Highlanders with them refuse to pay the taxes that Torstan Sharperson demands. That resistance is spreading throughout the Highlands, and his collectors are finding it harder and harder to do their jobs. As that resistance builds ..."

"It becomes a mechanism that could lead to a rebellion,"

finished Davin, catching up to Talia and Aislinn. He nodded toward Bryen. "Those two sound much like you. You took down a king. There's little difference in doing the same to a Governor."

Bryen smiled at that. "Perhaps so. That's why I'd really like to meet these Highlanders."

"As would I," murmured Lycia. "They sound quite driven."

"That they are," agreed Talia. "They're forces of nature, both in their own unique way."

"Let's step back for a moment," said Declan. "What have these two Highlanders done to defend against the Wraiths, Stalkers, and slavers? Why are they perceived as being successful with so many people coming here to the Isle of Mist rather than staying in the Highlands?"

"They've built a series of towers, what the Highlanders call brochs. Every village has one. When the fog comes, so do the Wraiths. When that happens, the Highlanders seek refuge in the brochs. When the Stalkers come, they seek refuge in the brochs."

"I would assume these towers also offer good protection against these slavers," said Lycia.

"They do," nodded Talia. "But from what I understand, Jakob and Duff have taken a more aggressive approach with respect to the slavers. They have no love for those cowardly thugs."

"What approach would that be exactly?" asked Lycia, now even more curious.

"They send out hunting squads."

"For the slavers?" asked Lycia, her eyes brightening with delight.

"Correct. They've placed a bounty on the head of any slaver who sets foot in the Highlands. Twenty golds."

"That sounds very literal," said Davin, intrigued.

"It is," Talia replied.

Declan nodded. Easier to carry a head than drag a body through the mountains.

"Twenty golds?" gasped Davin. "That's a small fortune. Where did they come across that kind of money?"

"I don't know, and I really don't want to ask them," replied Talia. "They aren't the kind of men you want to cross or get on their bad side. Clearly, they hold grudges."

"There is nothing wrong with that," replied Declan, "especially when there is good cause to do so."

"No, there isn't," agreed Talia. "Grudges can serve as good motivation. And the bounty has motivated some of the slavers to give up their trade. They know that there's a death sentence waiting for them if the Highlanders catch them."

"Simple and effective," said Lycia, "and very final. I definitely would like to meet those two."

"You might get that chance," said Bryen cryptically, but before he explained what he meant he turned his piercing gaze back to Talia. "Where do these Stalkers come from?"

"We don't know," admitted Talia, her tone revealing her frustration. She had been searching for the answer to that specific question for quite some time and had yet to find it. That was irritating her to no end. She needed to find out, because it was the only way to confirm who was responsible for her father's death. "And believe me, it's not for lack of trying."

"You must have some idea?" asked Rafia, catching the momentary flash behind her eyes.

"Rumors only."

"A good friend of mine liked to say that there was always a nugget of truth in every rumor," said Rafia, many of those gathered around the Stalker understanding that she was speaking of Sirius, "so I'd appreciate it if you shared what you know."

"The Stalkers always come from the north," replied Talia. "Having confirmed that fact, then logic suggests several possibilities that can't be ignored."

"They come from the Highlands?" asked Rafia.

"No. Farther north."

"The Northern Territory?" asked Aislinn, her mind already unavoidably moving down a path that she would have preferred not to walk yet having no choice but to do so.

"Yes, the rumors suggest the Stalkers come from somewhere within the Northern Peaks. I have no evidence to support that claim. Just stories. But I have no cause either to disbelieve that claim. Not yet anyway."

The nods that Bryen and Aislinn gave each other relayed that both were thinking the same thing. The necessity that they go to Shadow's Reach, what with the Stalkers possibly coming from that direction and the Wraiths definitely moving down through the Northern Peaks to make their way to the Highlands, just became that much more imperative, because it seemed that the answers to many of their questions would be found there.

"And these people here on the island?" asked Declan. "There's no one to protect them?"

What he had seen in the village had torn at his heart. They were farmers and craftspeople. They were not soldiers. They couldn't stay here and have any real chance of survival unless they made some very drastic changes that would be exceedingly difficult for many of them.

"No, they have no choice but to protect themselves. The Highlanders are stretched thin as it is across the channel."

Declan's face darkened upon hearing that. He had spoken with many of the people living on the island that morning, walking through the makeshift village, learning their stories, their concerns, their fears, their hopes. He had wanted to get the lay of the land, and what he had discovered had struck a chord that he thought had gone silent long ago.

The belief that the island was safe was a myth. The dead Stalker lying at his feet confirmed that. Moreover, there wasn't much game, and certainly not the type needed to feed a growing village. Also, there were only a few small lakes and streams for fresh water. The islanders could fish, but even that was a challenge because of the great whites.

Clearly, most of what these people required to survive was across the channel in the Highlands and Fal Carrach.

"The two Highlanders you mentioned, Jakob and Duff." Declan's volcanic expression suggested that his rage was beginning to simmer. "They haven't offered aid to the people taking refuge here?"

"They have," replied Talia. "They provide what they can. They send what foodstuffs and other materials the people here might need, such as clothes for the children and other necessities. But they have only so many resources themselves. They are focused on defending the Highlands, on freeing the Highlands actually, from the monsters and the man who views the Territory as his own private plaything. They've given every person here an open invitation to return to the Highlands. Duff and Jakob promised that they could build their own villages and that the Highlanders would build a tower for each one, providing protection as needed."

"Yet they're still here?"

"They're frightened. They feel safer here despite the fact that they're still under threat."

"What's on your mind, Declan?" asked Rafia. "I can see the wheels turning."

"Based on this conversation, I think it's quite clear that Bryen and Aislinn need to make for Shadow's Reach. They need to meet with Aislinn's uncle. More importantly, they need to find out what's going on in the north. They need to determine if the Lady Carlomin's rumors have some basis in truth."

"I couldn't agree more," replied Aislinn.

"At the same time, the Lady Carlomin has her own work to

do against the pirates. From what I can tell, she has that well in hand."

"I do," nodded Talia, "although there is still a great deal more work required before the Sea of Mist is free of that lice-ridden pestilence."

"Although I wonder, even with her success, if the Lady Carlomin might be willing to accept some assistance," continued Declan, nodding toward Bryen to tell him that he had the same thought as he did.

"Perhaps," Talia replied slowly. "That would require some discussion. I refuse to be in anyone's debt."

"Nor would you be," said Declan. He could understand her reluctance to take that risk, not after hearing about all that she needed to do to build her business and gather the resources to take on the pirates threatening to destroy her and the other merchants working along the coast. "And we face, as well, the challenge of helping the people who have come to the Isle of Mist seeking refuge. If we don't, these people are nothing more than sitting ducks for the Stalkers or the Wraiths if the Murk ever covers this island."

"You mean to keep the Blood Company here?" asked Rafia, although her comment was more a statement than a question. She had expected as much from him. He couldn't stand by and watch people in need suffer.

"For a time, yes," said Declan. "To help protect these people and to teach them how to protect themselves. As we just saw, the Stalkers are a continuing threat. And from what I gathered in the village, the slavers are turning their eye toward the people here as a source of labor since the Highlanders are making it so difficult for them across the channel."

Declan shook his head, his anger plain. "One of the people I talked to said that just last week a party of slavers tried to come across the channel only to lose control of the small skiff in the rough surf and become bait for the great whites. I can't say hearing that saddened me in any way, but I doubt that these people can depend on the weather or rough conditions on the water to keep those slavers away for much longer. If Jakob and Duff are enjoying as much success as you say they are, Lady Carlomin, then the slavers will have no choice but to turn their eyes toward the residents of this island."

"What you suggest makes sense," said Bryen. "Besides, we probably don't want to unleash the Blood Company on the mainland until we know what's really going on in the Territories."

"It all makes sense," said Rafia, "but then when Declan is putting forward his strategies when doesn't it make sense?" That comment drew the smiles of those standing around her, except for Talia, who still didn't know the Sergeant of the Blood Company very well to catch the humor. "I think I'll stay here with Declan and help him do what needs to be done. I'd also like to study these Stalkers a bit more. This seems the best place to do that."

"Then we're agreed," said Bryen, not surprised by Rafia's decision, and clearly Declan was pleased by it, although he refused to show it. He then turned his focus to the pirate hunter. "Talia, before we start putting these plans into motion, a moment of your time?"

"I can't believe that I'm actually considering this."

"Bryen can be quite persuasive," said Davin, who stood next to Talia, his shadow almost covering her. "Remember, he did overthrow a dynasty three hundred years in the making in just a few days."

"So I'm learning," huffed Talia.

They were walking along the beach in the small cove that protected the *Freedom* and Talia's three ships, the *Swift*, the

Resolution, and the *Revenge*. Her captains had reported that they were ready to sail, although they wouldn't be going to Ballinasloe. Not yet.

They still had some hunting to do. They wanted to improve on their current haul of five pirate frigates taken or sunk, two of those when aiding the *Freedom*.

"I'm sure that I could prove helpful to you. Have no fear of that."

"Because you're a good fighter?" wondered Talia. "Of that, I have no doubt. You couldn't have survived in the Pit otherwise. That is not my concern."

"Then why are you hesitating? Another blade at your back couldn't hurt, could it?"

"That's not what I'm worried about."

"Then what are you worried about?"

"Your judgment," replied Talia bluntly, turning toward Davin, seizing his eyes with her own. "I worry that you make bad decisions, and I don't want any of those decisions to affect me or my crews."

"My judgment? I don't understand what ..."

"You understand quite well what I mean," cut in Talia. "Don't try to deny it."

Davin was about to do just that. Smartly, though, he held back what he was going to say next. This woman had caught him out. There was nothing to do but speak honestly.

"Most of what you hear about me is exaggerated."

Talia doubted that. She didn't know whether the man walking beside her was remarkably brave, slightly insane, or a combination of both. Looking at his current grin, she thought probably both.

"You, gladiator, are reckless. Most people would question your judgment after the risks you've taken."

"I was just doing what I thought was necessary," Davin replied simply, shrugging his shoulders. "No more than that."

"And some of the other tales your friends shared on the way here?" asked Talia.

"You'd need to be more specific." He gave her a broad smile with the hope that it would ease the tension radiating from her. "As I said, most of the stories that you hear about me are exaggerated."

Obviously, it didn't. Instead, her eyes narrowed, and her lips tightened.

"The multiple times you put yourself in unnecessary danger while fighting the Ghoules. So many times, in fact, that those stories all blended into one. And that narrative tells a simple tale. You are willing to take risks that others are not." She held up her hands to delay the protest he was anxious to offer. "Yes, at times, such an approach can prove useful and necessary. But not every time. And I fear that you don't know the difference between when such risk taking is necessary and when it is more of a threat to those around you. To those depending on you."

"Yes, I understand what you're saying, but there was ..."

"And then you swinging on a vine across an acidic river while fighting whatever an Echidna is," continued Talia, overriding what Davin was going to say in his defense. "How you could view that as a good decision, I really have no idea."

"Yes, but there were extenuating ..."

"I know," said Talia, cutting him off again. "You were just doing what you thought was necessary."

"Exactly," replied Davin, although he said it with a weakening confidence.

Davin was distinctly uncomfortable, never having been in this position before with anyone else but his sister and Bryen. This woman had the ability to see through him. To perceive the person beneath the façade he preferred to present to the world.

"I don't know that I can trust you," Talia continued. She didn't say it as a judgment, simply as a fact. "It's as simple as that. As I said, I will not risk myself or my crews on someone I don't know. On someone who takes unnecessary risks just because they're bored."

"You can trust me," Davin replied with some heat. No one had ever challenged his loyalty before, and he didn't like it.

"To do what you think that you need to do or that you want to do?" asked Talia. "Or to do what I tell you to do?"

Davin opened his mouth to reply, then stopped himself. He understood now. She saw him not as an opportunity, a tool to be used in her endeavors against the pirates, but rather as a potential threat. A liability.

"You're lost," Talia said in a softer tone, this time with a note of unexpected empathy in her voice. "I can understand why. I might be much the same if I had been sentenced to the Pit. But you need to find yourself again, and I can't put the men and women I am responsible for in danger while you try to do that."

"You might be right," Davin sighed. "But you seem lost as well."

At that, Talia stared at Davin as if she were seeing him for the first time as something other than the Crimson Giant, a gladiator second only to the Volkun in the Pit.

He shrugged. "I know what I was when I was on the white sand. Now, you're right. I am trying to find myself. To determine what I should be. Perhaps working together, we can find ourselves again. Or maybe even discover who we are supposed to become."

Talia stared at Davin for almost a minute before looking away, having stopped at the far eastern border of the beach. How could he be so difficult and so intuitive at the same time?

Then she shook her head as if she were reaching a decision that she didn't like but she felt she had no choice but to make. "Are you certain you're one of the most feared gladiators to ever fight in the Pit?"

"It depends on who you talk to. Lycia probably wouldn't

agree with you. But that's my sister for you. She rarely agrees with anyone about anything."

Talia snorted at Davin's comment, even though he hadn't intended it as a joke. He was simply telling her the truth. Still, her smile made him smile as well.

"You make it very hard not to like you," murmured Talia.

"I'm sorry?" Davin wasn't quite sure how to respond to that.

Talia closed her eyes for a moment, suppressing the smile that wanted to break through the stern countenance that she was trying to project.

"If I allow you to join us, you doing what you think needs doing or what you want to do comes to an end. Do we understand each other?"

"Can we talk about that for a moment? I wanted to ask about a few specifics ..."

Once again, Talia interrupted him. "No, there is no need to continue a discussion on that topic. If you want to join the crew of one of my ships, you do as I say, when I say, as I say. It's as simple as that. Do we understand one another?"

Davin was about to ask another question. The hard expression Talia gave him suggested that they had reached the tipping point in their dialogue. How he responded now would determine whether he stayed on the Isle of Mist with Declan or got the chance to see more of the Territories.

Restraining his urge to be difficult, he nodded, then gave Talia a brief salute.

"Aye, aye, Captain."

12

MOMENT OF IMPATIENCE

"I still don't see how she does it," said Jakob.

"Who does what?"

"Tommie. She's as good as me with a bow, if not better, but she can barely see a thing without her spectacles."

"She is that," agreed Duff, pride evident in his voice. "You're the only person I've seen who can give Tommie a run for her money."

"Yet most of the time she doesn't wear her spectacles when she's shooting because she doesn't like the feel of them. She says they throw her aim off."

"She does say that. Tends to be a bit of a pain about that, in fact," nodded Duff. "Don't really know how she does it, but sometimes it's better to just leave things be and accept rather than question."

"You sound like my father," muttered Jakob.

Duff grinned at that. "You say that quite a lot. I'm surprised I never met him while I was in the Royal Guard."

"He served in Tintagel a very long time ago, and not for very long, at least from what he told me. When he did, he was usually stationed up by the Shattered Peaks."

"That would make sense," said Duff. "I stayed in the capital and enjoyed a few assignments to the south."

"I'd still love to know Tommie's secret. If she can't really see a target with any clarity beyond twenty yards, how can she possibly hit it so frequently? And always dead center. Never fail."

Jakob was still trying to figure out how he had lost the archery contest that he had engaged in with the veteran of the Royal Guard. Before the darkness fell last night, he and Tommie had shot from a distance of one hundred yards at a piece of wood that was no larger than a hand that they had set hanging from the bottom limb of a heart tree.

Duff and the other Highlanders had watched, enjoying the competition, cheering both archers on. Even placing a few wagers, though not in coins. Rather in chores.

Jakob and Tommie had shot ten quarrels at the small piece of wood. Neither had missed. Each shaft struck the middle of the target. Until the final round.

Tommie had hit the exact center of the small disk. Jakob had missed by the width of a knuckle. Excellent shooting, though not good enough to beat the woman widely recognized as the best archer to ever serve in the Royal Guard.

Because of that loss, Jakob had been tasked with cooking their dinner. He didn't mind. It was a fair price to pay for allowing himself to be distracted just slightly on the last shot, Duff grazing his ear with a stick in an attempt to throw him off.

Jakob's anger at Duff's maneuver was tempered by the fact that if he had struck true, Duff would have been the one cooking dinner last night.

That was something that Jakob wanted to avoid. Out of all the Highlanders in the small band, Duff's cooking left the most to be desired. Edible, yes. Although just barely.

Tommie had said that competing against Jakob without her

spectacles was a point of pride. Whether for Tommie or for Jakob, who could say?

Jakob just didn't understand how Tommie could shoot so well while keeping the spectacles she wore to accomplish most every other task in life in the leather bag that hung from around her neck.

"That's just the way of it sometimes," replied Duff, clapping Jakob on the back. "We all have our skills, even with our limitations, even when we make the challenges we face that much more difficult. It just so happens that Tommie can hit an ant at one hundred yards with her eyes closed. So, as I said, often it's just better to accept rather than question."

"I don't begrudge her that at all," Jakob replied. "I'd just like to know how she does it. When I asked her about it, Tommie avoided answering."

"She can be secretive, can't she?" nodded Duff. "I think she's that way not because she doesn't want to tell you, but because she doesn't know what to tell you. You want to know what I think?"

"Do I really have a choice if I say no?"

Duff grinned at that, then gave Jakob a lift of his eyebrows. "Funny. And no, you don't." Duff clapped Jakob on the back again. "In my opinion, with Tommie it all comes down to a combination of skill and luck."

"How so?"

"She's shooting more by feel than sight. She shoots better without the spectacles because those pieces of glass make her see the target too clearly."

"You do realize that you're not making much sense, right?"

"Patience, lad. Patience. I'm getting where I want to go, just in my own time."

Jakob was considering whether to tell Duff that once again he sounded just like his father. He didn't get the chance, as Duff continued with his explanation.

"Tommie says that the spectacles are an impediment to the true sight that she's seeking when she shoots."

Most would have scoffed at such an answer. Jakob didn't.

He remembered his father telling him of certain soldiers who had a unique skill with a particular weapon. An ability that no one else could match no matter how much they practiced.

One man could throw a battle axe on a curve around a shield wall, never missing his target. Another soldier could throw a dagger without even having to see the target, the woman never missing, allowing instinct and feel to guide her.

"True sight," repeated Jakob, allowing the phrase to percolate in his mind. He was beginning to think that what Tommie could do with a bow was similar to what a Magus was required to do while learning how to use the Talent.

While he was training with Aloysius, the old Magus hadn't called the need to narrow his focus so that he could touch the Talent true sight. He had called it seeking the void. Or seeking the calm. Or the quiet. He called it a lot of things actually, just not that.

The words that Aloysius used to describe the state that you needed to reach didn't matter, because it was all the same. You needed to clear your mind of everything. You needed to concentrate solely on the natural magic flowing through the world to tap into it for your use. You needed to see, sense, feel, hear, nothing else but that. A level of concentration that most people could never achieve.

Thinking about it now, he wouldn't be surprised if what Tommie did before she shot was similar to what Jakob did when he reached for the Talent. Seeking the true sight was the same as seeking the quiet. Two different tools to be employed, though in the same way.

"That's what Tommie calls it, just as her father called it, and her father before that, and so it goes all the way through her family's history." Duff grimaced as he remembered the conversation he had engaged in with Tommie when he had asked the archer much the same as Jakob was asking him now. "I wouldn't ask her too much about it, however. You'd be wasting a few hours of your life as she gave you a long lesson on her family tree."

Jakob smiled at that. He had already learned that talking with Tommie could take you down a road with so many splits and crossroads that you never knew where you were going to end up until you got there.

"I'll keep that in mind," Jakob finally said. "Whatever the reason, so long as she doesn't miss, I don't care how she does it."

"I'm with you on that," said Duff. "Now let's see if we can find what we need."

Bertie, Duff's former Corporal, was wandering along with Tommie through the market that was set up in the green that circled the broch, the Highland peaks surrounding the small valley. Following in their wake was Martin, a reluctant soldier who preferred to be a blacksmith. He had made the massive hammer that Duff now carried in his hand as if it were no more than a child's toy.

Benyen sat on a small barrow at the very edge of the green. The tracker had been at Duff's side as much as he could be ever since his former Sergeant and Jakob had decided on the need for more aggressive action against the Stalkers, slavers, and Wraiths.

Even after all the clashes he had fought in, Benyen still felt a debt to Duff. And with good reason, Jakob knew. The Highlander had saved the tracker's daughter Mari from the Wraiths.

So he continued to join them when he could even though Duff had told him multiple times, just a few minutes ago in fact, that he wanted the tracker to stay with his family and keep an eye on the broch and the surrounding countryside.

The Highlander was considering the request as he observed

all the activity on the green. He was reluctant to acquiesce because he felt as if he would be letting down his friends, even though his wife suffered from a chronic illness that would leave her in bed for days on end when it struck.

Jakob knew what the tracker was going to do, even though Benyen hadn't figured it out yet. The tug of family would get the best of him. Just as it should.

The tracker preferred not to spend too much time around so many people. Benyen said that the interaction and the noise was too distracting for him. It made it more difficult for the tracker to center himself when he was out in the wilderness and following a trail.

Jakob smiled at that thought. It seemed that every one of the men and the woman who followed Duff who had settled right back into their roles from their time in the Royal Guard had their own peccadilloes that needed to be accepted.

Jakob was sure that he had his own, although he likely was too new to the small company to have any of the Highlanders point them out to him.

Yet.

He assumed that it was only a matter of time.

When they did, and they would, he could handle it. His father had been more than happy to identify on a much too regular basis what he perceived to be his son's bad habits and minor faults.

When Duff's friends began to do that, actually he'd be pleased.

He valued the connections that he had made with Duff and his squad, needing something to fill the void left by the death of his father. And their ribbing him as they did each other would mean that he was no longer an outsider, but rather an accepted member of the small troop.

"How goes it, Lord Kestrel?" asked Donel. The shopkeeper was almost done measuring out the grain, seed, and other staples that Duff and Jakob were trading for with the two deer and one large elk they had taken down in just the last day.

They planned to bring those supplies to the Highlanders who had just taken up residence around the newest broch that had been built, which was only a few leagues to the west. The stores would help them get through the next few weeks while they finished building their cottages, clearing the fields, and planting their first crops, along with completing the myriad other tasks that would need to be done to ensure that their village thrived just like the one Donel governed as elected mayor.

"You don't need to call me that, Donel," Jakob replied, the title making him uncomfortable. "I've never called myself that, and I'm not a lord. I'm just the son of a soldier."

Duff tried to hold back the laugh that threatened to break free. When he saw Jakob's crestfallen face at how Donel addressed him, he could barely contain himself.

Duff should have regretted what he had done, especially after seeing how it had first affected the lad. But as more time passed, Duff realized that there was no time for regrets. He knew in his heart that he had done the right thing.

The lad hated being the center of attention. Even more so, he hated being anything other than himself.

Duff appreciated Jakob's modesty. It had served him well in the past just as it would in the future.

But it would only be a matter of time before Jakob began to see in himself what others already saw in him. And when he did, he would realize that the moniker Duff had given him was an appropriate one. A necessary one, in fact, for what was coming next.

"Being the son of a soldier clearly is a worthy birthright," Donel countered with a laugh. "Get used to the title, Lord Kestrel. All this," the mayor said, motioning to the bustle of activity around the dozens of stalls set out around the broch, "wouldn't be possible without all that you've done for us."

"You give me too much credit, Donel."

"I give you the credit you deserve because you earned it," the mayor of Winsome said, his voice a bit stronger now, carrying the weight of his office. "Without you, we couldn't live as we do now. As we choose to live and not in fear. We couldn't take on the Wraiths and Stalkers as we do now. To say nothing of the slavers. We'd still be hiding in the tower whenever they came around."

"You should still be taking refuge in the broch when there's a need to do so," urged Duff.

The former Sergeant was quite pleased by Donel's comments, which were nothing more than the truth. Jakob's arrival and then his desire to clear the Highlands of the slavers, Stalkers, and Wraiths had served as the catalyst for the transformation that was going on within these rugged peaks.

Torstan Sharperson, Governor of the Highlands, hid within the Stone, ruling from afar. Or rather he was attempting to do so.

Jakob was out among the people, doing all that he could to help them.

He wanted nothing from them. That was plain.

Everyone who met him could see it. Everyone in the Highlands was drawn to him as a result.

He had a quiet charisma that he couldn't see himself, even as it drew others to him.

That was a unique and valuable trait, and one that Duff meant to make use of. Jakob willing of course.

Duff wouldn't force the lad to do what needed to be done. He wouldn't have to.

Jakob would see on his own what was required and accept the responsibility that would be thrust upon him. It was in his blood. His sense of right and wrong was too deeply ingrained for him to ignore the tasks that only he could accomplish.

"Have no fear of that, Duff. We know what to do." Donel filled one last bag with the seed that the Sergeant was trading for, nodding to his younger sons to tie all the bags with the cords hanging from a nail sticking out from the edge of his table so that they could be carried over a shoulder. "But it's because of you and the young Lord Kestrel that so much has changed so quickly. Just a few months ago, none of this would have been possible."

"You're right, Donel. A great deal has changed thanks to the Lord Kestrel."

"You too?" demanded Jakob, annoyed by Duff's use of the title that was becoming more common every time he visited a village, his friend clearly enjoying his irritation. "All that we've accomplished has come about because we have all contributed to our success. I have only done my part. No more, no less."

"I'm only speaking the truth, Lord Kestrel," said Duff, his previous expression of amusement replaced by a seriousness that usually only appeared right before a fight. "Yes, all of us have contributed. That can't be denied, nor should it. The success of one is the success of all. The Highlanders have done a great deal for the Highlanders."

Duff leaned in toward Jakob, willing him to understand before he continued. Because this next part was crucial if the Highlanders were to have any chance of not only building on, but also maintaining the success that they had achieved. "Even so, Donel speaks truly. None of all that we have accomplished would have been possible if not for you. We know it. You know it too. Sometimes, whether you like it or not, you have to accept praise when it's deserved."

The Highlanders had been surviving before Jakob walked out of the Murk and began to aid their efforts against the monsters hunting them. Now, however, thanks to Jakob's unique skills the Highlanders were beginning to thrive.

The brochs and other measures Duff and his friends had put in place gave the Highlanders what they needed to defend themselves. Jakob, with his application of the Talent and his sharp grasp of strategy, allowed them to do much more than that.

For the first time since the Murk smothered the peaks and the Stalkers haunted the shadows, the Highlanders could fight back. Of course, the fact that many of the people who had settled in the Highlands had some experience in the Royal Guard or one of the Duchy Guards certainly didn't hurt.

In Duff's opinion, the title that he had bestowed upon Jakob -- in jest at first, because of Jakob's habit of staring at the kestrels flying through the sky, but then with greater seriousness when he began to understand the value and impact of what Jakob was doing -- was more than appropriate. It was deserved.

Jakob had earned it. And now, Duff's naming of the young Magus had become much more than just a title.

Duff knew from experience that a name was more than just a name. It could help to craft a new identity. It could give a downtrodden people hope and a new purpose. And it could be used to challenge those seeking to claim what didn't belong to them.

"Are you sure that you never met my father?" grumbled Jakob, clearly not pleased by the Sergeant's very gentle scolding.

"I have no doubt that he was a very wise man," replied Duff.

"You give yourself too much credit."

"As I should," Duff replied with a grin, glad to see that Jakob wasn't to put out by what Duff had done and what it had led to.

Duff appreciated Jakob's humility and his ability to laugh at himself even under the most trying of circumstances. Those two traits were well entrenched within the son of the former soldier who, like it or not, because of his deeds and his words, was becoming much more than that.

"Might I bother you for a favor, Lord Kestrel?" asked Donel.

At first Jakob didn't respond. He knew what was happening. The moniker was sticking. He knew as well what could happen if he continued to allow it.

He glanced quickly at Duff, giving him a look that could freeze the fast-rushing water of the stream that ran down from the peak on the western edge of the valley in which he now stood.

Duff ignored Jakob's glower, his eyes tracking the kestrel circling high above them.

Perception and reality. Two key factors to success, both often indistinguishable. His former Captain of the Royal Guard had taught Duff that. And so far, the perception that Duff had crafted was slowly becoming the reality that he wanted.

"Last night we rang the bell. Stalkers."

"Did everyone get to safety?" Jakob thought that he might have heard the bell, even though they had made camp for the night several leagues distant.

"Everyone in the village, yes," Donel replied. "We employed the training and tactics that you taught us. As soon as we were certain that all were safe and we saw the tracks, a squad went hunting."

"The result?"

"We killed the Stalker, Lord Kestrel. That monster never had the chance to do anyone harm."

"That's excellent news," replied Jakob.

"Yes, we were quite pleased with our success," sighed Donel, the elation that Jakob and Duff were expecting from the mayor's small victory missing.

"But ..." prodded Jakob, seeking to break through Donel's hesitation.

"After the squad killed the Stalker, they scouted around the village. They found more tracks."

"You think there was more than one Stalker?"

"We know that Stalkers usually hunt alone, but the tracks suggested that there might be more than one of those creatures lurking about."

"Did the squad follow the tracks?"

"No, the sun was coming up. The Stalkers hunt at night and hole up during the day. We weren't concerned about another attack. At least not then. We were concerned about what might happen if we started poking around in the caves to the west. We set a stronger guard just in case."

Jakob closed his eyes for a moment, beginning to understand. "Who didn't make it to the market this morning?"

"They live in the opposite direction the tracks led. From what we could tell, the Stalkers were heading into the wilderness, not toward them. We didn't think there was cause for concern until they failed to arrive when they usually do."

"Who, Donel?" asked Duff, his expression grim.

"Matten and his family. They live a league to the north. He's a carpenter by trade. Most of us own a piece of furniture he made. And his wife sells herbs and ointments that are quite effective."

"They never miss the market?" asked Jakob.

Donel shook his head sadly. "Never. Not even when one of their children is sick. One of them always makes it. Their sales here are a large part of their income."

Jakob turned to Duff. "Are you thinking what I'm thinking?"

"I am, unfortunately."

"Do you think Benyen can pick up the trail?"

"If he can't, then no one can."

"They were protecting their children," whispered Benyen.

The tracker stared a few seconds more through the shattered oak door into the room beyond before turning away. His face was white, his expression murderous. He was thinking of his own children.

"Why don't you take a look around, Benyen," Duff said quietly, grasping the soldier's shoulder warmly. "See what you can find."

Benyen nodded, closing his eyes and taking a deep breath before stalking off between the trees that rose right next to the small cottage. He hadn't known these Highlanders, but that didn't matter. They certainly hadn't deserved this. No one deserved this.

He would find the trail. He needed to. It was the only way to gain the vengeance that these good folks deserved.

Duff and Jakob stepped up onto the porch, pushing the broken door to the side. The scrape of the shattered wood across the doorstep sounded unnaturally loud in the silence that had fallen within the surrounding trees.

It only took a few seconds for them to determine the flow of events that composed this tragedy.

Matten and his wife had died right at the entrance to their home. They likely hoped that the door would hold.

They realized in seconds that it wouldn't. It couldn't. Their attacker was too powerful.

When the Stalker broke through the heavy oak, they did the best that they could to keep the monster from entering their home. Their efforts probably lasted for only a few seconds. Trained soldiers fighting on their own usually had little success against these monsters, and Matten and his wife hadn't been soldiers.

His wife's throat had been cut, the ragged slash confirming that the Stalker had run one of its claws across the soft flesh. A horrible death, and the terror in her staring eyes was still visible.

Although Jakob believed her terror wasn't for herself. Rather, it was for her family. For her children.

She hadn't gone down without a fight, however. She had gotten in a few good cuts of her own before she died. The dark blood that had congealed on the small cleaver she still held in her right hand testified to her success.

Matten had died next to his wife. He still held his sword in his left hand. The dagger that he carried in his right had slipped from his grip and lay between the couple.

The carpenter had enjoyed some success as well against their assailant. The same black blood stained the steel of his sword from tip to hilt.

Unfortunately, his efforts hadn't been enough. The Stalker had ripped open his chest, revealing in several places the white bone of his ribs.

"With any luck, Matten severely wounded the Stalker if he didn't kill it outright," said Jakob, nodding toward the sword. The blood on the blade suggested that the Highlander had skewered the beast, although whether chest or gut rather than leg or arm he couldn't say with any certainty.

"Aye," agreed Duff. "Though we can't count on luck when dealing with these monsters."

Martin stepped up next to them, only taking a brief glimpse of the murdered couple, not really desiring to see more. He didn't need this scene plaguing his dreams like all the others from his time while serving in the Royal Guard. "Where are the children?"

Duff and Jakob looked at one another. That question had been playing through both their minds as well.

Tommie stood at the bottom of the porch, arrow nocked to the string of her bow, her spectacles still in the leather pouch that hung around her neck.

The archer didn't think they'd face any additional threats here, not with Jakob having the ability to search around them and offer a warning if there was need. Still, better to be safe. Better to stick to her training.

Bertie was circling through the woods, moving in the opposite direction to Benyen. He hoped to speed up the process for finding the Stalker's tracks. He hadn't seen what had happened within the cottage, and after taking one look at Benyen's face, he didn't want to know.

"Stay here," said Jakob.

He pulled a bone white, double-bladed dagger from the sheath on his back, then stepped into the house. He avoided the door that hung from a single hinge, careful not to disturb the fallen Highlanders.

Duff followed, a dagger in his right hand.

They searched the small cottage quickly. Besides the kitchen and the family room, there was a bedroom at the back.

They didn't find anything useful.

The ladder off to their right that led to the loft beckoned.

Jakob climbed slowly, quietly, not feeling the need to rush. Not wanting to disturb the silence.

When he poked his head above the top of the rail, a wall of shadows hindered his gaze. Only a thin stream of dim light from the small window at the far end provided any illumination. It wasn't enough for him to see with any clarity, even with his flashing green eyes.

Calling on the Talent, he sent a small ball of light drifting through the large space.

Jakob identified the struts of the roof and the ceiling above. Matten certainly knew his craft. The woodworking was impressive.

Jakob judged the space in the loft that had served as the children's bedroom to be almost as large as the kitchen and the family room below.

He stepped up onto the landing, crouching so that he didn't hit his head on one of the beams. As he walked farther into the loft, he found what he hoped that he wouldn't find.

In the floor. Several deep gouges in the wood that ran all the way to the small window and then back again.

The Stalker had killed Matten and his wife and then searched up here as well. Yet nothing had been disturbed. There was nothing to suggest that the Stalker had found the prey that it had been seeking.

"Anything?" called Duff.

Jakob took one more look around before heading back toward the ladder. The children had been up here when the Stalker had attacked at the door. He was certain of that.

They had been sleeping. They had left their bedrolls quickly, the blankets strewn about, the toys still scattered across the floor.

Somehow the children had gotten out of the house before the Stalker could take them. Or so he hoped, since there was no sign of a struggle here or in any of the other rooms. No trail of blood that suggested that the Stalker had found them.

All five of them must have escaped. He had to believe that. He didn't want to think about what had occurred if he was wrong.

So where did they go?

"No," Jakob replied from the loft. He slid down the ladder, his dagger still in his hand. He turned his head slowly, taking in the family room.

Seeing everything and seeing nothing both at the same time. Just allowing his eyes and senses to roam.

It had to be close, Jakob thought. The children wouldn't have had much time to get down from the loft and go wherever they went to escape the Stalker, because it hadn't taken the monster very long to break through the door.

Maybe two or three kicks based on what Jakob had seen

when he examined the frame before walking into the cottage. Then another minute, maybe two at most, before the monster was past Matten and his wife.

Yes, it had to be close. Easy to hide. Easy to access. Easy to open. Just as easy to close behind them.

That's why Matten and his wife had died right in front of the door. They weren't just trying to protect their children. They were also attempting to give them the time that they needed to escape.

Just to be certain, Jakob started in the kitchen, walking slowly, eyes scanning everything around him. Then the bedroom in the back. Nothing caught his attention, so he headed back into the family room.

"What are you doing?" asked Duff.

Jakob ignored him, his gaze settling on a large table that had been pushed up against the far wall. There was a rug beneath it, the edge caught under one of the legs.

The house was immaculately clean. The only mess that was allowed had been up in the loft. Everything else had a place and was put in it. The rug bunched up under the table leg was the only anomaly.

The table had been pushed there quickly. It didn't belong there. Jakob could tell by the scratches along the floor that it belonged in the center of the family room.

He walked over to the table, then kneeled down, studying the floor beneath it.

"Jakob, what are you doing?" asked Duff.

Martin had poked his head through the doorway, curious as well as to what was taking them so long.

"Five children were here when the Stalker attacked," Jakob replied, his eyes finally locating what he was seeking. It was barely visible, and he would have missed it entirely if he hadn't known what he was looking for. "They aren't here anymore."

"The Stalker got them?" asked Martin, the thought of that

turning him green. Even veteran soldiers had a difficult time contemplating the violent death of a child.

"No," Jakob replied softly, a tinge of hope in his voice. He pushed himself back to his feet and sheathed his dagger.

Then he grasped the large table with both hands and pushed it away from the wall and toward the fireplace that had gone cold sometime during the night. Kneeling back down, he rolled up the rug where it had curled up on itself.

The floor beneath looked no different than anywhere else in the house. Except for that one tiny spot that he had almost missed.

Jakob reached for the Talent once again, extending his senses down below the cottage. He needed to make sure. He wanted to avoid any nasty surprises.

Nodding to himself that nothing waited for him beneath, he pushed down with a single finger on the small indentation. When he heard the click, he reached down with his other hand, pulling up the small cord that had been crafted into the floor and was only visible once Jakob had released the locking mechanism.

Clearly, Matten was quite skilled in his craft, as Jakob had seen when examining the door, which by all rights should have been flung from its hinges the first time that the Stalker had struck it.

But that hadn't happened because Matten had fashioned small pegs that ran along the frame that he had locked in place before the Stalker had attacked. The door had held through several more blows, and his and his wife's quick thinking and brave actions had allowed their children to get away.

Duff stood just over his shoulder when Jakob pulled up on the string, Martin coming up behind them. Jakob lifted up a small section of the floor, revealing a square of black.

"How did you know?" asked Duff.

Ingenious. And just large enough for a child or a small woman. A Stalker would never fit in this opening.

"I guessed," Jakob said quietly. "I'm just glad that I was right."

"What do you want to do?" None of their company would fit down in the tunnel.

"I'll follow it with the Talent. Then Benyen can take us to where the path comes up out of the ground," said Jakob. "Five children made it into the tunnel. Hopefully all five made it out safely and are still alive."

"IT COMES OUT JUST UP AHEAD," said Benyen. Duff, Jakob, and the other Highlanders followed behind the tracker. "This carpenter really knew what he was doing. You'd have no way to find it unless you knew exactly where to look."

Jakob already knew what he was going to find when they got there, having used the Talent to search ahead. He had been worried that they would come upon a gruesome slaughter.

Thankfully not. At least not yet.

His eyes followed the set of tracks that led away from the cottage. Several of the leaves that were larger than the shields favored by the soldiers of Caledonia that had fallen from the heart trees were crushed into the mud by large, clawed feet.

He had given Benyen the direction to follow, tracking the tunnel that ran about ten feet below the ground. He hadn't seen anyone still in the tunnel, so he assumed that all the children at least made it to the exit.

How far they had gotten after that, though, he had not yet determined.

The Highlanders came to a stop about one hundred yards from the cottage.

For some inexplicable reason there was a large boulder

resting on the ground. How it had gotten there, none of them having seen any rocky outcroppings since they had come this way from the village, was anyone's guess.

On the north side of the boulder, the side facing away from the cottage, there was a small patch of ferns that rose to the height of a tall man.

Benyen pushed some of the stalks away, already having searched the area. Jakob and Duff leaned in first, the other Highlanders taking a peek after the two had stepped back. There was a slit in the ground right beneath the base of the boulder. Again, just large enough for a child.

Jakob and Duff shifted their focus toward the north. They took a few steps, both staring at the soggy ground, yesterday afternoon's rain making their search much easier.

"They went that way," said Benyen, who came to stand next to them. He nodded toward the small imprints in the mud that led off through the wood, only the thick roots curling along the ground preventing them from identifying the very obvious path. "They at least made it this far."

"Yes, but how far did they get?" wondered Bertie, voicing the concern that played through all their minds.

They could all easily make out the Stalker's unmistakable prints that were mixed in with those of the children. The monster had found the trail and followed it.

"We might already be too late," whispered Martin, hoping that he wasn't right.

"That doesn't matter," said Jakob, his left hand tight on the grip of his bow. "Come what may, we find them."

"We find them," agreed Duff. The other Highlanders nodded their heads in agreement. "The Stalker as well. That monster needs to die."

Benyen took the lead, having little difficulty following the trail that led them in a consistent direction deeper into the wood. The children only diverged from the way they were going when a heart tree got in the way.

The path, which had been getting more difficult to see because the ground had become rockier, gradually sloped up toward a peak that put this section of the wood in a perpetual shadow at this time of the afternoon. The tracker didn't end his pursuit until almost an hour had passed, a massive heart tree near the top of the slope now blocking their way.

Benyen scouted to both sides, not rushing. Then he took another minute to swing around the hundred-foot circumference of the tree trunk.

He needed to make sure. At first, he didn't bother to say anything, just shaking his head.

"Nothing," he said. "The trail ends here."

Jakob stepped forward then, slowly approaching the trunk of the heart tree. Nothing caught his eye as he examined the massive conifer. Thinking back to what he had done in Matten's cottage to find the hidden tunnel, he took a similar approach now.

Clearing his mind. Closing his eyes. Running his hand along the bark.

Just because he couldn't see it didn't mean that it wasn't there. Not if Matten had once again demonstrated his unique inventiveness.

He knelt, his hand running along the bark just a few feet off the ground.

"What are you doing?" asked Duff.

Jakob held up his bow, a sign for the former Sergeant to give him a moment so that he could concentrate. He continued as he was doing, taking his time, allowing his fingers to slide across the rough bark.

He didn't see any claw marks in the wood. A good sign, perhaps. But he had yet to find the imperfection that he desperately hoped was there.

With a start, Jakob's hand stopped. He smiled.

Matten not only was a skilled carpenter but also a clever one. That much had been obvious. Why not do here as well what he had done to hide the tunnel beneath his home?

Pushing in on the small hole with just his pinkie finger, there was a soft click. A piece of wood disguised as bark swung out from the tree trunk.

"How did you know?" asked Bertie, amazed as he watched Jakob trail his hand a foot up the bark from the first rung, pushing in again on a small hole that was hidden by the shadow, another wooden bar swinging out and locking in place that when it was a part of the tree perfectly resembled the bark.

And then one more, and another, until finally there were ten steps sticking out from the trunk of the heart tree that gave access to the lowest branch that was about twenty feet above the ground. Once the children gained the limb, they would have little trouble reaching whatever hideaway their father had constructed for them farther up in the heart tree.

"I didn't know for sure," replied Jakob, shrugging his shoulders, simply glad that he had been right. "I just guessed based on what we found in the cottage."

The Highlanders stared up into the branches above them. They couldn't see much at all but for the large tree limbs fading into a murky darkness the farther up they gazed.

"Are they up there?" asked Martin.

Jakob extended his senses up into the tree. Fifty feet. One hundred feet. Nothing.

He was getting worried. Another fifty feet. Still nothing. Two hundred feet, about two thirds up the ancient heart tree.

He smiled, nodding to Martin. "They are. All five."

"Finally, some good news," he sighed, his relief plain.

The Highlander's eyes widened in shock before he even finished what he was going to say. Jakob had spun toward him so fast that he scarcely was able to follow the movement.

"Down!" Jakob shouted, bow raised, arrow already pulled from the sheath on his back and nocked to the string.

Martin crouched instinctively, although he was no more than a few inches closer to the ground when Jakob released. The steel-tipped shaft streaked through the air just above Martin's head.

The Highlander didn't need to turn and look to know that Jakob had hit his target, the punch of the barb slamming into the Stalker's chest sounding incredibly loud in the silent wood.

The force of the strike, Jakob shooting from only a dozen yards away, knocked the Stalker backwards, the monster collapsing against the bark of the heart tree to their right.

For just a heartbeat, all was silent again in the wood, the arrow sticking out from the Stalker's chest, a bloody wound visible on the beast's right side. Matten's work.

In an eruption of motion, the Stalker jumped up from the ground, shrieking in rage. The monster crouched so that it could leap toward its attacker.

The Stalker remained on its clawed feet for less than a second more, a second arrow sprouting from its right eye. The force of the blow snapped the Stalker's head back against the heart tree.

For just a breath the monster remained upright, wobbling, then fell backward again, crumpling against the massive roots that twisted away from the heart tree and across the ground.

Jakob took a deep breath, calming his nerves. His hands had been in the process of placing another shaft to his string, knowing that he wouldn't have been fast enough to fire again.

Thankfully, Tommie had been ready. The archer stood on one of those large, twisting roots, about six feet off the ground, using her perch to shoot right over Jakob's shoulder.

Jakob turned toward Tommie, offering her a nod of grati- tude. "You know, I'm really glad that you're not wearing your spectacles."

"WE NEED TO MOVE FASTER," urged Duff.

Jakob and the other Highlanders had found Matten's five children hiding in the heart tree. It had taken quite a while to get the three boys and two girls all back down on the ground.

Duff climbing up the branches first probably hadn't been the best idea. The children found his scarred visage almost as frightening as that of the Stalker. The oldest child, upon looking through the peep hole, refused to open the door to the large cubby their father had carved out of the trunk, not trusting him.

The Sergeant had scowled and cursed all the way back down. Not at the children. He could understand their hesitation.

Rather, he should have thought about what the reaction by a gaggle of terrified children might be and sent one of the other Highlanders up first. That mistake cost them valuable time.

The children didn't exit their hidey hole until Martin climbed up the several dozen limbs to reach where they were located, gaining their confidence with a big smile and some sweets that he found in his pocket that he had forgotten to give to his own children.

They lost more time on the climb down, Martin, Bertie, and Tommie needing to carry the younger ones.

Duff really couldn't blame the children. They had been through a great deal in just the last day, their terror still fresh and their fear always just on the edge of their awareness.

The children had seen the Stalker before slipping into the tunnel beneath their home, the monster about to break through the door. Duff was thankful that they were already gone before the Stalker killed their parents. If they had caught sight of that, they probably wouldn't have made it very far beyond the tunnel.

The oldest was only eight, the youngest four. Somehow, despite the harrowing nature of their situation, they had followed their father's instructions and made their way through the dark of night to get to this place of safety even though the Stalker was still hunting for them.

They had seen the monster again, the oldest said. Although not before they had all made it up into the heart tree.

Because of that, Martin hadn't been able to convince the oldest boy to allow his siblings to climb down until he had promised that he would show him the dead Stalker.

When the Stalker had remained near the bottom of the heart tree, the oldest boy had watched from outside their shelter for a time, worried that the creature would come after them. But it hadn't.

He didn't know why. The Stalker hunted around the base of the tree for a time and then stalked off into the gloom.

Either waiting for the children to come back down or for whomever might come after them, Duff assumed. A worrying thought. It demonstrated a cunning that Duff really didn't want to consider in that moment, having other things on his mind.

"I'm going as fast as I can," said Bertie. He was carrying the oldest boy on his shoulders, huffing and puffing his way through the thickening fog. "I haven't had to do this for quite a while."

"None of us have done this for quite some time," said Martin, running just ahead of Bertie. "You let yourself go and it's catching up to you."

"Winnie's a good cook," Bertie gasped. He didn't feel the need or the desire to defend himself, as he would be the first to admit that he'd put on a few pounds since leaving the Royal Guard and marrying his wife. "I don't want her to think I don't like the meals she makes for me."

"You can still eat," said Martin, the blacksmith looking no different than he had when he retired from the Royal Guard.

"Just don't eat so much. Winnie won't mind. And then maybe she'll be able put her arms around your waist again."

"Why are you talking about Winnie and my waist?" demanded Bertie, his voice taking on a dangerous tone, one that used to appear with greater frequency when he was younger, less so now.

"Just making a point," laughed Martin, who increased his pace, pleased to see that his needling Bertie had done the trick. His friend had forgotten his struggles as they ran through the wood, more interested in staying close to Martin so that he could give him a piece of his mind.

The Highlanders had been in a race ever since Martin had gotten the last of the children back onto the ground. That was when the first few faint wisps of the Murk began to drift through the forest.

Duff had hoped that they had gotten through the hardest part of their mission when they killed the Stalker. He should have known better, revising his perspective when he saw how swiftly the fog smothered the land, leaving them in a grey haze that turned them all into dim shadows at a distance of only a few feet.

The Murk was a challenge, but the Highlanders could manage that. What came with the mist was the greater concern.

Jakob had sensed the Wraiths immediately. The monsters were at the very cusp of the Murk, no more than a mile away from its grasping tendrils. Worse, they were coming fast.

That fact only added an even heavier weight to an already urgent situation.

To aid them in their goal of making it back safely to the broch, Jakob used the Talent to connect to Duff and the other Highlanders.

Now, thanks to Jakob's use of natural magic, they all could see what he saw. They could navigate the Murk as if it wasn't even there, needing only to worry about avoiding the massive roots that twisted out from the heart trees and turned the ground around them into an obstacle course, the challenge of making their way through it one that they really would have preferred to avoid with the lethal danger pursuing them.

Under most circumstances, because of the gift that Jakob gave them, they wouldn't have been concerned by the half dozen Wraiths coming their way. At least not overly so.

They had fought the Wraiths before with Jakob employing the Talent. All of them were chomping at the bit to have another go at the monsters in a fair combat, still relishing their most recent success.

But they couldn't do that. Not now.

They had a more overriding concern. They needed to get Matten's children to the broch before the Wraiths caught up to them, because they doubted that they could defend themselves and the children at the same time what with the monsters' remarkable agility and speed.

If they were to challenge such creatures, they needed to do so free to move and free to fight.

"They're coming faster now," said Jakob. "Just a few hundred yards behind us and gaining."

That bit of expected news gave the Highlanders another short burst of energy, running even faster as they dodged, jumped, or climbed over the roots as best as they could, each of them carrying a child. None of them wanted to think about what might happen if they were caught out by the Wraiths.

"Only one hundred yards now," Jakob called out just a minute later, not really needing to since the other Highlanders could track the location of their pursuers themselves.

Still, the announcement made the Highlanders pump their legs just a little faster, Tommie cursing as her foot caught the top of the root she was hurdling over. She stumbled when she hit the ground, almost dropping the little girl she was holding tightly in her arms. Somehow, she kept her feet, continuing to follow after her companions, not wanting to fall too far behind.

Just then, the Highlanders emerged from the forest. Escaping the last of the roots, they sprinted toward the boundary of the village that was just a few hundred yards to their front.

They reached the trail that led through the hamlet at the exact same moment the first Wraith emerged from the wood behind them. The other monsters were about fifty yards behind the scout.

They could turn and fight, but the safety of the children had to come first. That knowledge giving them another burst of speed, they raced down the path toward the broch.

"Come on, lads and lass!" urged Duff. "You can do it. We're almost there."

The Sergeant was right. Even though the scout and the Wraiths behind him were gaining, the green that circled the tower was just ahead. They would get to the broch before the Wraiths made it onto the grass.

Even so, Jakob knew that despite their best efforts it wouldn't be enough. The broch would be sealed by now. The only way to get inside would be a rope thrown down from the parapet.

The children wouldn't be able to climb to the top on their own. Duff and the other Highlanders would need to help them.

The Wraiths would be on them before the first of their small group even started climbing.

That meant that to ensure that these children didn't meet the same gruesome fate as their parents did, they needed time. A boon that the Wraiths wouldn't grant them, but perhaps Jakob could.

"Here," Jakob said when they reached the edge of the green, handing the little girl he was carrying to Duff. "Take her. I'll slow them down. I'll come after you once you get them all into the tower."

"What do you think you're doing?" questioned Duff as he skidded to a halt, having no choice but to take the little girl and cradle her to his chest, her older brother riding Duff's back. "How are you going to take on a half dozen of these monsters all by yourself? We can't stay with you. We need to climb the broch to get the children inside."

"I know," Jakob replied, already turning to face the Wraith scout even though he was only about fifty yards from the broch. "You need time. I can give that to you. However many Wraiths I need to take on doesn't matter. Just get the children inside."

"Jakob, you can't ..."

"Just get them inside, Duff." Jakob's voice was hard, his green eyes blazing brightly in the Murk. "This isn't the first time I've done this. I'll buy you the time you need. Now go!"

Duff was going to argue Jakob's decision some more, but he realized that giving in to that desire would do nothing other than ensure that several of them died rather than possibly just one. Shaking his head in frustration, he muttered, "I named you too well."

Offering Jakob a nod, he sped off.

Duff could sense where the Wraiths were. Jakob was right. They would need time to get the children to safety.

As he ran up to the stone of the broch, the other Highlanders already there, Tommie having begun the ascent with the rope that Donel and the Highlanders above had thrown down, Duff promised himself that if the Wraiths didn't kill Jakob, when this was all over he'd kill the lad himself for taking such a foolish risk.

Jakob couldn't seem to stop himself from playing the hero.

Blast it!

13

TAKING CONTROL

"Where is Kendric?" demanded Hakea Roosarian. "He called this meeting. He should be here."

"My husband, Lord Winborne, is where he needs to be," Ursina replied with a warm smile, although that warmth was absent from her frigid eyes.

"Your husband, Lord Winborne," said Hakea, a hint of spite coloring her tone, "needs to be here."

"My husband needs to be where he needs to be," Ursina repeated, her cool tone suggesting that she was unaffected by the younger woman's bad temper.

Hakea stared at Ursina for several seconds, her expression shifting from testiness to confusion. "What does that even mean?"

Ursina gave Hakea a sly smile, but she didn't reply immediately. She didn't really want to be here herself, although she knew that it couldn't be helped. And despite the location and the company, she was enjoying herself in a twisted sort of way.

She stood with Hakea Roosarian and Torstan Sharperson that frosty morning on the floating pier in one of the hidden coves along the New Caledonian coast that was called Smuggler's Cove. The name stayed the same, though the location changed weekly.

She had developed the system for several reasons. One of which was to give the Governors of the Eastern Territories a place to meet away from prying eyes. Where their plans within plans could be pursued without having to worry about being discovered by those who might try to thwart them. Without having to deal with people wondering why they were meeting distinct from the two times a year that all the Governors of the Territories were supposed to gather and deal with any issues relevant to New Caledonia.

Her frigate and those belonging to Sharperson and Roosarian were tied up on three sides of the dock. The open berth allowed the frigid wind to maneuver its way through the gap in the cliffs that led out to the Sea of Mist and strike her full force in the face.

The cold felt good after being cooped up in her cabin during the voyage of almost a day to get there. There were faster ways that she could have used to make the journey, but it was much too early to reveal all that she could do to these two. If she ever did.

For the thousandth time Ursina wondered how much longer this partnership needed to continue.

Roosarian and Sharperson had been given their power. They hadn't earned it.

As a result, they didn't know how to exercise their power. Rather, they only played with it. And poorly at that.

They were weak, which was why Ursina didn't mind being there. It served her purposes because they continued to serve her purposes. For now.

Nevertheless, a lesson was needed. A correction of sorts.

The icy stab that shot through the gap in the cliffs made Ursina smile. She studied Hakea for a few heartbeats.

The woman was shivering despite her wearing two heavy

coats and a cowled cloak. Hakea's biggest challenge was speaking and preventing her teeth from chattering. She was desperately trying to keep her two companions from knowing and taking any pleasure in how badly the cold was affecting her.

Ursina shook her head sadly, knowing what was going through Hakea's mind. She believed that demonstrating the impact of the cold could be perceived as a sign of weakness, and that was something that the Governor of Fal Carrach would never allow, especially not with Ursina and Sharperson standing there with her on the dock.

Hakea believed that their designs were much the same as hers. To become the most powerful Governor in New Caledonia. And then, perhaps, to become more than that.

Yet Hakea didn't seem to realize that her ambitions were built on a deck of cards.

Ursina watched Hakea fight her losing battle with the cold for a few seconds more. Foolish child. The woman had no concept of what real power was. She had no idea as to the true extent of Ursina's ambition. Of what she would do to achieve her objectives.

"He was unavoidably detained," Ursina replied in a calm voice that mimicked her mendaciously gentle eyes. "But have no fear. With me here, we can conduct our necessary business and be on our way. Clearly the weather doesn't suit you, my dear. We certainly don't want you to catch cold."

Ursina smiled sweetly at Hakea, taking a good deal of pleasure from how her veiled barb stoked the Governor of Fal Carrach's rising anger. Predictable.

A little discomfort and the woman gave free rein to her worst emotions rather than keeping them tightly under control. How very sad.

Hakea seemed to believe that anger was a sign of strength. As Ursina had learned the hard way, it was anything but.

She understood that allowing the venom that she so wanted to lace into her voice would offer her little benefit. In fact, it would only complicate matters more than they already were.

Better to keep your opponents and your partners, since there was rarely little difference between the two, off balance. Better to stay calm and composed at all times.

Ursina's words and posture certainly were designed to do just that. She was quite skilled in assuming and then maintaining the appearance of a kindly aunt, a caretaker for all those with her.

Always ready to give a kind word or necessary, gentle nudge to ensure their agreed upon plans continued to move forward, even when the circumstances swirling around her made it so difficult for her to do so when she would have much preferred to lash out instead. Just as was the case now.

She had grown tired of having to deal with these two pups playing a game they truly didn't understand. Yet she had no choice in the matter because of their grants from the Caledonian Crown.

She and Kendric were not in a position to adjust the parameters of their partnership. Not yet anyway.

So for the time being she allowed Hakea's irritation to wash off her, taking a great deal of pleasure in how easily her verbal jab had struck the arrogant and self-absorbed woman. Although she had expected as much. Hakea's anger seemed more forced than real, the Governor of Fal Carrach unable to function without it.

Demonstrating such patience as she was now could be tedious. Ursina would be the first to admit that.

It was made easier because she could sense that the time that she had been waiting for was almost upon her. Better to do it when her husband wasn't with her, so that their two supposed allies could better comprehend where the real power of this partnership rested.

"What could possibly be more important than this meeting?" challenged Hakea.

Ursina almost gave in to her desire right then. Yet still she held back. At least for a little while longer. If for no other reason than to test her strength of will. Another skill that she had practiced and improved upon over the years.

She believed, in fact, that if not for her determination, her unwavering need to achieve the goals she set for herself, she likely wouldn't be where she was now. She was certain that she would have crossed to the other side, and in the opinions of those seeking her death deservedly so.

"He battles the Wraiths who hunt in the Murk," Ursina replied serenely, giving Hakea a sweet smile that the other member of their trio almost snorted at. He stopped himself just in time, covering up his indiscretion with a cough.

Ursina shifted her gaze to the Governor of the Highlands, who had swathed his tall and broad frame in more robes and cloaks than she could count. Whether because of the cold or to hide his bulk, she didn't really know. Probably both.

She could tell that Torstan Sharperson was relishing how her tone and expression upset Hakea. Ursina nodded to herself.

She realized then that she had misjudged the young man. Hakea was straightforward with respect to her desires. A bull who would trample whatever lay before her to gain what she wanted.

Not so Torstan. Although his size suggested that he should be the bull, instead she viewed him as a snake, slithering around and over obstacles until he gained what he desired without revealing his true intentions until the very end.

Ursina could see that Sharperson knew what she was doing. He was enjoying her performance. He also knew that Ursina wasn't all that she seemed.

She realized that she would need to put him in his place.

She couldn't have him waiting in the shadows to stab her in the back.

"He's focusing on the Wraiths?" asked Torstan. "Have they not been dealt with yet? Last time we spoke, you said that ..."

"Must I repeat myself?" Ursina stared daggers at the young Lord.

Ursina observed the emotions playing across his face. Despite the fact that he stood half again as tall as she was, with just a few words and a look she had made him shrink in upon himself.

Watching him, it was clear that he hated the fact that he couldn't stop what he was doing, his shoulders curling, his back hunching. Hated her since she was the cause. Despised himself for his weakness.

That didn't bother Ursina in the least. That anger would make dealing with him much easier. In her experience, anger could quickly turn into fear when the correct amount of pressure was applied at the right point.

Ursina could tell quite clearly what was running through Torstan's mind as she refused to release his eyes with her own. Her gentle smile quirked just a little bit. Yes, this was going to be just as easy as she assumed that it would be.

He was really no different than Hakea. He had no idea what real strength was.

She believed that Torstan should have worn a knit cap with this frigid air blasting into the cove. His bald head was turning red and becoming chapped. She didn't think that frostbite would be that far behind if he didn't get out of the cold soon. Although his decision in that regard didn't surprise her and it would, in fact, aid her.

These two were all about appearances. Because of their youth and lack of experience they had yet to realize the importance of working from the shadows.

Why be the center of attention when that only ensured that

many more inquisitive and perhaps even grasping hands tried to latch on to you?

It was that callowness that prevented them from realizing that perception wasn't as important as reality if you had the means to control that reality.

"He fights the Wraiths," she continued. "Those monsters in the mist have become a major concern for Shadow's Reach. My husband is dealing with those nasty creatures so that they will no longer be a concern. That is why I am here in his place. What he does now in the Northern Territory he does for all of us."

"That's all well and good," said Torstan, trying to lift himself out of his self-imposed hunch so that he could claim a stronger position in this conversation. "And we certainly ..." Torstan's words drifted off as Ursina's sharp gaze caught his eyes. His shoulders came together again, and he started to bend even more at the waist. "And we certainly value the contribution that Lord Winborne is making to our partnership and to the Territories as a whole ..."

"But?" interrupted Ursina, her voice cold now, her feigned warmth vanishing in an instant, her patience draining away, replaced by a hardened, imposing imperiousness.

She was playing with the boy. That was true. But all for a good reason. It would get her closer to where she needed to go that much faster.

"But, with all that we need to discuss, all the challenges that we must overcome, it's just that ... you know, we need to ..."

"What the big lummox is trying to ask, Ursina, but can't because even as we speak his head is freezing into a massive ball of ice, is how are we supposed to get anything done without Kendric here?" demanded Hakea, her temper having increased from a simmer to a boil. A frequent occurrence whenever events weren't playing out in her favor. "Kendric is the partner in our little group. Not you. He is the Governor. He's the only one who can speak for the Northern Territory."

Ursina turned her keen eyes away from Torstan Sharperson, who had been sagging even more under her keen gaze, and toward Hakea Roosarian.

She didn't say anything. She didn't need to. It wasn't long before Hakea, after a great deal of effort, pulled her eyes away and looked down at the pier, taking an inordinate amount of interest in the wood. She began to shuffle her feet then.

The Lady of Shadow's Reach shook her head slowly, more in disappointment than anger. In just seconds, with just a glance, the dynamics of their relationship had changed. If Hakea had been a dog, she would have been lying on her back, exposing her belly, acknowledging Ursina as the leader of the pack.

These two pups truly were fools. They played with power, yet they did not really know how to use it. When to use it. When not to use it. And she doubted that they ever would.

That lack of understanding and impetuousness made what Ursina needed to do to ensure her success and that of her husband all the more difficult at times.

The need for the constant mind games, the coddling shifting to an iron hand and then back again, was exhausting.

Then again, better to deal with challenges such as those rather than having to scale more difficult obstacles that could have been put forward if these two were versed in the ways of power and wily to its many applications. It just meant that she would need to exercise greater patience in order to do what needed to be done.

She had done so before. She could do so again.

No matter how much it might pain her. Because she was getting closer and closer to achieving the goal that had been driving her ever since she set foot in the Territories.

"I am the Lady Winborne, and I speak for the Lord

Winborne," she replied, biting out the words so that Hakea understood that she would require formality when the young woman spoke to her and of her husband. "We are of the same mind on all matters of import. Is that clear, Hakea?"

"So you say, although I still don't understand the purpose of this meeting," replied the Governor of Fal Carrach, trying one last time to exercise her authority, which she felt draining away from her the longer she engaged with the older woman. "Why is it that Lord Winborne required that we meet here even though he couldn't?"

Ursina offered Hakea a serene gaze. Clearly, Hakea had not recognized or had ignored the warning signs that revealed that she was swiftly losing patience with her behavior. Either she was a fool or simply difficult. Likely both, Ursina believed.

"A matter of some urgency, Hakea. Why else would we all be here?"

Ursina offered nothing more beyond that. She knew that she was being petty. That she was treating the Governor of Fal Carrach much like a mother disappointed in her child would when that child was proving to be difficult.

Still, she couldn't help herself. Besides, it was necessary to put Hakea in the appropriate mood.

She would make Hakea pull the information from her. The effort required to do that would only irritate the Governor of Fal Carrach even more, which would prove useful to her purposes later in the conversation.

"Which would be?"

"Did I not mention it, my dear? I'm sorry, but with all these questions wasting what little time we have, I must have lost track."

Hakea bit back a harsh reply, seething at Ursina's masked disrespect.

Ursina broadened her smile, wanting to stick the needle in a little farther. She saw the impact her self-satisfied expression was having. Hakea's fury was continuing to build, and she was fighting to maintain control over her temper a little while longer, her face turning red from the effort.

"You did not."

"I'm so sorry, my dear," Ursina replied sweetly, as if she missed entirely Hakea's dissatisfaction.

Yet Ursina offered nothing else beyond that, making Hakea and Torstan continue to wait. Hakea's eyes began to bulge, her temper threatening to get the better of her. Just heartbeats away from bubbling free. Just as Ursina wanted.

Ursina was slightly amused when Torstan decided to step in before that happened. Obviously, he was cold. Freezing.

But he wasn't a fool. That much was obvious to her.

He knew what Ursina was doing to Hakea, and he believed that Hakea deserved it. So he didn't begrudge Ursina having her fun. But he had no desire to deal with the repercussions if Hakea lost her temper.

Ursina nodded to herself, realizing that Torstan was the more dangerous of the two. Smarter as well.

He just wanted to be done with this meeting and go. And not just because of the cold.

He could tell that something was going on here that he didn't understand, although he did understand that whatever it was, it wasn't a good thing for him.

Just then Ursina locked eyes with the Governor of the Highlands. It was there in the back. He saw the truth. He had figured her out, but he didn't want her to know that he did, hoping to avoid any unpleasant repercussions that might be associated with his newfound knowledge.

Ursina put herself forward as nothing more than a kind friend, someone who functioned as an intermediary to ensure that all was working as it should, always there to offer assistance if there was need.

Torstan had just recognized it for the farce that it was. He sensed the steel within her, and he was worried about what would happen if Ursina chose to remove the velvet that hid that steel.

Ursina watched all that play across his features, even as he tried to keep it to himself.

Good. That's exactly what she wanted him to see. It would make using Torstan that much easier.

"The problem that you and Lord Winborne have identified?" asked Torstan in as calm and composed a voice as he could manage after the terrible realization that had just struck him. "Would you be kind enough to tell us?"

The tension was building around him, building within him as well. And he didn't like it. He liked it even less than the frigid air whipping about the floating pier. So, he sought to dampen it if he could.

"Of course, Torstan, again my apologies," Ursina replied, the sweetness in her tone almost dripping out of her voice like syrup. "How could I not after being asked so respectfully." Ursina waited a few seconds more just to make her point once again, enjoying how Hakea fidgeted and so obviously struggled to contain her rage, before finally answering. "His niece is scheduled to arrive in Ballinasloe."

"And that should worry us why?" wondered Torstan.

"Aislinn Winborne is in line to assume power in the Southern Marches upon her father's death," explained Ursina. "It's quite obvious, isn't it?"

"Yes, but I still don't understand how that would affect what we're doing here," responded Torstan, raising his hands quickly upon seeing the unexpected spark of anger in the back of Ursina's eyes, the cold that he felt in the depths of his bones burned away with that one look. "I'm not trying to be difficult. I'm just trying to understand. The Southern Marches is a long way from New Caledonia."

"I'm with Torstan," Hakea added, finally having regained

some control over her temper. She promised that she wouldn't permit Ursina to get under her skin as easily as she had been doing. Then again, she made a lot of promises that she rarely kept, even to herself. "I don't understand the issue. Kendric's niece has no authority here. There is little that she can do."

"You both need to examine this situation with a more strategic eye. From a perspective that takes in not just the small world that you're trying to create for yourself. The Territories are a New Caledonia, true, but they are not yet free from Old Caledonia."

Ursina didn't offer any more of an explanation than that. Instead, she waited to see who would decipher it first. If she had placed a wager on the outcome, she would have won.

She saw that the hulking Governor of the Highlands had figured it out. "Would you care to explain it, Torstan, so that Hakea can catch up to us?"

"She's a Winborne," he nodded, "and as you said the heir to the Southern Marches. She would become the Duchess upon her father's passing."

"And if your husband dies," cut in Hakea, hating the fact that the big lug had figured it out before she did, "the charter to the Northern Territory reverts to Kevan Winborne. Which means the daughter ..."

"Can exercise full authority," finished Torstan. "She would have the authority to take control over the Territory. And from her position of power, if she chooses, she could decide ..."

"To use her control over the Northern Territory to make a play for all of New Caledonia," concluded Hakea.

"Just so," Ursina replied, not bothering to mention that doing that could require her removing her uncle from his current seat in the Northern Territory. Or at least trying to. "I'm glad that you both finally understand the seriousness of what all that could mean for us."

"Is the concern truly legitimate?" asked Torstan. He raised

his hands again hoping to ward off another of Ursina's looks. "I'm not asking just to be difficult. Truly. I just need to get a better sense of what we might be facing."

He didn't really know Aislinn Winborne. He had met her maybe once or twice when they were children and had little recollection of her.

It seemed that what Ursina was suggesting was a bit of a stretch. Then again, was he not doing exactly what Ursina feared Kendric's niece might do? Seeking to gain power if there was power to be gained? Filling any vacuum he identified whenever he could if it took him one step closer to what he truly wanted?

"Maybe, maybe not," offered Hakea. She was of a similar mind as Torstan. What Ursina suggested was certainly a possibility, though to her way of thinking still only a possibility. If Aislinn Winborne was in line to rule the Southern Marches, governing that Duchy and then governing the Northern Territory at the same time with the breadth of the Burnt Ocean between them would be incredibly difficult, although not necessarily out of the question. "But better to assume the worst and prepare for that."

Torstan nodded. He couldn't disagree with Hakea no matter how much he wanted to. Her logic was sound.

"What would you have us do?" he asked, turning toward Ursina.

"I want her eliminated. Swiftly. Silently."

"You want her eliminated or Kendric ... or Lord Winborne does?" Torstan corrected himself quickly, wanting to avoid her sharp gaze and even sharper tongue.

That hint of warning was growing even louder in the back of his mind. That sense that Ursina Winborne was much more than she seemed. He believed his concerns were justified, because when he looked into her eyes, he was beginning to think that she knew that he knew, and it didn't seem to bother

her in the least. In fact, she seemed to be pleased that he had figured it out.

"We want her eliminated," confirmed Ursina, her cool façade back in place, even as her eyes blazed brightly. "As I said, I speak for the Lord Winborne. In all matters our thoughts and decisions are the same."

"When is she supposed to dock in Ballinasloe?" asked Hakea.

Killing Aislinn Winborne didn't faze Hakea. She had done much worse as she sought to extend her power in Fal Carrach.

But she was tired of freezing on this dock. And she was tired of Ursina Winborne attempting to demonstrate her superiority. The sooner she was back in the warmth of her cabin and away from this annoying and irritating woman, the better.

"It's past time."

"So she's late," said Hakea, which in itself wasn't uncommon, what with the rough weather that tended to play across the Burnt Ocean. "How late?"

"By more than a month."

That response took Hakea by surprise. A week late, yes. Two, perhaps. More than that? Usually that meant only one thing.

"Then perhaps we don't have a problem at all," suggested Hakea. "When ships are delayed after that much time has passed, usually we never see them again. Your niece is probably already at the bottom of the Burnt Ocean."

"I am well aware of that possibility," Ursina replied.

Again, Ursina didn't offer any more than that, wanting Hakea to work harder for what she wanted to know. And she didn't allow the smile that wanted to become a smirk to break free. It was clear that she was requiring Hakea to exercise a level of patience and restraint with which she was unaccustomed and ill suited, and Ursina was quite enjoying that.

"Then why the concern? It sounds to me as if the sea has

dealt with her already. In fact, it makes me wonder why we're even having this conversation."

"Because I have a feeling that the girl isn't going to make things easy for us," replied Ursina, her voice a bit harder now.

She was finding it more and more difficult maintaining her own patience even as she tested Hakea's. She was beginning to think that it was time to let go of her natural reserve and forbearance. That it was time for these two pups to see who they were really dealing with.

"You believe that she's still alive?" asked Torstan.

"I do."

"Why?" asked Hakea.

Hakea was getting tired of Ursina's very brief responses that only served to require her or Torstan to ask more questions. She should have been aboard her ship and heading back toward Ballinasloe by now rather than being led by the nose by this woman who had assumed her place within their collaboration by charming a man desperate for affection who just so happened to be the brother to one of the most powerful rulers in Caledonia.

"Why is of little concern to you. What does concern you is making sure that when she lands in Ballinasloe -- and she will, of that I have no doubt -- she doesn't get much farther than that. I do not want her to set foot in the Northern Territory. I don't want her to even get a glimpse of the Northern Steppes. Therefore, both of you must be ready. Do I make myself clear? In this, there can be no misunderstandings."

Neither Hakea nor Torstan understood why Ursina was so concerned about this niece who was probably already feeding the crabs at the bottom of the Burnt Ocean. Still, despite their natural tendencies to challenge her claim, to be difficult simply for the sake of being difficult, after the last few minutes they didn't want to antagonize her.

It would simply mean staying on this dock longer. To avoid

that, they chose to acquiesce, wanting to finish this conversation and move on.

"What are we supposed to do if this woman appears in our Territory?" asked Hakea. "We can't use soldiers from our Guards to kill her. That would be too difficult to hide and would only lead to questions that we wouldn't want to answer. There are few Seekers in New Caledonia if any at all, and hiring thugs or cutthroats could come back to bite us as well."

"Finally, the voice of reason, Hakea," said Ursina, a gentle smile once again in place, what Torstan took to be a mask that he had no desire to see fully removed. "Thinking first before doing. I am impressed and quite proud of you."

Hakea bit back the sharp reply that immediately came to mind, not appreciating being talked down to. "I ask again. What are we supposed to do if Aislinn Winborne somehow manages to appear in Ballinasloe or at the Stone for that matter? We can't kill her ourselves."

"I wouldn't expect you to," replied Ursina. "So have no fear of that. I will give both of you the tools to do the job as it needs to be done. All you need to do is release those tools at the appropriate time. They will do the rest. Do you have any other questions? This is a simple task, I know, but as I said, we can't afford any mistakes."

Hakea and Torstan didn't feel the need to answer, simply shaking their heads, getting tired of the veiled insults. Yet understanding that with Ursina they weren't in a position to oppose her.

"Good, then there is one more matter that we must discuss before we can depart."

"What would that be?" asked Torstan, wanting to get this over with and back to the Stone. Whatever wasn't sitting right with him about this meeting was beginning to scream at him that it was time to go. Worse, he didn't know what was bothering him so much, and that's what bothered him the most.

Usually, he could interpret the intentions of others quite easily. Hakea was an excellent example of that. She wanted all of New Caledonia for herself just like he did, and she would do anything to attain it. Her primary failing was that she did such a terrible job of hiding that desire, her ambition much too obvious.

He assumed that Ursina and Kendric wanted the same as Hakea and he did. To rule all of New Caledonia. And that this partnership would only last for however long it continued to prove useful.

But that was an assumption only, because though he could read Kendric like a book, Ursina was quite a different matter entirely.

He expected that she wanted all of New Caledonia, in fact he would be disappointed if she didn't, but he believed that there was some other variable in play that she desired. He just couldn't identify what that might be.

"You," Ursina replied simply.

"Me," said Torstan, taken aback both by the claim and the challenge in Ursina's tone. "Why me?"

"Because you seem to be losing control over the Highlands."

"Who said that?" demanded Torstan, his voice revealing both his anger at being confronted in such a way and a hint of fear that there might be some truth in the claim.

"Who said it doesn't matter, does it? What matters is that it was said at all."

"Did you say it?" demanded Torstan, his face turning even redder, and not from the cold. In the heat of the moment, he had forgotten to whom he was speaking. "You and Kendric? Are you spreading rumors?"

Ursina ignored him. "What matters, my dear boy, is whether there is any truth to the rumors that we are hearing. As a former instructor of mine liked to say, in every rumor there is always a nugget of truth."

"I have no idea what you're talking about," grumbled Torstan. He was worried, but he couldn't let it show. He couldn't afford to demonstrate any weakness now, not with Hakea staring at him as if he was fresh bait in the water and she was the shark.

"You do know what I'm talking about, but you don't want to admit it," pressed Ursina.

She enjoyed watching Torstan squirm, his eyes frantic for a few heartbeats as the young man struggled to figure out all that she might know about what was really happening in his Territory. That was all useful information. That meant that there might be more than just what she had dug up. That there might be more that she and her husband could use against him when the time was right.

"I have no idea what you're talking about," Torstan replied in a sullen tone, refusing to take the bait Ursina had thrown into the water for him.

"No idea," nodded Ursina skeptically, her eyes narrowing, becoming predatory. "If that's the case, then why has production from the mines slowed?"

Torstan could only stare at Ursina, mouth open, not sure what to say. How could she possibly know that? No one knew that but him.

"I have no idea what you're talking about. That's not a rumor. That's a lie."

"Not much of a defense," murmured Hakea, a small smile breaking out on her usually sneering mug. She was enjoying her rival's discomfort a great deal, having hated being the center of Ursina's attention for so long.

Torstan flashed her a look of rage before turning back toward Ursina. "Production from the mines has not slowed ... at least not noticeably. We have experienced nothing more than a few small hiccups. It's only natural. We are working in a rugged and difficult environment."

"Hiccups? Really?" Ursina shook her head as if she was actually considering his answer. "These delays and problems seem to be more than just hiccups. Much more, in fact."

"I have no idea what you're talking about."

But even as Torstan tried to defend himself, he was spending just as much time wracking his brain, attempting to figure out how she could possibly have gained any information about what he was dealing with in the Highlands.

A spy? Some other method? He had to find out.

Production had slowed. But he had no desire to explain to Ursina or Hakea why that was the case.

Although from the look that Ursina was giving him, that confident sneer hidden behind her calm façade, she knew just as well as he did what the obstacle was to ramping production back up to the required level.

He breathed easier when she chose not to challenge him any further.

"I hope you're right."

"I am right. I know all that goes on in the Highlands."

"Even while you're hiding away in the Stone," smirked Hakea.

"I do not hide in the Stone," hissed Torstan, his anger plain now that he had a target other than Ursina. "I am ensuring that the construction of the Stone is completed by the end of the year. Once done, the Stone will be the choke-point through which all must travel to reach your Territories. The Stone gives us more power and the opportunity for more revenue."

"So you say," said Hakea.

Hakea couldn't dispute his logic. Placing that fortress where he did certainly would allow for the imposition of another tax.

Although she had her doubts as to whether Torstan would share that revenue equitably, if at all. If she were in his position, she wouldn't.

"I do," he replied, his temper boiling, fury dancing behind his eyes. "My word is good. No one can challenge it."

Hakea snorted and then shook her head sadly. His word was only good for however long it served his purposes.

She saw how red Torstan's face had become, almost as if his head was going to explode. She was about to make a joke to that effect when Ursina's soft voice cut her off.

With just a few words, Ursina smothered all of Torstan's anger, leaving behind only uncertainty and a fear that he tried and failed to hide.

"Then if you know all that's going on in the Territories, tell me of this Lord Kestrel."

"What are you talking about?" asked Torstan in a tortured whisper.

"You know of whom I speak. His name is on the lips of every person living in those desolate peaks. Who is this Lord Kestrel? This interloper they call the Lord of the Highlands?"

"He is not the Lord of the Highlands!" Torstan shouted, trying and failing to control himself, his face red with fury and fright. Some of it feigned, much of it real. He wasn't sure how to extract himself from this woman who knew more of what was going on in his Territory than he did. "I am the Lord of the Highlands!"

"You might believe that," Ursina said gently, a cunning grin breaking out on her always calm visage, "but the people you are supposed to be ruling apparently don't agree with you."

"Who is this Lord Kestrel?" asked Hakea, never having heard of him and not sure if she should be worried or curious.

"Shall I inform her?" asked Ursina. "Perhaps you could use a few minutes to cool down so that we can have a productive conversation."

Torstan was in no position to reply, needing to turn away so that he could compose himself.

He didn't like being challenged. And yet this woman did it

with impunity and in such a way that he didn't even realize what she was doing until he had no defense against her. This woman seemed to exercise more power and had more knowledge of what was going on in New Caledonia than her husband did.

How was that possible? How did she acquire her information?

"It seems that because Torstan has not provided an effective defense against the Wraiths, the Highlanders have taken that task upon themselves. Word of this Lord Kestrel, this Lord of the Highlands, who fights without fear in the fog against the Wraiths, is spreading. If Torstan is not careful, this Lord of the Highlands might seek to steal his Territory from him."

"He is nothing," hissed Torstan, whipping back around, his rage and doubt roiling within him. "He will be nothing but a memory once I kill him."

"Then I suggest you get to it before he takes your Territory. And while you're at it, increase production from the mines to where it should be. Delays won't be tolerated. Is that clear?"

Torstan could only nod in response to Ursina's demand, his eyes widening as the realization struck him at last, that worrisome, niggling feeling at the back of his brain finally giving him a much-needed clarity.

Kendric was the Governor of the Northern Territory in name only. It was this woman who ruled there. It was this woman who sought to rule him and Hakea as well.

What worried him the most was that he had no idea how to prevent her from achieving her objective. And even if he did, he doubted that he could stop her, because there was a potency to this woman that terrified him.

"Good, because if you can't accomplish what's expected of you, then perhaps we should approach this Lord Kestrel. Perhaps he will be able to do what you seem to falter at."

Realizing what would happen if he didn't stand up for

himself in that moment, if he didn't try to regain some control over the conversation despite the almost paralyzing fear that was threatening to consume him, if he didn't demonstrate to this woman that he wasn't what she thought him to be -- simply a steppingstone, a tool to be used and discarded, he walked right up to her, hovering over her, putting her in his shadow. Then he hissed out a response that he hoped would make her think twice about ever challenging him again.

"All our plans are based on what *my* slaves are digging out of the ground. Don't forget that."

"And don't forget who I am," Ursina replied in a deceptively calm voice. She stepped in even closer to the hulking Torstan, clearly not intimidated as she stared up at him, unblinking.

Torstan's eyes widened, his knees threatening to buckle.

Her dark eyes, which were completely black now, not a hint of white in them, bore into his. When he saw the wispy black threads of energy begin to swirl at the very edges of those piercing orbs, he tried to step back.

But he couldn't move. His fear rising, he knew that Hakea could see it and feel it as well.

Both were frozen in place, captured by the harsh gaze of Ursina that spoke of a power that they couldn't comprehend. A power that could destroy them in an instant. A power that in that moment tipped the balance between them toward this woman who smiled at them with a rapacious grin.

This woman who had walked a path that few dared to tread.

A path of shadow and corruption.

A path that if they ever dared to tread would destroy them utterly.

14

MAKING A POINT

"It's hard not to stare at it, isn't it?" asked Talia.

She stood next to Davin aboard the *Swift* as he leaned his forearms on the railing, staying out of the way of the sailors scrambling across the deck as they prepared to throw the ropes to the dockhands waiting to make the ship fast to the pier.

"Why isn't the keep finished? From all the stories I heard about the dangers to be found here in the Territories, I would have assumed that a citadel such as that one would have been one of the first structures to be completed."

He examined with a frown the fortress that dominated the small island that sat in the very center of the harbor. He wasn't all that impressed by what he saw. Actually, he was disappointed.

Little thought had been given to how the redoubt could be used to defend the harbor and the city. Rather, it appeared to have been designed with one purpose in mind.

To intimidate.

Based on the concept that bigger was better. And likely to feed the ego of the Governor of Fal Carrach.

The walls on two sides must have been at least two hundred

and fifty feet high, while those facing to the east and the west were about twenty feet higher than that. Apparently, however, they weren't tall enough.

Four cranes were mounted on the current balustrade, there for the express purpose of increasing the height of the fortress.

If attackers slipped in close to the redoubt, then whatever ballistae or trebuchets that were placed atop the parapets to defend the citadel would be useless, the angles working in favor of the assailants rather than the defenders.

And though it was clear that the Governor had designs to raise the walls even higher, none of that work was being done. In fact, nothing was happening on the island at all.

There were stacks of building supplies but no workers. Smelters and mixers stood idle. A few barges were tied up to the dock that stuck out into the harbor, yet even that pier hadn't been finished yet.

A few small ferries were going back and forth from a dock in the harbor to the island.

Davin assumed that the citadel was functioning as the administrative center for Fal Carrach. It appeared as if Governor Roosarian was trying to rule her Territory and exert her influence from an incomplete fortress.

The Rock would be quite massive when it was complete. Quite imposing as well. The redoubt certainly would serve that purpose. That couldn't be denied.

But it wouldn't serve as an effective barrier against an attack from the sea, and there was some aspect to the construction that didn't appeal to him.

The fortress didn't feel right to him. Just looking at it made him uncomfortable.

"Governor Roosarian is having a difficult time finding workers now. Very unfortunate." Talia failed to keep the hint of pleasure from her voice.

Davin nodded, even offering her a small smile, his thoughts

elsewhere for a few heartbeats. Maybe it was the sense of menace that he experienced when he looked at the redoubt that was bothering him. It wasn't the aesthetics of the citadel that troubled him. Rather, it was as if there was some darkness lurking behind those jagged stones.

Regardless, something was making the skin along the back of his neck prickle.

He was certain of it, even though he couldn't see it. And, in all honesty, he had no real desire to confirm it.

For the first time since he left the Isle of Mist, he wished that Bryen, Aislinn, or Rafia were with him. They'd be able to address his concern with the Talent. Tell him what was bothering him.

Then he grinned, allowing his discomfort to fade away.

It wasn't his problem. Not yet anyway.

He was on his own. For the first time in his life.

True, he had made a commitment to the woman standing next to him. Still, that wasn't preventing him from experiencing a freedom that had been rare if not entirely nonexistent up until this point in his life. As a result, he was enjoying immensely his time away from his friends and his sister.

He turned his thoughts away from the Rock, an apt name for the monstrous construction if ever there was one. The island upon which it sat dead and lifeless.

Everywhere else he looked, all he saw was activity. Vessels coming and going. Cargo being loaded and unloaded. Markets on the piers that stretched back into the city with crowds of people buying and selling. Taverns and inns doing a brisk business. Farriers, blacksmiths, suppliers, merchants, cobblers, carpenters, and so many other tradespeople all hard at work.

He was both impressed and excited. He had been yearning for a new adventure. He was getting the sense that he'd have little trouble finding one here.

Within just a few minutes of arriving in Ballinasloe, the

Swift was tied to the dock and the sailors were hustling up and down the multiple gangways that had been fixed in place before the dockhands even had completed their task. Davin realized that everything that he saw happening around him was occurring exactly how Talia Carlomin wanted it to happen.

There were a set of procedures in place for moving cargo on and off, for replenishing supplies, for making any necessary repairs. Because speed and efficiency were the distinguishing characteristics of the Carlomin Trading Company.

It only made sense since this ship would be going back out in just a few hours with a new crew.

He wouldn't have believed it if he hadn't seen it with his own eyes. The sailors and dockworkers accomplished their assigned tasks with a rhythm that made him think that he was observing a dance. And he enjoyed watching it for a short while, the precision of the movement that was so clearly chore-ographed appealing to him.

Finally able to tear his eyes away from the hustle and bustle, Davin focused on the large southern section of the harbor that belonged to Talia Carlomin and her mother. It was just as some of the sailors and soldiers he had befriended on the short voyage here had told him it would be.

A small city separated from the larger city by a thirty-foot wall, all the necessities for living in Ballinasloe safely behind the barrier.

Access to that smaller city was restricted by the gate on the pier that was closest to the rest of the harbor, the far southern side of the Carlomin holdings ending at a long, rocky beach that continued down along the coast. There was no way to enter the compound from that direction, the wall extending out over the water, a small watch tower built on top at the very end to ensure that no one tried to swim around the barricade.

Twenty-one vessels were docked along the three Carlomin piers. More than two-thirds were taking on or taking off cargo, all at the same time just as was occurring now on the ship that he had sailed in on.

At the far end of the longest dock, which reached out from the mainland and into the harbor for almost a quarter mile, three more ships were under construction. Multiple large sails were draped across the workspace to hide much of that building process so that no one on the vessels that passed by could see how the fastest ships in the Sea of Mist were being built and what new innovations Talia's Master Shipbuilder might be incorporating into their design.

Looking back toward the city, Davin easily picked out near the gates to the Carlomin enclave the seven new buildings that Talia and her mother were having built. He couldn't recall the purposes of each one.

Talia had explained in great detail that each building did indeed have a distinct purpose, but he hadn't been listening very carefully, at the time distracted by the game of dice playing out before him. He did remember that one was to be an infirmary, and another was to house new administrative offices so that the Carlomins could manage more effectively their rapidly growing business.

Most telling was that these new buildings were being built with stone. A stone of a similar color to that being used to construct the Rock.

Davin nodded with pleasure as he took it all in. There was nothing but motion here, a controlled freneticism matched with a solidity that tugged at him.

He definitely had made the right decision to leave his friends and accompany Talia Carlomin to Fal Carrach.

"You're the reason the Rock is as it is, aren't you?"

Davin's smile revealed his amusement at that finding. This young woman, who was no older than he was and already owned the most profitable shipping company along the coast of New Caledonia with ports of call across the Burnt Ocean, clearly was a force to be reckoned with. Even more intriguing, there was a hardness to her that made Davin think that she would have acquitted herself quite well on the white sand.

"Stonemasons, carpenters, and other skilled craftspeople prefer to work for employers they can trust. They also like to be paid on time and a fair wage." Talia shrugged. "I can only guarantee to anyone who works for me that they will receive a fair wage, get paid on time, and will be paid more than what Governor Roosarian might be willing or able to pay them. I have no control over who they decide to work for and when."

"Of course you don't." Davin glimpsed the small smile that played across her face, disappearing just as quickly as it had appeared. He was glad to see that Talia Carlomin actually had a sense of humor, because he had seen little evidence of that when he had first met her and then on the journey here. "Governor Roosarian must not be too happy with you."

Talia shrugged. "She wasn't happy with me to begin with, so what does it matter now if I make things more difficult for her?"

Davin nodded. She made a good point.

If the Governor wanted to take the Carlomins' business for her own and would do whatever was necessary to get her out of the way, why would Talia make it easy for her? Why not make the Governor's life as miserable as possible?

"It just seems like you're enjoying it all a little bit more than you should," proposed Davin.

"Are you suggesting that I have something of a mean streak, gladiator?" asked Talia, her eyebrows rising just a little bit. "That I hold grudges?"

"I'm not making a suggestion," he replied calmly. "I have no doubt that you hold grudges."

"Does that bother you, Davin?" Her eyes sparked, but whether from amusement or as a challenge wasn't clear.

He didn't reply immediately, in large part because she had addressed him by his first name, which was a rare occurrence.

In fact, he didn't think that she ever had before. "No, it doesn't. I'd be worried if you didn't. If I was in your position, I'd hold onto my grudges as well, and I'd do everything in my power to make the lives of my rivals as difficult as possible."

"And did you do that in the Pit? Make the lives of your opponents as difficult as possible?"

"Yes I did," Davin replied with a grim satisfaction. "If I hadn't, I'd be dead."

Talia stared at him. As she did so, he felt as if she were evaluating him as she would a business deal, making note of his strengths and weaknesses, her eyes hardening as she reached her conclusion. Then, much to his surprise, she nodded and smiled, seemingly satisfied with what she had discovered, before she walked toward the helm to talk with the Captain who had just come on board and would be taking over the vessel.

Left on his own, Davin continued to take in all that was occurring around him. He had never enjoyed feeling as if he were stuck in place, as had been the case when he fought in the Pit.

When he and his sister were brought to the Colosseum, he had assumed that they would both die there. They probably would have if not for Bryen and Declan.

Now that he was free of the white sand and the commitments that he had made and then kept in Caledonia, he wanted to keep moving forward. He wanted to see more of the world. He wanted to do new things. He wanted to reclaim that sense of adventure that was so much a part of who he was.

He needed some way to tap into the adrenaline that had served him so well in the Colosseum. Because without that energy sizzling through his blood, he didn't feel truly alive.

Here in Ballinasloe, working with Talia Carlomin, he was beginning to think that he might be able to do just that, at least for a time. Then, once the excitement of this new adventure waned just as it inevitably would, he could search for some other way to fill the hole that he felt inside himself now that he wasn't fighting for his life several times a week.

Still, that was a concern for later. He was here now with a new world to explore.

It had been a fast trip from the Isle of Mist, the ship remarkably swift, Davin understanding why it was so named. But after admiring the speed with which the *Swift* and the other two Carlomin vessels approached the *Freedom* while he and the Blood Company fought against the pirates, Davin had expected as much.

Because of that, he had enjoyed every second of the journey. Even when, as was her wont, Talia stared at him from atop the helm with a look that suggested that she didn't know what to do with him.

And that if she couldn't figure it out before they made port, she'd get rid of him somehow. Maybe throw him overboard.

That concern floating through his mind, he stayed away from her as much as he could while he was on the frigate. He spent his few free moments in the crow's nest, Talia only allowing him up there after he promised that he wouldn't dive into the sea with a rope tied around his waist.

Davin had learned much to his chagrin that Bryen had warned her of his risky predilection, so she had told him quite clearly to find something to do so that he didn't feel the need to beat his boredom by acting the fool.

He had to give Talia credit after that conversation. She certainly did speak her mind. And he didn't intimidate her, even though she only came halfway up his chest.

He liked that about her. He knew where he stood with her at all times. In fact, he valued that. Because, in that way, she was much like Declan.

Taking her advice, order, there didn't seem to be much

difference between the two with her – another similarity with Declan -- he had offered what assistance he could to the crew.

Just as he had observed while docking here in Ballinasloe, the crew of the *Swift* knew what they were doing. There was a rhythm to their actions that they didn't want a clumsy gladiator from the Pit to disrupt. They had made it clear to him that they had little desire for him to become involved.

Their stance softened when they learned that Davin had been well trained by Captain Gregson and the crew of the *Freedom* on the voyage across the Burnt Ocean. Once they saw what he could do, especially impressed a man of his height could scurry around the rigging as if he belonged there, they quickly adjusted their perspective and began treating him no differently than they would any other sailor.

As a result, Davin found sailing through the Sea of Mist to be quite enjoyable, although much too brief. He had to admit as well that it had been even more fun to demonstrate what he could do with a spear to the soldiers on board the ship.

Sirena Makarin, Captain of the Carlomin Guard, had her doubts about him. Much like her employer, she didn't hesitate to share her perspective.

He remembered the exchange and the combats that followed quite vividly.

Several of the soldiers had been practicing on the aft deck. Davin, having finished a shift working the sails and the rigging, asked if he could join them.

He hadn't trained as much in the circle during the journey from Caledonia as he probably should have, his focus on other endeavors, none of them particularly useful, and he found that he missed the camaraderie of and precision required in the practice ring.

Besides, he felt the need to hone his skills. He didn't know what might be waiting for him when they reached Ballinasloe.

Sirena had balked at first. "You're not a soldier. You're a gladiator."

"I'm a fighter," Davin had replied simply.

"Fighting on the white sand doesn't mean you're qualified to take on a trained soldier."

"Of course it does," he had replied, trying to remain calm even as his agitation began to percolate. "Keep in mind as well that as soon as I left the Pit upon the overthrow of Marden Beleron, I became a Corporal in the Blood Company."

"Corporal in a company of gladiators?" Sirena had been less than impressed.

"Corporal in the Company that played a key role not only in the overthrow of the monarchy, but also in ensuring that Caledonia remained free of the Ghoules. The Blood Company fought in the Winter Pass. We fought well."

"So did many other companies."

"How many other companies fought in the Trench? How many gladiators fought in the Lost Land?"

That last comment finally got Sirena's attention. "You fought in the Lost Land? By choice?"

"I did."

Davin knew that Sirena had expected more of a response from him. She likely had assumed that he would offer a colorful tale, maybe brag a little bit with the hope that he could convince her to change her mind.

If she had been to the Lost Land, home to the greatest enemy to ever threaten Caledonia, like most everyone else she probably would have. But he had kept his mouth shut instead.

He hadn't thought that boasting about his exploits would gain him much ground with her. Besides, he hated bluster.

The Captain of the Carlomin Guard had studied Davin with a more critical eye after that. She had liked him as soon as she met him, how he seemed to approach the world with a tired amusement, even as a seriousness that he tried to hide but couldn't be ignored sparked in the back of his eyes.

She also had appreciated how he had slipped in with the crew as if he had worked aboard a ship his entire life. And now, not bragging about what he had accomplished, finally had won her over.

"Then what are you doing here?" she had asked. "After all that you've done, you could be wherever you want to be. You could be doing whatever you want to do."

Sirena had been right. He could have gone wherever he wanted. He could have done anything that he had desired. But nothing had appealed to him other than to continue on with Bryen and his friends to the Territories.

A fresh start. That's what he needed.

"It's a long story and not worth your time," he had replied.

"I admit that seeing you fight in the practice ring certainly has a unique appeal," Sirena had said. "But Captain Carlomin was quite clear that she didn't want anything to happen to you while on board our vessel."

"She said that did she?" Davin had wondered about that briefly, whether because she worried about him or she didn't trust him, he really hadn't been able to tell. But Sirena's next comment had deflated his ego swiftly.

"She did. She feared what the Lord Keldragan might do if you were harmed in any way while under her care. Or you harmed yourself. By mistake, of course."

"Wait a moment. I'm under Talia Carlomin's care?"

At first Davin had been amused by that notion. Although the more he thought about it, the more his temper had begun to flare.

"Captain Carlomin's words, not mine," Sirena had clarified quickly, catching the glint of anger in his eyes and seeking to squash it swiftly. "If I allow you to fight in the practice circle – and I must admit that I would like to see your skills with a spear -- then I put you at risk. I need to think of Captain Carlomin's interests first."

"Of course." Davin hadn't been able to argue with her logic. And he hadn't wanted to put Sirena in a difficult position. Still, he really wanted to have a go at the soldiers and have a chance at sharpening his skills. The itch to match steel with steel was becoming more insistent within him. "What if I told you that I could defeat any of the soldiers you set against me without a single one even getting close to me. That you wouldn't have to worry about anything happening to me."

Sirena had laughed at that. "Words mean little in the practice ring."

"Only steel does, I know," Davin had replied.

"You need to understand that every soldier aboard this vessel is highly trained. They all have years of experience in various Duchy Guards, several spending their entire careers in the Royal Guard. To put it bluntly, these men and women know how to fight."

"Of that I have no doubt," Davin had replied, "but so do I. I'm sure I can show them a thing or two that might be of use to them without Captain Carlomin having to worry about me."

"She's not worried about you. She's worried about the promise she made to Lord Keldragan. You might do well against some of our soldiers, but keep in mind as well that Rorie over there," Sirena had said, motioning to a tall, slim soldier who had just stepped into the practice ring with two short swords, "has fought against Jurgen Klines, the Caledonian Blademaster. From what I understand, he lost by only a whisker."

"Impressive," Davin had replied, nodding to demonstrate his agreement. Nevertheless, he believed that he could do Rorie one better if he could persuade Sirena to allow him to enter the ring. "And what if I told you that I killed a Slayer? Would that convince you to allow me to have a go? I think killing a Slayer is just as if not more impressive than almost beating the Blademaster." Davin had raised his hands then, not wanting to come across as arrogant, simply seeking to create an opening for himself. "No disrespect intended toward Rorie. I just believe that I could serve as a worthy combatant for him. Give him a chance to really test his skills."

Sirena had stared at Davin for quite a long time. Once again, Davin had felt as if he were a commodity. Someone to be evaluated or measured.

He hadn't enjoyed the experience, but he had understood Sirena's caution. Besides, every day he had walked out onto the white sand he had been evaluated and measured, and if he had been found wanting, he would have died.

He hadn't. And this was nothing compared to that.

"What's a Slayer?" Sirena had asked finally, not having any idea what he had been talking about. Although the look in her eye had changed by then, suggesting that her perspective had as well. Davin had believed that now she was looking for a reason to grant his request rather than deny it.

"An assassin of the Ghoule Overlord. Nasty creature. Claws. Hardened scales. Whiplike tail with daggerlike protrusions on the end. Not a monster I want to come up against again."

Sirena's eyes had widened as she had listened to his explanation, her already impressive stare once again fixed upon him. He had given her a shrug, hoping that he was conveying to her that he was just telling her the truth. He had assumed that she didn't believe him when she had broken out into a laugh.

"You killed a Slayer? One of the Ghoule Overlord's assassins? Really?"

Davin had been certain that she didn't know what a Slayer was despite his description. Clearly, however, she had known of the Ghoule Overlord, most likely having heard the stories that had circulated within the taverns in Ballinasloe about the battles in the Winter Pass against the Ghoule Legions and how the Volkun had fought against the Master of the Curse.

Because everyone knew of the Volkun. Bryen's fame, something that he didn't want, obviously was warranted.

Davin wouldn't have been surprised if there had yet to be any mention of the Crimson Giant or the Crimson Devil or any other gladiators of the Blood Company in the tales being told. That was just the way of it when such a momentous event had just occurred, only months old.

The larger story always came first. The color and many individual threads would be incorporated later as some of the other major players were added to the growing legend.

Although Davin cared little for any of that. He just wanted to get into the practice ring.

And he had recognized then that Sirena was now giving his request serious consideration. Still, he had understood her hesitation. He had assumed at that moment that she was probably thinking that he, who came across as good natured but had a worrisome penchant for getting himself into trouble, wasn't being completely honest with her.

He had assumed as well that she was also probably thinking that more tales of the Second Ghoule War would make their way across the Burnt Ocean. Perhaps a few would reference him and what he might have done to stop the Ghoule Overlord and his Legions.

Who knew? She did know that Captain Carlomin would be very displeased if anything happened to him while she was responsible for him, a situation that had rankled at the time but now only amused him.

Nevertheless, he had let it go, because he had sensed that Sirena's resistance was beginning to waver. And all he cared about in that moment was gaining her approval.

Because he had been certain that Sirena was really beginning to think about what he had told her. And the fact that he had survived for so long on the white sand he had been sure would aid his efforts to gain what he wanted. She would be thinking that if he could fight in the Pit then clearly he was good with a weapon.

Maybe not as good as a trained soldier, probably rough around the edges, less disciplined, more prone to emotion and bad decisions, but he should be able to do well enough to not put his life needlessly at risk.

And if he took a slice or two across the arm or the thigh, what was the harm? He'd still be alive. He might even learn a much-needed lesson.

That's what Davin had believed was playing through her mind while she looked at him, finally searching for a reason to allow him to train. Yet despite all that he had offered, she had felt the need to throw down one more obstacle in front of him.

"I find it hard to believe that you killed a Slayer."

Davin had smiled then. Because he knew for a fact in that moment that she had wanted him to convince her. She had wanted him to give her the final push she needed to agree to his request.

"More than one in fact," he had said softly, without a hint of boasting in his voice. Just a simple statement, no more than that. And before Sirena had the chance to offer any more protests, he had continued, realizing that they finally had reached the tipping point. She had been balancing right on the edge.

"Just give me a chance. Pick whomever you want to take me on in the practice circle," Davin had proposed. "Rorie. Someone else. It doesn't matter. Just give me a chance. I either win or lose. And if I lose, if nothing else it should be amusing for your soldiers, and I won't bother you again. I promise you that."

"That sounds quite appealing," Sirena had said. "And if you win?"

"Then you allow me to train with the soldiers without complaint and if Talia Carlomin tries to stop me from doing that you support me."

"And even if I support you and she still won't allow you to work with the soldiers?"

"Then I'll leave you be and spend what free time I have in the crow's nest."

Sirena finally had smiled then, obviously pleased. "You have a deal."

She had kept Rorie in reserve, still worried that the skills that Davin had learned in the Pit, though possibly useful in a fight against the Ghoules, wouldn't translate well when facing a trained soldier in a combat. Davin had dissuaded her of that prejudice swiftly.

Rufus was a good-natured fellow. A veteran with more than a decade of experience. And he was big. So big that he reminded Davin of Jenus and Majdi, both gladiators who needed to duck and turn to the side in order to walk through a doorway.

Davin hadn't minded this first trial, even though he really had wanted to test his skills against Rorie now that he knew he had trained with the Blademaster. Even so, he had understood Sirena's decision. She hadn't wanted to throw him into the deep end without first seeing if he could really swim.

He would have done the same if he were in her position.

He and Rufus had become friends after the combat. Even though Davin had dispatched him quickly, in less than a minute in fact, no more than four moves required to get Rufus on his back and the blade of Davin's spear against his neck, he had treated the soldier with respect. Rufus' even temper and desire to learn what he could from Davin helped as well.

Sirena had simply nodded when that combat ended. Much sooner than she had anticipated, that was true, although she couldn't say that she had been surprised.

Davin had seen all that playing through her mind.

Rufus was all power. Davin was power but also speed.

She had sent Toni into the practice ring next. She reminded Davin of Asaia.

Driven. Almost obsessively so. And fast. Very fast.

It had taken him more than a minute to defeat her. Ninety seconds in fact.

She had assumed that she could beat him with the rapid-fire pace of her assault, attempting to catch him by surprise, because that's what had worked for her in her other combats. She hadn't realized until she too was on her back, steel against her throat, that though Davin didn't look it, he was even faster than she was.

When that combat had ended, Davin had stood in the practice ring, grinning broadly. Not because of his success, but rather because he had realized that he was back where he was meant to be.

Sirena had sent Rorie into the training circle next. The soldier who had trained with the Blademaster was more cautious than Rufus and Toni. He had watched both duels intently, looking for any weaknesses to exploit, then putting into practice all that he had learned while serving in the Royal Guard and working with the greatest swordsman in Caledonia.

Much to his dismay, Rorie hadn't found any flaws. He had discovered after just the first touch of steel between them that defeating this gladiator would be just as if not more difficult than defeating the Blademaster.

Stuck with that knowledge, Rorie had played for time. He hoped that he could entice Davin into making a mistake, thinking that perhaps a natural impatience might get the better of the gladiator and give Rorie the opening that he had wanted.

Davin had never given him the chance that he was looking for. He had defeated Rorie in just under five minutes, but it had only taken that long because Davin was enjoying the engagement and Rorie reminded him of Chesin. Just as fluid with a blade. Very precise. Very persistent. Though more even tempered.

After Rorie had regained his feet, Davin having offered his hand to help him up from the deck, the soldier had brought his blade to his forehead and given Davin a nod of respect. Davin had done the same with his spear.

The soldiers and the many sailors who had surrounded the training circle to watch the combats had stood there in silence, their awe at what they had just witnessed quite clear. They had never expected the gladiator to work his way through three skilled fighters in less than ten minutes.

Then the clapping had begun. Rufus first, Toni as well, Rorie right behind them, joined in by all those who had been observing.

Davin had been embarrassed by it all, smiling sheepishly. He had raised his hands, hoping that it would stop the acclaim. Unfortunately, his attempt at quelling the praise had only succeeded in making it last a little while longer.

When he had stepped out of the training circle, Davin had looked up at the helm. Talia Carlomin had stood there the entire time. Watching the contests.

She had worn a mysterious expression then, one that he hadn't known how to interpret. But she hadn't appeared to be angry, so he had been pleased by that.

The next day, Sirena had challenged him to a combat. The Captain of the Carlomin Guard was good, almost as fast as Toni, almost as skilled as Rorie. Still, she had made little headway against Davin.

He had trained with the Volkun, after all. And he had survived hundreds of combats in the Pit.

Davin had the capacity to adapt to any opponent no matter their natural abilities and then find the weak spot. That was the first thing that Bryen had taught him on the white sand, and it was a lesson that he had never forgotten.

Davin had been certain after just the first few minutes of their combat that Sirena's opinion of him had changed. That she had come to believe that as he had told her the day before, he was a fighter, not just a gladiator, and she had appeared to respect him for it.

His belief in that regard was confirmed when he had defeated her just a few minutes later, putting on a dazzling display with his spear, the steel slicing through the air so quickly that no one watching the combat could tell where he would attack next, least of all Sirena.

After she had yielded, rather than being angry she had smiled. Then she had asked him to take the contingent of soldiers aboard the *Swift* through a training session. He had done so gladly.

Several hours later, the combats completed, Davin had looked up at the helm once again. Talia Carlomin had been staring down at him, her expression the same as before. Just as difficult to read.

"Are you coming? Or are you going to stand there staring at everything for the rest of the day?" Talia's impatient voice brought him back to the present.

Davin grinned sheepishly as he set aside those pleasant memories. Nodding, he followed Talia down the gangplank, seeing an older version of Talia waiting for them on the pier.

This woman had to be Isana Carlomin. The only difference between mother and daughter was the pinkish hue to Talia's blonde hair.

"Who is this?"

"Davin ..." Talia began to reply, then she stopped herself. She turned toward the red-headed gladiator who carried a light pack over one shoulder and his spear in his hand. "I'm sorry, I don't know your last name."

"I don't have one."

"You don't have one?" asked Talia. She didn't want to embarrass Davin. Even so, she tried and failed to keep the surprise from her voice. "How could that be?"

"My sister and I were quite poor, so we didn't live in a part of the city where last names were important. In fact, we lived in the Dregs. You can guess by the name what it was like. In the Dregs it was better if no one knew your full name. Because if they did, they either wanted to kill you or they wanted to turn you in to the City Watch. Last names made it easier for them to find you."

"You're not making this up, are you?" asked Talia. She was worried that Davin might be trying to have some fun at her expense, not yet able to tell if the small glint of humor in his eyes was a permanent resident or just there for this particular engagement.

"He's not playing with you, Talia," said Isana. "He speaks truly." Talia's mother stepped up closer to Davin, taking a good look at him. "I take it that he didn't tell you too much about himself while he was aboard, did he?"

Davin offered a smile to Isana, although his eyes remained hard. Just as hard as hers, in fact.

Talia's mother was running her raptorial gaze over Davin, appraising him.

Others might have been bothered by the scrutiny. He wasn't. He was used to it after Talia and then Sirena had done the same. Although theirs was nothing compared to Declan's.

He actually appreciated it, because her close examination helped him to better comprehend the situation he had become a part of here in Ballinasloe. It helped him to better understand the mother and daughter who were poking the Governor of Fal Carrach in the eye as frequently as they could manage it.

The Carlomins focused on value, whether person, product, or business deal. If you could offer them value, then they would offer value to you in return. And if you couldn't or didn't want to, they weren't going to waste their time on you.

Davin's smile broadened then. That was something that he was used to, a legacy from his time in the Colosseum.

"No, he didn't," Talia replied. "What little I know of him was provided by the Lord Keldragan. Davin doesn't talk about himself all that much unless it's a requirement for getting into the training circle."

"You just never asked the right questions, Talia," Davin replied with a wink and nod. "Do that, and I'm an open book."

Isana chuckled when she saw her daughter's expression sour. "Oh, I like this one. The strong and silent type, but ready to offer a gentle quip when appropriate. Davin will be good for you."

"What do you mean by that?" demanded Talia, her face turning red. Her anger, never far from the surface, increased swiftly. Her mother simply ignored her.

"So tell me, Davin, did you always live in the Dregs?"

Davin shifted his focus back to Isana, smiling even more broadly, for some reason quite enjoying how irritated Talia had become. "When we were children, we did. Before my sister and I were thrown into the Pit, we lived on the streets of Tintagel for a time. Last names didn't mean much in those places either."

"And your sister's name?" Isana had watched the gladiatorial games once when she was younger while she visited the capital of Caledonia. She had refused to go again, finding the wanton bloodshed an atrocity and sickened by the barbarity.

"Lycia."

Isana nodded at that. "Twins, I take it?"

"How could you possibly know that?"

"It's just one of her unique skills," muttered Talia, still shaking her head in exasperation at her mother's comment.

"We are," Davin nodded in reply. "We're much the same,

although she's meaner than I am. She has a much more jaundiced view of the world than I do."

"Oh, I doubt that," Isana laughed again, this time louder. "That's just what you tell yourself." She was enjoying her conversation with the gladiator. She turned back toward her daughter, who had managed to finally gain better control over her temper. "Yes, Davin definitely will be good for you."

"What are you ..." But she cut herself off almost immediately, not wanting her mother's statement to burrow any further under her skin than it already had.

"What were you and your sister called in the Pit?" asked Isana, understanding the importance of names on the white sand.

"The crowd called me the Crimson Giant, my sister the Crimson Devil."

Isana nodded upon hearing that. "I assume that your red hair was only part of the reason you earned that name."

"Just so," Davin nodded self-consciously. "I tended to make my adversaries bleed."

"That doesn't surprise me," Isana replied. "You wouldn't be here otherwise."

Davin nodded to her, confirming that fact.

"I don't know that the Crimson Giant will serve you well here, although I take it based on my watching your practice sessions that you were well suited to the name," Talia added to the conversation, trying to demonstrate to her mother that she couldn't be diverted so easily.

"Some thought so."

"Be that as it may, as I said, the Crimson Giant probably isn't the best choice for you while working in service to the Carlomin Trading Company."

"I wasn't intending on using that name," Davin replied with a short laugh that only served to make Isana chuckle once again and helped to hide his own discomfort. If he never again heard the moniker given to him by the crowd in the Colosseum, he'd be quite happy.

Gritting her teeth, Talia took a moment before replying, knowing that she shouldn't say what immediately had come to mind. She still was trying to figure out whether Davin was teasing her.

Usually, she had no problem reading other people. But this gladiator was an enigma to her, and she didn't like that at all.

"I'm glad to hear it. Here, you can take whatever name you want. So at least there's that."

"Aye, aye, Captain," Davin replied with a nod. "I'll keep that in mind."

Talia gave him a sharp look then. She wanted to be angry with him, but she was finding it increasingly difficult to do so. Especially since she was struggling to hold back the smile that threatened to break free because of his comments and his own smile that had brought a spark of amusement to his eyes. At the very last moment, she forced out a grimace instead.

"So how is it that you have acquired Davin?" asked Isana. "Davin Noname I should say."

"We met while fighting pirates in the Sea of Mist."

"It sounds like the beginning of a love story," Isana said suggestively, giving her daughter a wink.

"Mother, I can't believe that you would suggest such a ..." Talia began, her face starting to color.

Isana cut off Talia's protest. "You see, Davin Noname, how easy it is to get under Talia's skin? You just need to have a little fun at her expense and she immediately takes issue."

"I hadn't really noticed," Davin replied with a shrug and a hint of dry wit. Giving Isana a lift of his eyebrows, he continued. "I tried not to pursue my natural inclination to ruffle her feathers, fearing that she would throw me overboard." Talia's glare at him suggested that he wasn't being entirely truthful, so he clarified his response. "At least not as much as I wanted to."

"Then more credit to you, Davin," said Isana. "Although I must say, despite your smile and that twinkle in your eye, I see the sadness in you. It's not for your current situation, I hope?"

Davin studied Isana for several seconds. He thought that he had Talia's mother figured out, but apparently not entirely. Then he shrugged. "No, being here doesn't sadden me. I'm pleased to be in Ballinasloe."

"Then the cause?"

At first, Davin thought not to reply. He didn't like to share much about himself to begin with. Yet this woman had a knack for seeing the truth behind the walls he had built around himself.

With other people, he might have been worried about that. But for whatever reason not with her. He got the feeling that some of her experiences in life were similar to his own.

"I've seen many things I never wanted to see," Davin replied. "I've done many things I never wanted to do."

"But you had to do them," said Isana, nodding, her understanding plain.

Davin gave her a short nod in return. "I had to do them."

Isana smiled again, apparently having completed her examination and identifying what it was she was looking for within him. "It is a pleasure to meet you, Davin. Be welcome here."

"Thank you, Lady Carlomin."

"Mrs. Carlomin or Isana will do just fine," corrected Talia's mother. "And why is it that you're here, Davin?"

Talia interrupted then, not knowing what to make of what seemed to be a very personal exchange between the gladiator and her mother, more said without words than with. In just a few minutes she explained with her normal succinctness the deal that she had struck with Bryen Keldragan and the role that Davin was to play in helping to achieve it.

Isana listened to it all, not saying a word, just taking it all in.

"You've had a much more productive journey than I thought possible, Talia."

"I did. Now we must see what we can make of it."

"If we have the chance," said Isana. "Hakea Roosarian has been more difficult the last few weeks. She has become almost obsessed with ..."

"Captain Carlomin," called Sirena, the Captain of the Guard working her way down the busy pier, trying to avoid the sailors, dockworkers, craftspeople, shipbuilders, and others who were all plying their trades along the long expanse. "We need you at the gate. We have a problem."

15

LIGHT IN THE DARK

The Wraith scout sprinted through the Murk, the mist parting for him, caressing him as he went by, urging him on. He was intent on the several targets he had identified just up ahead.

Eager to make the kill. To prove himself.

There were at least four humans to his front. Maybe more. He couldn't tell how many for sure.

He could only guess based on how the Murk swirled in front of him, the curl of the wispy grey threads pointing the way, and the muted sounds that traveled so well through the grey haze -- the pounding of the humans' feet against the ground, the curses when they slipped or stumbled -- allowing him to pinpoint their location.

The humans were desperate to escape him. He was certain of it. That thought sent a thrill through the Wraith that was unlike any other that he had experienced before.

The humans had entered a world that wasn't theirs. A world where they didn't belong.

The Wraith was a part of the Murk. The tendrils of grey hid him. Protected him. Nurtured him.

This was his hunting ground. The humans his prey. No matter how many there were, they didn't stand a chance against him.

The Wraith would take a great deal of pleasure when he cut across their throats with his daggers. And when he was done, he would taste their blood, just as he always did.

He had no doubt that it would be just as sweet as the blood of all the other humans that had touched his lips.

Perhaps even sweeter, if any of these vermin dared to put up a fight.

The Wraith increased his pace. He could sense the humans moving farther down the trail, now out in a larger space. He assumed that they were on the green that circled the tower.

He was almost past the last house before the cut grass.

His clawed fingers gripped his daggers tightly. He would be on them in just a heartbeat, before they even knew he was there, the last of their worthless lives now counted in mere seconds.

That thought sent another thrill of exhilaration through him.

The exact instant the Wraith stepped out onto the green, visions of the murder he was about to commit dancing through his mind, he caught a faint shift in the Murk just off to his left that shouldn't have been there. At the same time, he felt a strange warmth surging up from just below his chin.

The Wraith took a few more steps before skidding to a halt in the wet grass. He dropped one of his double-bladed daggers, bringing a clawed hand to his throat in shock.

It came away with a streak of blood. His blood.

The Wraith dropped to his knees, his energy draining out of him rapidly.

Looking down, he watched as a long stream of his blood flowed down his chest, staining his leather armor, pooling in the grass in front of him.

Before the Wraith could even begin to understand what had happened, how he had failed so terribly, he fell over onto his side, the last of his strength fading away.

As the Wraith's deep black eyes glazed over, a shadow stepped out of the Murk, staring down at him. At the hunter who had become the hunted, the Wraith too proud, too arrogant, to consider for even a moment that his prey might turn on him.

That his prey might become the predator.

A good kill, in Jakob's opinion, but only one kill. There were more Wraiths that required his attention.

He knelt down, wiping the steel stained with the Wraith's blood on the monster's leather armor. Then, rising back to his feet, he twirled in his hands the daggers he had acquired from the Wraith he had killed just weeks before.

Just as they did the first time he grasped them, just as they always did, the blades felt right, as if they belonged in his hands.

Who was to say? Maybe the Wraith who had named him had been right to do so. Maybe he belonged in the Murk.

Jakob pushed his thoughts to the side. He still had a lot to do. All with little chance of success. But that wouldn't stop him from trying.

One down, five more Wraiths coming his way.

He couldn't challenge that many monsters of the mist at one time. He would need to adopt a different strategy. One favored by the Wraiths, in fact.

He would hunt just as they did in the Murk.

If he succeeded, he would improve his odds.

If he failed, he would die.

Simple.

Eventually, the Wraiths would realize that they would need to adjust their tactics. Until then, he would make use of the

Wraiths' penchant for fighting as individuals, the monsters savoring every opportunity to engage in single combat.

That decided, using the Talent, he confirmed where all the Wraiths were in the Murk. One was coming down the trail that led through the village, though he was taking his time, not so desperate for the kill as the one now bloodying the grass behind him.

The other three monsters also weren't in a rush. Savoring the hunt.

They had spread out. They were working their way in among the cottages now, likely hoping that some of their prey hadn't made it into the tower in time.

Jakob would use their mix of caution and curiosity against them.

He glided farther up the trail, the Murk barely moving around him, until he was even with the last house before the green.

He focused on the Wraith coming down the path. The monster who was now no more than twenty yards away from him and had slowed. Then stopped.

Despite his best efforts to mask his approach, the monster must have caught his movement in the mist.

That was fine with Jakob. He had doubted that he could kill the second Wraith as easily as he had the first.

"I know you," hissed a raspy voice just to Jakob's front.

Jakob couldn't see the Wraith with his eyes. Not yet. But thanks to the Talent he didn't need to. He knew exactly where the monster stood.

Just thirty feet farther up the path. Right in the center.

"And I know you," Jakob replied.

With the other Wraiths slowly working their way through the village, he was more than happy to engage in a conversation. Every second that passed before the Wraiths killed him was another second that Duff and the others could use to get the children into the broch.

"Who am I?" asked the Wraith, the tone of his voice containing both curiosity and amusement.

"You are the Wraith I am about to kill next."

Jakob's comment was met with several seconds of silence. Then a raspy chuckle filtered through the grey haze, this time only twenty feet in front of Jakob.

The Wraith had snuck closer, Jakob not catching the movement with his eyes, only able to track the monster with the Talent as he moved stealthily through the Murk.

"You are either incredibly brave or incredibly foolish, boy. I can't decide which. But from the stories I have heard, I can't say that I'm surprised."

"Probably a little bit of both," Jakob replied.

Jakob used the Talent to confirm what was happening at the broch. Two of the children had reached the top of the parapet, Tommie sliding down the rope so that she could take up the third.

Only Bertie and Duff remained on the ground, Bertie preparing to begin the climb that would get the child who was clinging to his shoulders to safety once Tommie completed her second ascent.

"Maybe so," agreed the Wraith. "You know, I've been wondering about you."

Jakob shifted his gaze to his right. The Wraith remained twenty feet away, but he had glided to the other side of the trail without disturbing the mist.

"Really? And why would you be doing that?"

"Because I find you intriguing, human. Few are willing to stand against us."

"My father taught me that you must do what you must do."

There was another silence for a time, the monster apparently mulling what Jakob had just said. "Sage advice. Did we kill your father?"

Jakob bit back the curse that immediately came to mind, having to work to maintain his calm, a surge of anger seeking to break through. "No."

"A pity," replied the Wraith. "If he was anything like you, he would have been a worthy kill."

"He would have been, yes," Jakob confirmed, a hint of sadness in his voice.

"You know, there's a bounty on your head. The Wraith Hunter will honor the Wraith Scout who kills you."

"The Wraith Hunter doesn't have the courage to kill me himself?"

"Do not let your arrogance and luck at making it this far get the better of you, Wraith who is not a Wraith," hissed the Scout. "Do not make light of the Wraith Hunter. You are beneath him. Nothing more than an ant to be crushed beneath his boot."

"And yet the Wraith Hunter has felt the need to place a bounty on my head," murmured Jakob, his eyes tracking from right to left as he followed with the Talent the Wraith's movement back to the other side of the trail. The Wraith was testing him, trying to determine if Jakob could decipher his motion. "Curious, don't you think?"

"You won't have to concern yourself with it for much longer, human," promised the Wraith Scout. "I will kill you now and put you out of your misery."

"Promises, promises," Jakob replied.

The other Wraiths were still several hundred yards away, hunting carefully in among the houses. That was fine with Jakob. The more thorough their search, the longer it would take, and there was no one there for them to find.

Jakob had confirmed that already. Even better, Bertie had reached the top of the broch. Duff was the last Highlander on the green. Jakob only needed to delay a few minutes more, which he attempted to do.

"I use your weapons now, Wraith. I took them from another Scout who thought that he could kill me. Are you sure you want to try your luck against me? Are you ready to die by the blades that you make use of yourself?"

A low growl emanated out of the Murk just fifteen feet to Jakob's left.

He smiled briefly, pleased to have finally antagonized his adversary. More important, he had goaded the Wraith into an impetuous move.

In a blur the Wraith coalesced out of the fog, double-bladed dagger slicing through the air for Jakob's throat.

The monster wanted a quick kill. He had no desire to engage in the Dance of the Daggers for any longer than necessary, having heard more than enough about the Wraith who is not a Wraith and his lethal skill.

Jakob ducked the cut, allowing the weapon to pass over his head. In the same motion, he kicked out with his right foot and connected with the back of the Wraith's legs.

The monster, slightly off balance because of the wide arc of his swing, stumbled and then slid through the grass for several feet.

"Perhaps you should slink back into the fog," suggested Jakob as he stood behind the Wraith, not bothering to attack. Not yet. "You are no better than your brethren. You will die by my blade."

Jakob really wasn't as confident of his success regarding this combat as he sounded. But that didn't matter.

His goal right now was to delay, and he believed that his best chance to gain the time that he wanted, and perhaps even improve his chances of surviving this duel, was to anger the monster who swiftly regained his clawed feet. If the Wraith allowed his emotions to sway his reason, then that was all to the good for Jakob.

"I will take your head to the Wraith Hunter," hissed the Wraith Scout, the monster turning in a blur and sprinting toward Jakob.

Because of the unimaginable speed of the Wraith's attack, Jakob had no other option but to stand his ground. He greeted each slash of the Wraith's daggers with the steel of his own.

In just seconds, they had established a rhythm that rang out through the fog, the clang sounding like a hammer striking a bell to sound out the hours.

The Wraith tried time and time again to cut into Jakob's flesh yet failed to do so.

As a result, the Wraith's rage built within him. Despite all that he had heard about him, the monster never expected such a challenge from this boy.

With them so closely engaged, Jakob could see the monster clearly now. His anger and frustration were evident on his gaunt, skeleton-like face.

Still, despite his success at getting under the Wraith's skin, Jakob realized that wouldn't be enough. He knew that he couldn't keep doing this, not if he wanted to avoid a painful death, because the Wraith was just as good if not a better fighter than he was.

In fact, the only reason that Jakob was still standing was his use of the Talent. His natural magic quickened his own movements and allowed him to anticipate from which direction the Wraith's next attack would come.

"This is the best that you can do?" Jakob challenged his adversary through gritted teeth, bringing his dagger up in his right hand to parry the slice aimed for his ribs. Just as swiftly he pivoted and knocked away the Wraith's next attack, using his shoulder to nudge the monster a step to the left, the Wraith's other blade passing harmlessly through the space between them. "You dishonor your brethren."

Jakob's last comment had the effect that he wanted. He watched as the Wraith's eyes narrowed, the monster's rage burning brightly. He knew what his opponent planned to do next, and he was ready for it.

The Wraith, unable to control his fury, lunged for Jakob, long dagger leading, aimed for his heart.

Jakob twisted backward, avoiding the thrust, and then again, and again, the Wraith continuing his assault, the razor-sharp blades he held in each hand punching forward.

The monster was less interested now in a sophisticated approach to killing Jakob. He was more interested in trying to overwhelm him through sheer power and force.

"I am disappointed," said Jakob as he spun back another time, not bothering to raise his blades. Rather, he just let the Wraith's steel slip into the space where he had been standing just a moment before. "You dishonor not only your brethren, but you dishonor your master. You dishonor the Wraith Hunter."

"You will die, human," hissed the Wraith, no longer able to control his temper. The dagger in his left hand whipped around in a long, backward arc targeting Jakob's neck.

The Wraith's eyes widened in shock when his steel didn't meet the resistance he anticipated, his blade failing to cut into the human's flesh. His eyes almost bulged out of their sockets when instead he choked, feeling a painful stab through his throat.

"Not before you do," replied Jakob in a deathly quiet voice.

He stood right in front of the Wraith, one of his blades sticking all the way through the Wraith's neck.

Jakob watched as the Wraith choked on his own blood, the light leaving his eyes in only a few heartbeats. When Jakob pulled his steel free, the Wraith dropped right at his feet.

Pleased to have removed another Wraith from the fight, Jakob was about to make for the tower while he had the chance when he realized that he couldn't.

Duff had run into a problem. The rope running down from the top of the tower had snagged on the stone at the very edge and was in danger of snapping.

The Highlander was still stuck out in the open at the base of the tower, one child riding his back. Duff had to wait for another rope to give him a chance of escaping the Wraiths who were coming out of the village now and moving toward the broch from several directions.

Jakob should have assumed that his luck wouldn't hold. The Wraiths were streaming past him now in the fog, either not aware that he had just killed another of their brethren or not caring. They were probably seeking to eliminate the easier prey first before coming back to wreak their vengeance upon him.

There were four of the monsters in all. More than he could fight at one time.

But what did that matter?

He had come this far. If he was going to die this day, he was going to take as many of the Wraiths as he could to the other side with him.

Matten and his wife's children deserved the chance to grow older and make something of themselves. That would be his gift to the murdered Highlanders. But first, he needed to catch the Wraiths' attention.

"I am the Wraith who is not a Wraith!" Jakob roared, his voice shattering the silence of the Murk. "I have killed two of your Scouts. Do you run from me, Wraiths? Do you not have the courage to challenge me?"

Jakob watched it all happen with the Talent. The Wraiths who had been moving toward Duff stopped abruptly. Standing still in the fog.

Jakob waited uneasily for several seconds, worried that his

attempt to draw them toward him had failed. Concerned that the Wraiths would simply continue on toward the broch. Thankfully, his taunt had the desired effect.

With a sigh of relief, even as he began to wonder if he had lost his mind for taking such a risk, Jakob left the trail running through the village and walked out toward the center of the green. He wanted the additional space as he watched the Wraiths glide toward him, moving deftly through the mist, barely disturbing the grey haze. One of the monsters worked his way behind him so that his adversaries had taken up positions around him that mimicked the four cardinal points on the compass.

Jakob prepared himself for the combat that was about to begin, shaking his head in resignation. His plan wasn't going as well as he had hoped that it would.

Another half dozen Wraiths had just entered the village and were making their way toward the green, not bothering to search in and around the cottages, knowing that the Scouts who preceded them already had done so.

Jakob could only assume that these Wraiths had come here with the express purpose of hunting him down and putting to rest the legend he had crafted for himself in the Murk.

He didn't have any more time to think on all that as well as how he had gotten himself in the middle of such a mess. A soft hiss that sounded just a dozen feet to his front drew his attention.

"You will pay for your arrogance, Wraith who is not a Wraith. You will pay with your life."

"They're safe?" asked Duff.

He handed the oldest of Matten's children to an older

woman who whispered soothing words to the eight-year-old as she carried him down into the tower.

"Yes," Martin confirmed. "We did it. All five children are safe and sound."

"And we need to join them. It's not smart to be up here with the Murk all around."

Duff gave Donel a sharp look which made the merchant step back a half pace. He forced himself to soften his expression, not wanting that kind of reaction.

Duff didn't want to add to the fear that was already permeating the tower. The Highlander was a trader. He had never been a soldier.

That wasn't a criticism. It was simply a fact.

As a result, the Sergeant could understand Donel's desire to make use of the protection offered by steel and stone. The Wraiths were terrifying adversaries. Few survived an encounter with them when caught out in the Murk.

"We can't leave him down there on his own," protested Bertie.

His face was still red from the run and the climb. He was breathing heavily, and he was tired. More than tired, in fact. Exhausted. Even so, his eyes flashed with clarity and purpose.

They had made it to the broch with the children in tow because of the lad who now had the courage to face off against the Wraiths on his own. Bertie refused to repay Jakob's bravery and generosity by simply watching him die.

"Why doesn't the Lord Kestrel ask for the rope?" asked Donel, looking for some other way to get these fierce warriors to understand the gravity of their situation. He was mayor of the village. He was responsible for closing the trap door on the roof. And he was reluctant to leave it open for much longer, knowing how swiftly the Wraiths could climb the stone with their needle-sharp claws. "He knows that we need to seal the tower. It's the only way to ensure that we survive the attack."

The mayor of the hamlet was having a difficult time understanding what was occurring and why. The tower was there for a purpose. It should be used for that purpose when there was a need to do so.

The Lord Kestrel had demonstrated before that he could survive in the Murk. Donel had no doubt that he could again.

It was for these reasons that the Lord Kestrel was so well known and respected by the Highlanders. He did what others wouldn't or couldn't do. He did what the Highlanders wanted to do but didn't have the courage or skill to do themselves.

"There are other ways to fight Wraiths," said Tommie cryptically, bow in her hand, arrow fitted to the string. She stared into the swirling grey, unable to see beyond the grey stone of the parapet.

"He can't," Martin replied, answering Donel's question. He couldn't see with his eyes what was going on, but he could with the Talent, the connection between Jakob and the other Highlanders remaining in place. "There's a Wraith blocking his way, and more of those bastards are coming toward him now to ensure that he can't escape them."

"How can you even know that? I can barely see you, and you're only ten feet ..."

Donel jumped back a step, gasping, watching as Tommie pulled back on her bow and released an arrow into the fog. And then another, followed by a third. A fourth and a fifth came right behind.

Her movement was smooth and constant. Donel noticed that the archer was leaning farther over the battlements each time as she aimed closer and closer to the base of the broch.

"We have a problem," Tommie murmured, stretching out over the edge of the parapet, the grey haze greeting her. Even so, she could see through the Murk as if it was clear as day. "They're too close now. Too fast. They're coming for us."

"How can you expect to hit anything ..." Donel couldn't

even finish his statement, not really understanding what was happening, his face turning as grey as the haze. "What did you say? They're coming for us? What are you talking about?"

Tommie ignored Donel's questions, leaning over the parapet once again and firing almost straight down toward the ground. She welcomed the grunt of pain that drifted up from below. Nevertheless, the archer still cursed softly under her breath.

She hadn't killed the Wraith who had been about to climb the tower. The monster had sensed the arrow at the very last second, moving his body just enough to take the barbed tip in the top of his shoulder rather than his head.

Still, if Tommie was lucky and the wound severe enough, she had at least reduced by one the number of Wraiths capable of scaling the broch, which meant one less threat to deal with for the time being.

"What did she mean they're coming for us? The Wraiths? Now? Aren't they busy with the Lord Kestrel?" Donel looked at Duff in consternation, events moving too quickly for him. "We need to close the trapdoor. Now. Otherwise, we're putting the entire village at risk."

Duff shushed the merchant, needing a few moments to think. To figure out what their options were.

He hated the idea of hiding in the broch, and he realized in a flash that he couldn't do it. Not now. Not with Jakob still fighting for his life.

He and the other Highlanders linked to the Talent through Jakob stared into the Murk, hoping that the lad might be able to break free. If he did, they could help him get to safety.

But it wasn't to be.

Instead, their expressions darkened. The Wraiths had surrounded Jakob, and there was nothing that Duff and the other Highlanders could do.

Four of the monsters kept Jakob in place. Two more glided

across the green to tighten the noose. The other monsters streamed through the village, ignoring the standoff, intent on taking the tower.

Duff couldn't leave things as they were. He couldn't leave the lad to his fate.

Having no other options, he reached for the rope that was still tied to the steel ring that was set in the parapet. He needed to get down there fast. If it meant his own death, so be it.

He had never left a soldier behind when he served in the Royal Guard. He refused to do so now.

About to throw the rope back down, Bertie grasped Duff's forearm, preventing him from swinging a leg over the parapet.

"Don't," the large man said. "It's too late. We can't help him. Even if we went down there, we would only get in the way. He'd be more worried about us than himself."

"He can't take on so many by himself," Duff argued. "The lad is a surprise a second, yes, but even this is too much for him."

"You know I'm right, Duff," Bertie replied with a calm that he wasn't really feeling, but that he knew he needed to project. A composed tone now was the only way to get through to his Sergeant. "We don't want the lad to die. But we need to leave him be. If he's to have any chance of getting out of this mess, it's a chance that he'll have to create, not us."

Duff was going to protest again. He was going to shove his friend out of the way. But he realized that Bertie was right.

No matter how much he hated to admit it, he couldn't ignore the truth. If anyone had the capacity to extricate himself from such dire circumstances, it was Jakob. No one else.

The lad was on his own for now. Because they had their own battle to fight.

"There are more coming now," said Martin, his gaze tracking the movement of the Wraiths through the Murk as they approached the broch.

Duff saw it now as well, all of it playing out in the back of his mind. His desire to aid Jakob had blinded him to the larger threat that they faced.

In addition to the six Wraiths who were already on the green for the sole purpose of cornering Jakob, another six were approaching the broch, just seconds away from digging their claws into the stone so that they could scale the tower.

Worse, three more Wraiths had snuck around the back side of the broch and already had begun their ascent, the soft scrape of their claws digging into the stone and mortar the only give-away of their impending arrival.

"Get inside, Donel," Duff said, giving the mayor a gentle shove toward the trap door. He couldn't make decisions based on what he wanted. He needed to make decisions based on what was real. It was the only way to ensure that they survived the coming fight. "Seal the broch. Now."

"You're not coming?" The shock in Donel's voice was unmistakable.

"No," Bertie said. "No. We never leave a Highlander in need. Especially not the Lord of the Highlands."

"The Lord Kestrel refuses to go to the other side without a fight," Martin said, his pride evident. "Neither will we. We make our stand here."

Tommie didn't bother to say anything, only nodding at what her friends had said. Bow drawn, arrow nocked, she leaned over the parapet again, seeking another target.

Donel didn't know what to say. Staying out in the Murk with so many Wraiths was a death sentence. Everyone knew that. Everyone had friends and relatives who had suffered the consequences of making that mistake.

But what was he to do? These men and woman were soldiers. Had been, anyway.

Still were, in his opinion, as they radiated a quietude that he had no chance of attaining with so many monsters just yards away from gaining the top of the broch. Who was he to argue with them?

Nodding, Donel hustled over to the trap door, pulling it closed behind him as he descended the stairs.

The Highlanders looked at one another when they heard the loud clang of the bars being set in place below them and then the click of the lock. Their expressions were grim, although not fearful. No, rather a certainty flowed through them, both in terms of their actions and their decisions.

They were on their own now, yes, but they weren't defenseless. Far from it, in fact.

They still benefited from the gift that Jakob had given them, the sight that allowed them to navigate the Murk as if the fog wasn't even there.

Jakob would fight his battle.

They would fight theirs.

As one, Duff and the Highlanders turned toward the parapet, the Wraiths already climbing the stone.

By all rights, the human should already be dead.

Surrounded by Wraiths. No avenue for escape. A simple kill, just like all the others.

But he wasn't.

The human stood in the Murk, Wraiths all around him.

Despite his imminent demise, the human appeared to be the one in control of the situation, not the monsters of the Murk.

That's why the leader of the Wraith Scouts watched the first combat with such interest. After just the first slice of steel through the grey, he knew how it was going to end. For that matter, he had known before the duel had begun, even though his Wraith had not. Or his Wraith had chosen not to see it.

His Scout was blinded by his desire to kill the Wraith who is not a Wraith. By his lust to claim the recognition that would be bestowed upon him for collecting the bounty the Wraith Hunter had set on the boy's head.

One of his Wraiths already lay dead just twenty yards away, the Murk hiding his body. That Wraith had been much too confident, believing that the human he challenged could not stand against him.

The human had proven the Wraith wrong.

The Wraith had wanted acclaim. Just like the Wraith who was now fighting for his life.

Instead, because of his arrogance, the Wraith had done nothing more than earn himself a swift death.

It had taken no more than a few heartbeats, the Wraith seeking to slice the boy's throat with a single stroke.

The Wraith likely had attacked the same way before with great success.

Not so this time.

The human had been expecting the attack, and he was ready for it. The human pivoted to the side, barely needing to move as he punched one of the blades that he had stolen from another fallen Wraith right into his adversary's side.

The Wraith was dead before the boy had even withdrawn his steel.

The second Wraith was smarter, not as arrogant as the first. He demonstrated more patience. More reserve. He was trying to draw the Wraith who is not a Wraith into a mistake that he could capitalize on.

The Wraith didn't feel the need to end the combat rapidly. He only felt the need to end the combat in his favor.

The right approach, the leader of the Wraith Scouts believed. Yet as he observed the combat, he sensed that the Wraith really wasn't in control of the duel. That somehow the human had gained the upper hand and that he was deciding what would happen and when.

Maybe he felt this way because the Wraith had yet to create the opportunity that he was seeking. The boy made the Wraith circle around him, not giving him any chance to break through the defense he wove with his stolen steel.

The boy had struck the Wraith three times now, drawing blood with every slice of his blade.

Not so the Wraith. The boy had yet to bleed.

The leader of the Wraiths was impressed. The boy was performing the Dance of the Daggers better than his Wraith was.

He really shouldn't have been surprised, however. It simply confirmed that the boy was aptly named. It demonstrated that sending his Scouts after the boy was the right decision.

Just a second later, the Wraith leader closed his eyes, shaking his head in annoyance.

Assuming, of course, that they could kill him.

He had seen it even if the Wraith hadn't. The boy had lowered his right shoulder just enough to finally give the Wraith the opening that he wanted. It looked like the mistake that his Wraith was waiting for.

It wasn't.

The Wraith didn't realize that it was only a feint.

Too late.

The Wraith lunged. The boy danced away.

At the same time, the boy sliced backward with his stolen dagger with a speed that made it seem as if he was a part of the Murk.

His steel did no more than nick the Wraith's throat.

It didn't look like much of a wound at first, but the leader of the Wraiths understood what it meant.

The thin trickle of blood erupted into an uncontrollable spurt.

The boy had cut the Wraith's artery. Barely a slice. Even so, a perfectly placed slice.

The Wraith was dead, he just didn't know it yet.

～

JAKOB DIDN'T BOTHER to look around him, knowing what he would find. The six Wraiths hidden within the Murk, surrounding him, didn't worry him.

He had expected this to happen.

He had nowhere to go.

He had no chance of escape.

That was all right with him, because he had achieved his objective.

As a result, his life had become much, much simpler.

It had been reduced to a simple phrase that his father had shared with him. A phrase that his uncle had used quite a bit when they served together in the Royal Guard.

Kill or be killed.

That's what his life had become.

Jakob had killed one Wraith.

The second Wraith would be joining the first in just a few seconds. The monster had dropped to his knees, unable to stop the gushing flow of blood that cascaded from his neck, his already grey skin becoming even greyer as his life poured out onto the green.

Two Wraiths dead. Six more waiting to have a go at him. Probably even more, if the Wraiths attacking the tower had the chance to join the queue.

So be it.

Kill or be killed.

A simple philosophy.

A good philosophy.

The right philosophy for him right now.

Jakob took a breath, centering himself. The first two combats hadn't offered him much of a challenge. But these Wraiths standing around him had seen what he had done. He couldn't take them by surprise now.

The next combat would be more difficult. The one after that even more so, assuming he found a way to fight his way past his next challenger.

Jakob realized that he was lucky to still be alive. If the Wraiths came at him all at once, he stood little chance of defending himself. He would be dead in seconds.

For whatever reason, however, the monsters in the mist felt the need to engage in single combat with him. Every one of the monsters desired to be the one to take his head to the Wraith Hunter. All of them wanted the kill for themselves.

That was fine with him. The Wraiths' self-defeating insistence that they each be given the chance to kill him was why he was still alive.

It was a foolish approach. Better just to kill him and be done with it.

But until they figured that out, of course, he was more than willing to reap the benefits of their arrogance for as long as he could.

"Who are you to challenge me, boy?" demanded the Wraith Scout who stood right in front of Jakob, no more than twenty feet separating them.

The leader of the Wraiths felt the need to step in before the next combat began. He could feel the tension building among his hunters.

They wanted the kill for themselves, yes, but they were beginning to comprehend that earning that kill was less than certain. The bodies of their compatriots confirmed that for them.

The Wraith leader understood that. He had risen to his

current position because he had thrived within the warrior culture of his kind.

But he couldn't allow that culture to keep him from attaining his larger objective. He couldn't permit the boy to kill any more of his hunters.

"Who are you to challenge me?" Jakob responded in a similarly arrogant tone.

The Wraith Scout remained silent for a time, somewhat taken aback by the reply. Then he laughed, the scratchy noise audible all around the fog-shrouded green.

Despite the boy killing several of his Wraiths, this mission was proving to be more fun than he had anticipated. The boy truly was a worthy adversary.

"I was told that you were competent with a blade and that you were brave," said the Wraith Scout. "From what I have seen, those assumptions were both accurate. You have killed two of my Wraiths and you stand outside your tower. You do not cower behind the stone like the others of your kind."

"I do what needs to be done," Jakob shrugged, knowing that the Wraith could see the movement even with the fog billowing around them. "That's all. Nothing more, nothing less."

The Wraith Scout chose that moment to step out of the fog, no more than ten feet away from the Wraith who is not a Wraith.

He could see the boy clearly. He had heard that the boy used the weapons that the Wraiths preferred, so when he saw the haladie in his hands he wasn't surprised.

Such a waste, the Wraith leader thought. The boy should have been born a Wraith. He would have risen far within their ranks.

"That you do," the Wraith Scout agreed, "as do I. Your fun has come to an end. I have a task that must be completed, and you are keeping me from doing that."

"Killing me," said Jakob, his voice calm, betraying no emotion.

He had assumed as much. Word of the attacks that he had led against the Wraiths likely had returned with those monsters who had survived.

If the Wraiths wanted to maintain their dominance when hunting in the Highlands, then they had no choice but to eliminate him. They couldn't allow him to continue to challenge them.

To give the Highlanders hope. Belief.

He was the only reason that the balance of power had shifted away from the Wraiths and back to the Highlanders. Once he was dead, that balance of power would shift again, giving the Wraiths free rein in these peaks and to the south.

The Wraith Scout nodded. "Killing you, yes. But it seems that challenging you to a combat as is the way of the Wraith leads to only one end. I have no doubt that I can kill you, and the opportunity to do just that certainly is something that I relish, Wraith who is not a Wraith, but I have no more time to waste on you."

The Wraith Scout listened briefly to the fight taking place atop the tower. His other squad of hunters was seeking to climb the stone and force their way through the door in the roof, knowing that they stood little chance of breaking through the main entrance on the ground level.

He wanted to get up there himself. If his Wraiths could take this tower and get inside, they could find its weaknesses and learn how to take the others that the humans hid in whenever they came from the north. At least that's what he hoped.

"I'm sorry I made things so difficult for you," Jakob replied with a flick of his eyebrows.

As he stood there opposing this Wraith, he thanked Aloysius once again for all that he had taught him. Not just in terms of how to use the Talent, but also how to maintain his calm and composure in challenging circumstances.

If not for that training, if not for his ability to find that peace and drive away the emotions roiling within him so that he could look at the world through a stark and calculated reality, he had no doubt that he'd be pissing his pants right now.

"I doubt that," the Wraith Scout replied, the monster staring at Jakob for a few seconds more. He was intensely curious about this boy who challenged his hunters with so little fear. Who moved through the Murk as if he was born to it. But he didn't have time to continue this conversation, so he moved on to the conclusion. "What is it that your people call you, Wraith who is not a Wraith? I like to know the names of the ones I kill before I kill them."

"The Lord of the Highlands!" Duff shouted from the broch, even as he swung his hammer down toward the claw that appeared out of the fog and sought to grab hold of the stone parapet.

He and the other Highlanders were doing their best to prevent the Wraiths from gaining a foothold on the roof. But it was becoming more and more of a challenge for them. The Wraiths were too many and they were too fast.

Jakob grimaced when he heard Duff call down from the top of the broch. At first, he thought that the title Duff had given him was in jest, but as time passed, he had begun to under-stand what Duff was doing and why. That it was much more than an attempt to add a little humor to a hard existence.

Jakob didn't like what he was being called more frequently now, but he had no way to stop it. The new name was already taking on a life of its own. And he was absolutely certain that if he survived this clash, the title was going to stick. He'd never be able to escape it.

"Well, Lord of the Highlands, the time has come," said the Wraith Scout. "Are you ready to die?"

"You first," Jakob replied with a bravado that he didn't feel.

The Wraith Scout smiled, appreciating the boy's boldness. Then with a nod from their leader, the Wraiths surrounding Jakob moved toward him as one, daggers at the ready.

Jakob nodded to himself. He had been wondering if the Wraiths would adjust their strategy.

No longer able to play off their single-minded tactics, it was time for him to adjust his strategy as well.

Sheathing one of his double-bladed daggers behind his back, he reached for the Talent, a blazing sphere of energy dancing across his palm.

"Tommie!" Duff shouted at the exact moment that he raised his hammer in front of his face so that it was vertical to the ground, one hand near the end, the other halfway up the steel handle.

He used it to block the wickedly fast slash by the Wraith who had just reached the top of the tower. The monster didn't even bother to get his bearings, coming right for him as soon as he vaulted over the parapet.

The archer, standing near the center of the tower atop the locked and barred door that led down into the broch, responded immediately, a steel-tipped shaft streaking through the grey fog and punching through the Wraith's arm.

Tommie had aimed for the center of the monster's chest. Although the Wraith wasn't fast enough to get entirely out of the way since Tommie had been no more than a few dozen yards away when she fired, remarkably the monster sensed the projectile streaking toward him, dodging to the side to avoid the full force of the strike.

Even so, the barb did what Duff needed it to do. The Wraith hissed in pain and stepped back to examine the wound. The hiss became a growl as the Wraith reached down for the arrow and snapped the shaft in half, the feathered end dropping to the stone of the roof.

The monster then tried to yank free the end of the barb that was still lodged in his flesh. The growl became a roar. The Wraith couldn't pull it loose. It was caught in the bone.

Enraged, leaving the broken barb in place, the Wraith lunged for Duff, slashing and stabbing in a pattern that almost resembled a dance. Yet no matter what he tried, he couldn't get past his prey's defenses, the Wraith's options limited because he could only use one arm. The other hung limply by his side, a deep well of blood running down his clawed fingers and staining the stone.

Duff was more than happy to make use of that weakness. Employing his hammer deftly, he parried every attack, keeping the sharp steel the Wraith held in his left hand from slicing into him.

Although it was a hard fight, he was quite pleased. He was still alive as were all of his Highlanders. They were holding their own even though the Wraiths scaling the broch were having some success forcing them away from the parapet and more toward the center of the tower.

Duff knew that as soon as the Wraiths gained a foothold atop the broch, it was only a matter of time before the end came.

They were engaged in a losing fight. He had known it as soon as he had told Donel to shut and lock the trap door. His friends had known it as well.

The Wraiths were too many. They were too fast. They were too skilled.

Even with the gift that Jakob gave them, they could only stand for so long. Once one of them fell, the others would, their defensive circle broken.

Duff hated to admit it, but it was only a matter of time before that happened.

The fight atop the broch had been going on for only a few minutes, yet it felt like hours had passed. The Wraiths attacked with a controlled freneticism that was truly frightening and tested the very limits of their ability.

By all rights they should all be dead. If not for Tommie aiding them with her bow, intervening in the combats whenever the need was greatest, the Wraiths would have already claimed the top of the tower for their own.

Duff knew that for a fact. There was no denying it.

And there was really no reason to continue thinking about it. Better to focus on the present. Better to focus on prolonging the fight for as long as possible.

He and his friends had made their decision, and they certainly didn't regret it. Duff just wished that they didn't have to leave the lad all on his own to stand against so many Wraiths.

He wanted to help Jakob, but that was no more than a useless hope. He was disappointed by that conclusion, but not surprised.

Since he and his friends had no chance of going to Jakob's aid, they had lowered their expectations. Now, they just wanted to kill as many of the Wraiths as they could before the Wraiths killed them.

A simple objective.

And as the battle raged around him, Duff knew that simple was best.

"Duff, behind you!" shouted Martin.

The Highlander stood to Duff's right, having just succeeded in knocking a Wraith back off the parapet to fall to the ground below.

The Wraith had been intent on slicing his throat.

Martin, as was his way, didn't rush his attack. Instead, he allowed the monster to control the tempo of the combat while he looked for his enemy's weak point. When he found it, he struck wickedly fast.

With the Wraith overextending himself just an inch because of a slightly wild slash, Martin ducked beneath his steel, taking a knee himself as he drove his short sword clean through the monster's right knee.

The Wraith staggered backward, shrieking in agony, his leg beginning to buckle.

Martin was more than happy to make use of his adversary's impediment. As he pushed himself up off the stone, Martin slammed his shoulder into the Wraith's midsection, knocking the creature off the tower.

A good victory, but in his opinion, it had taken too long. He didn't have the time that he needed to help Duff. A Wraith who had just vaulted onto the roof was gliding through the fog, coming at his Sergeant from behind while Duff was engaged with another of the monsters.

Martin watched in horror as it all played out before him in slow motion. He knew what was going to happen, yet there was nothing that he could do to stop it.

In a flash of white light that scene disappeared from view.

Martin was thrown back toward Tommie and the locked trap door. The tower shook as if an earthquake had struck, all of the combatants atop the broch tumbling to the stone, a rumble of thunder echoing off the mountains.

Martin shook his head, trying to clear it of the ringing in his ears and the bright white spots that plagued his vision. Just then another bolt of lightning shot down from the sky, incinerating a Wraith who had been trying to push himself to his feet, intent on stabbing Duff in the back while he was engaged with his brethren, the Highlander somehow remaining on his feet despite the powerful blasts.

Not so for the first Wraith Duff had been fighting. The monster had fallen onto his back and was struggling to regain his bearings.

Duff didn't waste the opportunity granted to him, swinging

a powerful stroke down with his hammer and crushing the Wraith's skull.

Not knowing what had happened or why, Martin pushed himself to his feet, retaking his place next to Duff. Bertie, Benyen, and Tommie were there as well, although all of them were still feeling the aftereffects of the explosions, all of them staring at the stones scarred the color of ash where the lighting struck.

A brief respite for them, no more than that.

There were still too many Wraiths opposing them atop the broch, and several more of the monsters with their clawed hands already on the parapet were about to pull themselves over.

"Stand strong, lads and lass," Duff said in a flinty voice. "Make them earn it."

Duff could not explain the lightning that had struck. He could only assume that Jakob had something to do with it. After the two bolts hit the rooftop, Duff had glimpsed briefly what was going on around him.

It wasn't good.

A simple mathematical equation. Too many Wraiths, too few Highlanders.

Duff knew that the end had come for all of them.

He was ready. His only desire was to make some of the bastards bleed before they took him.

Yet before the Wraiths could begin their final attack, Duff sensed a rush of movement behind him. His eyes widened when he saw Donel running by him, a battle axe in his hand, screaming as loud as he could. Dozens more Highlanders followed, charging toward the Wraiths who had encircled the five friends.

Duff's look of shock turned to one of pleasure as he jumped back into the fight, joining the Highlanders who had bounded out of the trap door with spears, swords, daggers, and axes, even cleavers and carving knives, seeking to clear the top of the broch of the invaders.

He relished the exhilaration in their eyes, the same look that he had seen in the other Highlanders who had been joining him and Jakob outside the brochs, braving the Murk and the Wraiths.

A taste of freedom. A feeling that they were no longer held hostage by the coming of the mist and the monsters lurking within.

Thanks to Donel's frenzied charge, the battle atop the broch ended quickly. The Wraiths who were too slow to flee, not knowing what to do when challenged by so many humans at once, were cut down with a brutal efficiency. The Highlanders energized by a rage that allowed them to get past their fear.

Yet despite their victory, the Highlanders remained a somber lot. Because the clash wasn't over yet.

Once the Wraiths were cleared from the top of the tower, they turned their gaze to the Murk below.

Flashes of white light streaked with red burned through the grey haze.

There were still Wraiths that needed to die.

THE WRAITHS APPROACHED CALMLY through the Murk, their anticipation sparking in their depthless black orbs. They held their blades at the ready, a few even spinning their weapons in blurry circles of bone-white steel. With so many of them attacking at once, they seemed to have little concern now about killing the human who had stood against them with such frightening ease.

Jakob could almost feel the steel about to slice into his flesh.

He could sense the desire emanating from these monsters.

The hunger for the kill.

Each one was desperate to be the one to strike the killing blow. To be the one who killed the Wraith who is not a Wraith.

But they would have to wait a little while longer to gain that accolade.

They would have to earn that privilege and engage in a real fight.

Thankful to Aloysius for teaching him another skill with the Talent that he thought would be quite useful in this moment when his life could be counted in heartbeats, a skill that the old Magus had made him practice for hours, not allowing him to stop until he had perfected it, even as other weighty matters pressed down upon them, Jakob pulled in as much of the natural magic as he could hold. Then he laced that already immense power with that of the Blood Ruby, the artifact welcoming his touch and magnifying his strength a hundredfold.

His green eyes flashing brightly in the fog, Jakob threw the ball of energy that had been dancing across his palm at the Wraith to his front, the monster about to lunge at him with his dagger.

The white-hot energy tinged with the red of the jewel blasted right through the Wraith. The monster stood there for just a few seconds, forgetting his enemy standing before him, forgetting the daggers he still held in his claws, his focus entirely on the smoking hole burned through his chest and out his back.

The Wraith looked up from his devastating wound, catching his killer's eyes, the green fire burning there the last thing he saw before he fell onto his back.

For just a breath, everything stopped, the Wraiths stunned by the display of power.

Jakob was the first to act, using their surprise and hesitation against them.

Spheres of energy laced with red shot from his palms,

blasting through the Wraiths who just a moment before believed that they were going to make names for themselves by seizing the prize the Wraith Hunter sought.

No longer.

The dynamics of the combat had changed.

Now they were simply joining the list of Wraiths killed by the Wraith who is not a Wraith.

Four Wraiths died in seconds, only the leader of the monsters still standing on the green with Jakob, and he had a ball of energy already dancing across his palm.

The Wraith held his daggers in his clawed hands, ready for the combat to begin. However, he knew that was only a foolish hope now.

The boy had turned the tables on him. There was no cause for the Wraith who is not a Wraith to engage in the Dance of the Daggers with him.

The Wraith's death was certain now. He could see it in those blazing green eyes, and there was nothing that he could do to prevent it.

"We will continue to come for you," hissed the Wraith, his voice revealing the hint of fear and disappointment that had begun to work its way into him. "The Wraith Hunter will not stop until he has your head."

Jakob simply stared at the Wraith. Then he nodded, unaffected by the threat. "I welcome the challenge. And who knows, maybe your Wraith Hunter will have the courage to challenge me on his own rather than sending you to die for him."

Before the Wraith could respond, Jakob flicked the ball of energy at the monster.

The Wraith remained on his clawed feet just a second more, the monster's expression changing from one of anger to disbelief. His strength fading, the Wraith dropped his daggers to the grass and then crumpled to the ground, most of his chest missing.

Jakob should have felt some emotion as he surveyed the wreckage of his work. But he didn't.

Exhilaration? Satisfaction?

No, nothing. Not even regret.

These Wraiths came here for one reason and one reason only.

To kill him.

And then they were going to kill his friends and any other Highlanders they could sink their claws into.

He had succeeded where they had failed. It was as simple as that.

As his father and uncle had liked to say, kill or be killed.

Today he had survived. Tomorrow ...

Tomorrow was tomorrow.

The only thing that affected him was the odor of burning flesh that permeated the fog, the scent making him feel ill.

He wanted to breathe clean air that didn't remind him of death.

Yet despite his success Jakob wasn't done.

He needed to help Duff and the other Highlanders atop the tower.

Jakob understood that he needed to remain calm. It was essential to using the Talent effectively. But in that moment, he could barely control his anger, feeling as he did when the slaver murdered his father and he had no choice but to slip off into the Murk, leaving Dougal's body behind.

He realized, however, that for what he had in mind, he could release his rage. That he needed to release his rage, in fact, in order for him to have any chance of success.

Because for him to accomplish his goal, the precision that Aloysius had demanded of him during his training sessions needed to be tied to the power surging through him.

Raising his arms so that they were even with his shoulders,

he took a breath, trying to calm himself, hoping that what he was about to attempt actually worked.

He whipped his arms toward the ground.

He maintained his calm as the bolts of lightning slammed down onto the tower and then out into the glen.

Jakob guided the strikes as best as he could, focusing on the Wraiths who were around the broch before targeting those approaching through the Murk.

He had never done anything like that before with the Talent. He had never harnessed so much power at once. And he really didn't know how he had figured out how to call down lightning bolts from what had been a clear sky before the Murk had settled over the Highlands. He was just glad that his precision matched his power.

Maybe it was because of the Blood Ruby, the gem that was touching his chest filling him with a welcome warmth and a sense that he could accomplish anything that he set his mind to.

Maybe it was simply a natural progression as he explored what he could do with the Talent without the guidance of someone like Aloysius.

Of course, the why didn't really matter now. Only the how. Only the fact that he had succeeded.

He could think about all that later. There was one more task that he wanted to try.

If he succeeded, he would send a message to the Wraith Hunter and his Scouts that might make them question their decision to invade the mountains that Jakob had claimed as his home.

Closing his eyes and taking a few deep breaths to center himself, Jakob pulled in as much of the Talent as he could. The Blood Ruby lying against his chest grew warmer by the second, although thankfully not uncomfortably so.

Feeling himself reach the limit of his ability to control the energy flowing within him, he realized that now all he could do was hope that what he wanted to do worked. Otherwise, he got the feeling that he was well on his way to killing himself.

He started slowly, not wanting to rush, not wanting to make a mistake, recognizing that he needed to exercise the patience that was so often a challenge for him.

To make it easier, he visualized it. Slowly at first, beginning as no more than a dim glow, a nimbus of white light streaked by the red of the Blood Ruby formed around him and then streamed out in all directions.

Jakob smiled. He could sense what was happening. He could see it in his mind just as he could see it with his eyes.

It was working. He was reflecting outward the massive quantity of energy that raged within him.

Pleased with his initial efforts, Jakob then released more of the Talent he held, the energy intensifying the brightness of the nimbus that surrounded him.

In rough terms, he viewed it as turning himself into a human torch, the power so blinding now that if anyone could see him in the Murk, they'd have to turn away. He assumed it was much like staring at the sun.

And just as he had hoped, where the Talent touched the Murk, the tendrils of grey burned away into a flaky cinder that drifted down toward the green, disappearing entirely before the ashes hit the grass.

Confident now in what he was doing, Jakob released more and more of the Talent. The blazing energy surged out from him, forming a dome of white that reached from the very base of the broch to the trail that led through the village.

Where the overwhelming power of the Talent touched the Murk, the grey haze retreated or was destroyed, the Wraiths still on the green having no choice but to follow the fog as it began to retreat across the plateau.

Jakob continued to feed more power into the white-hot

energy that was centered on him, a wall of white pushing slowly but inexorably into the Murk, revealing the green and the broch, then the first few homes of the village, then the entire village, and then the entire plateau.

Jakob became more confident in what he was doing as he did it. The energy that he controlled reached out into the Murk, burning it away and returning the village and its surroundings to the Highlanders.

Certain now that he had mastered this new skill, he extended his reach swiftly, sensing the many other Wraiths still at the edge of the plateau who had been seeking to join the fight around the broch.

With a final push, the wall of light reached into the encircling mountains, the warm touch of the afternoon sun a welcome change to the smothering feel of the grasping grey.

For those Wraiths caught in Jakob's final surge, it was a painful and horrifying death. The touch of the sun set their flesh aflame, the only thing they could hope for a quick end to the torment.

Jakob felt no sympathy for the monsters.

They had come here anticipating an easy victory.

It hadn't worked out in their favor.

Such was the way of war.

Because it was a war, Jakob understanding what would happen to him and his Highlanders if they lost.

Having pushed as far as he could with the energy under his control, Jakob closed his eyes again, this time in thanks.

He had succeeded.

Aloysius would be proud.

Releasing his hold on the Talent, the power flowing through him, flaring around him, slowly dissipated.

Yet the Murk didn't try to move back into the leagues of territory that Jakob had reclaimed. Instead, the grey remained in place, unwilling to return to a place where so much of the evil mist had been destroyed. Where so many of the creatures the Murk nourished had perished.

When he opened his eyes, Jakob realized that silence had fallen over the green. He was struck by how quiet it was. Nothing and no one made a sound.

Feeling dozens of sets of eyes upon him, Jakob looked up.

The Highlanders stood atop the tower, the remnants of their battle, the charred husks of the Wraiths, littering the green around the base of the broch.

They were all staring at him.

Jakob's eyes moved from one face to the next until he found Duff, the Highlander standing right up against the parapet, his large hammer streaked in blood, a very large grin on his face.

He could tell that Duff was glad to see that he was still alive. He could tell by the spark in his eyes that the Sergeant was quite pleased for another reason as well.

Jakob had a feeling that he knew what it was, a touch of anxiety shooting through him. He didn't even get the chance to protest.

With one hand, Duff raised his hammer above his head. Then, in a stentorian voice that had served him so well as a Sergeant in the Royal Guard and that drifted out over the plateau, he let out a roar.

"Long live the Lord of the Highlands!"

The cries of the Highlanders standing atop the broch erupted across the plain, so loud that their voices echoed off the surrounding mountains, the cheers continuing for several minutes.

The Highlanders were consumed not only by Jakob's success, but also by their own. They had swept their tower clear of the Wraiths.

And then the Lord Kestrel had swept the plateau clear of the hated Murk and the monsters that came with it.

For the first time, the Highlanders had fought back. And they had won!

Thanks in large part to the young man who had hunted the Wraiths as the Wraiths had hunted him. The young man who had destroyed the Murk with a power that could not be denied.

Duff almost felt sorry for Jakob as he watched the lad. He noted how his expression changed gradually, Jakob grasping what had just happened to him. What it meant in the larger scheme.

That realization having struck him, Jakob didn't know what to do now.

Trying to help him, Duff gave Jakob a nod.

Jakob took the hint, nodding to the Highlanders screaming his name, hoping that doing so would end the cheering and what he viewed as undeserved acclaim.

It had the opposite effect.

The Highlanders' adulation increased in volume.

Once again, Jakob turned his blazing green eyes toward Duff, his expression desperate now, seeking guidance.

Duff almost broke out into a laugh, but he couldn't do that to the lad. He had already placed him in a difficult position, and in the weeks to come that position would only become more challenging.

Even so, it was necessary. Both for Jakob and for the Highlands.

He had seen it the first time he had met Jakob. And his belief in the lad had only become stronger as he had gotten to know him better.

Jakob's shy and uncertain reaction to what was happening to him now only confirmed it for the former Sergeant.

Trying to help him, Duff made a motion with his hand, simulating a wave.

Jakob nodded, getting the hint. He raised his right hand into the air, about to wave. But he had forgotten that he still held in his hand the double-bladed dagger he had claimed from one of the first Wraiths that he had killed.

Just as the weapon rose above his head, the sunlight flashed off the steel, bathing him in a white glow reminiscent of the power that he had used to force back the Murk.

That only led the Highlanders to raise their voices to a deafening crescendo.

Listening to the cheers, Duff knew the truth of it.

Jakob hadn't just defeated the Wraiths sent to kill him. He had done something even more important.

He had given the people of the Highlands hope. And, whether he wanted to or not, he had given them the leader that they needed.

QUITE AN INTRODUCTION

"By what right do you seek to enter our property?" demanded Talia, working her way between her soldiers to stand in front of the Captain who demanded entry. "You have no authority here."

Three squads of the Fal Carrachian Guard formed up into columns stood at the gate that led onto the Carlomin docks.

They hadn't tried to push their way through. Yet. Although based on how they were poised to move and how their hands were hovering over the hilts of their swords, they were preparing themselves to do just that.

Sirena and the Carlomin Guard had arrayed themselves right in front of the soldiers, careful not to step beyond the line that separated the Carlomin property from the city proper.

Sirena would stand strong, although she knew as well that she needed to be careful. She didn't want to provoke the soldiers who were paid by the Governor into using her obstinance as an excuse to do what they wanted.

She didn't mind a fight, so long as it was a fight that she could win. And in that moment, she had her doubts.

"By order of Governor Roosarian," the Captain replied in a

nasally voice, the man clearly bristling at being denied passage through the gate and being talked to with what he viewed as an utter lack of respect for his position in the Territory.

As the Captain stewed, Davin stepped forward to stand next to Talia. Isana came up behind her daughter and to the right.

Rorie, Rufus, and Toni, along with the other soldiers who had joined Davin on the journey from the Isle of Mist, filled in the space behind the gladiator, a solid wall of steel now arrayed against the soldiers seeking entry into the Carlomin enclave.

"Governor Roosarian rules Ballinasloe," Talia countered. "She does not rule on Carlomin property."

"You might want to rethink that perspective," hissed the Captain.

"I know the law. I speak the truth. I do not seek to challenge the Governor, I simply state clearly the rights enjoyed by any Caledonian who owns property in the Territories."

"In the Territories, missy, the law often doesn't hold as much sway as you might think," the Captain warned.

"Is that so?" Talia gave the soldier a look of scorn, ignoring how he attempted to belittle her. "And are you the one who's going to teach me the ways of the Territories?"

"I'll teach you whatever I think you need to learn, missy," replied the Captain, his tone sharp, also suggestive. "And I have no doubt that in the end you'll enjoy it and want another lesson."

"I doubt you could teach a fish to swim," challenged Talia, her sharp rebuke earning several snorts of laughter from the soldiers standing behind her.

Although not from Davin. He simply stared at the Captain, analyzing how he moved, ready if violence was called for. Words had little meaning to the gladiator. Only steel did when it came time for a fight.

"Do you know who I am, missy?" demanded the soldier. "Do you not know the power I hold in Fal Carrach?"

"No, who are you?" asked Davin, his natural curiosity tinged with a hint of disrespect.

The gladiator's question gained another round of laughter, although that wasn't his intention. He really didn't know who the man was, and he recognized that Talia's temper was rising. Never a good thing when there was the increasing urge to draw blades.

The Captain turned toward the man who had just interjected himself into the dialogue. In the past, the soldier's hard gaze, which he had spent a long time perfecting, had forced many an opponent to wilt under the pressure.

Not so the young man standing next to Talia Carlomin. Despite the tension of the situation, despite the steel and the adrenaline, the man stood there calmly, leaning against the longest spear the Captain had ever seen, seemingly completely at his ease.

"I am Vanion Oselnik," the soldier said, biting out each word. "I am the Captain of the Fal Carrachian Guard."

"Congratulations," replied Davin with a nod, his response earning another chuckle from the soldiers standing around him, even Talia and Isana cracking smiles now.

"You make fun of me, boy? Who are you to do that?"

"I'm Davin Noname. No more, no less."

Davin's response caught the Captain by surprise. "Davin who?"

"Davin Noname."

"Noname?"

"Noname," Davin repeated, wondering if the Captain had been hit one too many times in the head, just as his sister had claimed of him.

The Captain wasn't sure if the young man who displayed a unique calm despite the array of steel around him was making fun of him or simply responding to his question. As a result, for just a few seconds, he didn't know what to do.

"What kind of name is that?" the Captain finally asked, lacing his words with disdain.

"Just a name. A bit easier to say than Vanion Oselnik, in my opinion. That's really quite a mouthful."

The soldiers standing behind Davin laughed more heartily then, their increasing levity stoking the Captain's building rage. Before Oselnik could accelerate the confrontation as he so desperately wanted to do, his words died in his throat.

"Thank you for your efforts, Captain Oselnik," said a commanding voice from right behind him. Hakea Roosarian stepped between her soldiers so that she was now facing off against Talia Carlomin. She ignored Talia, however, her eyes lingering on the young man who had challenged her Captain without a second thought. "I believe you've outlived your usefulness to this conversation."

Davin ignored the woman's perusal of him, keeping his eyes fixed on the Captain. He knew that if the soldier was going to disobey his commander, now would be the time.

And clearly Oselnik was thinking about doing just that, not appreciating her last comment. He remained where he was, however, even as his right hand drifted down to the hilt of his sword.

"What can I do for you, Governor Roosarian?" Talia struggled not to utter a curse while addressing the woman, not believing that she deserved the respect that her position demanded.

"Is not my desire to visit one of my most loyal subjects reason enough to be here?"

"I am not your subject, Governor Roosarian," Talia corrected. "I am a citizen of Fal Carrach."

"It would be wise for you to remember, young lady, that semantics mean very little on this side of the Burnt Ocean. There is little difference between subject and citizen."

"On the contrary, I see a great deal of distinction between

those two words," replied Talia in a measured tone. "But it seems that we disagree on quite a lot, do we not? Such as the law as set forth in the charter giving you responsibility for Fal Carrach, a topic I was just discussing with your Captain."

Hakea nodded almost imperceptibly. "And there is the root of our difficulties. We interpret the world in a different way. Here, in Fal Carrach, in all of New Caledonia, in fact, it's good to remember that we are building the world that we want. Is that not what you and your mother are doing?"

"Building the world we want doesn't mean that we should ignore the rules that allow us to live together peacefully," said Talia.

"I couldn't agree with you more," smiled Hakea. "So with that in mind, why is it that you are trying to disrupt the peace that I am seeking to maintain in Fal Carrach?"

"By that you mean ..."

Hakea's smile transformed into a smirk. "You have not responded to my proposal, Talia Carlomin. I cannot allow you to continue to delay. For the good of the Territory, to ensure the peace that we both hope to enjoy here in Ballinasloe, I hope that you will be giving me the answer that I want to hear. The answer that will ensure that your fortunes and those of your family don't take a turn for the worse."

Davin watched the exchange between the two women with a great deal of interest, knowing which direction the verbal combat was going. The hate between them was almost a tangible thing.

"The answer is no," Talia replied, squaring up to Roosarian, her eyes locking onto the Governor's. "We do not accept your demand that masquerades as a proposal."

"Perhaps you should rethink that response, girl. We do want to maintain the peace, don't we? Who knows what could happen if all isn't as it should be?"

"You mean as you believe it should be," countered Talia, her expression becoming flintier.

"I am the Governor," replied Hakea with a shrug. "I do what is best for the Territory. No matter the cost."

"Do what you will," replied Talia, her voice strangely calm despite the Governor's obvious threat. "You will not take the company my father helped to build."

Roosarian stared at Talia for almost a minute, nodding her head ever so slightly as she did so. She really had expected no less from this foolish, headstrong, arrogant girl. Then she shrugged, as if to say that Talia's decision was of little consequence.

Hakea would get what she wanted. She always did. It would just require a bit more effort and time on her part.

"Then allow the consequences to fall on your head," Hakea said. "It's a pity, really. You've done so much. And to have it all fall down around you. Piece by piece. So very, very sad."

Davin watched as Talia's hand slipped toward her dagger, recognizing what she was going to do next. He could understand why she was angry, why she was thinking about drawing steel.

The Governor's veiled threat was unmistakable.

Moreover, he had learned from the sailors and soldiers during his journey to Ballinasloe that Hakea Roosarian owed Talia a debt in blood.

But now wasn't the time for Talia to collect. Not with several dozen soldiers just on the other side of the gate ready to rush forward. Not with the several more squads of soldiers who were trying to stay hidden in the crowd as they worked their way along the harbor to join their comrades.

He had no doubt that the soldiers in the Carlomin Guard would acquit themselves well if it came to a fight. But he also had no doubt that the sheer number of soldiers in the Fal

Carrachian Guard would win the day if this confrontation became one of steel rather than words.

"That's quite a fortress you're building on the island," Davin said, seeking to reduce the animosity growing between the two women, or at least delay its expression for a little while longer.

"I'm sorry, but what are you talking about?" demanded Hakea, turning her gaze toward Davin, her train of thought broken.

"Your fortress," continued Davin, nodding toward the island at his back. "Very impressive. Did you design it yourself? Very utilitarian. Very ... what's the word I'm looking for ... severe. Yes, that's it. Severe. Is there any particular reason you went in that direction?"

For several heartbeats, Hakea could only stare, taking in this newcomer's height and his hair that blazed red in the sunlight, his long spear held comfortably in one hand. She didn't know whether to be perturbed by the interruption or curious as to who this fellow was and why he was even here.

He didn't appear to be a sailor. Soldier, maybe, although he wasn't wearing the Carlomin uniform and leather armor.

"And you are again?" she demanded.

"Davin Noname," he replied with a big smile that even succeeded in lifting Hakea's lips into a twisted smirk of her own.

"Noname?"

"Yes."

Hakea opened her mouth to say something. She closed it just as quickly. For the first time in a very long time, she wasn't sure what to say next.

"And I ask again, who are you?"

"No one."

"Davin Noname is no one," Hakea replied, clearly amused by his response rather than angry.

Davin laughed with her even though everyone else around

them wasn't smiling. The tension and the threat of violence remained palpable.

"Where are you from, Davin Noname?" Hakea asked, allowing her curiosity to win out for a time. It was much more enjoyable talking to him than the woman who had frustrated her at every turn. And it gave her time to think about what to do next.

"Tintagel."

"And what did you do in Tintagel? You served in the Royal Guard?"

"No, I fought in the Pit."

That response caught Hakea's attention as well as that of the soldiers around her, a few even grasping the hilts of their swords and the hafts of their spears with a tighter grip, as if this gladiator was about to leap right into their midst.

She ignored them and looked past the spear he held, taking a closer look at him. She could see several of his scars extending out from beneath his shirt around his neck and at his shoulder as well as the many marks that crisscrossed his forearms, all of which attested to years of combat.

Next, she looked deeply into his eyes. There was a spark of mischief there that kept her smile on her face. There was another emotion there as well. At the very back. Only shared at certain times. Likely when he was about to drive that spear of his right into someone's chest.

A frostiness. A lack of feeling that both frightened Hakea and, strangely, excited her at the same time.

If he truly was a gladiator, and she had no reason to doubt him, then he must have been there during the Caledonian uprising. It's the only way that the man with a warm smile, which was completely in opposition to the frigid temperature of his eyes, could have escaped the white sand.

Intriguing. This soldier or gladiator or whatever he was had a quality that pulled at her.

She wasn't sure what it was. She wasn't sure why it was. And she wasn't sure that she wanted to pursue it. Even though she found it difficult to resist.

"Well, Davin Noname, allow me to welcome you to Ballinasloe." Hakea turned away then and began walking back into the city, her soldiers turning with her and preparing to follow.

Captain Oselnik gave Davin a hard look that was meant to intimidate him.

Davin just ignored him. After the combats that he had fought, no one had the ability to make him piss his pants.

Not even the Volkun, although Bryen wouldn't even bother to try. He'd just stab him and be done with it.

"Come see me in the next few days," Hakea called over her shoulder. "You've selected the wrong employer. You should come work for me. The world is changing, and I'm the one making that happen."

Davin watched her go, the tension near the gate finally easing as the Fal Carrachian soldiers were swallowed by the crowd that had gathered to watch the contest.

An interesting woman, he thought. Dangerous though. Definitely someone to steer clear of, although he had the feeling that was going to prove difficult in the days ahead.

"You had no right to do that," hissed Talia, rounding on Davin. She was right up against his chest because of the tight quarters, so she had to crane her neck to catch his eyes.

"I was just trying to help," Davin protested.

"I don't need your help."

Davin cut her off before she could say anything else. Talia reminded him of Lycia in several ways, and he really had no desire to listen to another diatribe.

"You did need my help. You were about to pull your dagger. I didn't think you wanted the situation to escalate to the point of bloodshed. This isn't the place to take on the Governor of Fal Carrach."

"I knew what I was doing," Talia countered.

"You were being impulsive. And I should know. Because I'm usually the impulsive one."

Talia was about to deny Davin's charge, yet she found that she couldn't. He had hit too close to the truth, and she didn't want to admit that to herself.

"I don't need your help," Talia whispered one more time for his ears only. Then she stalked off toward the warehouse that served as her quarters and her office.

Davin watched her go. That could have gone better, he admitted. Still, better Talia be angry with him rather than having a dozen or more bodies littering the Carlomin dock.

Isana came to stand next to him, her eyes following Talia as well. "You fought in the Pit. How would you judge the little contest we just enjoyed?"

Davin nodded. That was an excellent way to put it. "Emotional."

"Please explain."

Davin pulled his eyes away from Talia when she disappeared into the warehouse, giving his full attention to her mother. "I was trained to fight on the white sand without emotion. To focus on my steel and my opponent. To ignore the screams and curses from the crowd. To ignore whatever my adversary might do to distract me. To ensure that my focus was solely on killing. As quickly as I could."

"And this?"

"This was personal, and when it's personal you make mistakes," Davin replied. "Usually fatal ones."

"You know, as I said, I attended the combats at the Colosseum once," said Isana, linking her arm with his and drawing him away from the gate. "Not by choice, mind you. For business. I never went back again. Barbaric is too kind a word."

"I certainly thought so," agreed Davin.

"What was your name in the Pit again, Davin?"

"The Crimson Giant."

Isana nodded sagely. "Yes, a worthy title." She leaned in closer to him, as if she were going to share a secret. "As you have just seen, and as you probably already knew, Talia has a temper. Better to confront it head on just as you did. She just needs some time to cool off."

Davin nodded again.

"Your assessment was correct," Isana continued. "As you work more with my daughter, I would ask that you keep that in mind. There is something personal between my daughter and Hakea Roosarian. I worry that matter will get in the way of Talia making the decisions that she needs to make rather than the decisions that she wants to make."

"You want me to keep an eye on her?" asked Davin, somewhat surprised by the request.

"Isn't that what your Lord Keldragan asked you to do as part of this assignment?" Isana asked with a knowing look.

For just a moment, Davin didn't know what to say. Then he smiled. "I'll do the best that I can, but no promises. Your daughter doesn't want my help."

"Your assessment in that respect is correct as well. Now come on. I'll show you to your quarters."

They started walking past the warehouse toward a building on the pier to the north of the one where the *Swift* was moored.

"You know, I much prefer Davin Noname to the Crimson Giant," offered Isana.

"So do I," he agreed.

ANSWERING THE CALL

"I find that really hard to believe," scoffed Tamsin, shaking her head in a mix of amusement and disbelief, half expecting the Highlander she was speaking with to break out into laughter at any moment for making her look the fool so easily.

"You'll believe it if you see it for yourself," said Tenny. "I'm not trying to convince you. I'm just telling you what I saw."

"You saw it with your own eyes?" asked Tamsin, needing confirmation. The woman only came halfway up the broad Highlander's chest, yet the battle axe she leaned against, knob in her hand, sharp blades digging into the soft earth, dwarfed the one that he carried on his back.

"I have," confirmed Tenny, his tone serious, lacking the touch of humor that she could usually find there.

"And not just after you've had a few cups of ale?" wondered Tamsin. "We all know how much you enjoy your ale, Tenny."

Under other circumstances, Tenny might have laughed at a comment like that. Because he could only agree with her.

Tamsin was right. He did like his ale. But he didn't feel like laughing today.

Today he wasn't in a humorous mood. And he certainly didn't feel like drinking. He didn't think he'd feel like drinking ever again. He didn't want to miss the chance that the young man had given him, and he couldn't do that if he was sleeping it off in the back of a tavern.

No, he couldn't keep acting as he had been.

He needed to act differently.

And today he felt different. Because today felt different.

He wasn't sure why today of all days made him feel this way. A burst of energy, a surge of hope, residing in his chest, waiting to explode outward. But he was glad for it.

It took him a few seconds before his mind grabbed hold of the word that he had been searching for, all the while ignoring the laughter of the men and women around him. He refused to allow them to distract him.

He didn't care that they were making fun of him. In a good-natured way, of course. Because no one in their right mind dared to push Tenny over the edge.

He closed his eyes, pushing out the jokes and laughter.

Finally, the word came to him.

Momentous.

For whatever reason, today felt momentous.

And not just because so many Highlanders had answered the call. Thousands, in fact. Many had traveled several days or more to come to the Grove.

He knew that most of these people made the effort because of a story.

Just a story. No more than that.

But they wanted to hear that story.

For some, like Tenny, they came because they had played a part in that story. A small part, true. Yet he and all the others who had been with him then hoped for larger roles in the future.

Because they knew the truth. They knew the story that was

circulating among the gathered Highlanders was more than just a story.

They knew that the story actually was a path. If they had the courage to take it, they could gain what they most desired.

Their freedom.

So, he would allow the Highlanders around him, all curious for more information, to have their fun. He didn't mind.

They would find out what he had discovered soon enough.

Tenny shifted his gaze to the center of the plateau.

The Grove.

A peculiar name since only a single tree rose on this small plain.

Granted, this was the largest heart tree in the Highlands. Even so, it was just the one.

The rest of the plain was nothing more than long grass that kissed the slopes of the circling peaks and danced at the whim of the wind.

The heart tree did take his breath away. The monstrous conifer reached more than four hundred feet into the sky. Its branches extended out in all directions, putting more than a third of the plateau in shadow.

Its roots, most thicker than a man was tall, ran in all directions across the ground, twisting and curling as they chose. There were so many arches and corkscrews that it made him think of the powerful, breathtaking, somewhat frightening waves that he had braved several years before to reach the Highlands.

In fact, all of the people standing with Tenny had done the same. They had risked their lives and their fortunes to cross the Burnt Ocean so that they could come to these rugged, beautiful mountains.

Almost all had taken the risk for the same reason that he did.

They wanted to build something new. For themselves and for their families.

They wanted land to farm. They wanted a home to call their own. They wanted a place where they could make their own way in the world without the restrictions -- societal, economic, political, cultural -- that made creating a better life in Caledonia so difficult.

They had known that coming to this new, wild land would offer them challenges, frustrations, and obstacles that they would need to overcome.

They weren't fools, after all. They just wanted better lives. They wanted what they hadn't found in the Kingdom far to the east.

Still, Tenny and all the others with him had never expected that this new land, which had offered them so much promise when they had first arrived, would offer them so much terror and death as well.

Slavers kidnapping people and forcing them into the mines, never to emerge again.

Stalkers, what many viewed as walking nightmares, murdering good folk after the sun set.

Wraiths hunting within the Murk, slaughtering anyone foolish or unlucky enough to be caught in the mist.

And to add insult to injury, a Governor who cared nothing for them. A man who cared only for his Stone, a massive monument to his own vanity and visions of power.

He was supposed to govern here in this land that Tenny had claimed as his own with the primary goal of helping those in need. Yet during his time in this Territory, Torstan Sharperson had demonstrated time and time again that he was only good at helping himself at the expense of others.

"Laugh all you want," Tenny said. His gaze returned to the Highlanders around him, a larger crowd than had been there just a few minutes before having formed. It wasn't surprising.

He and Tamsin stood close to the path that led up through the mountains and onto the plateau, from here a straight shot to the gnarled knot near the trunk of the tree where the meeting would be called to order. "I know what I saw. I know the truth of what happened. I can't tell you any more than that."

"And what did you see, Tenny?" asked Tamsin, not having the heart to add a final barb before staring up at him expectantly, "assuming, of course, that the ale that flows in your veins didn't fog your vision."

Usually, he could take a few jibes. A joke here and there, especially when based on the truth, tended not to bother him. More than just a few, however, tended to rankle, especially when they questioned his integrity.

Yes, he drank too much. But he had good cause for doing so.

Even though his famous temper wanted to take control of his actions as Tamsin pushed him, he locked it down. Now wasn't the time.

Tenny once again chose to ignore Tamsin's attempt at humor, understanding the cause. He might have made jokes as well if their positions were reversed.

"I saw victory," Tenny replied softly, his eyes taking on a faraway look as he remembered that afternoon of just a few days past.

"You're going to have to be more specific, Tenny," prodded Tamsin. "You're sounding much too poetic for my tastes."

"When the Murk cleared, I saw Wraith bodies littering the grass around the broch," Tenny explained, reverence in his voice.

"That's not possible," countered Tamsin, having a difficult time believing what the Highlander was telling her, in large part because she really wanted to believe him. "The Wraiths never leave behind their dead. Besides, you can't even get a good strike in on them when they're hidden in the fog, much less actually kill them."

"That used to be impossible," said Tenny. "I can't and won't disagree with you on that. But no more. They can't hide anymore. It's a sight I'll never forget. A gruesome sight, true, yet also one that filled my heart with joy and hope."

"Can you give us a broader picture, Tenny?" asked one of the Highlanders standing to Tamsin's right, the woman clearly curious. Her hopeful tone suggested that she wanted to believe what the large Highlander said, so he smiled at her first before continuing.

"As I said, when the fog cleared, Wraith bodies covered the green that surrounds our broch. All of the Wraiths were burnt to a crisp as soon as the Murk drifted back toward the north and the sun touched them. Even then, though, you could see the wounds that killed them. In the gut. In the chest. A few across the throat. One an arrow through the eye. A difficult shot, yes, but if you don't shoot, you can't make your own luck."

"How do you know they were Wraiths?" asked Tamsin. "Most of us have never seen those monsters, and those who have can't tell us. They're dead."

"If you don't believe me, talk to Jona or Gretel or Freddi," said Tenny a bit more strongly than he intended, nodding toward the Highlanders standing at his back. He was getting tired of Tamsin's questions and her constant challenges. "Talk to Dooliy or Sereya or Loo. They were all there. They saw what I saw."

Tamsin and the others shifted their gaze to the men and women Tenny motioned toward. Much like the large Highlander, their expressions were grim. A few nodded to confirm the truth of Tenny's words.

Upon closer inspection, Tamsin and the others saw an emotion there that they hadn't seen in quite some time. The resignation that had drifted behind the eyes of so many Highlanders because of all that they had suffered through during the last few years wasn't there as they expected. Rather, it had been replaced with expectation and purpose, what could almost be described as hope. Maybe even belief.

Tenny shrugged then. "If you don't believe me, that's fine. If you don't believe my friends, that doesn't affect me one way or another. But I tell you now and I tell you true. We can fight the Wraiths in the Murk now. I've seen it and I've done it. And if you don't want to trust my word, then better that you experience it for yourself."

"What do you mean by that?" asked Tamsin, her natural sarcasm nowhere to be found when she asked her latest question. Because she really wanted to believe the Highlander who towered over her.

"When Duff and his crew of Highlanders came to the broch right before the fog came in two days past, the lad with him gave us the ability to see in the Murk. We saw what he saw. We saw the Wraiths before they saw us. It was the most incredible thing. The Murk was there but it didn't hinder us in any way."

"The one they call the Lord Kestrel?" asked one of the Highlanders to Tamsin's other side.

"Yes, the Lord Kestrel," nodded Tenny. "He doesn't like the name, hates it in fact, but everyone who's fought with him calls him that. He deserves the name because of what he can do."

"How did he do it?" asked Tamsin.

"He says he's not a Magus, but he is. It was because of him that we were able to stay outside the broch when the Wraiths appeared. It was because of the Lord Kestrel that we were able to fight the monsters in the mist."

"What happened?" asked a Highlander standing right behind Tamsin, his eyes as round as saucers. Until now, no one stood much chance of surviving in the Murk when the Wraiths came if they weren't locked safely behind the thick door and stone walls of a broch.

"It was no different than any other skirmish I fought in while I served in the Murcian Guard," shrugged Tenny, as if fighting and surviving against creatures that had gained a reputation for brutal, efficient killings was just a small matter. The Highlanders at his back, all veterans themselves, nodded their agreement in support of his statement. "When the fog came in, we took up a position around the main entrance to the broch, keeping the stone at our backs. Then we waited."

"How long?" asked Tamsin, feeling the need to regain control over the conversation.

"Only a few minutes, no more, before the Wraiths appeared."

"And you could see them?"

"We could," confirmed Loo in her musical voice, the woman standing at Tenny's right shoulder nodding. "As if the fog wasn't even there. In fact, we could see them better than they could see us."

"Did they come right at you?" asked Tamsin.

"Not at first, no," replied Tenny. "They waited. You know how the Wraiths like to do things. Taking their time. Never in a rush. Wanting to see what prey might be hiding in the fog that they can flush out."

"They were surprised more than anything else when they came upon us," added Greta, the Highlander standing next to Loo. "They didn't expect to see us waiting for them in the Murk."

"That they were," agreed Tenny, "though not as surprised as when Freddi and the other archers on the parapet started in on the monsters."

"I was tired of waiting," shrugged Freddi, although his eyes gleamed with delight as he recalled the fight.

"We all were," admitted Tenny. "As soon as the first of Freddi and the other archers' arrows struck home, one Wraith sprouting three in his chest one right after another, we advanced on the Wraiths. They held their ground for a time, tried to at least, but it wasn't long before they realized that they didn't stand a chance against us. We were too many and they couldn't get past us to get at the archers. They had no choice other than to retreat. Otherwise, we would have killed more of the bastards."

"How many dead?" asked Tamsin.

"Nine Wraiths." That led to a low murmur running through the crowd. "The others slunk off into the Murk when they realized they couldn't beat us. They headed back toward the north. We could see it all thanks to the Lord Kestrel."

"Did the Lord Kestrel fight with you?" asked a Highlander a few places to Tenny's left.

"He did. He killed two of the Wraiths on his own. Probably would have killed more if they hadn't retreated."

"Ran more like," interjected Loo.

Tenny smiled at that. Ran. Retreated. How it was described was of little importance. Only the final result was important.

For the first time since the mist had drifted down from the north, they fought and beat the Wraiths in the Murk. That's all that mattered.

"With those daggers of his?" asked the same Highlander.

"Yes, he used the Wraiths' daggers against them. I've never seen anything such as that before. It's like he was born to the white steel."

"It was like watching a Wraith," nodded Jona, the tall woman standing at Tenny's left shoulder. "Only faster. The monsters never knew what hit them, the Lord Kestrel was done with them so swiftly. And Tenny is right. The Lord Kestrel would have killed more of them if they hadn't run."

"You saw their bodies?" asked Tamsin.

"I did," confirmed Tenny, his voice carrying a hint of pique now. "I already told you about that." Tenny lifted his head to the sky and took a deep breath, not wanting his rising irritation to come to the forefront. Not on what he thought was going to be a momentous day. "We saw the bodies within the Murk and then without. When the fog cleared, we crafted a pyre and set the bodies aflame. It didn't take long. They were mostly ash already."

"How many Highlanders died during the fight?" asked Tamsin. That question had been on the minds of all the Highlanders who were listening to the conversation, which had grown to several dozen now. Killing Wraiths was all well and good, but dying to do it made for a harder decision when you had children to raise. "If that many Wraiths attacked, then you must have lost a good number of people from your broch."

"Just one."

"One?" Tamsin was incredulous. She was finding it incredibly difficult to believe what Tenny had just said. One Highlander killed while fighting in the Murk? That was close to impossible. "With that many Wraiths? You can't be serious."

"Just one," Tenny confirmed with a nod. "And she died because she didn't follow instructions. If she had adhered to the guidance that Duff gave her about how to fight the monsters in the mist, she would still be with us today. Instead, she wanted to fight against the beasts on her own and that cost her."

Tamsin stared at Tenny, an expression of disbelief still clouding her face. Then she swept her eyes over the Highlanders standing with her large friend. They simply nodded at her, supporting what he had said.

She knew then that they spoke the truth. She could see it in their eyes. Their postures. Their expressions.

Yet she was still struggling to believe what Tenny and the others told her. She wanted to believe. She really wanted to believe.

Because if Tenny was telling her the truth as she thought that he was, then that meant the Highlanders had a chance. She had a chance to gain the revenge that gnawed at her every waking second of the day.

Maybe that was why she was still hesitating to believe. She had lost her husband to a Wraith, so maybe having to bury what was left of him in the rocky ground behind their cottage was what was making this so difficult for her. She so desperately wanted to believe, but she feared that if she did and it all went sour, that would be the end of her.

Since the death of her husband more than a year before, there had been talk of the Highlanders rising up against the creatures terrorizing them, human and monster. But she and so many others had just laughed.

It had been no more than talk after all. She had been burned before. Hope had gotten the better of her.

Therefore, she had promised herself that she would not allow hope to drive her decisions in the future. Not when she had young children to care for.

But if Tenny was telling the truth ...

The hint of a smile began to appear on her lips, even while at the same time she tried to crush it. If Tenny was telling the truth, if this Lord Kestrel could do as so many Highlanders said he could, that would change everything within these mountains.

It would give them a chance. It would give them hope. And hope had been in short supply the last few years.

She understood how dangerous hope could be, yet she also knew how necessary it was.

"Even if you could see them, those Wraiths are still nasty fighters," challenged Tamsin, needing to offer one last argument before she allowed herself to take the risk of believing that perhaps the Highlanders might actually be able to begin charting their own course again. "How did you and the others from your broch manage to stay alive?"

Tenny stared at Tamsin for quite a long time before responding, his expression hardening. Although not in anger, because the sarcasm that he had anticipated from her was nowhere to be found.

It was an honest question, and he understood the source of Tamsin's unease. Why she was hesitating to believe. He had been much the same way until he had lived through it himself.

He had thought for quite a long time that believing in something was dangerous. Doing so only set you up for disappointment. His dead wife, caught too far from the tower when the Murk came in, was the best example of that.

But he had realized after he had allowed his anger at her fate to consume him, after he had turned to drink to ease the pain of her loss, that believing in something wasn't dangerous, so long as you believed in the right thing.

Having fought against the Wraiths in the Murk, having seen and experienced what the Lord Kestrel could do with the Talent, he now believed.

In himself.

In the Highlanders who had fought with him.

In the Lord Kestrel most of all.

"The Wraiths thought that we would be easy meat," Tenny finally replied. "I won't lie to you about that." Several of the Highlanders at his back who had been in that clash with him grumbled their agreement. "We showed them the falsity of their perspective. Duff and the Lord Kestrel gave us a strategy that we could use against the Wraiths to minimize the advantages those bastards enjoy. The formation we fought in, with the tower at our backs, helped to negate their speed. The archers atop the broch who found their targets despite the Murk prevented the Wraiths from coming at us as they would have liked. It wasn't a fair fight, and those monsters didn't know what to do about it, which was fine with all of us. We didn't want a fair fight. We just wanted a fight that we could win. And we did."

Tamsin nodded at his explanation, taking it all in, allowing her mind to start traveling down a road that she had avoided for quite some time. And for good reason, in her opinion.

"I was just like you, Tamsin," continued Tenny, the Highlander leaning down so that she no longer had to crane her neck to hold his eyes. "We all were." The Highlander motioned to the men and women standing behind him. "We had good cause to doubt."

"That we did," murmured Loo in agreement.

"We don't doubt anymore. We know what we can do. We know what the Lord Kestrel can do. We know that we can kill the Wraiths. And if we can kill the Wraiths, then we can kill the slavers and the Stalkers as well. We can take back the Highlands."

"You're asking for quite a lot," said Tamsin very softly.

Tenny nodded then, agreeing with her, understanding what she was struggling with because he had as well. "I am. I know. But I'm tired of living in fear. I'm tired of running whenever the Murk comes in or I hear the shriek of a Stalker or there's word that the slavers are coming. That's not the kind of life that I want to live. That's not the life I expected to live here."

Tenny shook his head to accentuate the point he was trying to make. "I won't live that life anymore, come what may. So, if the Lord Kestrel can help me live my life the way I want to, even for just a brief time, then I'll bleed for him. I'll die for him. Because at least then, I'm fighting for something I believe in. I'm fighting for me. I'm fighting for my friends. I'm fighting for the Highlands."

"Where is he then?" asked Tamsin, smiling for what seemed like the first time since her husband's death. "Duff called this Council. He should be here."

"He's right behind me," said Donel, the Highlander walking up the crowded trail that led toward the heart tree, pushing his way through the throng, many of the fighters from his broch coming right behind him.

"Yes, I'm right here," grouched Duff, the scarred Sergeant carrying over his shoulder a sack with a spreading stain on the bottom. Jakob followed him, Martin and Bertie walking at Jakob's shoulders, Tommie right at his back.

"Why are you late?" demanded one of the Highlanders as Duff passed.

"We were a little busy," Duff replied, having to slow his pace as Donel and his Highlanders continued to push their way through the crowd that wanted to get a good look at the reason they had gathered.

"What were you doing?" the same voice asked.

"They were killing Wraiths with us," Donel shouted, wanting to make sure that as many of the Highlanders who had gathered on the plateau heard him.

"You?" came a laugh to Donel's right.

"Yes, me, Regi." Donel stopped then, having little patience for the attempted jest.

He squared up to the Highlander he had done business with ever since he had settled in the Highlands. In the past, he might have tried to laugh off the comment. Not anymore. Now, he refused to back down.

He had charged right at the Wraiths, swinging his axe with wild abandon. Whether he actually hit one of the monsters didn't really matter to him. The only thing that mattered was that he had done it. He had thrown away the fear that had stalked him like the Wraiths in the Murk and found his courage.

He was a different man now. He felt it. He knew it. And he liked it.

"I fought against the Wraiths," Donel said with pride. "Every man and woman with me did."

"You're a merchant," scoffed Regi, not knowing whether to believe his friend.

"I'm a Highlander," Donel replied sharply.

Donel's strong reply said with an unanticipated heat got the attention of many of the people sitting and standing around the massive heart tree.

"And how many of these Wraiths did you kill?" asked Regi, not knowing what to make of Donel's swift change in character.

"All told, fifteen," shrugged Donel, as he and his Highlanders walked beneath the shade of the heart tree, needing to navigate their way around or climb over the twisting and turning roots so many Highlanders already occupied, "maybe more."

Laughter followed Donel and his Highlanders beneath the branches. Donel ignored it, not bothering to reply until he had reached an open spot right up against the trunk of the tree and just below the gnarled knob from which Highlanders usually addressed those who had gathered. And even then, he didn't say anything, simply turning around to face the curious crowd of thousands.

Because he didn't need to say anything, Duff providing the evidence that supported his claim.

The Highlander, who everyone knew, reached into the bloody sack and pulled out the severed head. He had placed it in the bag before the sun struck the dead Wraith, so it didn't shrivel into a dry husk like the rest of the body did.

Duff, having climbed atop the root that was more than six feet off the ground, held the severed head up into the air so that all those who had come to the plateau could see the prize.

Silence fell among the Highlanders as they stared at the gruesome display.

And for those who managed to look away from the stomach-churning sight, their gaze inevitably turned to the young man standing next to Duff on the thick root.

Most of the assembled Highlanders hadn't met him. They had heard of him, though. Of how he had gotten the scar that stretched from above his right eye all the way down to his jaw.

It was hard not to know of him, what with all the tales circulating throughout the mountain peaks about him.

About what he could do in the Murk.

About what he had done.

Seeing that Wraith's head confirmed it for them.

Because just like Tamsin, they wanted to believe. They needed to believe.

All the stories that Tenny and all the other Highlanders who had fought with him were sharing clearly were true. And now those stories were turning the Lord Kestrel into a legend before their very eyes.

Duff watched all those thoughts pass through the minds of the Highlanders. He could see what was happening, just as he knew that it would.

He was pleased. Events were moving in the direction that he wanted.

He was a little sad as well. Because if this played out how he hoped that it would, how he thought that it would, then the fate and future of the Highlands would change.

As would Jakob's fate and future.

Duff could only hope that the lad had the strength and tenacity to manage what was coming his way.

Once Duff was satisfied that he had everyone's attention, he threw the Wraith's head back against the trunk of the heart tree, a streak of blood splattering the limb that he was standing on.

"I call this Highland Council to order!" he shouted.

18

PRICE OF THE CURSE

"Come now, Kendric," Ursina whispered into her husband's ear, her hand rubbing gently along his arm, helping to calm him. She could sense his agitation with her other hand, which rested on his chest. His heart was beating much too rapidly. "You know this must be done. It's the only way."

"There's something about what we're doing that feels wrong, Ursina," Kendric replied softly, a hint of fear coloring his words.

He didn't like what was being required of him. Not in the least. He hated it, in fact. And he hated even more that he was being forced to do it much more frequently than he had in the past.

But he couldn't ignore his responsibility. He was an integral part of the process.

He would do what was necessary. For him. For his wife. "I know why we do this, but each time we do this I believe that more and more," he attempted to explain, "we are doing something that we shouldn't be doing."

"Kendric, my love, let your worry go," Ursina urged, trying

to soothe him. She began to rub his chest, sending a gentle stream of energy into her husband that helped to calm his beating heart, filling him with a warmth that she hoped would quell his anxiety. "There is nothing to concern you here. We are doing no different than we have done before. And what we do now we do for all of New Caledonia."

"Ursina, I'm sorry, I just can't get away from the feeling that this just isn't right."

"That's because of where we are, my love, what happened here," she argued gently. "Not because of what we are doing."

"And what of them?" Kendric asked, pointing to the five men and two women chained to the wall at the far end of the rough-hewn chamber. Their arms and legs were bracketed against the stone. Their mouths were gagged. Not because Kendric and his wife feared that anyone would hear them scream. They were too far below the Shadow Keep. No, rather Kendric couldn't stand the screams. Not anymore. "Are we doing the right thing to them?"

"It is necessary, Kendric," Ursina replied, a bit more harshly than she intended, although she forgave herself. She was losing patience with her husband. She needed him to stand strong, and too often now he was demonstrating a weakness that worried her. She hoped that if she shared her strength, it would become his.

"These men and women are doomed anyway," she explained. "They are murderers and thieves. Rather than hanging them we can give them a worthwhile purpose. They can help us. They can help all the people living in the Northern Territory."

"I know. I understand. Still, it doesn't seem right," Kendric groaned, his commitment to what he knew his wife was about to require of him wavering.

"Does it seem right to you that your lack of willingness to do what is needed might allow the Wraiths to slaughter every inhabitant of Shadow's Reach and the Northern Peaks?" wondered Ursina, a touch of steel creeping into her voice. She believed that it was necessary to challenge her husband now, to make him see that what they were about to do was about more than just them. "Because you know as well as I that the Northern Guard is not strong enough to hold back the Wraiths if they come in force."

She leaned in closer to her husband, touching her forehead to his. "We must challenge them. We must make them hesitate. This is the way to do that with little cost to us. If nothing else, it will make our enemies think more deeply about whether taking Shadow's Reach is worth the effort. In fact, if we make them pay too high a price, they will likely give up their quest."

Ursina and her husband were in the caves beneath Shadow's Reach. She had been the first to come here, having discovered one of the hidden caverns that led down to this haunting place when they began construction on the lower levels of the Shadow Keep.

Since then, no one but her and Kendric were permitted to visit what she sensed had once been a crypt.

Of course, she had little cause to fear that anyone would follow. The workers who had found the cavern all were dead. Once that was done, she had concealed the passageway with the Talent.

Whomever had lived on this plateau centuries before the Caledonians had arrived had conducted sacrifices in this grotto. Many sacrifices.

The skeletal remains were proof enough. The residue of death and torture seeping into the stone and creating a miasma of evil that permeated the chamber only served to confirm her belief.

Most anyone else who entered this small hall would have left, never to return. Too afraid of the feeling that terrible things had happened here, that terrible things would happen here again.

Not Ursina, of course. She wasn't afraid. She wasn't afraid of anything.

She was pleased actually.

She had found the perfect location for her to conduct her experiments.

The green moss that covered the walls and ceiling provided a strange, unique light. Yet the most distinctive feature was the pool of roiling black that churned within the massive, four-legged stone urn set into the wall at the back of the chamber.

The cistern had been here when she had first walked into this hideaway. The pool of black was Ursina's creation. It had started out as water. After she had gone through more than a hundred trials, finally she had succeeded.

Now what had once been water was more than just a liquid. It was power. It was an energy that she didn't believe anyone could stand against.

So far, that belief had proven correct.

She had taken a risk, and it had paid off.

And where she had taken that risk had aided her efforts.

The pain, anguish, hurt, and terror that pervaded the chamber from all those who were tortured and murdered here had imbued her creation with an unforeseen yet welcome potency.

Now she just needed her husband to take a risk.

Kendric took a deep breath, thinking of his wife's mild admonition. She was right. She was always right.

His nerves finally settling, Ursina continuing to rub his arm and his chest, he didn't fight the comfortable haze that slowly dulled his thoughts. Instead, he welcomed the warmth as it worked its way through him, allowing it to wipe away his concerns and fears.

"You're right, Ursina," Kendric said, patting the hand on his arm with his own. Kissing her forehead before she pulled away. "You're right. Thank you for reminding me as to why we do this. For the people of the Northern Territory, for all the people of New Caledonia in fact."

"I'm glad that I could help, my love," Ursina replied. "I know this is difficult for you. You have so much to worry about as it is. Better to leave certain matters to me."

"It is. It is," Kendric murmured several more times. "You're right. You're right."

"You have such a good heart I know that this pains you," said Ursina, "but as we've discussed many times before, you know that your position as Governor of the Northern Territory requires more from you than you may want to give. Unfortunately, you have no choice. If you are to assume your rightful place in New Caledonia, if you are to make this continent what you want it to be, what you believe it should be, then we have no choice."

"I know, Ursina," Kendric replied, a small smile finally playing across his face, his usual good humor returning even as his thoughts began to drift. "I don't know where I would be without you."

"Are you ready, my love? Shall we begin?"

"I am," he replied with a confidence that had been lacking just minutes before.

"Then let me do this quickly and I will let you go," promised Ursina. "Step a little closer."

Kendric nodded and nudged himself up against the cistern until he was standing right next to Ursina. He was mesmerized as soon as his eyes caught the roiling black water that moved as if it had a life of its own.

He didn't understand what power was held within this strange, boiling liquid that was always icy cold, and he didn't care. Not anymore. Not with the warmth of Ursina's touch still with him. He only cared that it worked.

The liquid contained the power to transform the prisoners into what he and his wife needed them to be. Into vessels that were more than themselves. Into tools that he could control and employ against monsters even more terrible than the monsters that they would become.

"This will only take a moment, my love," said Ursina. "Be brave."

Ursina pulled a long dagger from the sheath on her hip, then reached gently for her husband's wrist, turning his arm so that his inside forearm was tilted down toward the water. With a quick swipe, she sliced across his skin, a line of blood appearing that swiftly dripped down into the boiling black, those drops becoming a steady stream after Ursina sheathed her dagger. Then she used her free hand to squeeze her husband's wound, earning a hiss of pain from Kendric.

After almost a minute had passed, finally satisfied that she had taken enough blood from her husband, Ursina removed her hand from his wound, although she maintained her grip on his wrist.

With a thin stream of the Talent, she healed the slice. The skin knit itself back together until the only reminder of the injury was a thin, pale scar that could barely be seen that matched the many others that ran down both of his forearms.

"As good as new, my love," said Ursina, wiping away the blood stains from his arm with a cloth that she had pulled from a pocket. "A noble sacrifice on your part."

"Indeed. I don't know what I'd do without you, Ursina."

"You had mentioned that this time around we needed to create more than we usually do."

"Yes, I did," Kendric confirmed, stepping back from the cistern, though he kept a hand on the rim. Ursina had healed him, but he had given a large quantity of blood. He was tired and a little woozy. "Torstan has requested more. He didn't say as much, but I gathered from his missive that he's running out. He's not using the tools we've already given him wisely."

"He is losing the creatures that we sent into the Highlands?" asked Ursina, not quite believing that she even needed to ask such a question.

"That's how I interpreted his request," confirmed Kendric.

"Do you have any thoughts on what could be killing the beasts? That's no easy task."

"My guess?" asked Kendric. He continued after his wife nodded. "The Highlanders."

"The Highlanders? How could they be doing that? These creatures are virtually indestructible. It would take a unique skill to challenge them and have any chance at success."

"I don't know," Kendric replied with a shrug, "but Torstan was quite specific about what he wanted with the next few we send his way."

"How so?"

"He had a very specific request. However many we choose to send into the Highlands, he wanted them charged with the specific task of killing this Lord Kestrel we've been hearing about."

"Torstan believes that this upstart is the one killing the Stalkers?"

"He's not certain, but everything points in that direction." Kendric shrugged, admitting that he had very little else to offer. "He believes that the only way to find out is to remove him from the playing field."

Ursina nodded, thinking about what her husband had said. Or at least making it seem like she was. Because she already knew what Torstan had requested of her husband. She knew as well more of what was happening in the Highlands than the Governor responsible for the Territory did.

From what she had pieced together, she believed that there was some truth to Torstan's presumption. And if this upstart was, indeed, eliminating her creatures, and she had no reason to disbelieve that rumor, then he was a much greater threat than she had anticipated.

This Lord Kestrel, whomever he was, indeed was the cause of the Governor's many current troubles. But the upstart wasn't limiting his efforts to just killing the Stalkers.

He was going after the slavers as well. The first was bad enough, the second even worse. Because without the slavers production from the mines, already below the level that they required to obtain the necessary revenue, would be reduced to a trickle.

That was something that she could not permit. Not if she and her husband were to achieve their larger objective.

"Then I will do as he requests. I will make sure that three of these Stalkers target the one causing all this trouble for him. Perhaps even a few more in the next batch just to make certain. That many should be able to kill him swiftly."

Kendric nodded, pleased, although Ursina wasn't certain that she believed her own words. From what she had learned from her sources in the Highlands, this Lord Kestrel as he was being called – she had never heard of him before and had no recollection of him in Caledonia -- was quite a formidable opponent.

Not only hunting slavers and Stalkers without fear, but also staying within the Murk when it drifted down from the north and challenging the Wraiths in their own environment. Some even said that he used their own daggers against them.

Just rumors, of course. But she had learned from one of her mentors that in every rumor there lurked a nugget of truth.

"Good, thank you, Ursina. I appreciate it just as I'm sure Torstan will."

"Anything for you, my love," Ursina replied. "You look a little tired. Would you like to rest while I do what must be done?"

"I would be most grateful, Ursina."

Reaching out for his arm, Ursina guided Kendric out of the chamber and down a passageway cut roughly from the rock, green moss lighting the way for them. She then led him into a small room at the end of the corridor, helping him first take a seat and then lie down on a long, smooth rock shaped like a bench.

"Just rest for a while, my love. I will return to you when I'm done."

Kendric didn't reply, already asleep, exhausted by what had been taken from him, because the power in the basin of black always demanded more than just blood from him.

Giving him a kiss on the cheek, she headed back toward the chamber that she used for her work, thinking about what she needed to do next.

She understood the necessity of what was required. Still, a small part of her, a part of her that was slowly losing its agency and voice the more and more she engaged in this practice, rebelled against her actions.

There was nothing for it, however. She had traveled too far down this road to turn back now. She would do what needed to be done. Just as she always did.

Walking back into the chamber she ignored the seven people chained behind her, their eyes wide with terror. Unable to move. Unable to protest. Unable to plead for their lives.

Ursina stopped in front of the cistern, staring down at the roiling black.

She was worried. She had made several dozen Stalkers in just the last few weeks. What was required of them to do that was taking a toll on her and on Kendric.

But they could both handle the strain. At least for a little while longer. She hoped.

Because there was nothing for it. For her and Kendric to gain what they wanted, their creations needed to achieve the charges given to them. Yet unlike in the past, her Stalkers were running into complications that she hadn't foreseen.

Those failures -- she blamed this Lord Kestrel for most of them -- had forced her to engage in this practice more frequently than she wanted to. More than she believed was safe if they continued at this pace.

She needed to remedy this problem in order to eliminate her larger concern. And she believed that what she was doing now would help with that.

This latest batch would do the deed. She was certain of that.

Her recent lack of success irritated her to no end.

She didn't like that. She didn't like thinking that she was failing at the task she had set for herself. She liked surprises even less.

As another mentor had once said, she didn't like not knowing what she didn't know.

Ursina understood that was her greatest weakness, although she also viewed it as her greatest strength.

Her need to know.

Everything.

That's why her studies had pulled her toward the Curse. That and her belief that she was smarter than everyone else.

That she knew more than they did.

That she knew more than they ever would.

Because of those traits, she had believed that she could control the Curse. That she could make the Dark Magic work for her without having to deal with the consequences that had affected so many others.

She didn't recognize her arrogance and naivete until it was much too late.

She always saw the world through a specific lens, and she believed that she could do anything that she set her mind to.

It was that conceit and lack of perspective that had proven time and again to be her fatal flaw.

Yet still, even understanding that, she couldn't help herself.

She was who she was. She couldn't be anything other than that.

Ursina hated to admit it, but Rafia had been right about that. About so many things, in fact.

Rafia knew her much too well. If the Magus had been there when she attempted her escape from the Order, Ursina likely would have failed. Ursina either would be imprisoned in the Aeyrie or dead.

But Rafia had just missed her.

She considered those two possibilities for a second. Probably dead.

Rafia would have killed her. She wouldn't have wanted to. It would have been like sticking a dagger in her own heart. Nonetheless, Rafia would have done her duty.

She always did. No matter the cost to herself. No matter the cost to others.

Ursina couldn't fault her for that. They were too much alike. They each had their own duty.

And to accomplish her duty, Ursina had come to New Caledonia, seeking a fresh start and a place where she could hide away from those who might still be searching for her.

She had met Kendric soon after arriving in Shadow's Reach. She had fallen for him the moment she had laid eyes on him.

Ursina would move mountains for Kendric. And she had, countless times, doing all in her power to ensure that there was a clear path for Kendric to play a larger role in the future of the Territories. To potentially give him a throne rather than just a future Duchy.

Even though he had never asked for it, she knew that he would never turn down the gift if she presented it to him.

Understanding that, she had turned her efforts toward making that happen.

But she was worried now.

Despite all the knowledge that she had attained, despite her growing confidence that she had the strength and the ability to travel down a path that all other sensible, staid, and myopic Magii avoided like the plague, she sensed that she was losing herself to the power that she had convinced herself that she could control.

A power that much to her regret she had learned could not be tamed. Could not be managed. Could only be borrowed.

And at a very steep price. Because as soon as she began to employ this power, she had discovered that just as she was using this corrupt energy that made her feel more alive than she ever had before, it was using her as well. And she could do nothing to stop it.

She could feel the Curse worming its way through her. Consuming her. Slowly but surely. Making her its own.

She had yet to find a way to stop its spread. The more she tried and failed, the more she feared that she wouldn't. That she couldn't. That the Curse was too strong, too demanding. That her fate was sealed. That she would lose herself to the corrupt energy.

Even more, she feared losing Kendric, because she had touched him with the Curse to do what they were doing now.

For him to exercise any control over the Stalkers, it had been unavoidable. He had to be a part of the process. Their plans wouldn't work otherwise.

Now she worried more about him than about herself. She worried about what might happen to him because he didn't have the skill and the knowledge that she did to slow the terrible change that was taking place within him.

She had begun to see the signs, a hint of black in the back of his eyes every so often. Thankfully, it wasn't there permanently.

But that was just the start.

She understood that and she couldn't ignore it. She knew

what it meant, having already experienced what he might be forced to go through if she didn't find a way to stop and, barring that, ease the transition.

After battling the tainted power that she had allowed within herself and determining that she couldn't win, a conclusion that she hated yet couldn't deny, she had little hope that she would succeed. Still, she would do all that she could to help Kendric.

Kendric had saved her. She would save him by any means necessary.

She would never let the Curse take her husband. She would never allow Kendric to be taken from her. Not in that way.

He meant too much to her. He'd done too much for her.

That's why she had been using her skills as a healer on him as soon as she noticed the black spark, applying the Talent first in an attempt to stop the spread of the Curse, and then, after finding that she couldn't halt the inexorably encroaching taint entirely, seeking to slow its spread instead.

In that, she had proven successful. At least to a point.

She used her natural magic regularly in an effort to protect him from the taint that sought to take him. But it was a losing battle, the Curse constantly seeking to break through the barrier she had constructed within him. She could only delay the corruption's advance, and even then, incompletely because the barrier began to weaken and then dissipate as soon as she reset it.

Sadly, her constant application of the Talent along with the struggle playing out within Kendric had led to some complications that couldn't be avoided.

At certain times, more and more frequently unfortunately, Kendric was having a difficult time remembering things. He often couldn't keep his thoughts straight or maintain his focus or keep track of what was going on around him. He forgot names or why he was in a particular room or why he had gone somewhere or what he was supposed to do.

It was frustrating for him, terrifying at times, but Ursina could live with the side effects if she could continue to delay the full effects of the Curse. If she could continue to buy time to find some solution. Assuming that she could find a solution.

Of course, there had been a benefit that had resulted from her efforts, one that she hadn't anticipated.

Her constant use of the Talent upon him also made Kendric more malleable. A discovery that she had been more than willing to make use of when circumstances required.

After studying the bubbling black liquid for several minutes, the fluid that was like water but wasn't, that was never anything but frigidly cold, that swirled and flowed in a pattern of its own making, she judged that it was time, the last drops of Kendric's blood joining with the fluid that was the Curse made material.

That done, Ursina smiled. It was ready. It was time.

She reached down with a small glass vial, filling it with the black liquid. Turning, she walked carefully to the back of the cavern.

The five men and two women stared at her in terror, not knowing what was going to happen, not wanting to know, nevertheless concluding with a sickening inevitability that they had no chance of escape.

"Better not to resist," said Ursina with a smile. "It will go easier on you."

A few of the prisoners tried to scream through their gags. They failed.

Ursina simply watched, shaking her head in disappointment. It was always like this.

"You should be honored by what I and the Lord Winborne ask of you. It is a noble task. Certainly better than you deserve."

She stepped up to the man farthest on the end to her left. She would start with him and then work her way down.

Ursina pulled a small dropper out of the vial, then inserted the tip into the corner of the man's mouth. He could do nothing to stop her because of the gag, his eyes widening in terror as he tasted the one bitter drop that she placed on his tongue.

She then moved on to the next prisoner and then the next, moving down the line with a practiced efficiency. It didn't take long before all seven had tasted the solution laced with the Curse, and it didn't take long for the process to begin.

For a few seconds more, nothing happened. Then the eyes of all the prisoners widened in shock as their bodies began to shake and shiver, every single one of their muscles protesting.

The prisoners couldn't see what was happening to them, not yet, but they could turn their heads just enough to see what was happening to the men and women next to them.

Pulsing black threads that resembled a spider's web were forming on their foreheads and then rapidly spreading down their bodies.

The prisoners screamed in terror, struggling desperately to break free from their shackles.

Their efforts were useless.

They were stuck fast. And they were losing control over themselves. Their bodies and their minds. A new entity, a decaying influence, taking up residence within them.

Ursina watched it all impassively. She had done this so many times before that she knew exactly what was going to happen next as the Curse not only consumed the prisoners, but also transformed them. Made them more than what they were. Made them more than they could ever be if not for its touch.

Once the threads of black covered every inch of their bodies, their eyes completely black before settling into a blood red at the end of the metamorphosis, the physiological changes would begin. Their bones breaking and binding themselves back together again. Their bodies elongating. Their shoulders broadening. Their teeth lengthening into fangs. Their hands transforming into razor-sharp claws.

They would become an implement to be used so that she and her husband could achieve their objective of remaking the Territories into a New Caledonia that rivaled the old.

And for those who sought to oppose them, these Stalkers would be a nightmare come to life.

19

A SECRET REVEALED

"This is looking to be a waste of time," Jurgen Klines grumbled to himself, shaking his head in disappointment.

Arriving atop the knoll at midday, he had piled several of the rocks he had found scattered throughout the long grass into a small hide that protected him from view as he took up his vigil.

His gaze was fixed on the dark caves that peppered the base of the plateau upon which Shadow's Reach had been built. The outskirts of the city, placed perpetually in shadow by the monstrous peak that rose above it, were more than a league away from where he waited.

While working in Juliette's forge, the Blademaster had been hearing more and more about the Stalkers and the dangers they presented to the people living and working around Shadow's Reach as well as to the several other settlements in the Northern Peaks. It seemed that the Wraiths were old hat now, the residents of Shadow's Reach having grown accustomed to finding shelter and doing what was required to protect themselves when the fog arrived.

Or at least they believed that they were safe from the monsters in the mist.

The Blademaster didn't necessarily agree with them. He had heard the rumors that were spreading quickly in certain sections of the city that the Wraiths had gotten past the walls and into Shadow's Reach several times already, the Northern Guard unable to keep them beyond the parapet when the Murk drifted over the city.

Since he had fought one of the Wraiths in the street just a hundred yards from the wall less than a month before, he viewed those rumors for what they were. The truth.

The Wraith that he had dueled had been fast and exceedingly competent with those two double-bladed daggers of his. So much so that the Wraith even reminded him of the Volkun in several ways. Primarily his speed, his tenacity, and how he flowed more than moved when engaged in a combat.

After that experience, Klines could understand why Kendric Winborne and his soldiers had yet to claim even one Wraith body during one of the many attacks on the city walls. Just as he had expected, he had learned that these Wraiths were devilishly hard to kill.

He had heard as well through his many conversations with the people coming into the smith and in the taverns that he frequented that the Governor of the Northern Territory was attempting to cover up the fact that several families within the city proper had been slaughtered by the Wraiths. The monsters in the mist had not only scaled the wall and gotten into Shadow's Reach, but in a matter of minutes they had broken into newly constructed private residences that were built specifically to keep the inhabitants safe from any Wraith assault.

Of course, there was no evidence to support those claims. Whispers only. Even so, Klines tended to listen to whispers until they finally drifted away or were proven wrong. And these whispers were only getting louder.

But now wasn't the time to be thinking of the Wraiths. Klines hadn't seen any sign of the Murk in days.

Now was the time to concentrate on a different threat. One that was proving to be just as dangerous.

Vinson had talked about the Stalkers when he had come into the forge to pick up the spears that he had ordered. The farmer had taken a few minutes to explain why he wanted the weapons and why he was considering the purchase of a couple of crossbows as well, though he doubted that he could shoot with any accuracy in the dark and against an opponent said to be blazingly fast.

A Stalker had come for him and his family at dusk just a few days past. Vinson had been lucky to escape the beast that had hidden in his barn and attacked him when he came in to get the feed for his draft horses. He only had a pitchfork with him at the time, and he only made it back to his farmhouse and his family because the Stalker got tangled in some wire fencing that he had been working on that covered much of the barn's dirt floor.

It hadn't taken long for the Stalker to escape the timely and fortunate trap, but by then Vinson and his family had locked themselves within their home.

Vinson believed that the only reason they survived was because his farmhouse backed up against a stone ridge and its three walls were made from that same stone. Just as important, the roof was constructed with two-foot-thick solid beams that were spaced so closely together that the beast couldn't force its way through.

The Stalker had tried, easily ripping through the shingles of the roof, but the spars stymied the creature. That was after the Stalker failed to break through the oak door, which was a foot thick and wrapped in steel.

Vinson understood that he had been lucky. If the farmhouse hadn't first been built to serve as a guardhouse, he was certain that he and his family would have been nothing more than meat for the Stalker. The scratches in the door and on several of the beams that were inches deep proved it.

Klines asked him where he had seen the Stalker first appear. Vinson explained that he couldn't say for certain.

Even so, his property abutted some caves on the northeastern side of the plateau upon which Shadow's Reach sat. If he had to guess, he believed that the Stalker had come from there.

Klines knew exactly where Vinson lived since he had delivered a few plows to him just the month before. Upon hearing the farmer's story, he decided that it was time for him to take a look for himself. And that's why he was up on top of the tor.

He had been watching the caves for several hours. With the sun setting, knowing that he would have little chance of seeing anything once full dark fell over the land, he was about to leave. Beginning to push himself up from where he was lying between the stones, he stopped himself before he had gotten his chest off the ground.

Several shadows had just detached themselves from the darkness of the cave and were streaking off to the west and the forest that was only a mile away.

Vinson had been right, and he had good reason to be worried about his family.

Thankfully these beasts were moving off into the wild and away from the farmer's home. Nevertheless, once Klines was certain that no more of the monsters were going to emerge from the cave, he decided that on his way back to the city he would visit Vinson and warn him to keep his family inside tonight and every night thereafter.

Just because the Stalkers ran off toward the west didn't mean they wouldn't come back around or decide to hunt in the surrounding area.

It seemed that the theory that Vinson ascribed to, and one

that was gaining traction throughout the city in the last few months, was more than just a theory. The Stalkers were coming from beneath the rock upon which Shadow's Reach was built.

An important discovery. Still, that didn't confirm that the Governor had anything to do with these monsters – more rumors, just whispers actually – yet that didn't exonerate the man either.

It just meant that the Blademaster would need to do some more digging. At least now he knew where he needed to start.

Sliding carefully and slowly down the side of the knoll, wary of what was around him with the falling night limiting his visibility, he hiked a little more than a mile between the hills and was almost to Vinson's farmhouse when he stopped abruptly.

The back of his neck was prickling.

From long experience, he knew that there could be only one cause for that.

He was being hunted.

Klines pulled his sword free from the scabbard across his back just in time, the Stalker erupting from the darkness, ripping free from the shadows created by a fallen tree off to his left. If he hadn't had his sword in his hand, he would have been dead. Instead, he caught the monster's claws on his steel, then spun away, not wanting to get stuck in a battle of strength with the creature that towered several heads above him.

With full dark just minutes away, he could barely see the Stalker move. His only point of reference was the blood-red eyes. He focused on those burning pinpricks as the night fell, engaging his adversary based more on instinct than sight.

Klines ducked to the left and then back to the right, evading two swipes of the creature's razor-sharp claws. He took a step back and pivoted, allowing the Stalker to lunge through the space in which he had been standing.

When the Stalker tried to pull back so that it could reach

for him again, Klines struck. He drove the point of his sword down into the Stalker's clawed foot, eliciting a shriek of rage that failed to mask the pain of the wound.

Klines ducked, avoiding the claw that if it had connected would have ripped his head from his shoulders. Then he gave his sword a twist before he pulled it free, his action drawing a howl from the Stalker that echoed off the surrounding mountains.

That was the last sound the Stalker ever made, the Blademaster quick to take advantage of the hobbling monster's injury. He feinted another stab toward the Stalker's other clawed foot, the creature trying to dance back and failing, instead stumbling on a large branch that had broken off from the fallen tree.

The Stalker landed on its back at the exact same moment the Blademaster drove his sword through the monster's throat.

As the Stalker died, choking on its own blood, Klines stared down at the beast, finally getting a good look at one of these monsters.

He had no remorse about killing the beast. It was either the Stalker or him, or Vinson and his family or some unwary traveler.

After his examination, it was quite clear to Klines that this creature was made for killing. The monster made him think of the Slayers that Declan had told him about.

That, in itself, didn't bother him.

No, what unsettled him were the Stalker's eyes.

Blood red, yes, and certainly frightening, but at the very back of those orbs he discerned an all too human quality that made him wonder where these Stalkers truly came from.

20

THE REBELLION BEGINS

Jakob was enjoying the touch of warmth provided by the sun. The inconsistent rays of light that every so often snuck by the heart tree's massive branches and leaves that were larger than a soldier's shield provided some welcome relief from the chill of the breeze that curled off the surrounding mountains and swept across the small plateau.

Sitting next to Duff on the root that spiraled out from the trunk, he studied the unique protrusion that rose into the air just a few feet away. That knotted gnarl formed what the Highlanders had come to call the Speaker's Staff.

It rose five feet into the air, its top worn smooth. Whenever Highlanders visited the Grove, they liked to give the knob a rub for good luck.

Jakob assumed that there was little substance behind the need to do that. Even so, before he had taken his seat, he had followed Duff's example, brushing the top of the Speaker's Staff with his hand.

His gaze turned toward the branches above him, watching the play of light and shadow that streamed down. His mind was elsewhere, grappling with a decision that he knew that he needed to make.

He delayed for a little while longer because he wanted to consider any other options that might be available. What he was contemplating made him distinctly uncomfortable.

Yet there were no other scenarios that made sense as he mulled them.

There was one choice. One path.

The question wasn't whether there was another path. There wasn't.

The question was whether he had the courage to follow the only path open to him.

His thoughts consuming him, Jakob didn't really see the thousands of Highlanders who had answered Duff's call who now had taken up almost every available foot of space on the small plateau.

But those Highlanders did see him.

Many of the Highlanders, even as they listened to the men and women around them speak their mind, spent more time studying the one who Duff was calling the Lord Kestrel.

They peered over the shoulders of their compatriots, stood atop the roots, or sought a better position within the throng where they could get a glance at the young man who had gained so much acclaim so quickly. The young man who sent faint stirrings of belief through their hearts for the first time since the Wraiths appeared out of the Murk.

As he continued to watch the play of the light across the branches and leaves, all the voices swirling around Jakob were beginning to sound the same, so he allowed his mind to drift for a while longer. He didn't really hear the murmur of conversation rolling through the gathered crowd, one Highlander after another offering his or her opinion on what to do about the increasingly more challenging circumstances they faced.

The slavers and Stalkers were bad enough, everyone agreed. But at least the Highlanders had a chance against them, slim though that might be.

The Wraiths were another matter entirely. They had no way to defend themselves against the monsters in the mist. They had no choice but to make for the safety offered by the brochs, locking themselves away until the fog moved back to the north.

The Highlanders valued the protection the brochs gave them. They needed the towers.

But they hated those towers just as much as they hated the primary reason for their existence. Because every time they entered and locked the door behind them, they ceded their land to the Wraiths. Their homes. Their honor.

They were acknowledging their weakness. They were allowing the Wraiths to dictate how they lived their lives.

At least that's how Jakob perceived what was being said. No one was offering anything new. It was all different versions of the same story.

Jakob didn't really understand the purpose of the repetitive dialogue. It just seemed like they wanted to vent their concerns and their fears rather than discuss any solutions to their problems.

Duff had warned him that this was going to happen. He had said that as was the custom in the Highlands, anyone who wanted to speak before any decisions were to be made could do so.

Jakob understood the value of that, especially since they were all coming from a Kingdom where more often than not dialogue was a useless exercise and potentially one that could lead to imprisonment or execution depending on the topic discussed. Where decisions were made for them, usually without their input.

Here everyone deserved a voice. Everyone deserved to be heard.

Jakob liked that, but it also required a patience that wasn't always easy for him to exercise.

And that's what he struggled with now. Staying patient.

That was why he had shifted his focus.

Because he had heard everything the gathered Highlanders had to say in the first twenty minutes after Duff started things off by talking briefly on the need for the Highlanders to come up with a better approach for defending themselves against the many threats they faced and then opening the floor to any Highlander who wanted to offer their opinion on that matter.

The hour that had followed was simply a regurgitation of what had already been said. Even so, several arguments broke out, Duff having to interject himself into the proceedings a few times to quell tempers and get everyone back on track.

At first, Jakob had wondered why Duff had not demonstrated more control over this gathering, what his friend had called a Highland Council. He had provided very little guidance once he had started the proceedings.

Every now and then he looked at Jakob with an expectant eye, seemingly content to allow all those who had made it to the plateau to have their say despite having nothing to say.

In Jakob's opinion, it seemed that Duff's strategy for this meeting, because his friend always had a strategy, was to have the Highlanders talk themselves out before the real business began. Of course, he didn't offer that perspective to Duff. The Sergeant would simply shrug off the suggestion and give him that aggravating grin of his.

Jakob wasn't sure what exactly Duff was up to, but he was certain that he was up to something. He was always up to something.

He never did anything without a plan, and usually within that plan there was another plan, and another plan within that. It was just who he was, how his mind worked. Duff couldn't help himself.

On its own, that didn't bother Jakob. There was a value to how Duff approached the world.

What irritated him, more often than he cared to admit, in fact, was that the Sergeant rarely shared his plans with anyone. Not unless he had no choice but to do so. Even when those plans might affect them.

That was aggravating. Because Jakob preferred to be prepared for whatever was going to come next.

And before they had made their way to the Grove, Duff hadn't said a word to Jakob or Bertie or Martin or Tommie about what he had in mind for when they got there.

That failing had made Jakob distinctly uncomfortable. He didn't like surprises. Especially in this moment, because for some strange reason that he didn't understand fully he felt as if he had a larger role to play in whatever was going to happen here today. He just hadn't figured out yet what that role would be.

That wasn't entirely true, he admitted to himself. He knew the role that he could play. He knew the role that Duff wanted him to play.

Jakob just needed to decide if he was willing to take on that role.

Jakob turned his gaze away from the light playing across the heart tree to the kestrels soaring in the air far above him. He loved watching the raptors who claimed the Highlands as their home. The grace and power they demonstrated. The freedom.

A freedom that he wanted. That his father had wanted even more but could never have now.

That thought brought several memories of Dougal to the forefront. All the time that they had spent together in the wilderness behind their small cottage in the very northernmost section of Roo's Nest.

Dougal teaching him how to navigate the woods. How to

hunt. How to survive in even the harshest weather and under the worst possible conditions. How to track. How to fight. How to make split-second decisions without even needing to think about them. How to know when to go with his gut and when to listen to reason.

As all those and many more lessons that masqueraded as memories played through his mind, Jakob could only smile. Everything with his father always had contained a lesson. Sometimes obvious. Sometimes hidden away for him to find later. Whether in the woods or at the dinner table or when buying supplies in Hardholm or while reading before bed, there was always some new piece of information that Dougal wanted to impart to him.

Jakob had the sense that there was more to his father's efforts to educate him than just ensuring that he knew how to make his way in the world. Rather, he believed that Dougal had been trying to prepare him for something important.

What, though, he could never determine. And he had never asked.

Jakob never minded. He had enjoyed spending time with his father, even when his pedantic tone began to grate on Jakob's nerves.

Jakob had enjoyed learning everything that Dougal had been willing to share with him. Sometimes reluctantly. But he always adhered to the standards his father had set for him.

Even with the tension that would rise between them at times, a tension that Jakob assumed was common between father and son.

Those memories saddened him as well.

He missed his father. More than he cared to admit.

Right then, when the sun blasted in between the ruffling leaves to warm every inch of him, Jakob didn't want to think about the day his father had sacrificed himself so that he would have a chance to escape the slavers hunting them. That memory played through his head every time he slept. He didn't need to experience it again now.

Forcing that nightmare back down into the darkness, knowing that it would visit him again that night, instead his thoughts turned toward the last day he had spent in Caledonia before he and his father had been forced to take ship the very next morning, needing to escape the cloud of suspicion that inevitably would smother them if they had stayed in Roo's Nest.

That day had started out well and then soured quickly. For Jakob, it was a day of loss in so many different ways.

He remembered the combat against the Ghoules. The creatures had tried to waylay him and his father not too far from their cottage, but Jakob had sniffed them out. And just in time too.

From there making it to Senna's farm, wanting to warn her and her family of the threat that he and his father had discovered. Wanting to make sure that they were careful and kept an eye out for any more of those creatures that might be haunting the wood that bordered the Shattered Peaks.

Not realizing when he arrived that his day of horror had only begun, Jakob forced to battle monsters even worse than the Ghoules.

Monsters that he had thought were no more than stories. But he had found that these stories were all too real when he came up against them in the flesh.

Jakob had been terrified when he had entered the farmhouse that he had visited so many times before. He knew that some evil essence lurked within, but he had no idea what it could be.

He remembered that moment with a remarkable vividness. Mixed in with his fear strangely there had been anger as well. At his father, no less, because this was one situation that Dougal hadn't prepared him for.

How to kill a monster that was already dead.

Not wanting to think too much on that memory, he smiled sadly as he recalled the beautiful young woman who had captured his heart the second he had met her in the market in Hardholm.

He fixed in his mind the image that he had of her from the night before that terrible day. The gleam in her eyes. Her bright, beguiling smile that only got bigger while she listened to his proposal.

He refused to think about what she looked like the last time he gazed down upon her. When he had to leave her. Giving her a final kiss on her forehead even though she had already gone to the other side.

And then from there to Aloysius' cottage. After what he had fought and destroyed at Senna's farmhouse, he knew that he needed to warn the old Magus. He also had been hoping to find some refuge there from the terror of his day, if only for a brief time.

Yet he had only found a new menace that was even more terrifying than the last.

His day of horror had only continued when he had stopped in front of the shattered door that led into his instructor's cottage.

Because when he arrived, Aloysius was fending off a crea-ture more dangerous and frightening than the Draugr. What, after Jakob had succeeded in driving away the monster, the old Magus told him was a Skath.

A servant of the Ancient One.

As it always did when he remembered that evening, a much too common occurrence but one that he couldn't control, his hand drifted to the artifact hanging from his neck that he always kept beneath his shirt. His fingers tightened around the Blood Ruby.

Every so often, he needed to feel the jewel in his palm, the sharpness of its facets, the warmth that was always there in the very center of the artifact. The warmth that called to him and warned him when a threat from the Spirit World was nearby.

Because the Blood Ruby was something real, something tangible. Because just like the Draugr, the Skath and the Ancient One had been no more than stories as well until that fateful day. Stories that he had found difficult to believe until they had come to life.

Much as was the case with the Highlanders, who were seeking to come to grips with the stories that were circulating throughout the Highlands. Stories that they wanted to believe. But still only stories, at least for a little while longer.

Stories about him.

That thought brought him back from his reverie. Someone near the back of the crowd who was standing at the very edge of the shadow created by the heart tree was shouting out an argument that Jakob couldn't hear, an argument that he didn't need to hear, because he had heard it all before.

Although he had lost interest in the already much discussed concern the Highlander offered, he did care about what was driving the woman's concerns. She had started to shout, some of those farther away from her telling her that they couldn't hear her.

Jakob was one of them. He couldn't hear what she was saying, the grumbles among the crowd that accompanied her comments keeping her words from his ears.

Nevertheless, he could see her eyes. Even from this far away.

He could see the fear that resided there.

That almost took his breath away. Branded him in some respects.

He looked around then at the gathered Highlanders, studying those who had trekked to this remote plateau. A journey that for many was several days at least.

A journey that had taken them from the safety of their brochs. Forcing them to risk the coming of the Murk and what lurked within.

He examined their eyes. Their mannerisms. How they said what they had to say but without words.

The Highlanders were hardy folk. Strong. Brave. Adventurous.

He had learned that quickly. And after all that he had been through upon entering these beautiful peaks, he believed that he was just like them.

The Highlanders had to be as they were. Only people like them would take the potentially fatal risk of sailing across the Burnt Ocean and settling into wild land virtually on their own. A people like him.

Yet there was more to these Highlanders than just that. He had experienced it himself ever since he had escaped the slavers and then the Wraiths.

The Highlanders understood the value of working together. Of looking out for their neighbors.

They had to. They had no choice.

It was the only way to ensure that they survived in this rugged, dangerous land.

And despite all the challenges facing them, they had done well for themselves. They had started to create the world that they wanted here in the Highlands.

But now that world, barely built on this rocky ground, was under threat. Their lives and those of their families were in danger.

The world that they wanted, that they had worked so hard to attain, was just a hair's width away from being taken from them.

Because of that, these brave people were afraid.

As the last of the woman's words and then those of the man

who followed her washed over him, that realization only accelerated Jakob's thinking.

Was it better to live in fear, terrified of what might happen, so long as you were still alive? Still safe? Or as safe as you could be?

As if he was talking only with himself, Jakob shook his head.

That wasn't freedom. That was a form of servitude.

Fear was a part of life, yes. He knew that.

You couldn't escape fear.

But you could acknowledge it. You could harness it.

You had to.

Because fear was inextricably linked to freedom. You couldn't have one without the other.

That led Jakob to his next conclusion.

You had to fight through your fear.

It was the only way to achieve freedom.

The freedom that his father could never have.

Thinking about that depressing fact sent another bolt of sadness through him. He didn't allow it to stay with him, however, because even though his father could never have the freedom that he had wanted, perhaps Jakob could attain the freedom that Dougal had wanted for the both of them.

The freedom that perhaps these Highlanders could have. If they were willing to fight for it.

He corrected himself immediately.

The Highlanders would fight for their freedom. They wanted to fight for their freedom. He had no doubt about that. They just needed to be given a fair chance in the fight.

That was what the Highlanders didn't have right now. The odds were tilted heavily in favor of those trying to slaughter them.

And as Jakob had demonstrated, at least on a small scale, he had the power to potentially push those odds back in favor of the Highlanders.

Jakob looked at Duff, knowing what he needed to do.

The former Sergeant was staring at him.

Duff's eyes were difficult to read, but there was a hint there for him if he could interpret it.

After just a few heartbeats, he thought that he could make out what was flitting about in the very back.

Jakob's eyebrows rose, and he nodded. Not surprised.

Hope.

Why would Duff be hopeful? Now of all times?

Nothing was getting done here. Everyone was talking in a circle, more than happy to continue along the path that only served to bring them back to where they started.

Jakob's eyes widened. It hit him harder than the massive Ghoule he had fought back in Roo's Nest.

Duff had known what Jakob needed to do. He had known for quite some time.

Jakob just had to come to that realization on his own. And Duff somehow had the patience to allow that to happen.

He gave Duff a nod that the Sergeant returned.

"This is all in your hands, lad," Duff whispered to him, leaning in close so that Jakob could hear over the rumble of voices around them. "You needed to figure all this out on your own. You're the only person who can do anything about the challenges and perils that we face in the Highlands. You're the only one who can give us any chance of success."

Duff reached over and gripped Jakob's shoulder, giving him a companionable squeeze. "But you need to be aware that if you take on this responsibility, there's a heavy cost. It's unavoidable, and you'll be paying the bulk of it. Even so, if you don't take up the mantle, then the cost will be even heavier, the only difference being that everyone in the Highlands will be paying that. Not just you. So make sure you're certain of what you're about to do next."

"You're not making this sound very appealing," Jakob whispered back.

"I'm not trying to," Duff replied, releasing his hold. "I just want to make sure that you're aware of all the ramifications of the next step that I expect you'll take. Of the price that you'll likely have to pay, even if we succeed."

Jakob stared at Duff for quite a long time, hearing the truth in his words. Appreciating his friend's honesty.

He was the only one who could offer the Highlanders a solution to the dangers that threatened them.

Only him.

That was quite a burden. Heavier, in fact, than he expected it would be.

For just a few breaths, he thought that the weight that had settled on his shoulders as he considered accepting the challenge was going to crush him.

Then he looked at Duff again. The Highlander gave him another nod of support, telling him that he would be there with him every step of the way.

He saw Bertie, Tommie, and Martin looking at him as well. Their expressions were set, hard, confident. And just like Duff, hopeful. They would be at his side when he needed them.

He looked just past Martin to Donel and the other Highlanders who sat near the merchant. Donel had been quite clear when they arrived. He wasn't just a merchant. He was a Highlander. The bloody axe that he had yet to clean and still carried as a mark of pride confirmed it.

Donel turned his gaze toward him and gave him a look as well, then a nod, mimicking Duff. He was waiting just as Martin, Bertie, and Tommie were. He was just as hopeful as they were.

Jakob understood what they were thinking. They had already begun to fight back against those oppressing them.

The slavers. The Stalkers. The Wraiths.

Because of him.

They couldn't do it without him.

And if they were to stand any chance at all of continuing along that track, they needed him to lead them. They couldn't do it on their own.

But they understood as well that they couldn't force him onto that track.

No, Jakob needed to decide for himself.

Was he going to join them?

Was he going to lead them?

He tore his eyes away from his friends, sweeping his gaze across the Highlanders sitting and standing around him.

They'd worked through the same issues, the same conversations, multiple times. They still hadn't reached any conclusions.

However, he had.

Jakob stared one more time at the kestrels, the raptors soaring through the sky as if they owned it.

He wanted the freedom that the kestrels had. The only way to gain that freedom was to fight for it.

If these Highlanders wanted to fight with him, they could. And if they didn't, well, he'd still fight for his freedom.

His father had died to give Jakob his freedom. He couldn't turn away from a gift such as that.

One way or the other, he would do what was necessary. Whether he lived or died, he would do what was necessary.

JAKOB'S HAND wrapped around the Speaker's Staff as he pulled himself to his feet.

He had made his decision.

Now he was impatient.

He wanted to get moving. He wanted to do what needed to be done.

"What's the matter?" asked Duff.

"This isn't working."

"You mean all these people trying to offer their thoughts on what to do? You don't think it's working?"

Jakob ignored Duff's sarcasm. "Why did you do this? Why would you bring all these people together knowing that this would be the result?"

"I didn't do this entirely for them," Duff replied, giving Jakob a meaningful look. "Although it was a part of the process."

"Then who did you do it for?"

"I did it for you."

"Me? Why me?"

"You needed to see their passion," Duff explained. "Their desire. Their willingness to do what's necessary so that they can live the lives they want to live. So that they can claim the Highlands as their own."

"That passion is obvious, but that doesn't help me kill more Wraiths," countered Jakob. "Passion doesn't help me kill all the Stalkers or remove the slavers from the Highlands. Passion without purpose and discipline just ensures failure. All three need to be combined effectively."

"No, passion doesn't help us clear the Highlands. You're absolutely right. Purpose and discipline are essential parts of that mix. But you can use that passion. You can harness that passion and you can give them the purpose. You can give them the discipline. If you do that, they'll help us kill more Wraiths. They'll help us kill the Stalkers. They'll help us drive the slavers from the Highlands."

"You think that I can give them all that?" Jakob had wanted

to include some sarcasm in his tone, but he failed, trying to fight off one last bout of doubt.

Duff pushed himself up from his seat to stand next to Jakob. He motioned to the thousands of Highlanders gathered around them.

"You needed to see this. You needed to understand that everything that you need to do what you want to do is right here."

"That I need?"

"Yes, that you need, and they needed to see that everything they need to do what they want to do is right here," Duff confirmed, staring pointedly at Jakob, giving him a light tap on the chest with a finger.

"What do they need?" Jakob already knew the answer before he asked the question. He just dreaded hearing it, hoping that he was mistaken, sighing in resignation when he wasn't.

"A leader."

Jakob stared at his friend. He should have anticipated that this was Duff's play right from the start.

He had, in fact, and he had allowed it to happen, nonetheless.

A plan within a plan. And then a plan within that plan. That was always the way it was with Duff.

His calling this Highland Council wasn't to find a solution to the challenge bedeviling the Highlanders.

The people of the Highlands already had a solution. They just needed to see that solution for themselves.

That's why Duff had done this. That's why Duff had brought him here.

The stories that were circulating throughout the Highlands were not enough, no matter how fast they spread. The Highlanders needed to see the lead character in those stories in flesh and bone.

They needed to believe in something.

They needed to believe in someone.

They needed to believe in Jakob.

Because if he could give them hope, then he could capture their hearts. And then their passion could be put to work for the benefit of the Highlands. With a purpose. With discipline.

Mix those three together effectively and they stood a chance.

Jakob should have been irritated with Duff for placing him in this position. But he wasn't. Actually, he appreciated what his friend had done for him.

"You must do what you must do."

His father's words, something that Dougal had told him so many times before, played through his mind just then. A reminder from the other side.

Jakob already had decided. He knew what he had to do.

Now there was only one question left to answer.

What would the Highlanders decide?

Jakob was about to ask Duff how best to capture everyone's attention when a loud screech cut through the murmur of conversation, bringing an immediate silence to the throng.

A massive kestrel alighted on the branch right above Jakob, the majestic raptor staring out at the gathered Highlanders with an imperiousness and dignity that few had ever seen before.

Jakob looked up at the kestrel, the raptor staring right back at him. Then the huge predator appeared to nod before launching himself back into the sky.

Jakob watched the kestrel soar away, tilting a wing and beginning to glide around the heart tree under which he stood.

When he dropped his gaze back down toward the High-landers, the silence that had fallen remained. No one said a word. They only wanted to hear from one person now.

For just a moment Jakob felt more nervous than he had that

last night he had spent with Senna before his life had been turned upside down. But thinking back on that and all that had occurred since, he realized that there was no cause to feel this way.

He would do what he needed to do.

If the Highlanders chose the same path as he had, then all the better. And if not, although that would disappoint him, it wouldn't stop him from following the path that he believed he needed to trod.

As he gathered his thoughts, the silence began to drag.

How to start?

Then Jakob knew. These Highlanders had come here because of a story. They had come here to hear his story.

"I didn't want to come to the Highlands," Jakob began. "Not at first."

Jakob stepped forward on the root, not needing to hold onto the Speaker's Staff. He wasn't nervous now. He knew what he wanted to say.

Rather than think about the fact that he was addressing several thousand people, his gaze drifted throughout the crowd. He sought to lock onto the eyes of as many Highlanders as he could, so that it seemed like he was only talking to one person at a time.

"I had a life in Roo's Nest. Or at least I did until it was taken from me."

Feeling more comfortable, Jakob began to walk along the root, his eyes scanning the crowd. He tried to make as many of the Highlanders as he could feel as if he was talking to them directly as he wandered among them, stepping carefully around those who stood or sat on the bark.

"I understand now why my father wanted to come here. Because you're just like him. Just like me. You wanted a new start. For you. For your families. And you were willing to make whatever sacrifice was necessary to gain the freedom that you deserve. The freedom that my father wanted. The freedom that my father wanted me to have."

Jakob stopped walking for just a few heartbeats, looking down at the rough bark, gathering his thoughts, the emotion welling up within him as he thought about his father threatening to break through.

"My father will never earn the freedom that he so desperately wanted. That he so desperately deserved. But I will. I promise you that. Because I won't allow my father's sacrifice to be in vain."

Jakob began to walk slowly again along the root that was at least six feet above the ground, sometimes more as it arced and curled along the plateau. He followed the track of the bark through the crowd, attempting to bring the Highlanders into the conversation. And from what he could see by the looks on their faces, he believed that he was succeeding.

"My first night in New Caledonia was a memorable one. My father and I had set up a small campsite atop a tor just a mile or so into the Highlands. I was staring at the stars as they glimmered above the peaks. A beautiful sight. I had been in the Highlands no more than a few hours. But already these mountains felt right. They felt like home."

He paused for just a moment, recognizing that many of the Highlanders who were observing him had experienced much the same when they first entered these rugged, beautiful spires.

"I knew that I was in the right place. That this was where I was supposed to be. And I can see that many of you felt the same thing that I did."

Several of the Highlanders in the crowd nodded to him, smiling, enjoying a similar memory as Jakob did. Their expressions changed to shock in a flash.

"Less than an hour after that I had killed my first Stalker. A few minutes after that I was enslaved."

Jakob raised his arms into the air, displaying the manacles

that still encircled his wrists so that every Highlander could see them. Several times he had thought about removing the shackles. Yet each time that thought came into his mind, he chose to ignore it.

Removing his irons didn't feel right. Not yet. Not until he was truly free.

Besides, the steel around his wrists had proven quite useful in several combats since he had escaped the slavers.

"The next few weeks were the worst of my life. My father and I were forced through the Highlands toward the mines. We were forced toward a fate that was worse than death."

Jakob smiled then, despite the anguish that swept through him as he remembered what happened next.

"My father didn't give up. Even after the slavers beat him. Even after we escaped and he could barely walk. Even after we had fought our way through the Murk and the Wraiths. My father never gave up. Because he had one hope. Just one."

Jakob closed his eyes for a few heartbeats, allowing the sun to warm his face, needing a moment to steel himself for what he was going to say next.

"My father knew that he was dying, his injuries too severe. But he didn't care. The only thing that he cared about was not dying too soon. He didn't want to die until he had helped me to get free. And he did just that. My father sacrificed himself so that I could escape. And I know that since you've come to the Highlands, many of you have been forced to make sacrifices. Many of you have lost loved ones because they made the ultimate sacrifice for you. Just as my father did for me."

Jakob saw several heads nodding as his eyes worked their way through the crowd. He began walking along the length of the root once again.

"I lost my father because he would do anything for me. My father gave his life for mine. And that's a debt that I can never repay, no matter what I might try."

Jakob stared at the bark for a few seconds as he walked along the root so that his words had time to sink in.

"I should hate the Highlands. I should hate these peaks for all that happened to my father. For all that has happened to me. But I don't. I can't. Despite the loss of my father, despite the pain and suffering, despite the terror, I can't escape the truth. I know that I belong here. I belong in the Highlands. These mountains are my home."

Jakob waited a few seconds for the murmurs of agreement and even a few shouts of support to quiet down.

"Some of you have talked to Duff, to Donel, to Fenri, to Alanna, to the many other Highlanders who know me. Who know what I have done to fight those who would slaughter us or enslave us. They know how I've given them not only the assistance they need to fight the slavers and the Stalkers, but also the ability to combat the Wraiths in the Murk. To take the fight to those monsters in the mist. To ensure that we no longer have to hide in our brochs when the fog comes in from the north."

Jakob stopped pacing then, becoming silent for a time. No one said a word, every eye drawn to him. Everyone desperate to hear what he was going to say next.

"Whatever you decide to do here today, I will continue to help you as best as I can. I will continue to fight the slavers. I will continue to fight the Stalkers. I will continue to fight the Wraiths."

Jakob began to walk along the root again, wandering in and out of the shade provided by the heart tree.

"I have nowhere else to go, and I have nowhere else that I want to go. As I said, this is my home now. I don't care what I have to do to protect my home. I'll do whatever I need to do. No matter what it might cost me."

That earned several nods and growls from the Highlanders.

"Now I want to be completely honest with you. What I am

going to ask of you, there is no guarantee of success. I'm sure you know that, but still, I must say it. The monsters and men seeking to claim the Highlands for themselves will not be easy to defeat. They might take my life, I admit that. But I will make you a promise. Before they do that, I will make them bleed first."

A plethora of shouts burst forth from the crowd, a hundred or more fists punching into the air in support of Jakob.

"Even so, the truth is that I can't truly be successful without you. Only if we work together, only if we decide to fight together to free the Highlands, do we have any chance of making these mountains the home that we want them to be."

Jakob reached one hand up to his face, his fingers touching the scar that ran from his right eye all the way down to his jaw.

"A Wraith did this to me. Every day, I feel it. Every second, I know it's there because every time I think of the monster who did this to me it burns. And I think about that Wraith quite a bit. Because I haven't killed him yet." That earned a rumble of approval from the watching Highlanders. "But I value this scar, because every second of every day it reminds me of what's required to succeed in freeing the Highlands."

Jakob increased the volume of his voice so that it was almost a shout. "The Highlands belong to us. I don't really care what it says on a piece of paper signed by a king living on the other side of the Burnt Ocean. These mountains don't belong to Torstan Sharperson. The Highlands belong to us! If we are willing to fight!"

A roar of approval rang out from the Highlanders that echoed off the surrounding peaks. Jakob waited for almost a minute before raising his hands for silence, allowing the people around him to vent the kaleidoscope of emotions raging through them. The crowd quieted quickly.

"My father had many sayings, and he was always willing to share them with me. Much too willing, in fact."

That comment drew a rumble of welcome laughter from the crowd, priming them for what Jakob was going to say next.

"One saying seems particularly appropriate as to why we're here now. What we want to do now."

Jakob waited before offering one of his father's favorite aphorisms, wanting every eye on him, not minding in the least how the tension was building within the Grove, understanding that as every second passed that rising tension would only work in his favor.

"Stand fast. Stand strong. Stand free."

Jakob nodded, allowing his words to wash over the Highlanders. Then he repeated them with more force.

"Stand fast. Stand strong. Stand free."

He saw every single Highlander staring at him, almost all of them nodding.

"My father is right. If we want to make the Highlands our own, if we want to expel a lord who seeks only to subjugate us, if we want to rid ourselves of the slavers and the Stalkers and the Wraiths, then we must stand fast! We must stand strong! We must stand free! And we, together, relying on one another, helping one another, must fight for *our* Highlands!"

Another roar erupted from the Highlanders, Tenny and Tamsin and all those around them raising their fists into the sky, shouting their approval and their agreement.

Jakob allowed the cacophony to continue for several minutes before finally raising his hands above his head. Silence descended immediately.

Every eye was on him. Expectant. Hopeful. The thousands of Highlanders barely breathed.

"Once again, I must caution you that this will not be easy. So don't assume that it will be. It will take our blood, our sweat, and our tears. It will take the lives of some of us. But if we are to create the homeland that we want, then those are the risks that we must take."

"What would you have us do, Lord Kestrel?" asked Duff in a voice loud enough for all those who stood on the small plateau to hear.

"We wake the Highlands!" Jakob replied, pulling one of the double-bladed daggers that he had mastered from the sheath on his back and thrusting it into the sky, the bright sunlight setting the bone-white steel gleaming. "Because the High-landers go to war!"

This time Jakob didn't bother to stop the roars of support that rushed out from those gathered in the Grove, relishing the clamor of emotion, realizing that Duff was right.

Passion was key to their success, and the Highlanders certainly didn't lack that.

Then much to Jakob's surprise a handful of kestrels landed in the tree just above his head. The massive raptors added their own screeches to the cries now drifting out across the Highlands.

Jakob caught the sharp gaze of the raptor that had settled closest to him, not quite believing what he was seeing.

There was an understanding there. An acceptance. A strange but strong link that filled Jakob with a confidence that he had never experienced before.

When he nodded to the kestrel, the predator dipped her head as well, before raising her razor-sharp beak to the sky and adding her shrieks to those of her brethren.

Jakob had never been one for showmanship, but he did understand the value of it. So, he stood there for a moment longer, shaking his fist, the dagger shining brightly in the light, screaming with the people who had chosen to support him, all the while thinking of what they needed to do next.

They needed to push back against the slavers, the Stalkers, and the Wraiths. They needed to ensure that these invaders could no longer enter the Highlands with impunity. Their enemies needed to understand that taking that risk guaranteed an immediate and bloody response from the Highlanders.

And then the harder work would begin. They would take on the potentially even larger challenge they faced.

Because if the Highlanders truly were to claim these mountain peaks for their own, there was only one real solution.

Rebellion.

THE END OF BOOK 3.

I HOPE you enjoyed Book 3 of *The Tales of the Territories*. Keep reading for scenes from Book 4, *The Bloody Hunt for Freedom*.

BONUS MATERIAL

If you really enjoyed this story, I need you to do me a HUGE favor – please follow me on Amazon and BookBub. And if you have a few minutes, consider writing a review.

Keep reading for two chapters from *The Bloody Hunt for Freedom,* Book 4 in my series *The Tales of the Territories*. Order Book 4 from Amazon or my author website PeterWachtBooks.com.

PETER WACHT

THE
BLOODY
HUNT FOR
FREEDOM

ISBN: 978-1-950236-38-1

eBook ISBN: 978-1-950236-39-8

Library of Congress Control Number: 2023909943

❋ Created with Vellum

1. THE FIRST STEP

"Keep the men awake, Dooley. I don't trust these Highlanders any farther than I can throw them."

"Of course, Sergeant Henriks," Dooley replied. "A slippery lot, I agree. Worse than eels out of water."

"Just be ready," the Sergeant ordered as the village of Anhold came into view. "I don't want any problems. The sooner we're done with this, the sooner we're out of here. Get me?"

"Yes, Sergeant Henriks. Of course, Sergeant Henriks."

Henriks led several squads of soldiers from Governor Sharperson's Guard down the road -- really no more than a trail and a rough one -- that curled its way toward the tower that was under construction on the windswept plateau.

He didn't relish the task that the Governor had given him. Even so, better that he be the one doing the dirty work rather than being forced to take the place of one of these poor slobs himself.

A distinct possibility if he didn't meet the quota for this assignment. One hundred men. No less than that. More would be better. But at minimum one hundred men. One way or another. Healthy and whole. Or rather healthy enough.

Reining in his horse a few yards onto the green that encircled the broch, Sergeant Henriks awkwardly slipped down from his mount, saddle sore from the long journey, the pain in his lower back flaring up. Working the blood back into his legs with his hands, he walked with a pronounced limp toward the center of the village.

The wound to his knee hadn't healed properly, and just as it always did after just a little exertion, it was driving him to distraction. He hadn't gotten a good night's sleep since the dagger had slipped between the bones of the joint, severing the ligaments and leaving him unsteady on his feet.

Coming to a stop when he was ten yards away, he stared up at the broch. Even though he knew that it was a useless attempt to ease the pain, he rubbed his aching knee as he studied the tower. He was impressed by both its size and its construction.

Simply done. Well done as well. He knew from experience that the redoubt would perform the function for which it was designed.

The broch looked to be almost complete. A handful of Highlanders were dismantling the crane they had used to get the larger stones to the top so that they could construct the parapet. Several other Highlanders were straining to set in place the massive oak door that was wrapped in iron.

That final piece, along with the impenetrable stone, would offer these Highlanders protection against the Wraiths who came with the fog ... and men like him.

He nodded as he took in all the work going on around him. Yes, it was definitely a good thing that he got here when he did. Before his job got any harder than it already was.

"You," Henriks called, nodding toward a bald man standing near the entrance to the broch who was wiping his hands on a rag. "Highlander. We need to talk."

The man didn't bother to acknowledge Henriks other than to motion with a hand that he would be with him in a minute.

"Highlander!" shouted Henriks. His raised voice caused some rustling behind him as his soldiers dropped down from their horses. They eyed warily the Highlanders completing the broch as well as the many more building a row of cottages along the border of the green. "I'm talking to you!"

Sergeant Henriks' anger had flamed in a flash. A common occurrence for him these days. It didn't take much to get his blood boiling. Not now. Not when his leg throbbed and burned every second of the day.

It didn't help that he wasn't used to being ignored. That only irritated him to an even greater degree.

The Highlander waved at him one more time to let him know that he needed to wait a little while longer. Then he had the gall to turn his back on him, not even bothering to acknowledge a Sergeant of the Highland Guard as he continued to help the two men with him adjust the placement of the door.

Henriks' face grew redder and redder as the insult took root within him. He considered walking over and grabbing the Highlander by the shoulder, then decided against it, the pain in his leg keeping him in place.

Finally, the door positioned correctly and after giving the two men working with him companionable pats on the shoulder for a job well done, the Highlander turned and walked over to Henriks.

"What can I do you for?"

"You will address me as Sergeant," Henriks ordered, grimacing as he took in the nasty scar that ran down the Highlander's scalp all the way to his cheek.

"Of course, Sergeant," replied the Highlander, a hint of amusement in his voice and in the back of his eyes. The man actually had the temerity to salute him with a lazy hand to his brow, dirty rag still in his grip, before he started laughing softly as he shook his head. "What can I do you for ... Sergeant?"

Henriks' initial instinct was to make an example of the

Highlander. To put him in his place. He had done it before. Several times because it was necessary. More often just because he wanted to.

He certainly had the right men at his back for doing just that. But Henriks hesitated. A few of his men enjoyed that kind of work a bit too much.

Mulling that course of action for a few more seconds, Henriks decided against it. He would hold on to that option. Just in case it proved necessary. Or his leg bothered him so badly that he needed the diversion.

Besides, he had no doubt that the tenor of this engagement would change soon enough. There was no need to rush it along.

"First, you can answer a question," replied Henriks. "If you can do that, then you might be able to avoid the flogging that you deserve."

"What would that question be?" the Highlander asked, the man clearly not intimidated by the threat, his smile still in place, actually growing a bit bigger.

"Why the tower?" Henriks asked, nodding to the stone rising to his front. "I've seen several from a distance as I made my way here."

"It's fairly obvious, don't you think ... Sergeant."

Henriks stared at the Highlander, his blood pressure slowly rising, his face shifting from a light to a deep red. The scarred man had waited an awfully long time to add his rank. Almost like he offered it as an insult.

The Sergeant was beginning to think that this was the man he would, indeed, make an example of. Moreover, a flogging would be too kind. He and his men would need to employ more drastic measures so that these Highlanders were properly cowed before they began the journey to their new home.

Mollified enough by that thought to keep his temper in

check, Henriks took a deep breath before he hissed, "Explain it to me."

"In big words or little words, Sergeant, since I'm surprised that you seem to have some difficulty understanding the purpose of brochs."

The Sergeant's temper flashed, his hand reaching down and grasping the hilt of his sword. He heard a similar movement occurring in the twin column of soldiers at his back, several even pulling free their steel.

Strangely, the threat of violence had no effect on the Highlander. He remained in place, standing calmly in front of the broch as the other Highlanders with him continued their work. None of them seemed to be worried in the least that several dozen soldiers had entered their village.

"No more of your attempted humor, Highlander," ordered Henriks through gritted teeth. "Explain."

The Highlander shrugged, clearly not understanding why the Sergeant was so vexed. "Brochs are towers."

Henriks' eyes threatened to bulge out of their sockets, the red coloring his face shifting to a shade of purple. The Highlander was looking at him as if he were a fool. He didn't like that. Not in the least.

"I know they're towers!" Henriks roared, gesturing toward the massive construction standing before him. "Why are you building the brochs?"

"We're building the brochs for protection," the Highlander replied. He spoke slowly, as if he were talking to someone who had been kicked in the head by a horse when he was a child. The Highlander appeared to be about to continue with his explanation. Then he stopped himself, giving Henriks a quizzical look. "How long have you been a soldier? You do know what towers are used for, right?"

Henriks could only stare at the Highlander, completely taken aback. He had not had to deal with someone like him, someone so full of himself, someone so insolent, in quite some time. Someone whose every word was laced with disrespect.

His eyes narrowed. It was his turn to shake his head. Try to have a civil discourse with these Highlanders and this is what you got. An almost palpable contempt.

The Sergeant was beginning to think that the time for that example was almost upon him. He could be pushed only so far.

"Don't step beyond your place, Highlander," Henriks said as he struggled to keep his temper under control, taking in several deep breaths and blowing them out slowly through his nose. He was leading this mission. Even though it felt like there was broken glass in his knee every time he moved the joint, he couldn't allow his simmering rage that was amplified by his pain get in the way of his decisions. "Of course I know what brochs are used for. I want to know why you're building them."

The Highlander stared at the Sergeant for several seconds, trying to figure out if the man was for real. He started to say something, but stopped himself. And then again. He certainly enjoyed irritating the Sergeant, however it was far too easy. Finally, the Highlander shrugged and harrumphed.

"We're building the brochs so that we can protect ourselves from the Stalkers and the Wraiths," replied the Highlander, deciding that it was best to humor the soldier. "Slavers too."

The Highlander said the last with a nod and a knowing wink.

Henriks glared at the scarred fellow for a time. He should have assumed that the Highlanders would have sussed out why Henriks and his men were there.

The Highlanders were known for being difficult, just like this one was being. They were not known for being fools.

"I assumed as much," the Sergeant hissed. "Perhaps I wasn't specific enough, Highlander, since you seem to have such a difficult time responding to my questions."

"Maybe it's the questions and not me," the Highlander interjected. "They are quite simple, after all. Questions that really don't need to be asked because you already know the answers."

Henrik bit his lip to keep the sharp retort that was just on the tip of his tongue from flying from his lips. He could only assume that the Highlander was trying to have some fun before the fate that awaited crashed down upon him.

"Then I'll speak slowly, Highlander. Why are you building brochs when these mountains are under the protection of Governor Sharperson and his Highland Guard?"

For almost a minute the Highlander, brow furrowed, stared at the Sergeant as if he didn't understand the question. The Highlander's lips started to twitch, his eyes sparkling with either delight or derision.

Henriks couldn't tell which as both possibilities set his simmering anger back to a boil.

Then the man placed his hands on his knees and burst out laughing.

The Sergeant's expression darkened, a large blood vessel pulsing on his purple forehead.

The Highlander didn't care. "Martin, Bertie, did you hear what the Sergeant just asked me?"

"No, what?" asked Martin, a large hammer in his grip as he was about to drive a nail that was almost a foot long into the stone to help lock the door frame in place.

"The good Sergeant here wants to know why we are building brochs when we are under the protection of Governor Sharperson and his Guard?"

The Highlander's comment was met with absolute silence by the two men finishing their work on the doorjamb, then every single man and woman working around the broch started to laugh.

Henriks stood there frozen, stunned, then shook his head in

wonder. These people dared to insult him? With so many soldiers at his back?

He needed to correct his assessment of these Highlanders. Difficult, yes. But fools as well.

He was going to enjoy this. And he was going to let his men have their fun before they got underway. A little payback for the insults.

Having had enough of this recalcitrant Highlander, Henriks pulled his sword and demonstrated a surprising agility for someone with a bad leg, taking two steps forward in just a breath and placing the point of the blade against the man's chest.

As soon as the sharp steel pressed into his flesh, the Highlander's expression changed. The humor disappeared, replaced by a coldness that almost took the Sergeant's breath away.

"Don't test me, Highlander," hissed Henriks. "Before I have you hung up by your toes and your flesh sliced off piece by piece, tell me your name."

The Highlander stared at Henriks for a moment longer. The Sergeant could almost read the scarred Highlander's mind. The man was working through the various ways that he could kill Henriks if he didn't have a sword pressed against his chest.

To dissuade him from doing anything stupid, Henriks pushed the tip of his blade a little harder against the man's chest, piercing his shirt and the first few layers of skin.

"Duff."

"Now was that so hard?" asked Henriks.

"You could have asked me before, you know," shrugged the Highlander. "It might have helped to avoid the coming unpleasantness."

Henriks was about to reply, thinking that he had an excellent retort. Instead, he stopped himself.

He stared a little harder at the Highlander. By the tone of his voice, the man under his sword seemed to be suggesting that the unpleasantness would be experienced by him and not the Highlander.

Forcing that disturbing thought out of his mind, Henriks kept his sword in place. He swept his gaze from the left to the right, taking in all that was happening in his line of sight.

The Sergeant had sensed the change in the mood of the village as soon as he had drawn his blade. All of the Highlanders who had been working at their various tasks despite the appearance of his soldiers had stopped.

They were glaring at him now. Eyes cold. Expressions hard. Bodies tense.

None of the Highlanders looked very pleased. That didn't bother Henriks.

What bothered him was that the Highlanders staring back at him seemed hopeful. Expectant. Almost chomping at the bit.

"Duff," the Sergeant said, seeking to regain control of a situation that he realized could deteriorate rather quickly if he wasn't careful. "I'm going to keep this simple so we don't have any misunderstandings."

"Please do," the Highlander requested, his voice sounding more like a cold breeze.

"The men at my back," the Sergeant said, nodding toward the soldiers who had stepped away from their mounts, all of whom now held their swords in their hands, "will not hesitate to do what I command, even killing everyone here if I order it. Do you understand?"

"I do," Duff replied with a nod, giving Henriks an indecipherable look.

What bothered the Sergeant wasn't the speed with which the Highlander had replied. He had expected that. A show of force tended to do that.

What worried Henriks was that when Duff confirmed his comprehension, there wasn't a hint of fear in his voice or his expression, even though there were four squads of veteran soldiers, almost fifty men in all, ready and willing to do whatever he ordered them to do -- whether it was to make an example of the Highlander or burn down all the homes under construction -- and many of them more than willing to go well beyond that.

If that happened, so be it. This Highlander had pushed him too far. Whatever happened next, he and his friends had brought it upon themselves.

Henriks had a job to do. He needed to do it.

"Good. You will do two things for me. Without complaint. Without question. Do you understand?"

Duff's eyes hardened. He wiggled his fingers as if he was preparing to deal with the sword pressed into his chest. Not because it was hurting him. More because it seemed to be irritating him.

Henriks was ready for whatever the Highlander might try, anticipating that their confrontation would reach this point. But the Highlander kept his hands down by his sides, instead replying in a very calm voice.

"I do."

"Good," nodded the Sergeant. "First, you will call to the green every able-bodied man in this village and the surrounding countryside. They will be standing on the green in thirty minutes. No weapons. Just the clothes on their backs. Do you understand?"

Henriks had expected the obstreperous Highlander to ask why he wanted him to do that. He almost hoped that the man named Duff would.

Because that would give him a chance to demonstrate that he was serious. The Sergeant would enjoy doing that since this Highlander had proven to be such a challenge. Much to his disappointment, Henriks didn't get the chance to take that next step.

"I do," Duff replied simply.

"Good," Henriks nodded again, beginning to think that this Highlander finally might understand the situation in which he found himself. "Second, this village has not paid its taxes."

"Taxes for what?" Duff couldn't stop himself from asking even as the Sergeant pushed harder with his blade, the point of the steel cutting through the next few layers of his skin, a trickle of blood leaking out and staining his shirt.

"For the protection and many other services that Governor Sharperson, out of the goodness of his heart, provides to all those living in the Highlands."

Duff smiled, barely able to contain his amusement, even as his eyes remained cold. "That's it, then? Those are your two requirements? I'm assuming you'll collect the taxes after you've collected the men."

"They are. They're quite simple. So let's get started. Men first, then the taxes."

"And I'm assuming that these men, once they pay these taxes that you say they owe to the good Governor Sharperson, will be accompanying you to whatever mine you have in mind for them?"

It was Henriks' turn to smile. "And here I was taking you for a fool. It seems that you've gotten a lot smarter in just the last few minutes."

"That's kind of you to say," Duff replied. He nodded his head as if he was actually pleased by that comment and was considering the demand that the Sergeant had made of him. After making up his mind, he spoke bluntly. "I'm sorry, but I can't help you."

"What do you mean you can't help me?" demanded the Sergeant, pressing the tip of his blade deeper into Duff's chest in a final attempt to demonstrate his conviction. "I wasn't asking for your help. I was telling you what to do. I gave you an order."

"Sorry, but I still can't help you," Duff replied, ignoring the pinch of pain that radiated out from the center of his chest. He refused to move. He wouldn't show any sign of weakness to this soldier.

"You do realize that I'm within my rights to take your head from your shoulders for your impertinence."

"You can try," Duff replied with a mildness that befuddled the Sergeant. "I don't think you'll like the result if you try. Then again, you're not going to like the result even if you step back and stop acting the fool."

"Meaning what?" demanded Henriks, not quite believing how the Highlander was speaking to him. Not sure what to do next.

"Have you ever taken a head from someone's shoulders?" asked Duff, his expression revealing his belief that the Sergeant hadn't, in fact, taken someone's head from their shoulders with a blade.

"Why would you ask a question like that? I've got a sword pressed against your chest and that's what you ask me? Forget what I just said. You are a fool."

"Because it's not an easy thing to do," Duff continued, ignoring the Sergeant. "It's very difficult, in fact, if you don't have the experience and you don't have the muscle. And by the looks of you, you don't have either. Especially with that knee of yours. You need some leverage and it doesn't look like you can plant very well." Duff's eyes narrowed. "So who did that to you anyway? I'm assuming that it was a dagger right into the center of your knee."

The Sergeant closed his eyes for a few seconds, trying to comprehend how he had lost control of this conversation. He used to be a master at intimidation. However, his skill in that specialty seemed to have diminished since he had acquired his limp.

That blasted boy! He almost wished that he was still alive. If he had survived the Murk, Henriks could have paid back the boy tenfold for the injury he caused him.

It had to be the pain in his leg as to why he was failing so miserably with this Highlander. Henriks couldn't remedy the pain. He had learned that the hard way. But he could do something about this wretch standing before him who was so good at aggravating him.

"I will demonstrate my ability to take your head from your shoulders once I'm done here. In the meantime, do what I've ordered you to do."

"I'm sorry, but I can't," Duff replied, shrugging his shoulders apologetically.

"What do you mean you can't?"

"I answer to the Lord of the Highlands, not to you."

"What are you talking about? I'm a Sergeant in the Highland Guard. I take my orders from Governor Sharperson. He is the Lord of the Highlands. That means you take your orders from me."

"I take my orders from the Lord of the Highlands," Duff replied calmly. "Torstan Sharperson is not the Lord of the Highlands. He's no more than an overgrown boy playing at being a lord."

"I have no more patience for any of this, Highlander," hissed Henriks, the blood vessel in his forehead pumping savagely as his anger rose to a level rarely reached. Of course, the rational part of his mind agreed with the Highlander's perspective on the Governor. Still, what he believed didn't matter. He had a job to do.

Henriks pulled his sword away from Duff and stepped in close. He grabbed the Highlander's shirt with his free hand, wanting to pull him off balance.

He realized too late that wasn't going to happen since Duff was broader, clearly stronger, and much more stable on his feet. Nevertheless, he was committed, so he refused to let go.

"Get all the able-bodied men in the village and in the surrounding fields here on the green in thirty minutes or I'll hang you from the tower you've spent so much time building."

"I don't think you want to do that."

"Why wouldn't I?" demanded the Sergeant. "The soldiers behind me say otherwise. I know many of my men are just raring to have a go at you. They'll take their time, make it as painful as possible. Make you wish that you started off our conversation on better footing. I promise you that."

"That's all well and good," Duff replied calmly, ignoring the soldier's grip on his shirt, "and I'm sorry to disappoint, but the Lord of the Highlands won't like it. He doesn't have the patience that I do. That's why I've been talking with you rather than him. He would have already killed you. Me, on the other hand, I'm more than willing to engage in dialogue before the bloodletting begins. It helps to calm my nerves."

"And just who is this supposed Lord of the Highlands?" demanded Henriks, having no idea who this fool was talking about. "If there's going to be bloodletting, it's going to be his. After I cut him open so his entrails spill out and his blood stains the grass we're standing on, I'm going to hang him right after I hang you. Then I'm going to raze this village you're trying to build, and while it's burning, I'm going to tear your tower apart stone by stone."

Duff snorted and then smiled at the soldier. He didn't mind how the Sergeant was wrinkling his shirt, because it gave him a chance to look the man directly in the eyes.

The humor that had flashed in the back of Duff's eyes at the appearance of the Sergeant and his patrol was nowhere to be found now. It had been replaced with a cold calculation.

"That really doesn't make sense, you know," Duff said. "If you cut out his entrails, there's no point in hanging him. He'll already be dead. So why waste the effort?"

Once again, all Hendriks could do was stare at this Highlander who had proven to be nothing but difficult. "Even now, your death all but assured, you are unruly and headstrong. Truly remarkable."

"It's in my nature, thus very hard to contain," Duff shrugged, as if to say that there was nothing that he could do about it, "or so I've been told."

"It's going to be the death of you. I promise you that. Now where is your Lord of the Highlands? It's time to end his reign."

"Lord Kestrel," Duff called, nodding at the Sergeant with an expression that suggested that the soldier was going to regret coming to this village. "I've got a man here who wants to talk to you. Something about cutting out your entrails and then hanging you. Although it does seem like a bit of overkill."

Henriks' eyes and those of all his men were drawn toward the broch's doorway, all of them focusing on the young man with his back turned who appeared to have been ignoring the conversation that had drawn the attention of every other man and woman on the green.

The young man didn't appear to be in a rush as he made a few final adjustments to the lock, filing down some of the mechanism's pieces. That done, he tested it several times to ensure that it worked as he wanted.

Satisfied with the quality of his work as demonstrated by his nod, with his back still turned the young man placed his tools on the small table set next to the entrance and then pivoted to face the Sergeant and his soldiers.

"You!" shouted the Sergeant, his heart skipping a beat. "You should be dead!"

"Perhaps, but that's your own fault," Jakob Kestrel replied.

2. THE RIGHT BAIT

"What are we looking for?" asked Davin as he stared at the forbidding coastline. It was nothing more than sheer cliffs that extended hundreds of feet into the sky, the boundary between Fal Carrach and Benewyn ten to twelve leagues to the south.

Talia stood next to the gladiator at the *Swift's* helm. She held her spyglass up to her right eye. A common sight these last few hours.

As she studied the bluffs, she took her time, knowing that what she was looking for would not be easy to find. It couldn't be. Otherwise, it would defeat the purpose of the prize.

"Smuggler's Cove."

"You know where it is, right? You said you got the information out of one of the pirates." He motioned with his hand. "What's his name."

"Captain Blackbeard," Talia replied softly.

She ran her spyglass from north to south as the *Swift* cut through the ten-foot swells. With a quick turn, she brought the spyglass back to the north, thinking that she might have found the concealed entrance.

She shook her head in aggravation. No such luck.

"Right, Captain Blackbeard." Davin leaned back against the railing, shifting his gaze to Talia. He gave her a broad grin, although she didn't return it. Apparently she found it quite easy to ignore him since she was so intent on her task. "If that fellow named himself because of the color of his hair, then maybe I should do the same when I get my own ship."

"You're going to acquire a ship?" Talia snorted, unable to contain her amusement at the thought, even as she kept her spyglass focused on the cliffs.

She hadn't known Davin for more than a few weeks. Yet, in that time, she had seen little to make her believe that he had the desire or the capability to captain a seafaring vessel. In fact, just the thought of him commanding a rowboat gave her cause for concern.

"It's not beyond the realm of possibility."

"That's one way to put it," Talia agreed.

"You don't think I've got the money to buy my own ship?"

Talia clamped her lips together, not allowing herself to utter the first thing that came to mind. There was no reason to stoke his temper so early in the morning. "Buying or building a ship is expensive. I can tell you that based on my own experience."

"I have no doubt about that," Davin replied. "I went through it all with Master Hari."

"You spoke with Master Hari?" asked Talia, surprised to hear that the gladiator was spending time with her Master Shipbuilder.

"I did. I do. Almost every day," Davin replied, either not noticing or choosing to ignore the disbelief apparent in her voice.

"You're talking with Master Hari about building ships?"

"No, about how to construct wagons."

"Wagons?" That response almost made Talia pull the

spyglass from her eye. She didn't, although it was a struggle, too afraid that she would miss the hidden cove.

"Of course not," Davin replied. "I just wanted to see if you were paying attention."

Talia bit her lip, cutting off the curse that she wanted to expel. "You know, Davin, Lord Keldragan said that you could be difficult."

"He's right. He can be difficult as well. That's why we get along so well." Davin pushed off the railing and turned back around, leaning his forearms on the wood, gazing in the direction that Talia was searching. He saw very little that might give them a hint that what they were hunting was anywhere nearby. "And Bryen doesn't like to be called Lord Keldragan."

"I got that feeling," Talia replied, "but he will need to get used to it. And you reminding me of that is just another example of you being difficult."

"You are quite right, oh great Huntress of the Seas," Davin confirmed with a grin and a self-deprecating nod.

This time Talia had to fight to prevent the smile that wanted to break free. She had acquired that name because of her efforts and exploits against the pirates. Although she refused to admit it, she kind of liked the title. "Why are you talking with Master Hari?"

"Who else would I talk to if I wanted to learn about building ships. In my free time, he's been allowing me to apprentice."

"You? Really?" Talia found that hard to believe.

"Just because I was a gladiator doesn't mean that I don't have other interests." This time Talia could tell that Davin didn't appreciate the skepticism that was quite obvious in her tone. "He's not giving me anything too difficult to do. Just letting me get my feet wet. He wants to see if I'll be a fit for his team."

"He said that?"

"He did."

"And the fact that he is testing you doesn't bother you?"

"Not in the least," Davin replied. "I've been tested all my life. Why would it bother me now? Besides, it's the sensible thing for Master Hari to do."

Talia was about to respond, then she stopped herself. Why did she think that he might not respond well to a requirement like that?

She had learned that Davin was many things, but he was not arrogant and he didn't expect to be given anything. He believed that he needed to earn what he wanted in life. An admirable trait. In her opinion, too rare in too many people.

"I just thought that based on your experience you didn't like it when people told you what you could or couldn't do." She hoped that he took what she thought was a diplomatic answer as such.

"You mean because you believe that all gladiators are hotheads and are only interested in blood and killing and hearing the roars of the crowd."

Davin spoke evenly, not a hint of emotion in his voice. Even so, Talia sensed the hint of disappointment there. That she might think such a thing of him.

"I don't really know much about gladiators. I'd never met a gladiator until I met you. I don't know what to think."

"That's understandable," Davin replied evenly, evidently not too upset by her comment. "You know the saying don't judge a book by its cover?"

"You can read?" Talia asked, a smile cracking her usually serious expression. "I didn't know you could teach a gladiator to read."

"Funny," Davin grumbled. "Enjoy yourself at the expense of the lowly gladiator."

"Sorry, I couldn't help myself."

"You could have helped yourself," Davin countered. "You just didn't want to." Before Talia could protest that she meant her joke in good fun, Davin continued. "Anyway, my point is, you can't judge a gladiator just by what you see. We're more complex, more sophisticated, more nuanced, than you might think. We're not all blood and guts and steel."

Talia nodded, her gaze continuing to sweep across the cliffs that sped by on their starboard side. "I'll keep that in mind. Although you diving off the crow's nest to surf behind a ship makes it hard to believe that a gladiator can be sophisticated or nuanced."

"A momentary lapse," Davin admitted with a smile. "I was lacking maturity back then."

"From what I understand, you were diving off the crow's nest a month ago. So since then, in that very brief time frame, you now have attained the maturity that you should have had to begin with?"

"A lot can happen in a month."

"Don't I know it," murmured Talia. "A month ago, when you were diving into the ocean, I was sailing free and clear on the Sea of Mist, making runs, going after a pirate whenever I had the chance."

"And now you're saddled with a gladiator and you don't know what to do with him."

"Your words, not mine."

"True words, nonetheless."

"True words," admitted Talia with a shrug. "I made a promise to Lord Keldragan, and I keep my promises."

"Just put me to work," Davin replied. "You saw what I can do on the passage from the Isle of Mist to Ballinasloe. Master Hari can vouch for me as well."

"I'll keep that in mind," Talia promised, her lips scrunching up.

She was beginning to feel the first touch of frustration, and not because of her conversation. Actually, she quite enjoyed speaking with Davin. Rather, she was getting antsy because she should have spotted Smuggler's Cove by now.

"Thank you," Davin replied graciously. "You know, I'm still stuck on this Captain Blackbeard. He really should have selected a more exciting name rather than one based on the color of his beard. That really shows a lack of imagination."

"He didn't come across as the most creative person," Talia said. "Although it would make it easier for you."

"What do you mean?"

"Well, if you ever buy or build a ship larger than a rowboat, you can call yourself Captain Red."

"Helpful," Davin replied, rolling his eyes even though Talia couldn't see him do it. "Another lame attempt at humor."

"Or maybe Captain Crimson," Talia offered, for some reason feeling freer with Davin than she did with anyone else aboard the ship. Maybe it was because she didn't believe that she was responsible for him while she was for the rest of her crew. Or maybe it was because he never seemed to be judging her, and even if he did she wouldn't have cared. "That would be more appropriate based on the name you acquired in the Colosseum."

"That's better," Davin admitted. "Although I'm more partial to Captain Blood."

"I think we have the winner right there," agreed Talia. "Gives you a hint of menace. You need that if you're going to captain a ship."

"Which is why you don't mind the moniker the Huntress."

"Just so," Talia said.

"You're certain that Captain Blackbeard told you the truth? He didn't try to misdirect you?" Davin worried that they should have found what they were looking for by now. The ingress to the bay couldn't be so well hidden as to not be visible from seaward.

"Of course he told me the truth. He didn't have a choice."

"You're certain?"

Talia scrunched up her lips again, not liking how Davin was challenging her. She would have upbraided him if he were one of her crew.

But he wasn't, although that wasn't what stopped her. Rather, she feared that in the few seconds it would take to do that she might miss what she was looking for.

She took a few deep breaths before replying. She didn't want her growing aggravation, which was more with herself and her current failure than Davin's questions, to be made plain.

"Completely certain."

"Why so confident?"

"Because if he was lying to me – and I know he wasn't lying to me – then I would have fed him to the sharks that were swimming right beneath him."

"You're probably correct then," Davin nodded. "If you had me in that position I'd tell you the truth as well."

"Really," Talia said with a soft chuckle. She was laughing more in just this one conversation than she had since her father had been murdered. "You're lying. I have a nose for these things. You wouldn't break as easily as the infamous Captain Blackbeard."

"That's kind of you to say."

"Although I would still break you. Have no doubt of that."

"Promises, promises," Davin replied. Seeing the faint blush that began to spread across Talia's cheeks, Davin decided that it was time to shift the conversation to a more comfortable topic. "If Captain Blackbeard told you where Smuggler's Cove is, then why are you having such a hard time finding it?"

"Because Smuggler's Cove moves," Talia explained. This was a fact that very few people beyond the community of pirates haunting the Sea of Mist knew. "There are four, maybe five locations along the New Caledonian coast that all serve as Smuggler's Cove. They all look relatively the same. A slit in the cliffs just wide enough for a frigate to pass through leading into a small bay, an anchored pier sitting in the center that's large enough for three or four cutters to tie up to so that business can be conducted."

"Clever."

"Very. That's why we're having a hard time. Captain Blackbeard wasn't certain which Smuggler's Cove would be in use this week. We captured him before that information was circulated among the pirate captains."

"He told you where they were all located so that you wouldn't throw him to the sharks."

"Correct."

"And where is Captain Blackbeard now?"

"You want to know if I threw him to the sharks even though he gave me what I wanted."

"That thought had crossed my mind." Davin raised his hands quickly. "Not that you doing that would have bothered me."

"Do you really think that I would discard him so easily?" asked Talia, not knowing whether she should feel insulted or pleased that he believed that she could be so merciless.

Davin took his time before responding. "I do," he replied finally with a shrug. "If Captain Blackbeard had outlived his usefulness, then I think you would get rid of him."

"That's very cold-blooded of you."

Davin shrugged again, a common habit for him. "Maybe. I view it more as realistic rather than cold-blooded. It's the smartest course of action for you to take."

"Realistic? Really? Are you certain your bloodthirstiness didn't travel with you from the Pit?"

Davin laughed at that. "Bloodthirsty? No, I'm not bloodthirsty. I've only killed to stay alive."

"You truly believe that?" Talia asked.

"I believe it because I know it." Davin said it with such certainty that Talia couldn't dispute him. "Besides, Captain Blackbeard is a pirate, is he not?"

"He is," Talia confirmed.

"Then there's only one end for a pirate. Wringing what information you could out of him gave him more time to breathe. If he's still alive because you have a use for him, then he's getting even more breaths. But I have absolutely no doubt that once you're done with Captain Blackbeard, you'll hang him. Just as he should be hanged."

Talia was about to reply. Once again, she stopped herself before she said something that she shouldn't.

She wasn't sure why Davin perplexed her. Maybe it was because her initial read of him didn't match with reality.

That both annoyed her, because she was an excellent judge of character and she seemed to have failed with him, and pleased her, because the more she learned about him, the more he piqued her interest. Although that last worried her in an entirely unexpected way.

Not wanting to think on that, she continued to sweep her spyglass across the seemingly unending cliff face, looking for the slit that would give away Smuggler's Cove.

"Why do you say that about me with such conviction?" she asked.

"Because in many ways you're just like my friend Bryen."

"Lord Keldragan? How so?" She wasn't certain that she liked being compared to the man responsible for taking down the Beleron dynasty or, as he perhaps was better known, the Volkun. A gladiator with a reputation that was even bloodier and fiercer than that of the Crimson Giant, although not by much.

"Bryen will always do what's right, even when he doesn't want to. Hanging Captain Blackbeard at the right time is the right thing to do. That's why I'm so certain that when that time comes you will do it."

"You think you know me so well," Talia challenged.

Davin raised his hands again, hoping that he hadn't offended her. "I didn't say that. Although I do have a good sense of who you are."

"You do?" challenged Talia.

"I do," Davin confirmed. "I see you."

"You see me," said Talia, finally dropping the spyglass and turning toward Davin. He pushed himself off the railing and took a step back, not sure if she was angry because of what he just said or curious. "What does that even mean?"

"It means what it means," Davin answered with another shrug of his shoulders.

"That's not an answer," Talia said with some heat, not quite understanding why she felt so uncomfortable in that moment.

"It is an answer. A good one, too." Definitely anger rather than curiosity, Davin decided, which meant that it was time to shift the topic of the conversation once again. "So we're not just looking for Smuggler's Cove. We're looking for the one that's currently in use."

"There you go," grouched Talia, who shook her head in irritation and turned back toward the cliffs that sped by swiftly, spyglass fixed to her eye once again.

"You know, you could have just told me that instead of making me work for it."

"Where's the fun in that?" asked Talia.

Davin looked at her, his expression of surprise becoming a grin. "More humor from the Huntress. Who would have thought? Was that to get back at me for my comment?"

Talia's lips puckered together again as she considered her reply. He was always testing her, and she didn't understand why his doing that appealed to her.

She had taken Davin aboard at the request of Lord Keldragan, understanding the importance of maintaining that budding relationship. Yet she had never expected this type of engagement with a gladiator.

Davin was right. She had thought that he would be all about the blood, guts, and glory. One word responses mixed in with a few grunts.

But he wasn't like that at all. He was thoughtful. Articulate. Insightful.

The constant aggravation she felt because of Davin, first raised by her misinterpretation of him, was only made worse because he was more than happy to challenge her and her every decision.

Well, not every decision. And not really challenge. Just question. And she had to admit, if only to herself, that some of his questions often were good ones.

She had to admit as well that Captain Kenworthy had voiced privately the same concern as Davin did when she told the crew that they'd be hunting pirates on their own. So there was some legitimacy to at least some of what Davin had to say.

And she couldn't blame them for both feeling uncomfortable, since Carlomin ships usually pursued pirates in a squadron of three vessels. Now, however, because they were searching for the current location of Smuggler's Cove, their resources were stretched thin.

Although Captain Kenworthy continued to grumble, at least to himself, Davin had listened to her explanation of why she was ignoring her own stricture and then moved on. Thinking about it some more, and based on their current conversation, she was beginning to think that maybe she had the gladiator all wrong.

Maybe he wasn't challenging her. Maybe he was just curious. Maybe he just wanted to learn, and the best way to do that was to ask questions. Just as he was doing with Master Hari, who seemed to have taken the gladiator under his sail.

"There!" Talia pointed. They were just beginning to sail by one of the slits. At this distance it was barely visible, just a jagged cut in the cliff face, easily missed if you didn't know what you were looking for.

Talia handed the spyglass to Davin. Taking a glimpse through the lens, he could just make out one side of the anchored float. He nodded in appreciation.

"You said there were four or five of these Smuggler's Coves. How do you know this is the right one? There's no one there."

"Did you see the small black flag at the end of the pier?"

"Yes, although I could scarcely make it out."

"That means that this week this is Smuggler's Cove."

Davin nodded. A simple, effective system. "So you expect a pirate or two to show up here?"

"I do," Talia confirmed. "Captain Blackbeard said that they conduct daily meets to trade information and move goods around."

"What if today's meet has already happened?" asked Davin.

"Then we have to wait longer than we want."

Davin nodded. They couldn't really expect the pirates to adhere to a schedule that was convenient for them. "What do you want to do?"

"I've got an idea," Talia began.

"But ..." Davin prompted, sensing her hesitation, a tingling of warning along the back of his neck worrying him.

"But it depends on whether you're willing to take a risk."

"So you don't want me to serve as a sailor. Rather you want me to be ..."

"Bait. Yes, exactly so."

Davin closed his eyes and shook his head in disgust. "I hate being bait."

THE END OF CHAPTER.

To keep reading *The Bloody Hunt for Freedom*, visit my author website at PeterWachtBooks or Amazon to get your copy.

LOOKING FOR MORE …

This short story is a prelude to the events in my new series *The Tales of the Territories* and is FREE to readers who receive my newsletter.

Learn more at PeterWachtBooks.com.

www.ingramcontent.com/pod-product-compliance
Lightning Source LLC
Chambersburg PA
CBHW070232200726
48293CB00005B/1591